Also by Lori Gold

Love, Theodosia
Romantic Friction

Praise for *Romantic Friction* also by Lori Gold

An NPR Book of the Day
A Zibby Media 2025 Summer Reads Pick
A Zibby Media Most Anticipated Book of 2025

"Smart, funny, and unpredictable—*Romantic Friction* is a wild ride that kept me guessing until the end. Readers will love this irreverent, timely novel!"

—Amy Tintera, *New York Times* bestselling author of *Listen for the Lie*

"Sharply written and impossible to put down. Kept me squirming in my seat with the unrelenting real-ness of it all!"

—Jesse Q. Sutanto, *USA TODAY* bestselling author of *Vera Wong's Unsolicited Advice for Murderers*

"Witty, heartfelt, and delightful with a side-serve of AI drama and book-world insider gossip—what's not to love about this book? Relatable characters, sharp writing, and emotional turbulence will make you laugh and cry."

—Sally Hepworth, *New York Times* bestselling author of *Darling Girls*

"With prose that crackles and wit that leaps off the page, *Romantic Friction* opens the curtain to an irreverent, hilarious, and yet decidedly loving behind-the-scenes look at the world of publishing. Lori is a writer readers will be thrilled to discover."

—Chandler Baker, *New York Times* bestselling author of *Whisper Network*

"A fun romp through the book world, full of humor, hijinks, and envy."

—Catherine Mack, *USA TODAY* bestselling author of *Every Time I Go on Vacation, Someone Dies*

"A singularly original, no-holds-barred exploration of art, life, and everything in between. You won't want to miss this dynamic, unapologetic, highly entertaining book."

—Laurie Elizabeth Flynn, *USA TODAY* bestselling author of *Till Death Do Us Part*

"*Romantic Friction* is a delightful romp that will be catnip for writers and book lovers alike. Lori Gold takes affectionate aim at the publishing industry with sly humor, fun twists, and plenty of hijinks."

—Laura Hankin, author of *One-Star Romance*

"When the literary world and AI collide, laughable drama ensues. *Romantic Friction* is a devilishly fun look inside the publishing industry. Gold seamlessly blends heart and wit with a timely dose of reality."

—Dana Elmendorf, author of *In the Hour of Crows*

"Not since Elizabeth Peters' *Die for Love* (1984) has there been such a hilarious insider's take on the world of publishing as Sofie and her closest cadre of author friends plot an *Ocean's 8*–style takedown of her literary nemesis. In between all the laughs, Gold also offers up a serious exploration of the role AI could play in publishing, for better or worse."

—*Booklist*

Kiss

a novel

MARRY

KILL

LORI GOLD

PARK ROW BOOKS

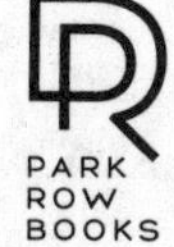

ISBN-13: 978-0-7783-0578-1

Kiss, Marry, Kill

Park Row Books
22 Adelaide St. West, 41st Floor
Toronto, Ontario M5H 4E3, Canada
ParkRowBooks.com

HarperCollins Publishers
Macken House, 39/40 Mayor Street Upper,
Dublin 1, D01 C9W8, Ireland
www.HarperCollins.com

Printed in U.S.A.

26 27 28 29 30 LBC 5 4 3 2 1

For Marc, in every universe

They were on opposite sides of the street.

It wasn't right.

Nothing should have been able to separate them. Certainly not him.

Then one of them yelled something I couldn't hear. But I didn't need to. Their body language said everything.

It was dark. It was quiet. It was fast. I wasn't sure it deserved to be, but there's only so much one can control. We do what we can. We make our choices. We have to let the universe handle the rest.

So we did.

And he died because of it.

Even though all of us saw, none of us said. Because secrets are like oxygen. They give life to friendships. And honestly, should it be any other way?

ONE YEAR EARLIER

Subject: [Internal Email] Revised Launch Copy
To: Aubrey Miller, Ilena Cohen, Mallory Latham
Reply to: marketing@AIM.com

Below, find the revised speech for the launch of the new (super exciting!) feature of our beloved AIM app, the undisputed leader in the booming health and wellness space. We're smiling wide over this (and users will too!). Promise! Our focus groups love it! (We mean *love,* love!)

Body language counts! Make sure you're smiling like a Cheshire cat (whatever that is!).

You already know how to AIM Higher and now . . . AIM Wider! You've followed the health programs, you've adopted the daily habits, you've been buoyed by the inspiring stories from everyone from former First Lady Michelle Obama (love!) to Olympian Simone Biles (love, love!) to media mogul Reese Witherspoon (love, love, *love!*)!

And *you* made "Seven Days to Your Resting Beach Face!" AIM's most successful in-app challenge yet! *Confetti cannons!*

But now... sad faces, because your five-minute daily meditations and ten-minute turmeric face masks and (the-longer-the-better!) pleasuring-yourself-without-guilt sessions don't seem quite as fulfilling without those points they earned you.

Your strong, happy voices have reached our perky *[note: word choice pending]* ears. And we AIM to please!

You keep on doing you, and you'll keep on earning those points for *A-MA-ZING!* discounts and *OMG-can-it-be!* freebies from our beloved partners. But that's not all! Because on this quest for a more fulfilling life, you shouldn't have to go it alone. This is a community—*your* community.

Today, we introduce "How Wide's My Smile"! Our newest and happiest feature invites you to encourage, support, and validate the journeys of your fellow users by *awarding points to one another*. And this isn't a challenge, it's a new, permanent feature of the AIM app you know and love (love, love!).

So raise those DIY cocktails! A happier self, here we come!

Mallory: I'm not saying this.

Ilena: You wanted to be CEO.

Mallory: Because *you* didn't want to be.

Mallory: WTF's a DIY cocktail? And why are there so many "!!!!!!" ??????

Mallory: We should fire the entire team.

Ilena: I declined to be CEO because I knew, as chief operating officer, one day I'd get the pleasure of seeing you stand in front of tipsy twentysomethings shouting "confetti cannons". *Love, love!*

Ilena: Aubrey, thoughts?

Aubrey: It's cute. Or maybe not?

1
AUBREY

Present Day
Thursday Evening

Aubrey stands before a path made of crushed oyster shells and all she wants to do is turn around. She's not ready. She thought she was, or at least hoped she was, or at the very least hoped she would be once she got here.

That's a lie. All of it. She knew she wasn't ready, but she also knew Ilena and Mallory needed her to be.

She presses her waterproof flip-flops into the crustacean husks, which crunch like shattered glass or broken bones, making her cringe. She breathes, but still one hand reflexively reaches for the phone in her pocket. One swipe, a couple of taps, and a rideshare would whisk her back home. She'd curl up on her brown microfiber sofa under the afghan her grandmother knitted for her to take to college, neither of them realizing how much a fuzzy orange blanket would make Aubrey stand out rather than fit in.

A trio of summer interns, unaware of the kid gloves with which everyone now treats Aubrey, materializes in front of her.

"Is it true the valuation is more than two billion?"

"Did you really come up with the name over kale salads?"

"Are Michelle Obama's triceps that GOAT in person?"

They bounce with enthusiasm, nervously clasping their elbows in awe of all this, maybe even of Aubrey as one of the founders of a company that everyone says is about to make history. But she's not a trailblazer. The only place Aubrey leads rather than follows is the *A* in *AIM*.

The young women wait, their anticipation morphing into discomfort, as Aubrey simply smiles politely to avoid saying the wrong thing. She's saved by Mallory's resounding "*Spectacular day for a summer outing! Cue those confetti cannons!*"

The interns dissipate like the dry ice coming off the raw bar, joining the other employees responding to Mallory's siren call or taking in the cornhole and bocce and giant Jenga, the dock with paddleboards and kayaks stacked one atop the other in a rainbow of reds and blues and yellows and greens, the inflatable flamingo two stories high that Aubrey's not sure is on trend or meant to be ironic.

Aubrey can hear Ethan's chortle of a laugh in her head. She misses it. She misses him. If he were here, would she chuckle lightly beside him, his likely sarcastic take on it all making her second-guess the signature cocktail, the life-size tic-tac-toe, the Instagram influencers documenting the entire outing in exchange for a lifetime subscription to AIM?

So what if AIM's a cliché? Being a cliché means they made it. They made AIM what they always hoped it would be. Didn't they?

Across the lawn, Aubrey watches as Mallory greets Ilena. They hide their strained smiles as they pause for pecks on cheeks because all eyes are on them. How could all eyes *not* be on them? Both tall and slim and commanding attention. Mallory may not be traditionally beautiful with her angular chin and thin, almost pointy nose, but she has an aura that ensnares all. Ilena has always been more reserved, with deep blue eyes and lashes that seem to reach out and shake your hand. As gorgeous as Mallory is charismatic, and Aubrey is the opposite of them both.

A drink, she should get a drink, calm her nerves, soften that unrelenting urge to flee. Because women cannot collapse under pressure.

Aubrey forces her feet to move, determined to be in the present despite how very much she wants to be in the past. Or even the future. Anywhere but here, where Ethan's no longer her Ethan and her best friends are letting a disagreement about taking their company public overshadow everything else.

She'll do what they asked, join them for the toast, hover awkwardly beside them during their practiced banter about creating AIM over those salads, and be free to return to her fuzzy homespun blanket.

As she heads for the bar, her wave to Noreen goes unnoticed. The woman is in full-on executive assistant mode, simultaneously posting sign-up sheets for a ladder ball tournament and scratching shellfish, gluten, dairy, egg, sesame, soy, peanut, tree nut, and who-knows-what-other-allergen warnings on the chalkboard menu. Beside the dock, marketing and legal pick teams for a paddleboard race. Felix, AIM's general counsel, bounces his one-year-old daughter on his hip as his husband organizes the selection process alongside Ella, head of marketing. Felix's husband, James, is an ideal wrangler thanks to being a first grade teacher. Either Felix used his status as GC to demand their toddler's entry or, more likely, he found a way to sneak the girl past Mallory.

Not surprisingly, there's a bottleneck at the bar, but Aubrey dismisses the invitations to cut the line. She loses herself in the hum of the crowd until a "*Kiss, Marry, Kill! New round!*" jars her. It's followed by a swift "*Gosling, Reynolds, Seacrest. Go!*" from someone she vaguely recognizes as part of the sales department. Another young woman snorts and rolls off: "Gosling, kiss, obviously, Reynolds, totes marry, and Seacrest? I'll offer mercy—instead of death, let's just cut off his scrotum!" Shrieks and giggles follow until the young woman realizes her boss has been listening. "Aubrey . . . um, hi."

A shroud of silence descends, Aubrey's newly developed superpower, and she issues a soft smile to free them from having to change their behavior on account of her. Chatter and giggles resume, and Aubrey breathes in the vanilla of someone's lotion and the rosemary of someone's shampoo and the mint of someone's mojito and lets herself relax into the warmth of the bodies that flank her. When it's her turn, she orders the signature cocktail, unsure what they decided on this year. And by "they," she means Mallory and Ilena. Aubrey's not known for her decision-making abilities in the best of times, and these are far from that.

As she waits, she takes in the carnival-like lawn of this gastropub across from the Charles River. Last year they rented out the cider house in the Boston shipyard. They'd never fit this year, Mallory was right about that.

Aubrey can see her from here, laughing at something said by a balding man in a blazer made by Armani or Prada or some other brand that costs as much as a month's rent. He's one of AIM's early investors and has clearly wanted to sleep with Mallory from the moment her kitten heels crossed into his VC conference room. She squeezes his arm, masterfully excusing herself, as she plucks a glass of sparkling wine from a server's tray.

She spies Aubrey and gives a warm smile, just as Grayson

Fields appears beside her. Another VC, but this one broad-shouldered with biceps that threaten to split his shirt seams. Mallory has wanted to sleep with him since the moment her kitten heels led him into their conference room—though she refuses to admit it. Even now, Aubrey senses a tension between them. Grayson's hand reaches for Mallory before pulling back. Mallory sinks her teeth into her bottom lip, tightening her arms across her chest, barely contained by the faux wrap of her aubergine jumpsuit. It's a brushed jersey that gives the aura of silk yet lives firmly in the realm of casual attire. Gifted from some designer, no doubt. Mallory's vivacious smile accompanies all their press, her larger-than-life personality an attraction for brand sponsors.

Meanwhile, Aubrey paired her company-issued coral "AIM Higher" tee with dark-wash skinny jeans. Only now, amid these striped maxi dresses and short rompers and white linen pants, does she remember some meme about skinny jeans. Saying she shouldn't be wearing them. Which maybe means that she should? She's really tired of never knowing what's meant to be ironic.

"Strawberry mule. Totally lit."

The voice comes from behind Aubrey just as the bartender sets down her drink.

Aubrey considers the frosted glass of pink liquid as well as the "lit." "That's what this is?"

Kai, a new part-time hire, places his identical empty glass on the bar top. "So I was told, though it seems a bit insulting."

"To the original?"

"To the alpaca." He juts his rounded chin to the three white Muppet-looking creatures ruminating on hay and presumably the ridiculousness of the line of AIM employees waiting to take selfies with them.

For the first time since she arrived, Aubrey smiles. He seems young, but an infusion of frivolity might be just what she and her team need right now. The bartender hands him another strawberry mule. As he clinks Aubrey's glass, she tries to remember if he's part-time because he's still in grad school. Or is it college? Is he even old enough to drink? Does she have to report him to HR? To herself? Should she do something or say something or—

"Don't tell me," he says. "Your favorite animal's the mule, and now I've gone and completely offended my new boss."

"I'm—no, no, that's not . . ." Her face betrays her again. Every Christmas, every birthday, her mom always said Aubrey never needed to verbalize whether she liked a gift or not because it was written in her every crease, lip curl, and blink. She couldn't fake it even when she wanted to. "It's just, are you sure you should be having one?"

Kai lifts his goody bag, and Aubrey realizes Grayson Fields has little on him by way of those biceps. Stick a surfboard under his arm, and Kai is a living, breathing travel poster for Hawaii, where he grew up. "The owners of this company kindly gave us all coupons for free rideshares. And this." He pulls out a fluffy white Koozie. "Explains the alpaca at least."

"Nothing explains the alpaca," Aubrey says, before she realizes she said it and takes a swig of her drink.

Kai laughs, his skin flushing with the barest undertone of peach. It sounds nothing like Ethan's laugh, but still, that's who she thinks of because she can't not think of Ethan.

She's fallen in love twice in her life. Once, nearly a year ago, when she attended a speech by Grayson Fields and was introduced to Ethan Sonders, and seven years before that, when she clinked forks loaded with microgreens at a table in Silicon Valley with Ilena and Mallory and created AIM.

She nervously excuses herself from Kai and heads for them,

both now seated in Adirondack chairs surrounding a sandbox. Her best friends, her colleagues, the women she'll make history with. If they don't kill each other first.

Aubrey settles into her Adirondack and forces herself to sip her strawberry mule slowly. She isn't the biggest drinker, even less so since Ethan, and the gin's already making her scalp tingle. But Kai was right; it is lit, if *lit* means refreshing, something desperately needed since the microclimate surrounding these Adirondack chairs is stifling.

If she'd known going public would cause so much discord, she'd have never said yes. Though in truth, there's no version of Aubrey that wouldn't say yes to Mallory and Ilena.

Ilena is the first person you'd call if you needed a lawyer to get you out of jail and the first person to lecture you for needing a lawyer to get you out of jail. Whatever got you into the mess in the first place was likely Mallory's idea. They would brave ice storms and nor'easters, Boston traffic on graduation weekends in May, and the subway on a ninety-five-degree day if you needed them. They knew what wine to order to complement everything from oysters to French fries, how to make hibiscus palomas, how to tie a scarf a hundred ways, how to build a company into an empire. They also knew how to be a best friend. Something a young Aubrey never knew mattered as much as it does. Something this Aubrey is scared of losing.

Mallory polishes off her bubbly and whips out her phone. "Is it rude to text Noreen to bring me another?"

"Yes," Aubrey says at the same time as Ilena rolls her eyes.

It's the latter, Aubrey's sure, that sends Mallory's thumbs tapping. They sit around the sandbox filled with plastic shovels and molds for castles and starfish, and Aubrey searches to make sure there aren't any pitchforks.

"All this . . ." Ilena presses her hand against the arm of the whitewashed chair made of reclaimed barn doors. "Is this truly the vibe you want AIM to have?"

"First, it's *we*," Mallory says, "and second, it's the vibe they expect. It's not just our user base that's half our age, Ilena, it's our employees. You never exactly were the life of the party, but parties do require life. Besides, just think how it'll look on social media."

"I know exactly how it will look. Like some of us don't take things seriously."

The air stretches taut like a rubber band about to snap.

"Well, it's too late now," Mallory says as she brushes her hair off her shoulder. The dirty-blond bob she had when Aubrey first met her has become brighter, longer, and more bronze over the years. Her waves now cascade down her back, more fitting for someone with the bravado of a wild peacock in perpetual preen. "You should have weighed in when Noreen sent the email. Even Aubrey did."

Ilena shrugs. Unlike Mallory, the dark, flowing hair Ilena had back then has gotten progressively shorter, now nearly a pixie cut. "Sorry if my life has bigger issues than party planning."

Aubrey lifts her drink to take a sip, but the tremble in her hand makes the glass ting against her front teeth.

Ilena's face pales. "Oh, I'm sorry, Aubrey. I wasn't thinking."

But she was. Just not about the same thing as Aubrey. They're all drowning in something. Aubrey and Ethan, Mallory and taking AIM public, Ilena and her ovulation cycles.

Aubrey feels the weight of their stares, wishing she knew what to say to tighten this widening gap between them, but all she can do is place her hand on top of the good-luck stone in her pocket—jerking back when Mallory slaps it.

"Mosquito," Mallory says.

"Oh, Aubrey, now you're going to blow up. Did you bring your Benadryl?" Ilena opens her bag. "I knew I shouldn't have switched into this small purse. I think I took out my pill case."

Mallory reaches for her own sailcloth clutch. "I might have that aloe lotion."

"It's okay," Aubrey says, despite the bite on her thumb already swelling to the size of a blueberry. "I'm okay, really."

They mean well, but it's this type of stuff that sometimes makes Aubrey, seven years their junior, feel like a toddler. They've always treated her as something that might break. And she's let them.

"Hey, hey, y'all!" Noreen approaches with a cheery smile and a round, wooden tray full of drinks.

Mallory looks up from her clutch and claps her hands. "There she is. My favorite assistant in all of assistant-dom."

Noreen's blond ponytail bounces as she hands another sparkling wine to Mallory. "How nice. Y'all deserve some 'me' time." She slips on those kid gloves and gives an empathetic nod to Aubrey.

Originally from Dallas, Noreen Parra made her way to AIM via Smith College, starting with the same web design rotation on Aubrey's team that now belongs to Kai. Mallory swooped in and nabbed Noreen to be her executive assistant before the rotation even ended.

Aubrey has never asked if Noreen likes it, same as Mallory never asked if Aubrey minded.

"Beaut of a spot, isn't it?" Noreen shuffles her white-sneakered feet against the grass as she passes strawberry mules to Ilena and Aubrey. "Great for celebrating today's valuation! Two point two billion? That's just . . ." She shivers, and one of the thin straps of her flouncy white sundress slips off her shoulder. "Ooh, wait, y'all *have* to do this! My family's tradition is to call on Lady Luck for something new by paying homage to something old. Good thing my mom baked her famous chocolate pecan pie before my first day of kindergarten instead of her muesli muffins. Had a slice every first day since, wearing a pair of overalls just like when I was five. And that includes the day I walked through the doors of AIM. So clearly, it works! Y'all should come back the night before you go public. Water view, strawberry drinks, and each other!"

"Don't forget the giant pink bird," Ilena says flatly.

Mallory narrows her eyes. "It makes a statement."

"And what statement is that?"

"We're fierce."

Ilena cocks her head. "And that's the reputation you want for AIM?"

"Yes, because it's not just AIM's reputation, it's ours. We *are* AIM. We are three women running what they used to call a unicorn company until all the unicorns were slaughtered by founders embezzling or lying to investors or testifying in front of Congress. The level of scrutiny on the tech world now . . . and for us? A thousand-fold. The number of female-owned-and-run companies traded on Wall Street can fit in the palm of my hand. So, yes, fierce flamingos it is. They can survive the harshest of conditions. They can even drink boiling water, did you know that?"

Noreen nods. "And they can stand in a lake as it freezes and scoot away unscathed when it thaws." Her eyes float to each of them. "They also live in flocks. They do everything together. And I mean *everything*." She gives a sexy bat of her eyelashes. "Squad goals, am I right?"

Aubrey's eyes widen. *Did she just tout "squad goals" for group sex?*

Mallory's smirk is mirrored on Ilena's face. Aubrey wants to reach out and grab this bond between the three of them and let it erase everything else.

"Oh, and, Mallory?" Noreen says. "The restaurant's general manager just told me that our rental fee doesn't cover dung cleanup. Alpaca or any other kind."

Ilena frowns.

And the moment is gone.

"No worries." Noreen twiddles her fingers. "I'll handle it. Now, how 'bout I round y'all up when it's time for the toast?"

Mallory lifts her sparkling wine in thanks, but Aubrey, welcoming the distraction, says, "Or you could join us."

Noreen balances the tray in one hand same as she balances everything at AIM. She's the kind of nice that you think must be put on. No one actually wants to bicycle to work in the rain to test out AIM's "Move, Don't Snooze!" challenge or grind five different beans for the coffee bar or send reminders to turn off your video when you take your Zoom meeting into the toilet. If AIM gave bonuses for being a team player, Noreen would be retired by now.

"As lovely as that would be . . ." Mallory says. "I think we forgot that splinter warning on the Jenga?"

Noreen flattens her palm against her chest. "My oversight, Mallory. I'll see to it faster than small-town gossip. Holler if you need anything."

Like a trip back in time to before everything began to change? Aubrey's gaze travels between her two best friends.

"Don't you look at me like that," Mallory says.

Aubrey trails a finger around the rim of her glass. "I didn't say anything."

"But you should," Ilena says.

A high-pitched squeal negates Aubrey's response, which is just as well. Such is the life of the youngest of four, with nearly ten years between Aubrey and her next sibling. Aubrey's thirty-two, of average height and average(ish) weight, from a family of professional and near-professional athletes, though the only competitive streak she had was for mathletes. Growing up, her siblings' games and practices and pancake breakfasts became her games and practices and pancake breakfasts. Her day planned for her before she woke up. Every decision made for her by someone else. Routines become habits and habits become a way of life.

AIM's way of life has always been Mallory as the public front, Ilena as the strategic core, and Aubrey behind the scenes as the master of all things tech, the only role she ever wanted. Except ever since Ethan she's found herself drifting, unable to focus, with little interest in the day-to-day of AIM.

Another shriek, followed by infectious giggling. At the end of the dock, Felix and James's daughter claps her hands in delight as Kai teeters on a paddleboard, playfully splaying his arms to the sides, mouth hanging open, exaggerating his risk of splashing into the murky river.

Mallory's teeth clench. "The invitation specifically said no kids. Where's Noreen? Oh, good, she's still close." Mallory raises her voice. "Nor—" The rustling of Ilena pushing herself out of her chair makes Mallory pause. "You know what, never mind. It's a good look for us, right? Let me just text those influencers to get a couple of shots. Hashtag family friendly?"

Aubrey digs a nail into the mosquito bite on her thumb as Ilena pauses, then slowly slides back into the seat. Her index finger taps against her mule, still untouched.

Her nails are painted their usual neutral beige. Mallory's sparkle in gold. Aubrey's are gnawed with jagged cuticles, just as they were the day the three of them met. It was eight years ago at a start-up program in Silicon Valley. Aubrey had been there as part of another team, but Mallory and Ilena had seen potential in her that her own team hadn't. Though Mallory and Ilena's alumna mentoring idea hadn't exactly been the program darling, buzz had still surrounded Mallory Latham and Ilena Cohen: smart, confident, extraordinary women who had bonded as freshman roommates at Harvard. An hour and a half into their first lunch, Aubrey had finally gotten past her nausea to eat some cilantro microgreens and those strange but delicious little squares of pancetta.

"After the program, you should join us," Ilena had said, to which Mallory had immediately added, "You *are* joining us."

Instead of her nausea returning, all Aubrey had felt was a dizzying desire to say "yes." Her brain slotted things into place as if it were code. "Aubrey, Ilena, and Mallory. We could be 'AIM.'"

Mallory smiled. "We're so going to make FU money."

"And show everyone that women can make FU money," Ilena had added.

Aubrey had toyed with her napkin. "And, maybe, show women that they should?"

Have they? Aubrey wonders now, looking out at the lawn full of employees who are all counting on them.

Has Aubrey? As chief technology officer she keeps the paid subscription base that could now support a moderate-sized Boston skyscraper running. That growth, which is responsible for AIM's astronomical Wall Street valuation, is partly due to last year's introduction of "How Wide's My Smile," one of Aubrey's grandmother's sayings and the buzziest feature of their app. The motivational talks from celebrities and "organic," "word-of-mouth" influencer campaigns (which are anything but) are all Mallory's doing. While Ilena ensures the inclusion of menstrual tracking and health proxies. All of it intended to help users find and stay on the path that will make them happy, healthy, and wise, guided and overseen by experts, teams of doctors and therapists and mindfulness specialists that provide the authoritative foundation that's come to set AIM apart from others in the niche.

Aubrey takes a mouthful of her strawberry mule, rolling it over her tongue, the sweet, savory blend rounding the edges that so much tension have made sharp. The three of them have always worked best when they work together. They need to be reminded of that.

"Maybe Noreen's right," Aubrey says. "Today's announcement deserves more than one celebration, doesn't it? Seems like the perfect thing to usher in good luck for AIM, right?"

"Yes!" Mallory says with more enthusiasm than Aubrey would have expected. "The night before we go public? We come back here, strawberry drinks and all. I'll take any excuse to wear this jumpsuit again. Stella McCartney sent it herself." Something lurks in Mallory's bravado, an undercurrent of insecurity. She tips her glass toward Ilena, waiting for her to agree.

But she doesn't, not immediately, and so Aubrey nudges Ilena's elbow. "Bring Jonah if you want, if he doesn't have a shift at the hospital like tonight."

A glistening sparks in Ilena's eyes, and she blinks. "No Jonah. Just us. I'll be there."

"Perfect," Mallory says.

"But about the direct listing," Ilena says slowly. "After AIM goes public, I'm—"

"This isn't the time," Mallory interrupts, eyeing Aubrey.

Tug, tug, tug on Aubrey's left.

"Because it's past time." Ilena raises an eyebrow at Aubrey.

Tug, tug, tug on Aubrey's right.

This is the way it's been. Mallory hell-bent on going public, Ilena wanting to hit pause, and both trying to get Aubrey to voice her opinion. Except what they want isn't an opinion but for her to choose a side. Whether they don't see that or can't or choose not to, it's not fair, same as it's not fair for her best friends to be acting like they aren't.

"The Lannisters," Aubrey blurts out. "Cersei, Jaime, Tywin, go!"

Ilena's brow crinkles. "I honestly have no idea what you just said."

A whisper of a smile plays on Mallory's lips. "Well, look at that, finally, we agree on something."

Aubrey scratches the mosquito bite. "A game. They were playing it at the bar. You know, that 'Marry, Kiss, or Kill' thing, and I just thought we could . . ." Could what? Be as free and playful as Kai? That's not really any of them. Especially now. She hears the collective thrum of everyone having a good time, and her lower lip twitches. "Forget it, it's silly."

Mallory's eyes drift to Ilena, and they have one of their silent conversations that always reminds Aubrey of how much longer the two have known each other.

"Not at all," Mallory says. "A little loosening up can't hurt. The hype has become overwhelming. It's like they're setting us up to fail."

"They?" comes Ilena's clipped response.

Mallory and Ilena hold each other's gaze for a beat that borders on uncomfortable.

Ilena inhales, chest rising, as she turns to Aubrey, whose face as always must say everything she's thinking, which is a *please, please, please*, because they're unraveling and have been unraveling and maybe it is her fault for not choosing a side, but the last choice she made brought her here, to this thread so frayed that she's not sure she can hold on much longer.

Ilena takes a long sip of her strawberry mule. "Okay."

Aubrey smiles the smile she learned she was capable of after meeting these two women, so real and full that she feels the truth of it in her toes. Despite it all, they're here for her. Aubrey both knew they would be and doubted they would be because these things live simultaneously in Aubrey. She never imagined being a part of something like this. Surrounded by people like this. She used to put herself to sleep writing imaginary code, variables and functions waltzing across the popcorn ceiling of her childhood bedroom, the placement of each something she knew instinctively, felt in the marrow of her bones. And now, she's in charge of employees she still can't think of as "hers," even after years of being their boss.

Ilena faces Mallory. "I'll play, but I need the rules."

"No, you don't." Mallory rubs her hands together. "At least not *the* rules, you need *my* rules. Because what we need is to make this interesting."

Of all the words that don't go together, *Mallory* and *rules* top the list. Aubrey is beginning to think this was a bad idea. "Actually, maybe this isn't the time, we should mingle . . . shouldn't we mingle?"

Mallory gives a dismissive wave as her eyes search the lawn. "Ooh, you are going to love this."

"Somehow I doubt that," Ilena says.

Mallory ignores her. "This will be spectacular, promise. The rule is AIM. Specifically, anyone who's here." Her eyes are pulled to Grayson like a magnet, and yet, unexpectedly, the excitement in them fades. She shakes her head and snaps back to Ilena and Aubrey. "Right, okay, so, out of everyone here, who would you fuck?" She points to Aubrey. "You. Go."

Aubrey's heart thumps. *Fuck?* Not Kiss?

"Mallory!" Ilena cries. "Inappropriate on every level. We're with our employees! Were you not at that sexual harassment training? We're not doing this."

"We are," Mallory insists. "My version, my rules. And Aubrey wants to."

"No. Aubrey doesn't." Ilena cups her hands around the arm of the chair, and her eyes swaddle Aubrey. "Come on, Aubrey, let's go."

Aubrey twists her hands in her lap. She suddenly realizes how very much she doesn't want to play this game, most certainly not this version of this game, and even more certainly, not this *part* of this version of this game. Mallory being Mallory doesn't excuse her from seeing that. Even the idea of answering makes Aubrey's heart burn with betrayal. But she's also being treated like the rope in her best friends' game of tug-of-war, and she just can't anymore.

Aubrey downs the rest of her strawberry mule, presses the cool glass against her mosquito bite, and resists the urge to make one of her signature pro-con lists. She simply says, "Kai."

"Sold," Mallory says.

Ilena stands. "Happy? We're done, then?"

"No," Aubrey says sharply, surprising herself. But her cheeks are on fire, and the alcohol's making her stomach churn, and she'll be damned if she's going to be the only one of them sent for remedial training on their sexual harassment policies.

Ilena nods slowly as if dropping Aubrey into a papoose on her chest. "Fine. Then, who's next?"

Mallory responds instantly, "You. Marry."

"Naturally, because irony is alive and well," Ilena mutters, reflexively spinning the opal wedding ring from Jonah around her finger. She steps forward, beyond the edge of the sandbox, and sets a hand on each of her hips. A perfect, sophisticated silhouette in her long-sleeved white linen shirt, navy blue shorts, and flats that she's pressing hard against the ground. Ilena sways slightly, neck rotating, until another shriek cuts through the music and the clank of tumbling giant Jenga blocks. The night is so full of happiness that it pinches Aubrey's heart.

Ilena's shoulders pull back as she angles herself toward the paddleboards where Felix and James each hold one of their daughter's hands, helping her balance.

"Felix," Ilena says. "I'd marry Felix."

Mallory gives a mischievous smile. "Which leaves just one thing for me."

2
ILENA

Friday Morning
*One Day **After** the Outing*

Ilena awakens to too much light. Did Jonah get up before her? Is he back on those 4 a.m. runs? Even so, his lifting of the blackout shades is definitely a passive-aggressive reaction to their last conversation.

Though technically, their last conversation wasn't a conversation at all. It was a request. One she said yes to, easily, more easily than she expected considering the request was to end their marriage.

She sits up, feeling groggy, like when she takes a sleeping pill too late and doesn't log enough hours. She tries to open her eyes, but the light's so bright, she can't focus. She aches everywhere. She had that one strawberry mule, just the one. She didn't drink enough to warrant feeling like this. It's Mallory's fault. Somehow. Everything is Mallory's fault lately.

Ilena searches for her silk eye mask. Finding nothing, she pulls the covers higher. The sheets slip through her fingers, the surface slicker than usual. She opens her eyes fully, the sheen of what should be her normally soft bamboo sheets registering behind the fact that they're a light blue, not white.

The xylophone tone of her cell precedes its buzzing against the nightstand. She shakes her head, trying to reconcile that Jonah not only changed the sheets but *changed* the sheets as she checks the clock beside the bed. The bright red numbers of 8:08 glare at her. What the hell is Jonah up to? They bought her round analog clock together in that store in Newburyport that smelled like Earl Grey tea and old wood. Neither had known what the rose compass inside was called, and it leaned more heavily on the kitsch side than Ilena's sophisticated tendencies. But Jonah had been the one to suggest it, a memento of the weekend spent on Plum Island, the weekend they were sure they exceeded the world record for number of orgasms in a single day. They rolled in ocean waves and cotton sheets and promised they'd return every year. That was four years ago. They've never been back. All they had to show for it was the clock, which Jonah apparently passive-aggressively moved, and a straw beach bag that came with the hotel room. They use it to hold guest towels, though they haven't had any guests in a long time. Still, she'll take the tote. And the clock. Is this her life now? Tagging twenty-one years of knickknacks and plates like they were at an estate sale?

Her phone continues its escalating ringtone, and she reaches for it. Aubrey's name scrolls across the lock screen, and Ilena hesitates. As much as she understands and sympathizes with her friend's fear of making choices, not having a belief of her own is costing them all. It may even cost them AIM.

Except Ilena can't honestly expect Aubrey to weigh in on canceling the direct listing when she doesn't have all the facts—let alone the key fact: that AIM's explosive success isn't real. AIM's exponential growth in users and subsequent high valuation is partly due to a computer error replicating accounts instead of actual humans signing up in droves. And only Ilena and Mallory know.

Pushing AIM into the spotlight now, without reconciling the fake accounts, isn't a risk, it's an unpinned grenade. It will go off. It will ruin AIM and everyone who gave up ski weekends and Cabo vacations and having kids when they were young to help build it.

But Mallory keeps on shoving, no matter what Ilena says.

Entwined as rope and as disparate as oil and water. That's been her relationship with Mallory since the beginning. Ilena's self-aware enough to realize that her judgmental nature, the thing she can't seem to fully unlearn from her mother, can be as detrimental as Mallory's no-holds-barred approach. Their long friendship has been a system of checks and balances for them both.

But the system has broken. The weight of their secrets has shattered it.

When Mallory came to Ilena a little over a month ago with the discovery of the duplicate accounts, they mourned together. The AIM they'd built was a success. Just not at the level they thought it was.

Still, it was theirs, the manifestation of twenty-one years of friendship and partnership. It had been incredible and fulfilling and hard, and this would be the hardest. But they wouldn't let a software malfunction be their end. They'd fix it together. They agreed on that. What they couldn't agree on was how. Aubrey's fragile state after Ethan meant keeping the truth from her, which meant keeping the truth from everyone, a decision that united Ilena and Mallory, that justified Ilena giving Mallory the time she'd asked for to try to make it right—part of Ilena perhaps truly believing that Mallory *could* fix it because Mallory's determination made her capable of anything. They are now a week out from going public. Nothing is fixed. And this, this is wrong.

Except not to Mallory, who isn't bound by rules or guilt or

right or wrong. It's who she's always been. Ilena loves her because of and in spite of it.

But that's not Ilena, and she won't let it become her. Ilena has every choice in the world, but yesterday, before the outing, she gave just one to Mallory: *Either we cancel the direct listing or I'm leaving AIM.*

And with the issuing of that ultimatum, Ilena erased decades of sophisticated decorating and baking her own rugelach and loving the man she's married to, all things done partly to ensure she is nothing like her mother.

Ilena refuses to be a woman on the cusp of forty, divorced, with a grenade of a company in her pocket.

The barrage comes like an assault.

The red spreading across his shirt. The smell of alcohol. The shattering of glass.

Ilena shoves the ensuing nausea away. She crushes the still-ringing phone in her hand, and guilt makes her answer Aubrey's call.

"Ilena! Is that you? Do I have you? Please tell me it's you. I have no idea what to do, and I must have really messed up and—"

"Aubrey." Ilena tries to cut her off, but the nonstop rambling continues, intensifying the throbbing in Ilena's head. She tries to sit up, but her lower back screams at her.

"But I'm naked, and I can't find my clothes, and—"

Naked?

"Aubrey!" Ilena propels herself into a seated position. She bangs her head against a panel of hard wood behind her where the upholstered linen should be and a wetness spreads beneath her. She thinks she may have just peed herself a little. Which makes her snap, "Aubrey, slow down, just slow down."

Ilena breathes deeply, but each inhale somehow squeezes her lungs.

"Okay, okay," Aubrey says. "It's just . . . I have no idea what to do. I mean, I think, I must have slept with him. Oh, Ilena, how could I have slept with him? With . . . with anyone?"

"Who, Aubrey, who?" Ilena blinks as her eyes finally begin to adjust to the brightness of the room—a brightness whose intensity she begins to understand as she takes in the gleaming white walls and shiny metal sconces and reflective glass dresser all where her Coventry Gray walls and blue porcelain lamps and driftwood chest should be. Either Jonah completely redecorated overnight or she spent the night somewhere else.

"Kai, didn't I say that? My new employee? My maybe-college-aged new employee. Oh god, please tell me he's eighteen. Employees have to at least be eighteen, right?"

"Are you sure?"

"That's what I'm asking you!"

"I meant are you sure you slept with him."

"I think so? I don't remember." Aubrey scoffs. "I'm a thirty-two-year-old cliché. Blackout drunk at a summer outing. I had those mules, two of them, and I guess I haven't really been drinking much since Ethan, but I don't even remember getting home last night."

"Neither do I," Ilena realizes, starting to wonder if someone slipped something into their drinks just as she's seized by a desperate urge to pee—that bit of wetness a warning. She presses her hand against her bladder. It's hard and full, so full, so . . . huge, actually. She looks down and can no longer hear Aubrey, just a buzzing in her ears, and her head swims and dark spots float before her eyes, and the phone falls from her hand.

She gently swings one leg, then the other off the mattress, her feet landing on an ebony hardwood floor instead of a crisp, white rug. She lifts her tent of a nightshirt. Sets a hand on her bare skin, a too-tight, diamond-crusted emerald the size of a kidney bean on her ring finger where her opal should be and the swollen belly of a pregnant woman in place of her Pilates-toned stomach.

Circled dates on calendars and endless data input into apps and contradicting trackers and choreographed sex and a diet of bee pollen and no caffeine and piles of peed-on sticks blaring one line, never two, and hope and sorrow and heartache and fights and fights and fights and this can't be . . . can't be . . .

Be what?

She skims her palm along her stretched skin, barely touching, as if the weight of her hand will make what's underneath disappear.

She lowers a pinkie. *Hard.* Her ring finger. *Like a soccer ball.* Her middle and index fingers. *Warm, so warm.* Then her thumb and the flat of her palm, and this thing that can't be real insists on proving the opposite because *it moves.* A flutter of bubbles grazing her skin. She stills. She wants it to happen again, she needs it to, because this isn't real. She's dreaming a dream that she can only make reality in the confines of her mind. Her mind is cruel.

She calls out, "Aubrey, you're dreaming. Go back to sleep. I'll see you at work."

Ilena finds her phone and presses the red button to end the call. She sets the phone on the nightstand and curls herself back under the sheets she'd never have purchased that actually feel glorious against her skin. Jonah would relish stealing these, rolling them to his side of the bed like always while simultaneously knocking one of his sci-fi novels onto the floor, waking her, but not himself. She's settling in to savor whatever is left of this dream when she hears the tapping of footsteps. If she weren't dreaming, this would be yet another passive-aggressive act by Jonah. He knows he's supposed to take his shoes off at the door. The exorbitantly expensive free-trade, sustainable, bamboo baskets were purchased for that very purpose, with the bonus of helping the women of the community that weaves them get free bicycles for safer journeys to retrieve fresh water.

Even in her dreams, she can't escape fighting with Jonah.

"Where are those confetti cannons when you need them?" Felix Singh strolls into the bedroom, a banana in one hand and an enormous smile pushing back the light brown skin of his cheeks. "You finally listened to me and let yourself sleep in, a full night of baby rest. Bravo!"

"Baby rest?" Ilena's brow furrows.

"What do you think?" He peels back the skin of the banana. "Decided I'd invent a new saying since you, my treasure, are by no means in need of beauty rest." He waves the banana in front of her face, and nausea clenches her stomach. "Still no?" He swiftly moves it away. "Figured it was worth a shot. I'll get you something else. Egg? Yogurt?"

"What? Why?" *Why are you here in my dream, in my house, in my bedroom . . . calling me "treasure"?*

"I walked into that one, didn't I?" He gives a warm smile. "However, I am fairly confident that a man is allowed to make his pregnant wife breakfast and have it not be a condemnation of her ability to get it herself. But if you'd prefer, we can invest in a drone."

"We?"

"Got me again. Yes, I'm the one who wants the drone. Sorry for being such a man."

This is bizarre, too bizarre. Ilena's ready to wake up. Just *wake up*. She pushes herself to her feet and turns to face Felix, but his back is to her. Beside him, the sun streams in through floor-to-ceiling windows that offer a breathtaking view of Boston Harbor. Boats and cargo ships and the Seaport Harbor Walk instead of the oak trees and white hydrangeas enclosing her small yard in Newton.

"Did I sleep here?" she finds herself asking, as if that would explain away the rest of it.

Felix spins around in front of the glass-topped dresser, confusion tilting his head. "Oh, you mean, well? Did you sleep well?" He closes the dresser drawer, a Stanford baseball hat in his hand even though she's positive that Felix went to Yale.

Felix walks toward her in his white polo and white shorts. "You slept like our baby."

She gasps, and he chuckles knowingly. "I'm already doing dad jokes. Pathetic, I know." He leans in and his lips graze her cheek. "Maybe I can work it out with a few strong backhands. I'll see you in a bit? You know how James gets when anyone's late."

"Your husband," Ilena blurts out, though as she says it, she sees the photograph on the dresser of Felix in a black suit, white shirt, black tie, and herself in a high-waisted cream gown with beaded embroidery trailing down the full skirt. Her wedding photo with Jonah shows her in an off-blue strapless shift and Jonah in a beige suit, both of which her mother had declared as "tacky" despite the ceremony taking place on the beach.

Felix laughs again, giving a bit of an embarrassed shrug. "Bit silly to have a work husband, I know, I know."

But James doesn't work at AIM. James is a first grade teacher who loves teaching six-year-olds decoupage and subtraction tables.

"I—I've got to pee," she says, then can't believe she said "pee" in front of AIM's general counsel.

"I'll take a bagel out of the freezer for you," Felix says, before stepping aside. "Take a bath, and if you get stuck again, use the voice commands to text me."

She really, really wants to wake up now. But then comes a pressure in her bladder and a tingling between her legs, and she takes off for the door on the side of the room, grateful she found the en suite on the first try.

This is what her life has come to: nearly peeing herself in her dreams, a lack of control that's a perfectly apt metaphor for everything. It's all Mallory's fault. Somehow, it just is.

She fights to yank off the emerald ring, a battle she loses with the platinum wedding band. She's washing her hands at the sink when she looks in the mirror to see the round bump of a bun on top of her head. She carefully releases the elastic, and hair that should be in a pixie cut spills to her shoulders. She jerks back as her phone rings again. She finds it beside the bed.

It's Aubrey. "Ilena, I'm sorry, I know what you said, but it's just . . . something's not right. I'm in my apartment, but it's not *my* apartment. There's no low tide smell and there's so much light, this might even be the top floor? But the Women Who Code print you got me is here and my grandmother's afghan too, but the couch is white and everything in the fridge is labeled 'vegan' and there's a naked kid in my bed that's not really my bed."

White couch, vegan fridge, naked kid.

Blackout shade, digital clock, Felix making dad jokes.

Ilena and Aubrey are in homes that are theirs but that aren't theirs, with people they shouldn't be with, people they simply work with. People who were at the summer outing, just like they were.

Ilena places a hand on her stomach that shouldn't be her stomach. But is. "Aubrey, what's the last thing you remember before waking up?"

"The outing, we were at the sandbox, but we hadn't even had dinner yet or done the toast and Mallory would have never let us not do the toast—"

"Aubrey! Just slow down. Focus. The last thing."

She inhales a breath. "The game. We were playing Kiss, Marry, Kill. Sorry, I mean *Fuck*. Fuck, Marry, Kill."

Ilena goes quiet.

With a tremble in her voice, Aubrey says, "Tell me you remember more. Because if you don't, then . . . wait, Ilena, are you with Jonah?"

Ilena's throat goes dry.

"Ilena? What is this?" Aubrey says.

Aubrey slept with Kai. Ilena's married to Felix, and that means . . .

"Mallory," Ilena chokes out.

"No," Aubrey says, her voice tight, "you can't think—"

"I'll meet you there." Ilena hangs up and stares at her phone, the past twenty-one years of Mallory rotating through her brain, black turtleneck and round glasses as Steve Jobs at Halloween, "time-sharing" the Burberry coat they jointly splurged on after depositing their first investor check, eating latkes on Hanukkah, oysters on July Fourth, cupcakes for every birthday . . . Mallory. Her Mallory.

Ilena shoves herself off the mattress, a wave of dizziness making her stumble. What if "there" isn't where they think it is? What if Mallory's not in the same apartment? This isn't Ilena's house in Newton, and it sounds like that's not Aubrey's basement apartment by the river she refuses to upgrade. Ilena grabs her phone and searches her contacts. Mallory's address is the same, but she has no idea if the number is because who knows anyone's cell number anymore? She's lucky she remembers her own.

Ilena rushes to the other closed door in the bedroom that she correctly guesses is the closet and fumbles to find clothes to fit this strange, new body. She dials and redials the number marked as Mallory as she wrestles on a pair of jeans with a kangaroo pouch, getting no answer, only the incessant greeting of Mallory's voicemail, taunting her. Because whatever this is, it's one hundred percent Mallory's fault.

3
ILENA

Harvard University
*Twenty-One Years **Before** the Outing*

Ilena met Mallory when she handed her a roll of duct tape.

She followed it with an idea, knowing if things went badly, it would be one hundred percent her fault. As Mallory listened, her left eyebrow, dark and thick like a couture model's, rose. They were her best feature, framing those doe eyes of hers, her second-best feature.

"You really think it's strong enough?" Mallory asked.

Ilena assessed this skyscraper of a girl who was to be her freshman roommate. She was all boobs and knew she was all boobs, but she must have been more than just boobs because boobs didn't get you into Harvard. "If it isn't, I'll spring for the rest of your shirt."

Mallory fingered the hem of her black, cropped tee that barely covered the hot pink of her underwire as she took in Ilena's conservative white button-down, khaki skirt, and tennis sneakers. "Well, well, well, who knew a country mouse could have so much spunk?"

"The roommate assignment sheet clearly says I'm from Lexington."

"Right, sorry. You're a rich country mouse."

"And where are you from again?"

"East Cambridge," Mallory said.

"And that explains the chip on your shoulder."

They stared at one another, each knowing that this was the moment that would define them as archenemies or lifelong friends.

Mallory began to use her gold manicured fingernail to pry the end of the duct tape loose. She paused, released the tape, and held her finger out to Ilena. "I've got your back."

Ilena hooked her own beige-painted fingernail around Mallory's. "And I've got yours."

In unison they said, "Pinky swear."

"Now . . ." Mallory returned to the tape. "Let's do this thing."

4
MALLORY

Friday Morning
*One Day **After** the Outing*

Mallory swore she'd never sleep with Grayson Fields again, no matter how tight training for all those marathons makes his ass. She's not into angry sex and not in a forgiving enough mood that would allow for any other kind.

But then how to explain waking up, curled in the corner of his bedroom with his apricot-colored Smurf of a dog huddled beside her? Still bizarre. Grayson always seemed more the German shepherd type. Nearly a year ago, when he'd escorted her into this apartment whose HVAC pumps filtered air and testosterone and scooped up the cockapoo, Mallory was convinced it was part of some practical joke. But the monogrammed Harley water bowl and the ridiculous Wi-Fi–enabled collar let her know it wasn't. She reads people, she's staked her career on doing it well. Surprises like that are rare.

And yet everything about Grayson has been a surprise—and not in a good way.

Grayson's the devil. She now realizes she willingly sold her soul to him the day she accepted his investment in AIM.

Unethical behavior is one thing (she should know), but his actions are potentially illegal. She wanted to ask Noreen to google if they could go to jail, but that would mean telling Noreen about the fake accounts.

This is Mallory's company. Not his. She's the first to smile through mansplaining to get a discount on server storage or tweak a department's performance quota to cut loose entitled Gen Z–ers without a hassle from HR. But this is outside her control, outside Grayson's. Why can't he see that? Probably because he's made sure it won't be his waxed balls on the line if the fake valuation comes to light.

She rises to her feet, a wooziness making her seek out the corner of the dresser, but it's one of those trendy mid-century deals and it's too low. She wobbles, and her bare foot lands right on the cockapoo's tail. *Fuck.* She braces for a bark or howl that will give away that she's awake. She intends to sneak out before Grayson comes back from the toilet or kitchen or wherever the hell he is, off collecting souls in this three-thousand-square-foot penthouse. But instead of a bark or a howl, the squiggly furball releases the barest of whimpers and tries to curl itself around her foot. Dammit. She's not a dog person. Or a cat person. Or, when it comes right down to it, a people person. Ilena and Aubrey, yes. But otherwise, people are like Wet-Naps, essential when you need them, but otherwise entirely forgettable.

Mallory scans the bedroom for her shoes and sailcloth clutch, finding neither. The gray comforter is pulled taut. Square pillows in a yellow-and-gray fleur-de-lis pattern that are new since she was last here sit perfectly propped.

Grayson shopping for throw pillows is as hard to imagine as Grayson sitting with this stuffed animal of a dog in his lap.

She slides past the ten-thousand-dollar Eames chair, still searching for her shoes and bag. She doesn't exactly feel like she had sex—that usual postcoital soreness that seems to linger longer and longer the closer she gets to forty nonexistent. She bends to look under the bed, and Harley leaps into her arms. Instinctually, she catches him.

That's when she sees the marks on her forearm. Long, red, deep. Like fingers. A handprint.

Well, no matter what her vulva's telling her, looks like they sure as shit did something last night. How could this have happened? Mallory perfected the ratio of food to alcohol when she was nineteen after waking inside the Fox Club's yellow Colonial on JFK Street not knowing how she got there.

Screw sneaking out. She sets Harley on the floor and marches out of the bedroom. She swings left to head for the living room and nearly collides with a four-foot-tall fountain, water flowing up and over into a bed of polished rocks that Grayson's more likely to use as a urinal than decor.

She storms down the hall, not past images of Muhammad Ali and Serena Williams and Tom Brady but canvas prints of ocean waves and a lighthouse. And, Christ, a pink sunset? A fucking gnome would fit in better with Grayson's minimalist design aesthetic than this woo-woo crap.

Her chest clenches. He's dating someone. Someone else. Her breathing grows rapid, but she pushes against it. She doesn't care. (Even though she does.)

Whatever, so he's dating someone. Some leggy yoga instructor who's namaste-ing this place, and yet here he is proving he's as much of a leech as her least favorite VC, Mr. Tom Ford Blazer, because he's dating someone else and still slept with Mallory after yesterday's outing.

She grits her teeth just as her cell begins to ring. Like a beacon, it brings her to a bamboo tote on the table against the back wall of the living room. She peers inside. Sticky notes line the fabric walls, reminders of bills to pay and which train line goes where and her mom's birthday? But no clutch. Yet everything else she'd normally carry with her, including her phone, is here. She reaches for it, pushing aside a fuzzy white Koozie she doesn't remember taking from the outing. The ringing stops, but on the screen are voicemail notifications—two of them, both from Ilena. And three missed calls before that—all from Ilena.

Ilena's thoughts on the direct listing are as clear as the glass on the John Hancock Tower outside the penthouse's windows and just as faulty. Her threatening to leave AIM led Mallory here, wondering if she had angry sex with Grayson after attempting to blackmail him at the outing.

Blackmail, like out of some B movie. But worse because Mallory only had a ghostly tendril of proof: snippets overheard a little over a month ago at his penthouse, the day she'd discovered the computer error. Though not entirely conclusive, it was damning enough to suggest that Grayson had created the error—on purpose—to make AIM appear even more successful than it already was. She needed more time to investigate, to fully understand what she'd heard, but Ilena's ultimatum had forced Mallory to play her empty hand. When she'd confronted Grayson at yesterday's outing, trying to force him to admit he was involved in creating the error, he'd turned the tables on her. In that moment, she'd never hated anyone as much, not even her pissant of a father.

A ding, not for another voicemail but a text.

Ilena: We're at your condo.

Shit.

Mallory turns to Grayson's living room. She's been secretly sleeping with Grayson for the past year. Not even Ilena knows.

Mallory texts back: Running late. Don't wait for me. See you at the office.

But it crosses with Ilena's: We're letting ourselves in.

Shit, shit, shit.

One of Ilena's lectures, Mallory could handle, her best friend's judgmental nature nothing new. But Ilena's disappointment . . . that's another thing entirely.

Mallory returns her phone to the bag and takes in the great room that, like the hallway and bedroom, has the same unfathomable Grayson Version 2.0 update. Air plants hang from the ceiling over a rainbow of floor cushions and a diffuser spewing lavender-eucalyptus mist straight out of one of AIM's meditation corner how-tos. But Grayson has never actually used the AIM app. That should have been her first clue that he doesn't believe in it. Or in her.

"Grayson?" she calls out to no response, though the flatscreen is on, muted, tuned to the same morning show her mom used to watch—probably still does—her mother's loyalty unwavering through anchors having oral sex with interns and pontificating on the uniforms of female athletes.

Mallory is staring at the somehow both puffed and skeletal face of the female anchor Shandy Shane, feeling good about her own decision to steer clear of fillers and Botox, when a blocky, distorted version of the AIM logo flashes on the screen. Panic gathers in Mallory's chest like a funnel cloud. She spies the remote on the side table and lunges for it, jamming her finger on the button to unmute.

"AIM Higher, they said, and, my, are they! And now you can too. Everyone's favorite wellness app is opening its shares to the public next week. Already a fan fave in the health and wellness space, AIM went wider and higher last year with its newest and buzziest feature, 'How Wide's My Smile.' Curl up with a book instead of your earbuds? Ten points! Bubble bath instead of doomscrolling? Fifteen

points! What's more all-American than your pursuit of happiness getting a seal of approval from your virtual friends?"

"Research, coaching—it's not only about the points!" Mallory can't help but shout.

"Speaking of friends, eight-year-old AIM isn't the first company founded and led solely by women to debut on Wall Street, but its valuation shatters records as the highest for any company in its sector to date. In this world where the tech bubble is going pop, pop, pop *with every massive layoff and embezzlement scandal, that's a feat worth a heck of a lot of points! Hahahaha!"*

Mallory's hands clench.

"But seriously, all eyes are on AIM, partly thanks to its crafty decision to opt for the less traditional direct listing rather than straight IPO. In just one week, the company will be selling shares to the public without the assistance of intermediaries—a high-risk, high-reward gamble that just might pay off. In fact, with four million subscribers and counting, industry insiders expect records to be made. And when they are, this is the place you want to be. We've just gotten word that one of the three smart, savvy, sparkling besties behind AIM will be here next week. How wide's our *smile to be sitting down with CEO Mallory Latham and Chairman of AIM's Board of Directors Grayson Fields!"*

Holy.

Shit.

"Grayson!" Mallory cries out, her heart thrumming. That PR firm they hired nailed it. AIM on *The Shandy Shane Show*!

She rushes to the tote and roots around past her empty emergency snack bag and makeup case and reclaims her phone. This must be why Ilena was calling. She mutes the television and is about to hit Ilena's number. They have to celebrate this—AIM is going to be on morning television!

But it's not AIM. It's not Ilena and Aubrey. It's only Mallory.

And Grayson. Why Grayson? Everything inside her seizes. Now the changes in the apartment make sense. B-roll footage.

He's preparing for it. Which means, he arranged it. To let her know what he's capable of, maybe even to prove in his warped mind how much she and AIM need him. But Grayson Fields doesn't do anything for anyone but Grayson Fields.

Bastard.

Then again . . . she and Grayson *would* be on national television, discussing AIM at the time when every fund manager and investor was watching.

Buzz, exactly what they needed. She'd always believed the press around going public would increase their user base. Something necessary now more than ever. It was the perfect domino effect: buzz would lead to more users, which would lead to the high stock valuation being entirely accurate. After they went public, they could fix the computer error, end and eliminate the fake replicating accounts, and have an entirely honest user base, no one the wiser. No need, then, for Mallory to tell Ilena her suspicions about Grayson being behind it all.

Mallory still believed in that course of action. And what better buzz could there be than Shandy Shane? The show could solve everything.

And yet, odds are, Ilena won't see it that way. She won't want to take the risk.

Mallory pockets her phone. She needs coffee if she's going to take on Ilena. And then it's time to schedule appointments for hair and nails, and she should probably get a new suit and maybe shoes, definitely a pair of summer heels, and a bra, this one feels scratchy with more sag than usual. Mallory moves toward the kitchen, confused by the black granite countertop and coffee machine that looks like it was invented by NASA. Though that's a worthy upgrade since her last visit. She circles the island to retrieve one of the Simon Pearce mugs, and her foot hits something hard. She looks down to see a thousand-dollar loafer.

"Grayson?" she says more softly, coming around the island. "Gray—"

He's on the floor, right leg bent at an unnatural angle, body still, eyes open, opaque, and not moving. Not moving.

She should drop to her knees, press her fingers to his neck, trying for a pulse like they do in the movies, but she has no idea where to actually put her fingers, and even if she knew where to put her fingers, how could she put her fingers on him when he's a greenish, grayish blue? He's blue.

Grayson Fields is dead.

5

MALLORY

Harvard University
*Twenty-One Years **Before** the Outing*

"Is he dead?" Mallory asked, staring at the Harvard boy hanging beside the largest dorm room in Straus.

Ilena slid closer and placed a finger under his nose. "Sleeping." She pursed her lips, anger drawing lines around them. "Such male privilege. As if a woman could ever fall asleep *duct-taped to a wall*. Arrogant bastard."

"Still . . . male arrogance isn't all bad. I mean, we won the bet."

"Yeah, we did." Ilena grinned.

This boy of at least a hundred and fifty pounds with a smattering of freckles and an abundance of hubris underestimated them. All he'd seen were legs, breasts, and flowing hair despite the fact that both Mallory and Ilena had gotten into Harvard just like he had.

When Ilena had given him the terms of the bet—their small dorm room on the first floor in exchange for his double the size of a quad with its own bathroom and two sinks—he'd snickered and held out his hand to shake, ready to be duct-taped to a wall. Ilena was wicked smart and a bit devious. Mallory had underestimated her too. Somehow, Ilena knew that the duct tape would hold. She bet that it would, saying they'd do the boy's laundry all semester if it didn't. And now this pompous boy's new roommate wearing a hoodie so low it skimmed his nose was mumbling under his breath and carrying Ilena's luggage and Mallory's box and duffel up these four flights of stairs.

Mallory turned to this girl she couldn't wait to get to know better. "Let's say he were dead . . ."

"Okay," Ilena said, not skipping a beat, and Mallory thanked the Harvard dorm lottery gods a thousandfold.

"Right, so he's dead. Are we the kind of friends who'd help each other hide a dead body?"

"Not yet," Ilena said. "But here's hoping."

6
MALLORY

Friday Morning
*One Day **After** the Outing*

Mallory's fingers get lost in apricot fur. She strokes in circles, easing the trembling of the cockapoo now curled in her lap but having no effect on her own. Her eyes want to close, yet every time she gives in, she sees his slack jaw and swollen lips and cloudy eyes and her stomach heaves like after she swallowed an ocean of seawater.

The accident happened when she was eleven. She'd been walking the beach with her mom on one of those days when the single-parent guilt proved overwhelming. Her mom had dropped everything so they could hop the subway to the Wonderland stop where sand and waves met grime and seedy parking lots.

She remembers they were halfway down the three-mile stretch when her mom's eyes fixed on a figure in the distance, tall and lumbering, barely able to maintain his balance, barefoot on the hot grains of sand. Her mother couldn't look away. Her mom didn't date, had never had a relationship, instead seemed to be holding on to a man who had left her and their only child when that child was so young that she was still wobbly on her own feet. And this was him.

Her dad.

Mallory had been sure of it. She convinced herself that *this* was the reason they'd come to the beach that day. Mallory was young enough to believe that wanting something could make it so.

Her eleven-year-old self had sprinted into the white break and swam out to where the line of surfers in wetsuits flexed their patience as much as their muscles. Swells do not make Massachusetts their home like they do in California or Hawaii. But Mallory had been lucky. A wave came to her as if she'd commanded it, rising and cresting, the white trails beckoning like fingers. She seized a board out from under a cursing teenager and dug in her skinny arms, the chill of the water no match for her adrenaline.

Her father would see her. He would be proud. He would stay.

She nearly drowned. Black and blue and gnarly shades of purple bruises on her stomach and back and shins and twelve stitches behind her ear from where her head met rock. They'd had to shave a section of her hair off, which made her a badass to the boys in school and a freak to the girls. Such easy lines for fifth graders. Of course, it hadn't been her father. Her mother had simply been seized by her own singular thought: the work deadline she'd forgotten that the impromptu beach day would cause her to miss.

The first time Mallory spoke of it again was the day before Ilena's wedding. Ilena's own father lived in California. His current wife wasn't the woman he'd originally cheated with, but his decision to have that affair (and let's be honest, probably more) had led him to palm trees and endless sun and Ilena with no one to walk her down the aisle. He had said he would come. And then, he didn't.

Mallory sat on the bed in the studio apartment she'd rented straight out of college and pulled back her duvet. Nestled beneath it, Mallory held Ilena until her shuddering subsided and then told her the story about her own dad. And then Ilena held Mallory. They never made it to the bachelorette party neither of them had really wanted Mallory to plan. Their friends and coworkers hopped on the bus to the orchard winery and sipped syrupy wine made from blueberries while Mallory and Ilena debated which dangerous animal they'd have as a pet if they were guaranteed it wouldn't hurt them. (A velociraptor for Mallory, an orangutan for Ilena.) And the next day, Mallory had walked Ilena down the aisle.

On the floor on the other side of the kitchen island, Mallory looks up. Her fingers stop moving, and Harley presses himself harder into her thighs as she scans the penthouse's command center: intercom, door buzzer, camera linked to the security desk. The one monitored twenty-four hours a day. They must have seen her coming up with Grayson last night. They'll know she hasn't left. They'll know she was the last person to see him alive.

She leaps to her feet, sending Harley scurrying under the dining room table. She flicks open her phone. The friend-tracking app shows that Ilena, who is in a cab with Aubrey, is only a few minutes out. Not knowing what else to do, she'd texted Ilena to meet her here, though she didn't explain why. Not over text.

Mallory faces away from Grayson's loafer and paces. *Was* she the last person to see him alive? She wraps her hand around her forearm, her fingers too slender to match up with the red marks. *Was* she the last thing he touched? Acid shoots up her throat, and she racks her brain to remember something, anything, about getting here or being here, but the last memory she has is sitting at the sandbox with Ilena and Aubrey.

Which leaves just one thing for me.

She'd grinned, and then she'd said the last thing she *can* remember: *Grayson*.

As the two syllables left her lips she'd felt a weight lifting, the tightness in her chest these past few weeks vanishing, the sting of his betrayal of AIM eased by her own of him. She hadn't even felt bad. No guilt.

This is a coincidence. He must have drunk too much and tripped. Hit his head on the granite island. Don't people die from falls in their homes all the time? Yes, yes, yes, of course, a drunken fall! A tragic drunken fall.

She hurries to the kitchen, her fingers opening her phone app, the "9" and first "1" already entered when she sees the artisan wood board on the counter beside the sink. A soft Brie or Camembert melted into a pool of white, orange cubes of an aged Gouda or Manchego crusting over, rolled prosciutto dried out, a flattened puddle of honey, a pile of crackers. She keeps her head forward, eyes on the cheese board as she moves closer. Something sharp digs into the bottom of her foot. She draws her heel back and bends to pick up one of the broken pieces of cracker littering the floor.

She brings it to her nose and sniffs. Her tongue reaches out, the salt hits her, and her head spins to the counter. She squints, trying to make out the shape and the color, but it's the little dark toasted specks that give it away. Sweat breaks out under her arms.

It can't be. She forces the piece of cracker into her mouth, and her teeth don't even need to bite down before she knows. She spits the macerated cracker into her palm and lets it fall to the floor. She clutches her phone and exits the kitchen, inhaling slowly to steady herself, to lower her heart rate, to let her mind try to make sense of this.

The crackers, gluten-free, low calorie, high protein, used to be her favorite, a staple of her emergency snack bag, one she stopped packing when she started sleeping with Grayson.

Harley creeps out from beneath the table and sits on her feet. She pulls her foot back; he inches forward and sits. She does it again. So does Harley.

Shit, shit, shit.

"Go!" she shouts, "just go!" She yanks her foot, sending Harley skittering and releasing that same low whimper that she's now sure he knows the effect of. Her lungs clench as she erases the "1" and the "9." She checks Ilena's status, sees she's nearly there, and texts a breezy Brunch! How fun! We've been waiting, bubbly popped! The dots of Ilena's response blink in and out, but Mallory cuts her off. No apologies necessary for being late!

Mallory squeezes the phone in her hand, willing Ilena to understand, to not do or say or write anything incriminating. Incriminating like the marks on Mallory's forearm.

When the doorman rings to announce Ilena and Aubrey, Mallory answers, using the performance skills honed through her every interaction with condescending investors and patronizing start-up founders to put on a show. Laughing to some unuttered joke, pausing as if Grayson's calling to her, responding to him as her heartbeat echoes in her ears, excitedly welcoming Ilena and Aubrey up.

In the penthouse's vestibule, the elevator dings, and Mallory holds her breath. The doors slide open. Mallory feels herself relax as her eyes meet Ilena's—her best friend, her partner in everything since they were eighteen-year-olds boasting that one day it'd be their names being whispered in the halls of Straus for having once claimed the biggest room as their own. The sight of her nearly sends Mallory into a fit of giggles. This is ridiculous. She's being ridiculous. Grayson fell. This has nothing to do with the outing and the game or the crackers that couldn't possibly have come from her.

"Oh, Ilena, you won't believe—" Mallory starts.

Ilena waddles forward, and Mallory's eyes take in Ilena's balloon of a belly.

"Ilena? Is this some joke, tell me this is a joke or . . ." Mallory's gaze travels from Ilena's worried brow to Aubrey's twisting hands.

This is . . . what is . . . this can't be . . . *real.* Mallory pinches her eyes shut and breathes, deeply, inflating her chest, releasing the tightness across her shoulders, knowing when she opens her eyes, all of this will be gone. She opens her eyes. Nothing's gone. Except maybe her sanity. "Well, fuck. Fuck, fuck, fuck."

Aubrey gives a half wave as she steps out of the elevator, letting the doors close behind her. "That was me. Apparently."

"But that's not . . ." Mallory's voice disappears, unable to choke out the *possible.* Ilena's stomach means anything is possible.

"I know, but I'm fairly sure." Aubrey's shoulders round as if she's trying to fold in on herself. "I don't remember, but there was . . . evidence."

Guilt wells in Mallory's throat. "Kai?"

Aubrey nods, her finger rubbing a spot on her thumb.

Mallory's breath grows shallow as she steps toward Ilena. She places a hand on the shelf of Ilena's stomach. "And?"

Ilena encases Mallory's hand with her own, displaying a platinum wedding band instead of her usual gold one. "Felix made a corny dad joke this morning."

Felix. It's like being dropped in a black hole with not even a pinprick of light to suggest a way out. "But how?"

Ilena releases Mallory's hand. "That's a question, but not *the* question. *The* question is . . ." Her soft fingertips glide over the red marks on Mallory's forearm. "Have you . . . did you . . . ?"

"*Kill* Grayson?" Aubrey says. "Of course she didn't."

They wait for a confirmation that Mallory cannot give. She steps back, allowing them to enter the penthouse.

Ilena moves with a speed that, though not swift, must be her top in this state. Aubrey follows a reluctant several paces behind. A humming clogs Mallory's ears, but soon through the fuzziness comes the scuffling of knees on a floor, a long cry, a gasp, a "Grayson!"

Mallory remains still. Ilena appears in the hall, her face tight, her eyes wide, but somehow still managing to exude her usual calm. She extends her hand. "Come."

So Mallory does. She lets Ilena take her hand and guide her to the couch where Aubrey's sitting with tears in her eyes and Harley in her lap. The television's still on, the morning show continuing to play on mute, and Mallory wants to turn back the clock and live in that brilliant span before she saw Grayson when the only thing on her mind was AIM being on *The Shandy Shane Show*.

Ilena settles herself in the armchair beside the couch. "I'm assuming you haven't called the police?"

Mallory shakes her head.

"And you have no memory of last night? Of . . ." Ilena gestures toward the kitchen, swallowing audibly.

Again, Mallory shakes her head, a chill starting in her toes and snaking up her legs.

"Then you have no idea how?" Ilena says.

That chill shrouds her torso, seizing her lungs. Grayson was always careful. He never ate anything without checking. Organic, GMO-free, grass-fed, all of that, for his health, sure, but also for his allergen and that "slight" complication of anaphylactic shock.

"Mallory?" Ilena prods. "Do you?"

"No," she lies, pressing her teeth into her bottom lip. "I just woke up and found him. I don't—I just woke up." The weight of Ilena's stare nearly suffocates her.

Finally, Ilena's eyes detach from Mallory's. They flicker to the red lines on Mallory's arm before Ilena says, "Okay." She takes out her phone and starts dialing. Mallory sees the "9" on the screen and snatches the phone out of Ilena's hand. "Mallory!"

"What, Ilena, what? You actually want to call the police? You think they're going to believe I just happened to wake up in a dead man's apartment with no memory of the past fourteen hours?"

Aubrey's hand quakes as she adjusts Harley. "But it's not just you, it's all of us."

Details follow of Aubrey and Ilena waking up to homes and lives that are a degree or two or a hundred off from their own. None of this should be possible. Have they all been drugged for some practical joke? But it's so elaborate, involving so many people and the renting and staging of apartments. And how could anything of this magnitude be done in that short amount of time? And Ilena would have to be in on it, wearing a fake belly and—

"How can the world just change overnight?" Aubrey asks.

"It can't," Ilena says. "Life is logical. Which is why I never believed in Santa Claus or the Tooth Fairy or monsters under the bed. There must be a perfectly reasonable explanation—"

"One that also explains this?" Aubrey holds up her hand. "I remember everything up to the sandbox, including the mosquito bite on my thumb from last night that's magically gone."

Ilena peers at Aubrey's skin. "But you swell up for days."

"I know." Aubrey sticks out her thumb. "But nothing. Unlike my nails. Pink polish? Did I sleepwalk and paint my nails? And look at my cuticles. As perfect as yours. And this?" Aubrey pulls on the waistband of her pants. "Two sizes smaller, but they fit. Not even snug." She reaches across the couch and pulls an elastic out of Ilena's hair. "And unless this is a wig . . ."

Ilena's ballooned belly overshadowed it, but her hair is longer, nearly to her shoulders, and Aubrey's face does look thinner, her wrists, chest, waist, all just a bit smaller, yes. Mallory reaches for her own hair, the same length as it's been for the past ten years. Her body feels like her body, feels the same, but is it different? Besides her jumpsuit not being aubergine but a rather hideous shade of Crayola crayon grape? She rubs the fabric, cheap and fit for a clown. The one she wore yesterday was couture. Thanks to AIM, she's become a public figure, one people pay attention to, down to her shoes.

Mallory's mind churns, trying to put this in some box that makes sense. "We agree we're alive, right? Not in some sort of joint hallucination or purgatory?"

Ilena's hand reaches for the ends of her long hair. "Logic would say so."

Logic. Right, okay, logic. Logically, what do they know? They were at their summer outing last night. They played a game. They woke up with no memories of anything in between. Except they woke up *here*. In this place. This place with these differences. These differences that are all connected to the game.

Aubrey sleeping with Kai. Ilena married to Felix—and pregnant. And Grayson. No matter the how, he's no longer alive. Mallory's stomach twists, and her heart clenches, and she has to put it aside. She can't care, not now, not here, not amid all this. She sticks Ilena's phone under her thigh, bouncing against it. She stares at the meditation corner and breathes through the storm raging inside of her.

She then faces her two best friends and lets logic guide her. "You both know I'm the last one to go for any kind of mystical crap." She also never believed in Santa Claus or the Tooth Fairy but pretended to for the benefits. And yet, she finds herself saying the impossible: "Fuck, Marry, Kill. We each did exactly that."

Ilena says, "I said there has to be a reasonable explanation for this."

"Then let's reason this out." Mallory assesses the changes in her friends, trying to quash the screaming in her head and sort through the thoughts firing one after another. "If this is real, actually real, then one of two things is going on. Either the place we call home has changed, and we're still us, in which case, Aubrey's thumb should be the size of an heirloom tomato and Ilena's hair shouldn't be touching her shoulders and her stomach shouldn't have another human squatting inside of it. Or this isn't home. And we're not us."

"Not us?" Aubrey says. "What does that mean, 'not us'?"

Mallory looks between Ilena and Aubrey. "I think, if we agree that this is *a* reality, then we have to consider that it might not be ours."

Ilena tries to clamp her shaking hands together in her lap, but her belly stops her. "That's just not . . . possible?"

Ilena's voice trembles, her tone as unsure as Mallory's ever heard it, and it steals her breath and rattles her bones, and *this*, this is the sound a rock makes when it breaks.

Mallory fights the sob rising in her throat and turns away from Ilena. A silence fills the room, broken by an actual soft cry from Aubrey and a matching one from Harley. Ilena then releases a long exhale. Mallory returns her gaze to her best friend, and they lock eyes, grounding them both in the people they have always been.

"We're clearly us in mind," Ilena says, in a way that is quintessentially Ilena—with a "but" coming.

One that Aubrey steals. "But in other bodies. So what's happened to our bodies? At home? Do we think they . . . I mean, we . . . still exist? As us? Or as, what? *Them?* And who's them anyway and—"

"Breathe," Ilena says softly. "Let's all just breathe. Because there's no way to answer any of that yet." She turns to Mallory. "But I think no matter where this is or what this is, an unexplained death still requires a call to the police. And this unexplained death is Grayson, Mallory, Grayson Fields. You chose him in the game, what? On a whim, to be funny, or was there another reason?"

Mallory's skin grows cold. She slowly lets her eyes drift to the kitchen . . . to Grayson's loafer . . . to Grayson.

Grayson sliding a check with more zeroes than she could imagine across the conference room table, wrapping his arm around her waist at the bar that night in celebration, her thigh against his during board of directors meetings, his grin pumping up his cheek, hand on a glass of wine at that vegan restaurant in the South End, fingertips wiping ketchup from her lips at the Shake Shack where their grumbling stomachs led them after, the half walk, half run to his building, where Grayson took her around back and punched in the code for the service elevator, whose secret ride let hands and fingers and lips go everywhere they'd been longing to go, stumbling over Harley, tearing off shirts and shoes and pulling back sheets and laughing and backs arching and oh, god, Grayson.

Her lips begin to quiver, and a deep hole of sadness opens in her chest. It grows and widens and threatens to swallow her whole. She can't let it. She can't acknowledge it. She can't give in to it. There's nothing more she can do for him. She has to stay focused on what she can control. And no matter what this is and what's going on, what they can control is their response to it all.

"I was just being my outrageous self," Mallory says. Admitting that she'd been sleeping with Grayson in their world would have made their relationship real. Here, it gives her motive. "He's not going anywhere, and we need time to figure out what happened, what this is . . ." *Time to not see that bent leg or feel the cold of his skin, to wonder if she might have . . .* "And we certainly can't do all of that if we're stuck in a police station trying to answer questions we have no way of answering."

Ilena's lips remain thin as she attempts to retrieve her phone. Unaccustomed to her new center of gravity, she falls back into the chair. Those same peacock-blue eyes that grabbed hold of Mallory twenty-one years ago take the measure of her now. Ilena is well aware of the lengths Mallory's willing to go to get what she wants but equally as aware of who Mallory is and what she holds dear. And that's everyone in this room.

With the barest of movements, Ilena dips her chin in agreement. Mallory knows how hard that is, especially since it's not the first time she's had to ask her best friend to set aside her morals recently. (Or the second.) Mallory returns Ilena's phone and then searches Aubrey's face for signs of a panic attack or worse. But Aubrey is simply staring straight ahead, eyes tinged with red, clutching the dog like he's a life preserver.

Mallory breathes in. "Who knows, we could wake up tomorrow back at the sandbox." *Or somewhere else entirely.* Mallory pushes through a wave of nausea.

"We could—?" Aubrey sneezes, but instead of Harley flinching or jumping off of her, he only burrows in deeper. "Do you think we could, Ilena?"

"I don't know," Ilena says, slowly. "I honestly don't know anything." Her hand floats to her round stomach, hovering as if afraid to let herself feel what's right in front of her.

Mallory looks at the marks on her own forearm and understands completely. "For now, let's get our bearings. Let's act normal. Go to work, go to . . . to . . . prenatal yoga, whatever, let's just get out of this goddamn apartment and away from this *(him)* so we *(I)* can think. Think and see what's here and who's here and what here *is* before anything else happens."

Aubrey remains still, holding on to Harley, but Ilena again bobs her head in agreement, her hand still unable to settle on the impossibility inside of her. All the years stretching between the two of them never included what it does now.

Mallory slides to the edge of the couch, puts her hand on top of Ilena's, and presses both to her belly. "A baby, Christ, Ilena, a fucking baby."

Mallory doesn't know if this is a dream or a trick or some supernatural anomaly or maybe some Groundhog Day loop, but she's not spending the time it'll take to figure it out in jail for feeding Grayson Fields nut crackers. Her friends need her, AIM needs her, and the goddamn *Shandy Shane Show* needs her.

7
AUBREY

Friday Morning
*One Day **After** the Outing*

Aubrey sits on Grayson Fields's bed with his orphaned dog in her lap while her best friends debate what to do with the body. The body, like it's a thing, an old armchair with peeling leather and a saggy cushion kept around because you can't remember how it got through the door in the first place. *He's a person*, Aubrey wants to scream, but doesn't. She doesn't have anything to follow it with. No solution to offer.

She's seen enough movies and TV shows to know that there's still a window of time where they can make this right, not get in any deeper, call the police and justify Mallory not doing so sooner because she was in shock. Shock can do all sorts of things to a person. Something she learned with Ethan. She pictures him, his sandy hair falling into his light green eyes, and drops of sweat erupt along her hairline. Her vision narrows as if traveling through a darkening tunnel, and she roots herself deeper into the mattress to stay upright.

She senses another sneeze coming on and tries to stifle it, as if by being quiet she can offset the fact that she's in here with a hypoallergenic dog she's somehow allergic to while her best friends deal with a dead body.

"Ilena, your legs." Mallory's order filters through the crack of the bedroom door. "Lift with your legs."

"Legs? My legs?" Ilena says. "Oh, of course, wait, there they are. It's hard to see them past my honeydew melon of a stomach."

Lifting? Ilena's lifting Gray—the body? Isn't that bad? Aren't pregnant women not supposed to lift heavy things? Or is it carry? Or is it—

The sneeze refuses to be stopped and the dog leaps from her lap, a blur of orange disappearing through the door before Aubrey can unfold herself. "Harley, no!" she shouts.

Keeping the dog calm and contained, that's all Aubrey was tasked with doing. Both of her friends had taken one look at the queasiness all over her face and sent her away. Aubrey was relegated once again to the place she's lived in her whole life as the youngest, quietest member of a family of Teflon-strength personalities. By the time she'd come along, birthday cakes were always chocolate even though the caffeine gave her headaches, pets were always of the feather variety even though their jerky necks gave her nightmares, and afterschool activities involved balls of any size, not wires or motherboards. She believed in Santa Claus and the Tooth Fairy for far too long because she wanted to believe the impossible could be possible. Like her grandmother did. If it weren't for her grandmother convincing Aubrey's parents that Williams College was a place that wouldn't swallow Aubrey whole, she might not have gone. She might not have majored in computer science and wound up at the Silicon Valley start-up program, filling in for a co-worker who dropped out. She might never have met Mallory and Ilena. Or wound up here.

"Harley!" Ilena cries. "Careful, Mallory!"

Aubrey untucks her legs and swings them to the floor. She

presses her hands into the mattress, a reflexive pro-con list forming in her mind, and of all the pro-con lists that have formed in her mind or will ever form in her mind, this has to be the most surreal.

She clears her throat and tries to choke out a "Do you need help?" but of course they need help. But they won't ask. Because she's too fragile.

"Your left foot, Mallory, watch your left . . . your other left!" Ilena says.

"Christ, this dog, where's Aubrey? Aubrey!" Mallory shrieks.

And Aubrey forces herself off the bed and into the hall.

Ilena faces her full on. "Aubrey, we're fine. Grab the dog and go back into the bedroom. We've got this."

A striped blanket in the shape of a body lies on the floor between Mallory and Ilena. Aubrey takes in the block of a torso in the middle, the limbs spreading to either side, the thrust of a nose making the blanket protrude, and her face must relay every ounce of her fear and grief and uncertainty, but she says, "I can help. I—I want to help."

Ilena sets her jaw, a refusal coming, but then begins one of those silent conversations with Mallory, their friendship of more than twenty years intimidating and inspiring, and still it's entirely dumbfounding how Aubrey's been a part of it for the past eight. Ilena steps back and says, "Okay, then."

"Spectacular." Mallory tugs down the hem of a white shirt that must be Grayson's. She slipped it over her jumpsuit, for warmth, maybe, or maybe to cover those marks on her arm.

A week out from taking their company public and potentially filling their bank accounts with more money than Aubrey could spend in three lifetimes, they are placing a dead man in a freezer custom-built to look like a blanket chest. It's gorgeous, a deep red mahogany with chiseled wood inlays and a compressor that's nearly silent. You'd never know it was storing not extra sheets and pillows and duvets but organic, raw dog food and grass-fed beef and cauliflower pizza crusts. You'd never guess it was about to be home to one of the most successful venture capitalists in the country.

To make room for Aubrey, Mallory shoves the garbage bag full of frozen food aside with her foot. "Just for now. Until we figure out what's happening. Then we'll make it right."

They'll want to, maybe they'll even try, but they won't be able to. Some wrongs are only wrong after the fact, when consequences and perspective give you hindsight you'd have otherwise never had. Like Ethan. Other wrongs can be seen from a mile away. This is one of those.

The three of them heave Grayson Fields into the freezer with a fair amount of difficulty given Ilena's current situation and the fact that Aubrey's hands can't stop shaking. Without the need to say it, Mallory is the one who makes the final adjustments and closes the lid.

Mallory turns to face them. "Okay, we need some rules. It goes without saying, we tell no one." Her eyes dart to Ilena, who reluctantly nods. "We stay vigilant, ears open, eyes wide, taking in everything but offering little. We need to let others lead and direct the conversation. Just like Aubrey already does."

This isn't meant as a criticism despite it feeling that way.

"We maintain our normal routines, whatever those are here," Mallory continues, ticking things off as if she's done this before. "Check calendars and emails and cancel things that seem dangerous."

Aubrey stiffens. "Dangerous? What's dangerous?"

Mallory shrugs. "I don't know, like a high school reunion? Where people will know too many things we don't."

Isn't that basically everything here? Everyone?

Mallory pushes on. "We don't draw attention, we don't post on social media, we don't deplete our other selves' bank accounts. What's that thing Jonah made us do when he forced us to go camping?"

Ilena hugs her arms. "Leave no trace?"

Mallory nods. "That's it. That's what we do. As best we can." She pauses. "But AIM's still going public in this reality, and we owe it to all versions of ourselves to support that. We can't be absent from work."

Ilena's jaw tightens.

Mallory ignores her and fixes her gaze on Aubrey. "We're here, together, in one piece. One step at a time. Okay?"

Aubrey. The weak link. Always.

She starts to nod, then says, suddenly, "Someone's got to take the dog. I think I might be allergic, and Ilena—" She gestures to Ilena's belly. "So, Mallory. Mallory's got to take the dog."

It's the first decision Aubrey's made without hesitating in a long time.

Aubrey cannot believe she's here. At AIM. Their AIM, but not. The office seems real, everything seems real, the slight rock of her desk chair, the smell of microwave popcorn wafting from the communal kitchen, the wave from the receptionist she doesn't know, the people looking at her like she belongs. But she doesn't. Does she?

Outside Grayson's building, they confirmed AIM's location was in the same spot and called up a rideshare app on Mallory's phone. "Hitch," apparently, short for *hitchhike*, which is either totally cute or totally creepy. Aubrey can't decide.

On the ride to AIM, Aubrey nearly stuck her head out the window like Harley to take it all in.

Starbucks, stifling humidity, summer tourists sightseeing via the lens of their phones. Brick sidewalks, ritzy shops on Newbury Street, traffic clogging every route out of Boston and into Cambridge. Everything seemed the same.

But there's also a grocery store called Eat Me and the Charles River looks clean enough to drink from and the contact list in Aubrey's phone is twice its normal size.

At her desk, she hides behind the three huge monitors. One more than usual. Is she more talented here or less? Does an extra monitor help her do more work efficiently or does she need the extra monitor just to keep up?

Like everything else, the office here is slightly off. Desks of wood not white, coworker faces she recognizes, names she knows, ones she forgets—though that's the same as in her world. "Her world" is how she's come to think of the place she was before she woke up here.

Woke up here and helped hide a dead body and kidnap a dog. That's what they did, isn't it? They strolled through the art deco lobby with the jittery pup on a leash, Mallory breezily giving the doorman a friendly wave and the explanation of "watching the dog while Mr. Fields goes on an unexpected trip." Aubrey speed-walked ahead of Ilena and Mallory so as to not ruin everything by vomiting right there on the black-and-white geometric tile. She ran out the door with her head down, nearly colliding with a set of legs in white linen whose owner quickly leaped out of harm's way.

They have Mallory's rules, easily followed behind the closed door of Grayson's penthouse, but here, with people who will assume things and ask things and need things, with people who don't know she just touched . . . a body, Aubrey's not sure she can remember the rules, let alone follow them.

A chill settles in. Aubrey tugs at the jacket draped over the back of her chair. White denim. This Aubrey not only has a white couch but also a white coat? Is she a wild risk-taker or does she never eat blueberries or avocados? Does she only drink clear liquids? Or maybe this Aubrey is just especially hygienic?

Aubrey wipes her hands on her pants and carefully slips her

arms through the jacket. She then opens her calendar app to see what she's supposed to do today. Mallory insisted they act normal until they figure out what's going on, but how is she supposed to act normal when they're in, what? An alternate reality? She's going to spill. She's going to say the wrong thing. She says the wrong thing in their world all the time, "Aubrey-isms," Ethan had called them. Usually, Aubreyisms resulted in a brief moment of social awkwardness, but here, she's going to get them all arrested or taken for psychiatric evaluation or locked away for revealing some secret government experiment they're all a part of, which honestly seems like the most rational explanation of all.

Focus, Aubrey, just focus.

She spins away from her open office door, an unfamiliar feeling. She almost always sits at a station amid her team in her world. It makes her feel less like their manager, a title that always hung heavy on her. But here, she's grateful not to find a space carved out for her among them. She needs the privacy. She's not Mallory. One look and they'll all know she doesn't belong.

With any luck her Aubreyisms are alive and well and she can chalk up any missteps and mis-speaks, like forever mixing up the difference between 180 and 360 degrees, to Aubrey being Aubrey. Especially when it comes to Kai. She hasn't seen him yet. When she snuck out of her apartment to meet Ilena, he was still asleep.

Aubrey flicks on all three monitors and loses herself in the nitty-gritty of what makes AIM one of the most stellar examples of a mobile app in the marketplace. Based on a prioritized to-do list this other version of herself has on the desk, Aubrey begins by trying to figure out why some users' apps crash when they select the new meditation guided by Matthew McConaughey, which her world also has and which was working just fine there, when the familiar smell of eucalyptus wafts over her. Either an affinity for the same shampoo is what bonded them here or Kai must have used her shower. It's strangely intimate, the idea of him standing naked looking at her razor and scalp mask.

"Sorry I'm late," he says, entering her office wearing a grin that makes Aubrey's cheeks flush and ignites an arousal like some sort of muscle memory. His jet-black, eucalyptus-smelling hair is pulled to a knot at the back of his head and he looks even younger than she remembers.

"No worries. I mean, the outing and all," she says before it occurs to her that the outing from her world might not have happened here.

"*And all*," he says, flirtatiously.

She takes him not cocking his head or furrowing his brows as confirmation that the outing happened. Disaster averted, but many, many more live on the tip of her tongue.

"Which includes those lit strawberry mules and this." Kai slips a hand into his pocket and sets a small glass figurine on her desk.

"An octopus?" she says.

"*The* octopus." He raises an eyebrow, expecting her to understand.

"Yes, well . . ." Aubrey pauses, doing as Mallory said and letting Kai guide the conversation. Except he just keeps staring at her. "I really should get back." She vaguely gestures to her three monitors, but before she spins back to them, she sees Kai's face fall.

"Oh, I thought . . . the octopus and the succulent, I thought we were . . ." He moves to put the octopus back in his pocket and changes his mind, pushing it toward her. "It's okay, I know how busy you are, boss."

Boss. Super, just super. On top of having no idea what this

private joke is all about, she is indeed his boss. Part of her was hoping she wasn't his manager here and didn't have to add sexual harassment to her growing list of offenses. "About that, all that, are you okay with that or do you need to talk to someone or maybe you don't feel comfortable admitting to me that you need to talk to someone, so should I have you talk to someone else to see if there's something you need to talk to someone about?"

"Wow, that was awesome. Your mind's like a bullet train."

"Yes, well . . ." She wishes Mallory were here to tell her what to say. "Okay, so then, about all that?"

"All that . . ." Kai swivels his head, checking to make sure no one's in earshot as if to emphasize how wrong this all is. Satisfied, he leans over the desk, his head in line with hers, pretending to look at the monitor in front of them. She feels the warmth of his shoulder against her own. She hasn't touched anyone other than Mallory and Ilena in what seems like a lifetime. Except that's not true, she touched Grayson this morning. And apparently Kai last night.

"*All that* was incredible," Kai whispers, his voice confident yet also somehow seeking confirmation she cannot give. "*That* was something—"

"Don't, just don't."

Kai's warmth contradicts Grayson's cold; the suppleness of his limbs a sick contrast to the rigidness of Grayson's; Kai's dancing eyes a mocking of the lifeless ones whose lids Mallory closed with the tip of her finger as the dog whimpered at their feet.

"Aubrey, I'm sorry, did I misinterpret—"

"It's just . . ." Aubrey wrings her hands in her lap before shoving her chair back. "You're just so, so—" *alive!* "—young!"

Kai's face contorts like he's been stung by a jellyfish. "It didn't bother you last night."

But it should have! "I've got to go."

Aubrey hops up from her chair and rushes to her door just as the head of marketing arrives. Or at least, someone she normally knows as the head of marketing.

"Aubrey, we know how busy you are," Ella says, nervously pushing back her overly short bangs, making Aubrey wonder if she's only recently gotten them here. "But a half hour is a record for you! Honestly, we just wanted to make sure you were all right."

Aubrey bites the inside of her cheek. "Uh, yeah, sure."

"Sure on the summer sunset or the river blues?" Ella says, raising a color swatch of each.

Aubrey stares at her blankly.

Ella's eyes dart. "More options, maybe? Certainly, we can do that. We should have thought of that. *I* should have." She presses a hand to her chest. "I apologize, Aubrey. Your decisions are always instantaneous and spot-on when you have all the information."

Instantaneous and *Aubrey* are two words that would never go together. Unlike *Aubrey* and *pro-con list*.

Aubrey's palms begin to sweat. And is the floor tilting?

"Oh no," Ella says. "Perhaps you delegated the color palette for the listing party to someone else? Of course you did, what with all you need to decide in a single day—hour! Our interns, they're new, we must have missed—"

"Aubrey?" Kai says, approaching. "Is there anything I can—"

"Stop," she says, fighting the black polka dots clouding her vision. "Just stop!" Ella and Kai draw back, fumbling for the door. "Oh, no, no, it's not you, it's . . ." This can't happen, this can't happen here, she can't let Mallory and Ilena down by having a panic attack. "I've got to just—"

Aubrey brushes past them, through the room full of coding

pods, past the kitchen where a redheaded Noreen pauses her filling of custom tea bags to enthusiastically wave, and to the elevator, jamming on the button, accidentally calling the up instead of the down, pivoting and throwing herself at the door for the stairs and sprinting down the four floors past the rehab center on the first floor and out the building, spilling into the plaza and barreling into a man in jeans and a short-sleeved, slim-fitted collared shirt she knows is from Banana Republic because she bought it there.

"Ethan?" Her mind's playing tricks on her in this dream or hallucination or coma or—

"Yes?" His head tilts to the side like it did during every single one of her Aubreyisms and she can't draw in a breath, can't see straight because Ethan? Ethan?

"What are you doing here?" she blurts out.

His sandy hair's shorter, clipped tighter to his head, but his eyes are still pale green, and his cheeks have that slight ruddiness and he's the same, he's Ethan, *her* Ethan.

He looks at her quizzically, those same two vertical lines that come when he's sorting something out etching themselves in the space between his eyes, clearly visible despite the new addition of dark-rimmed glasses. "Autumn, right?" He points at her. "The arcade? What was it? Must have been six months ago?"

"Six months?"

"More? Don't you remember? We talked about the coincidence." He juts a thumb behind him. "This is my building."

She nods. Of course she remembers that his building is opposite AIM, just as she remembers that their first date was at the adult arcade in Boston. His choice. But their first date was more than a year ago. They were together ever since. Except not here. Here, apparently, they had the one date and he left it thinking her name was Autumn.

"Actually," she says, "it's Aubrey."

"Aubrey, that's it. You're right. Aubrey."

He slides his hands in his pockets, and she takes in that shirt she bought him but didn't and the fact that they're not together in this world, same as they aren't together in hers. But in this world, they could be. Because in this world, Ethan isn't dead.

8
AUBREY

*Four Weeks **Before** the Outing*

Aubrey stood between Ilena and Mallory waiting for the tears to come.

They hadn't yet, not when she'd gotten the call from the hospital, not in the back seat of Ilena's SUV as they crossed the Salt and Pepper Bridge to Mass General Hospital, not even as she'd nearly collapsed in the emergency room when that intern led her to the bed and pulled back the mint-green curtain, then the white sheet. Giving her an image she would trade anything not to have. She was his emergency contact, but not yet his next of kin. The proposal she'd accepted, the ring still to come.

Today she'd chosen black slip-on mules, not trusting herself to balance on heels. Though honestly, they were sneakers. The same ones she'd worn when she and Ethan had taken the ferry to Martha's Vineyard and rented bikes for the day, stopping for lobster rolls and the obligatory photo op on the bridge from *Jaws*. That trip was her first experience with sex outdoors, which after the initial forbidden thrill, left her with sand in her underwear and a renewed appreciation for mattresses.

The ground was hard beneath her feet in this cemetery on Long Island. They'd taken the train to his hometown, Ilena handling the ticket and settling her into a seat, and Mallory carrying the bag she'd packed for Aubrey and slipping her the Xanax that softened the edges just enough for her to withstand the crippling guilt that almost prevented her from coming to Ethan's funeral.

It was all her fault. If she hadn't kept texting him, if she'd just let that one text be enough and not sent an impulsive, uncharacteristic second that must have made him feel compelled to respond even though he was walking across the street. If she had just let things be, not made that one, selfish choice, she wouldn't be meeting the Sonders family for the first time in a cemetery.

But Mallory had been waiting for them in the bar. The drink she'd insisted was the perfect one for Aubrey and Ethan's wedding reception already ordered. Aubrey was on her way, but she hadn't gotten anything back from Ethan, not a "can't wait" or "almost there" or thumbs-up or even just a smiley face to acknowledge the fact that his fiancée had texted him.

Aubrey was embarrassed, afraid of looking stupid in front of Mallory. Of all the things Mallory was good at pretending, liking Ethan wasn't one of them. So she'd done it, sent that second text, and in the middle of a response to her left forever unfinished, he'd been hit by a bus. And do you have any idea how many jokes there are about being hit by a bus?

She vowed, there at her fiancé's grave site, in between Mallory and Ilena, to never text again. She'd need some excuse to read but not reply. She couldn't tell anyone, she couldn't stand the way they'd all look at her if they knew she'd killed her fiancé.

9
ILENA

Friday Afternoon
*One Day **After** the Outing*

A stuffed giraffe. Two BabyBjörns. A running stroller overflowing with diapers. Ilena's office could double as a baby boutique. From the stack of cards and Polaroids on her desk, she gathers that AIM hosted a baby shower recently. For her and Felix. And apparently, Ilena was the life of the party.

Blindfolded playing pin-the-sperm-on-the-egg.

How mortifying.

In a chair, spinning a baby bottle on the conference table around which a dozen AIM employees are sitting.

Can you say "lawsuit"?

Cheering Felix on as he winds his way through some sort of diaper obstacle course.

No one at AIM will ever take them seriously again.

This Ilena must not have gone to Harvard, she thinks, channeling her snob of a mother. She rotates in her chair, and, well, that theory's blown as her Harvard undergrad degree hangs on the wall. She squints. Bingo: no cum laude, let alone magna.

Ilena shoves the cards and photos in a drawer and places a

nursing pillow underneath her, hoping to ease the pain in her lower back, knowing she won't erase its horrific cause: Grayson. It could also be from the honeydew in her stomach, but if she attributes it to Grayson, it remains Mallory's fault. Though the honeydew's technically Mallory's doing too—she came up with the twisted spin on the game that somehow led them here.

Wherever here is. This place . . . this place where a man she worked with is dead, where, in agreeing to conceal it, she once again made a choice that went against her every belief, where she let Mallory's decisions dictate her own.

Except, if she were being honest, not calling the police wasn't solely for Mallory's sake. Ilena has more to take into consideration than just Mallory.

Ilena rests her hand on her stomach, wondering how far along she is. Six months, maybe seven, she's guessing from the size and the persistent kicking. It's weirder than she imagined, though in truth, Ilena's always been more focused on the getting pregnant than being pregnant—something that's not going to change despite the soccer player inside her stomach. This isn't real. She'll be back to her actual life soon, and Grayson will be alive, and Mallory won't be a murderer, and she . . .

She won't be about to become a mother. She removes her hand from her stomach. The baby kicks as if calling her back, but she keeps her hands flat on her desk.

In front of her is a receipt from the gastropub where they held their summer outing last night in their world, and from the size of the bill, apparently in this one too. She riffles through the invoices and papers beneath it. Raw bar, paddleboards, dung cleanup, everything but the flamingo. Perhaps this Ilena weighed in before they signed the rental agreement.

"Knock, knock," precedes an actual rapping against the open office door. Felix smiles. He's wearing his usual office attire of slacks and a pressed button-down, and she can't help thinking how good he looks. So does James, who enters behind him. His freckled skin is more deeply tanned, his red hair more ginger, like he lets himself spend more time in the sun here. Perhaps playing tennis with her husband.

"Brought the real muscle to finally get this stuff home now that the nursery's painted." Felix grips James's upper arm, and his cheeks flush.

Ilena feels like a fraud, an intruder, and she really has to pee—again. "Thanks," she says. "Thank you, James."

"My pleasure. And last night's party was quite the shindig. As always with you," James says sweetly, though she's pretty sure, as he picks up a Diaper Genie, he rolls his eyes.

The baby kicks, and her body jerks, less from the honeydew's foot and more from the realization that James may not be a teacher in this world, but he's still in love with Felix. This isn't right. She's not like Mallory, immune to guilt, able to pick and choose what lies to tell and what truths to keep secret.

But then Felix is at her side, kneeling, hand on her belly. "You've always been fun in a bottle."

No, she hasn't. Not even in college, not really. And especially not compared to Mallory.

Felix adds, "Pop the cork, and we're off! Runs in the Cohen family."

She stiffens. The only thing that runs in her family is Chardonnay.

"I really should get back to work," she says brusquely.

Felix jerks back, confused, before nodding slowly. "Oh, Ilena, it's just us. No need to put up a front that the baby isn't as important as it is."

"The complex life of a working mom. So on trend," James says, smiling politely, but those eyes judge every inch of her, and she feels like James knows she's a fraud.

The baby lobs a grenade at her midsection, and she places her hand on the spot. Felix covers it with his, laughing and smiling and making her smile. Then she looks up. James's jaw tightens as he rolls the diaper-filled stroller out the door. Felix dated both men and women in her world before settling down with James, and James's reaction is making her wonder if the same is true here. And if it is, how could he have possibly wound up with her instead of James?

Felix stands and begins gathering more baby gifts. He snuggles the giraffe in the BabyBjörn on his chest and piles baby clothes in the one he slides onto his back. All the items are neutral colors, no pinks or blues, no indication of the baby's sex, which is fine, which is good. She doesn't want to get attached to what isn't hers.

Felix leans in to kiss her goodbye, and she tenses, but his lips simply brush against her cheek. *Act normal*, Mallory had said, but she's not the one carrying the child of a man who should be living a life with someone else. She takes a deep breath, readying herself to confront Mallory, when she sees a clear plastic box on her desk. Encased inside is a pregnancy stick, those two lines she's been desperate to see staring right at her. Underneath is a note signed by Felix: *I'm now positive too.*

Which could mean there was a time when he wasn't. When he was scared. Just like her.

10
ILENA

Harvard University
*Nineteen Years **Before** the Outing*

Ilena sat, scared, on a toilet surrounded by empty bottles—water and beer, a fairly even proportion because Mallory suggested it, and Ilena needed both the hydration and the liquid courage. Though guilt twisted her insides with each sip of the cheap, watery beer. Because what if it hurt the baby? Mallory searched the internet and told her it wouldn't, that it was too early. And, she pointed out, Ilena wasn't keeping the baby even if there was a baby anyway. But one, Mallory lies, and two, *was* Ilena not keeping the baby?

She had fallen for Jonah the moment he'd stuck his arm in between the closing doors of the Red Line train at the MGH stop two years ago when they were both freshmen. He'd kept the subway at the station long enough for Ilena to run across the platform, arms laden with the artisanal cupcakes she'd special ordered for Mallory's birthday. She'd thanked him by opening the box and letting him choose one. He hadn't hesitated. Chocolate–peanut butter, he'd said, if Ilena didn't mind. She did. That was her favorite too. But then she caught a glimpse of those unruly brown cowlicks and suddenly she didn't mind so much. They ended up sharing the cupcake on the train. Jonah later admitted he had purposely missed his stop so they could keep talking. And it was talking, but it was also the most arousing foreplay she'd ever experienced.

She'd never been able to look at cupcakes quite the same way again.

The artisanal confection had been her father's go-to "surprise" when she was little—every birthday, every Hanukkah, chocolate–peanut butter and lemon-raspberry and key lime. That was, until her dad stopped being there for every birthday and every Hanukkah.

Jonah had reminded her of her dad, or her dad before he became a word, simply a noun, something she knew of but that had no bearing on her life, like Vegemite. She saw her dad not in Jonah's cowlicks that would forever curl every which way, but in his motivational-poster way of looking at life.

On the train, Jonah had pulled a coffee shop napkin from his backpack before Ilena could reach for the one in hers. He'd split the napkin in two, and they'd each wiped their fingers.

Then he'd said, "If I kept a bucket list, I'd be able to check off 'eating the perfect cupcake.'"

"Oh, are you morally opposed to bucket lists?" Ilena had asked.

"Principally. I prefer to be focused on what's right in front of me."

Ilena groaned. "Could you have a more cliché pickup line?"

"Probably? If you give me the chance."

Jonah was all about mindset and finding pleasure in everything. Alone, Ilena would breeze past the buskers in Harvard Square, but when Jonah was with her, he would stop and listen, really listen, not a polite pause and nod but staying through to the end of the song, two, three, tossing in tips or buying their homemade CD. He was the optimist to her realist, the rule bender to her follower, and he didn't mind that Ilena was outspoken or dogged when she knew she was right, which she nearly always was. He was okay with that too. But he was also ambitious, loading down his schedule at MIT with extra classes and internships just like Ilena did at Harvard. He wanted a future. One that didn't include a baby before they were even old enough to legally buy alcohol.

"I think that's enough," Mallory said as the timer went off and she picked up the pregnancy stick. "Twelve negative tests in a row. You're just late."

Ilena couldn't let the relief take over yet. "But I'm never late."

"There are some things even you can't control, and that includes the expulsion of your uterine lining. Now, come on, let's celebrate."

"Thanks, Mal." Ilena wanted to wrap her arms around her best friend and squeeze her tight. But she was still her mother's daughter and had to wash her hands first.

"You'd do it for me." Mallory scooped up the dozen pregnancy sticks and dropped them in the trash, not bothering to try to hide them with tissues like Ilena would have. "Of course, you'd have only had to sit through one test, not the entire inventory from CVS." She winked, then said, "This calls for champagne!"

Ilena's hand shot out and rested on Mallory's forearm. "Wait."

"No, for this, for our future staying intact, real champagne. None of that headache-inducing imitation crap that Jonah loves."

"It's not that." Ilena looked at the trash, all those single lines on the plastic tests adding up to nothing. "It's just, a part of me, a tiny part, but a part, is disappointed."

Mallory stilled, then gently placed her hand on top of Ilena's. "I know."

They stayed that way, listening to the voices in the hallway making plans to study or get pizza or down Jell-O shots, having no idea that inside this bathroom, Ilena's life had taken one path instead of another.

11
MALLORY

Friday Afternoon
*One Day **After** the Outing*

Mallory's phone buzzes. Mid-stride, she swipes to switch from her search engine to her messages.

Ilena: You're not in your office.

A question in statement form that makes the inherent judgment more pronounced.

Ilena: We need to talk.

Mallory's grip on the soft-sided carrier tightens. She actually should be at the office by now. But her decidedly Barney-colored jumpsuit garners attention. In terms of evidence, the Koozie may be circumstantial, but if there was an outing here last night, she couldn't very well show up in the same outfit. Especially the outfit that leaves the fading, though still visible, handprint on her arm for all to see.

After the car service had dropped Ilena and Aubrey off at

AIM, Mallory continued on to "her" condo on the far side of Harvard Square. She entered with a level of trepidation, but the changes were more subtle than the ones at Grayson's, less evocative of a personality adjustment and more in line with what she assumes are current trends. Capiz honeycomb chandelier instead of a linen drum pendant, absurdly bright colored tanks and blouses instead of sleek grays, whitewashed farmhouse floors instead of wide pine planks. Thankfully no evidence of another living being—not a partner, not a furry pet, not even a goldfish.

She hurriedly changed, leaving Harley in his carrier, unwilling to turn her well-manicured condo over to a dog. And yet as she began her walk to AIM, she realized that having him in the office wouldn't be much better, especially since she's the one who nixed the pets-in-the-office proposal a couple of years ago.

She texts Ilena an On my way. Traffic traverses universes! and slides her ringer off.

She increases her pace, resisting the aroma of coffee from two of her favorite shops and one she hasn't seen before that's trying a bit too hard with its 1980s decor. She longs to stop for a takeaway cup, rich and strong enough to make her dizzy, but between her phone and the furball, she doesn't have enough hands.

She closes the tab on *The New York Times*, which exists here too. But it matters less if this place has the same president and climate change and reality star scandals and more what this place *is*.

She needs that coffee. She backtracks, crosses the street, and slips into the '80s café, cringing at the "take one, leave one" neon plastic bracelets at the register.

When her order is ready, she clutches the cutesy Garfield mug and sits on a stool by the window, Harley at her feet. She starts by typing in "A place that is the same but different," which leads her to "the weirdness of Austin" and "islands that are really peninsulas" and "how to make your au pair feel at home," but also to what had been rattling around in her brain since the three of them sat on Grayson's couch, ten feet from his corpse, with memories of the lives they led that were slightly off from the ones they appeared to be in. She couldn't remember the term, but now, here it is: parallel universes.

One of the top hits is a link to the movie *Sliding Doors*, and it gives her an odd sort of comfort to know that not just the movie but Gwyneth exists here. (Sans Goop, which makes her an ideal asset to entice to AIM.)

A fact that Mallory files away just in case. Even amid all this, whatever "this" is, Mallory's brain never fully disconnects from her career. She refuses to apologize for being ambitious, for wanting her company to succeed, for the hope that AIM being on the morning show was happening at home. She's worked half her life for this, and she deserves it. They deserve it. And maybe it will be the key to changing Ilena's mind about leaving AIM. Because one thing *The Shandy Shane Show* made clear is that Mallory can and will take AIM public without Ilena. The thought punches a hole in her heart, same as the thought of taking AIM public *here*. Because here isn't home. Here is where Grayson Fields is dead.

She steadies her racing pulse and types "theories for parallel universes" into her browser. She watches the links pop up and begins skimming articles, her heart pounding in time with her scrolling, her brain hurting with every article she attempts to read. By the time she sets down her phone and drinks her untouched coffee, it's long past cold. She blinks, trying to reinvigorate her tired eyes. She searches the tote she grabbed at Grayson's for drops and finds a pair of cat-eyed reading glasses. Oh, for Chrissake. Her oval face is entirely the wrong shape for cat eyes. Still, she puts them on, and instantly the shaky letters sharpen. Is it possible that this Mallory is older?

Feeling superior physically, Mallory wonders which of them is lacking mentally. Trying to make sense of all this is about to give her an aneurysm.

She's been here nearly an hour. Ilena's going to send out the National Guard, or at the very least, Noreen. *Noreen.* Mallory better have Noreen here, or a Noreen equivalent. As Harley wriggles inside the carrier, Mallory finishes her cold coffee, tucks her phone in her bag, and hits the sidewalk.

She follows her mental grid of the city streets and chews on "Schrödinger's cat" and "Copenhagen interpretation" and "Einstein's wormholes" and "collapsing wave functions." Terms and theories that make her long for Jonah's science fiction–honed mind. She should have paid more attention when he recounted his latest geeky read.

Still, no matter her level of comprehension, everything she scrolled through points to the same conclusion: parallel universes are theoretically possible. Controversial, complicated, for sure, but not solely the stuff of science fiction books and movies. As much as, logically, the multiverse theory screams otherwise.

How is this physics and math and not woo-woo crap? That every time a decision is made, the outcome not taken branches off into a different reality? *Every time.* That means the universe, Mallory's universe—the one where Grayson's alive and her wardrobe doesn't appear to come from a cruise ship's gift shop—has split and is still splitting into near-infinite alternatives, each slightly or wildly different from one another. That's what this is. But then again, it *can't* be what this is. Every article she read and those she simply scanned and searched for terms like *collide* or *meet* or *cross* said the same thing: they shouldn't be able to intersect.

But what if they can?

What if they have?

Is there a third and a fourth and a fifth Mallory about to approach an animal shelter with hands shaking from having possibly, probably, potentially just committed intentional or unintentional murder?

At her feet, Harley gives that same small whimper, and Mallory bends before the carrier. Her trembling fingers unzip the flap. What if the thing has to go? She can't let him soil himself in there. The shelter might not take a dog with crap matted into its fur.

The dog creeps forward, and Mallory's fingertips graze its soft hair, not fur. He tilts his head to look at her, and she reaches into the carrier's side pocket for the bag of dried minnows. The security guard, Archie, had given the treats to her as the three of them left Grayson's building, Mallory quelling the tremble in her voice at the image of Grayson underneath that blanket. She nodded along as if dogs eating fish was something she knew, otherwise she might have undermined her whole dog-sitting story.

Harley sniffs the stinky creature but doesn't move to eat it. He pads closer to Mallory. She never thought puppy dog eyes were real until this moment.

"It's temporary," she says.

Harley places a paw on her leg, and all Mallory can see is Grayson's loafer, his leg bent in a way it couldn't possibly be.

But was.

Because he was dead. Most likely of anaphylactic shock. Yet the question is how that could have happened. She both wants to know and doesn't want to know. Because she'd have never put out the crackers by mistake. Sure, sure, because of her position as CEO of a health and wellness company, but also because of what nearly happened a year ago. The night of the launch party for "How Wide's My Smile," the night she and Grayson went to that vegan restaurant. The server had been new. Rather disturbing to wonder what he must have thought it referred to, he hadn't known the chef's reference of "Brazilians" in the amuse-bouche of a shot glass of carrot soup meant "Brazilian nuts." Thankfully, the host who'd taken the reservation and noted Grayson's nut allergy had intervened right before Grayson lifted the glass.

Grayson didn't carry an EpiPen. Hubris or stupidity or both. He could have died. While Mallory watched. They hadn't slept together yet, that would happen hours later, but the image had curdled the launch party cocktail in her stomach.

After, she had Noreen poll the entire company on allergies, each one noted in a searchable database and listed on foods served at every AIM event since. And that day, Mallory swore off the nut crackers that had once been her snack bag staple.

Her breaths shorten, echoing in her ears, and she wants to focus on the sound. If she focuses on the sound, she's not focusing on Grayson, her hands on his cold skin, her fingertips on his lifeless eyelids, his palm on her warm inner thigh, their synchronous fist pumps when they got their first valuation for AIM. All replaced by their clipped tones at the outing. He was the first investor who had truly believed in her. They are so very alike. *Were* so very alike.

"It's temporary," she says again.

Screw the internet. If these worlds intersected once, they can intersect again, which means she'll be back in her world with Grayson alive and everything will be as it was. Maybe not good, but also not this.

She leans over the dog, and he scurries into her lap, those goddamn puppy dog eyes so trusting, so searching, so sad. Or maybe she's projecting that last part.

She needs to do a hell of a lot more googling. Including on

how to take care of a dog. And get urine out of linen because the furball did have to go. *Christ.*

Now, why hadn't she thought of that? This Mallory punched through the walls on either side of her original office to make a suite. A lounge area with a couch, wet bar, kitchenette—she could live here. Or at least, Harley could.

She opens the front of the carrier, and he lazily stretches himself out of it, as if knowing he's won. She needs to set a reminder to walk him, or better yet, have Noreen set a reminder, and she really, really hopes she has not just a Noreen equivalent here but *her* Noreen, craving the familiarity. The shaking of her hands has traveled up her arms and into her neck, and she's on the verge of becoming one of those plastic bobbleheads.

Mallory breathes in and out as she circles her office suite, Harley her shadow. Her eyes land on a glass bowl filled with individually wrapped chocolates bearing the blocky AIM logo she saw on the morning show. It's not the sleek, somewhat abstract logo the three of them had landed on all those years ago. It's better.

Shit. She shoves the bowl, and chocolates fall to the floor. Harley scurries back. Yet his nose quickly overcomes his fear, and he begins to flip one, end over end. Mallory picks up the chocolate, peels the paper back, and Harley sits. A slight smile creeps in as she imagines Grayson training him, or more likely, paying someone to train him. *Those cloudy eyes. That blue skin.* Mallory can't breathe. She breaks off a piece of the chocolate.

"Don't!" echoes through the office as Ilena comes rushing in, though Mallory mentally puts air quotes around the "rushing."

"What?" Mallory says. "I know the no-pets rule was mine, but it's not like I could leave him in my condo."

"So instead you decided to kill him too?"

Mallory recoils. "You think I killed Grayson? You actually think that?"

(Because Mallory does too. A little.)

"Why shouldn't I?" Ilena shoves a long strand of hair behind her ear. "The rest of it happened, didn't it?"

Mallory grips the chocolate and blinks through an uncharacteristic stinging in her eyes.

Ilena stares at her, the two of them suspended in a silence that holds their history of more than twenty years, filled with broken hearts and broken toes, Tequila Tuesdays and Hangover Wednesdays, wedding vows and watering each other's plants (Mallory forgetting to), and absent fathers and birthday after birthday, so many things, big and small, but nothing like this.

Ilena's tone still carries an edge as she says, "You push boundaries, Mallory, you always have. But this? Can I believe you killed Grayson on purpose?" A sigh inflates her chest, which is now approaching Mallory's cup size thanks to the fetus inside of her. "Of course not. And yet none of us meant to do the things we've done here. But they've happened all the same." Ilena's eyes settle on Mallory's arm and the red fingerprints now covered by a long-sleeved orange blouse that completely washes her out but was the least offensive thing she could find. "We need to figure out how to deal with it. And I say that as someone who's spent the morning peeing herself every time she breathes too deeply." Ilena reaches for the chocolate in Mallory's hand. "Chocolate's toxic to dogs. Onions too. If you're going to watch him, you should probably do some due diligence."

Mallory swallows hard. "Right, thanks."

"Yes, well, at least we're here together."

"Wasn't sure you'd think that was a good thing."

"Twenty-one years, Mallory. We don't abandon one another, no matter what."

Except Ilena had threatened to do just that.

Ilena had presented her ultimatum as a choice, but it wasn't a choice at all. The direct listing or her. Mallory could call her on it, but then they'd start fighting and the only fight left in Mallory is for getting the fuck out of here. And back to their world, where Grayson isn't dead. But where she has reason to want him to be.

Mallory juts her chin at Ilena. "You've always been a self-righteous snob."

"Same as you've always been a self-centered egomaniac."

They stare at each other until Mallory gives her signature grin, and Ilena rolls her eyes. She lowers herself into one of the coral brushed-velvet chairs across from the sofa with her usual grace. Ilena's rich dark hair is the longest it's been in years. Seeing Ilena's skin smooth and dewy, her eyes weighed down with worry but still with a brightness that's long been missing, Mallory thinks the cliché of glowing when pregnant maybe isn't a cliché after all.

Mallory softens. "Ilena . . . a baby. After everything."

Ilena's hand reflexively cradles her stomach, and she gives a half smile before her face returns to its neutral state. "It's not right, Felix and all this. I'm not sure, but I think I—or she . . . this Ilena . . . well, something's off. There was a note on my desk, and James clearly despises me. I understand why you think we shouldn't call the police, but pretending to be people we aren't isn't going to work. Do you honestly think Aubrey can do it?"

Mallory wraps her arms around her torso. She thinks of those goddamn impossible nut crackers, and she isn't sure *she* can do it, let alone Aubrey. "We have to at least try. Besides, it's only temporary."

Ilena's eyebrow arches. "Grayson's *temporary*?"

"Temporarily what?" a chipper voice says. "Oh, sorry. I should have knocked." A sturdy-looking woman in her late fifties with poofy white hair and rosy cheeks ambles through the office door she opened without asking.

Mallory curbs the flaring of her nostrils and offers a generous smile to this woman who belongs in a yarn store, not at AIM. "Good morning."

"More like afternoon!" The Mrs. Claus lookalike taps an analog watch on her wrist. "Mr. Fields may not always be on time, but he's never a no-show. He lets me know if he's going to be late. Did you say he's temporarily delayed, Ms. Latham?"

This woman knows her, which means Mallory must know her too. "You haven't heard from him?"

"Not since last night. He let me in on your little secret." Mallory's face momentarily falters, and the woman hurries to add, "Oh, I swore not to tell a soul until the news was out this morning. But my gosh, how I wanted to call my sister. I dare her to go on about how I can do better than being the secretary to the man about to become the most well-known VC in the country now!"

So Mrs. Claus is Grayson's secretary, the complete opposite of Patrick, the crisply dressed and expertly groomed twenty-five-year-old Stanford graduate he poached from Snapchat's CIO in their world.

"I never doubted you for a moment," Mallory says.

"Thank you, Ms. Latham. Heidi Hoffman doesn't let you down." When neither Mallory nor Ilena responds, she continues, "And there I go talking about myself in the third person again." The woman—Heidi Hoffman, it seems—places a hand to her heart. "Mea culpa. Mr. Fields hates that."

"Well," Mallory says, "fortunately he's not here. At the moment, I mean."

The woman's brow furrows. "I have to admit, I'm starting to worry. He said a prep session had to begin first thing."

Ilena's head cocks, and Mallory realizes she never told her about *The Shandy Shane Show*, about only Mallory and Grayson being on it.

Mallory steps forward to escort Heidi Hoffman the hell out of her office. "Yes, well, schedules are—"

"Cleared," Heidi Hoffman says. "Noreen and I made sure of it."

Noreen.

Relief floods Mallory's veins.

Heidi adds, "She knows how flighty you can be."

Flighty? Mallory draws back, and Ilena laughs like it's a joke, but Heidi Hoffman just keeps on going.

"So we put appointments in everyone's calendars to meet in the AIM conference room, and I've got the nut-free rice bagels all set out."

Is that a brag or an indictment?

What it is, at the very least, is confirmation of Grayson's nut allergy and AIM's commitment to their employees' health in this world, same as in hers. That's good. Great. Terrific for AIM, more than a little worrying for Mallory. Because odds are, this Mallory also knew about Grayson's allergy.

"And now . . ." Heidi claps. "Where's my little munchkin?"

This draws Harley out from under the desk, which, unlike in Mallory's office in her world, is positioned to give her a view of AIM's interior, not the river.

"Harley!" Heidi Hoffman says. "There you are!" She holds up her phone. "Wi-Fi collar never fails. It's why I thought Mr. Fields was here. He dropped Harley off, then?"

"Not exactly," Ilena says. "He's—"

"On an unexpected trip," Mallory says.

Heidi Hoffman's forehead could double as a topographic map. "But he didn't mention anything to me."

"It was very sudden."

Skepticism clouds Heidi's eyes. "Business or pleasure?"

"I didn't want to pry," Mallory says.

Heidi dips her chin. "Oh, yes, yes, certainly not."

Mallory hadn't meant it as a criticism of the woman, but if that's what it takes to make her relent, so be it. "Right then, so any materials you have regarding preparation can be directed to me." Ilena's lips part, and Mallory adds, "Us, to us."

"You can count on me, Ms. Latham, Mrs. Singh."

Ilena winces at being called by Felix's surname, and Mallory covers with, "Another Braxton-Hicks?"

Heidi swoops in, arms extended, as if ready to wrap Ilena in a chunky wool blanket. "Come now, Mrs. Singh, just breathe through it." She sets a hand on Ilena's shoulder, pressing down, and counting.

Ilena mercifully fakes it, though her eyes bore into Mallory's.

"That's it, Mrs. Singh." Heidi pats Ilena's shoulder as Harley scampers toward her. She bends to tickle his chin. "What a sweetie you are."

Mallory realizes her opportunity. "Perhaps you might take—"

"If only my building allowed pets, I'd steal Mr. Harley right out from under you!" Her jaw slackens. "Mea culpa, Ms. Latham, that was inappropriate. But how about while I'm here I take him for a jaunt? Feed him his raw chicken nuggets?" Heidi gestures to the wet bar.

Mallory shakes her head. "I need to stop at a pet store, I guess."

"Oh, no, no. Mr. Fields only feeds Harley an organic, allergen-free raw diet. I have a subscription sent to his home each month." That brow draws the Eastern seaboard. "He must have been in *quite* the rush, indeed." She straightens her spine. "No matter. I'll just scoot on over to his penthouse, pop open his cold chest, and be back before Harley's tummy can grumble."

Shit, shit, shit.

Mallory digs into the side of the carrier and presses the leash into Heidi's hand, wishing she'd paid more attention to the pile of frozen foods they'd sifted through in the chest in Grayson's apartment, stuffing some into his normal freezer, tossing the rest. "I couldn't ask you to do that. Walking him is more than enough."

"Nonsense. I'll even use the code for the service elevator so I don't get waylaid by Archie."

Mallory crosses her arms in front of her chest. That first night, in their world, after the nut-free vegan meatballs and greasy Shake Shack burgers, Grayson had taken her up the service elevator, explaining after the tearing off of shirts and arching of backs that he often used the service elevator to avoid getting drawn into an interminable conversation about the security guard's sciatica, and other times when he needed to sneak in a repair company not on the condo association's approved list. Some ongoing conflict with the cleaning staff and the condo board meant no cameras had been installed at the back of the building or in the service elevator. Grayson had said riding in that elevator, unencumbered by stock tip solicitations and pleas for angel investments, was one of the few times he felt free to truly be himself.

He became someone else in that moment, someone she understood on a level she didn't even want to admit to herself. She'd traced her fingertip down his cheek, across his lips, parting them slowly, letting their kiss begin softly this time, and their touches followed suit until they could no longer go slow. She shivered beneath him, the second time even better than the first. She felt so close to him, in a way she hadn't with anyone, not since she and Ilena first met.

"Actually . . ." Mallory makes a show of opening her phone. "Let me. It would be hyperefficient for us both. Ilena and I have an appointment right near Grayson's building, and I'm sure you have a lot to do, rescheduling Grayson's commitments."

Heidi, who's been burying her fingers into Harley's underbelly, snaps her head up. "Of course, thank you, Ms. Latham. Role reversal today. Me off my game and you spot-on!"

Mallory grits her teeth, missing Patrick, but plays into whatever this Mallory's got going on here. "Well, to stay that way, I better not risk Archie."

Heidi nods emphatically. "His disc history alone will have you there until next Tuesday." She pulls a sticky and a pen from her pocket. "Use the service elevator."

Perfect. Code in hand, Mallory closes the door behind the cooing Heidi Hoffman and this stuffed animal of a dog that won't stop with those goddamn puppy dog eyes.

"Just what are you up to?" Ilena says.

Mallory's and Ilena's approaches to life increasingly diverged as the years went on, Ilena's black-and-white rules growing thicker while Mallory's philosophy of "ask forgiveness not permission" turned to "ask forgiveness never." Grayson understood that, didn't judge it. They were both always on, waiting for the right moment or cataloging information that might be useful later. It's a skill that brought them together and separated them, starting with the moment she overheard Grayson in his penthouse and ending at the outing when he threatened to ruin her best friend.

"Text Aubrey to meet us."

"Why?"

"Because if this morning's any indication, you're in no shape to help me move a body."

12
MALLORY

*Four and a Half Weeks **Before** the Outing*

He shifted the weight of his body so as not to crush her, the first step in their well-honed dance to transition Mallory on top. Because she was close. But this time, as his torso rotated, he cupped the back of her head with his hand. Briefly. Gently. Intentionally. So when Mallory climaxed it was with the force of a battalion of confetti cannons and the realization that they were no longer simply fucking. She and Grayson Fields had just made love for the first time.

Well, shit.

But also, spectacular.

Mallory didn't quite meet his eyes as she moved off of him. She was still somewhat surprised she was here rather than with Ilena. But as much as Ilena understood Mallory, Grayson understood this. The impossibility of failure.

She was a strong woman who didn't squeal at mice (much) or need help changing a tire (except for the tire part), and she had never needed a romantic relationship before and she didn't need one now. And yet, she'd come to Grayson, just wanting him to make everything right. But to do that, she'd have to tell him that AIM's growth wasn't real. Saying the words out loud seemed like a betrayal to this company she needed like oxygen.

Still, he knew something was wrong. Grayson leaned against the headboard, his gelled dark hair a slick contrast against the tweed fabric. "Ah, Mallory, you and I are so much alike that our only options are to fall desperately in love or kill each other. Perhaps both." He grinned, and those dark brown eyes that had drawn her in nearly a year ago did so again. "You're taking your company public. The pressure is overwhelming, I know. The night before my first IPO, I vomited blood. I clutched that toilet bowl and vowed not to let it get the better of me. My stomach lining couldn't take it. And even though it wasn't just nerves, and it turns out I'd broken a rib the night before during an impromptu triathlon . . . Still, a lesson learned."

He was cocky and arrogant, and it wasn't a turnoff, not then. Grayson pulled Mallory to him, and his fingers trailed the bare skin of her upper arm. She yearned for more of the physical connection, which was uncomplicated and satisfying and should have been enough. Yet her mind couldn't let go of the reason she was there. AIM wasn't the success she thought it was. (Which meant, neither was she.)

Grayson kissed her cheek before hopping out of bed to feed Harley. Mallory gnawed on her lower lip, growing impatient. She slipped on his robe, hurried down the hall with its photo homage to the sports elite, and entered the great room overlooking Boston's Copley Square. The white marble of the kitchen counter made her want to lie naked on it, cool her flushed skin. She was about to call for Grayson to suggest just that when a gravelly voice fluctuating in volume stopped her.

". . . user base . . . deep-seated error . . . unchecked . . ."

The voice wasn't Grayson's. She strained to hear the next low rumble of words, drawing in a sharp breath at the last ones: "suspicious accounts."

"Not here." A terse response unmistakably from Grayson.

And the scream that had been lodged in Mallory's throat since that afternoon nearly choked her.

"That meant 'leave,'" Grayson said.

"Your call, as always," came the first voice, definitely in person, louder, with a bit less gravel, and familiar? "AIM's valuation lives and dies by the mighty Grayson Fields. And here's where one must proceed with caution because you can't pluck feathers from a bald chicken—AIM's valuation also happens to hang on my ability to keep a secret."

A chill snaked down Mallory's spine. She heard the clank of the service elevator, the same one she and Grayson had come up the first night he'd brought her here all those months ago, where they'd shared their first kiss, a word too innocent and sweet to accurately describe the lust with which they'd attacked each other.

She hurried back inside the bedroom, trying to understand how Grayson could know something Mallory had only confirmed that afternoon. She stifled her gasp. Her every organ shut down, she grew cold and numb, felt as though she were floating outside of her body. He must have known before she did. And never said a word.

As he reentered the bedroom, she kept a smile on her face despite the roar rising inside of her. "Our board might be a bit concerned if they knew you were doing both sides of a conversation with your dog."

Grayson buried his nose in Harley's fur, laughing. "If only. Instead I was too busy cursing out another of those blasted Instagram ads. Nine hundred dollars for a beach chair with a deep seat? Criminal, no matter what they say about their user base. As I live and die, I will not pay a smidge more than five hundred for a beach chair."

Was he testing her? Did he know she'd overheard? Was he

truly arrogant enough to think she'd buy this? Instead of the truth she was piecing together: that he purposely created what she'd thought was a glitch for his own financial gain, knowing an increase in users would send AIM's stock soaring. And now he was what? Being blackmailed by someone who'd found out? And hiding it from her?

Mallory had long ago perfected the art of playing along. With someone like Grayson, nothing could be gained without concrete proof. As so, she stayed silent, her cheeks remained full, her lips extended into that smile, but her gut twisted and she fought a surge of acid up her throat.

She saw herself hanging cardigans in his walk-in closet, the two of them nestling against the headboard, him forcing her to read the *Times* in paper form, her complaining about the ink staining the sheets, her pushing him to switch out his utilitarian coffee machine for one that made espressos and cappuccinos and her gently nudging him into Harley spending weekends at a dog sitter's. Turkeys carved and menorahs lit and a beach house in Wellfleet where they'd seed their own oysters and laugh about how they became people who wear Hunter boots and in less time than it took Harley to lick Grayson's hand, Mallory had created an entire life. A life where she was happier than her mother. But maybe nature was more powerful than nurture because both Mallory and her mother fell for assholes who lie.

13 AUBREY

Friday Afternoon
*One Day **After** the Outing*

Meet us out front.

That's all Ilena's text says, so Aubrey does. Not just because of her vow not to text but because that's what Aubrey does. She follows. Maybe the Aubrey of here doesn't or doesn't as easily, but the Aubrey of here *isn't* here.

Aubrey's chest seizes. Is the Aubrey of here in her world? Is this some *Freaky Friday*, *Invasion of the Body Snatchers* thing? The thought sends a chill down her spine. That would mean the Aubrey of here is in her world not mourning Ethan. She wouldn't know not to wash the mug with the "My Favorite Unique Visitor" that Aubrey had custom-made for him, the coffee ring around the bottom and drips down the side left from the last time he'd used it on the morning he died. She'd have no idea that the sand in the vase beside the bed was from Martha's Vineyard and not HomeGoods. She wouldn't understand why it was beside the bed. She wouldn't feel the way Aubrey has been feeling for the past few weeks. She'd be both lucky and unlucky at the same time.

Aubrey tries not to think about that mug being stacked in the dishwasher next to bowls crusted over with vanilla yogurt and pasta sauce. She rocks back and forth on her heels, willing Ilena and Mallory to appear. But what she seems to will instead is her one-night stand. It was just the one night, wasn't it? They haven't done that before, have they?

Kai crosses the plaza, iced drink in one hand and a paper bag with the name of a deli Aubrey doesn't recognize in the other. He's with Noreen, hair red instead of blond, back held a bit straighter, smile as energetic as ever, widening as she approaches Aubrey.

Kai laughs as they walk, his stride as long as his legs, his lips fixed in a gentle upturn, and shame and guilt claw at Aubrey's insides for seeing not all of that but him naked in her bed. When he sees her, his smile thins out. Apparently that's the reaction she elicits regardless of what universe she is in. It had happened with Ethan too. Months of her Aubreyisms taking their toll.

She wipes her clammy hands on the sides of the cargo pants she yanked off the hanger in the dark, not realizing they were bright pink. "Hey," she says.

"Ms. Miller," Noreen responds, with more formality than their Noreen. She's also taller thanks to the skinny heels that are the opposite of the white sneakers their Noreen preferred. "Fresh air's good for the pores. Or so AIM's total health feature tells me." She laughs, and Aubrey's not sure if she's being ironic, and she just really, really hates that she can't tell. And she also kind of hates that Kai smiles at Noreen, but not at Aubrey. "Y'all decide on the color palette?"

Aubrey forces a swallow. "I . . . What were the choices again?"

Noreen shifts her cup into her opposite hand. "All the things you have to keep in your head, I swear . . . no disrespect, but support staff needs to earn its name. Ella's so worried about making the wrong choice that she makes no choice at all. Passes the buck, which, incidentally, is a choice too, isn't it?"

Aubrey can only stare at her feet, at these wedge sandals she found by the front door.

A ding from Noreen's phone. "Ms. Latham. Gotta scoot. She needs me! Bye, y'all!" She gives Aubrey's arm a squeeze, something she'd never done in their world, before twiddling her fingers at Kai and rushing toward the building, leaving an awkward silence.

Aubrey finally points to the drink. "Any good?"

Kai's head tilts to one side. "You promised it'd change my life."

And this is why Mallory said to let others lead and direct the conversation. Aubrey doesn't drink coffee. She never outgrew the inability to handle caffeine. "Yes, well, it is only coffee, so perhaps I oversold."

He takes a sip. "Not by much. It's good. But it's that rooibos tea. You don't drink anything with caffeine."

"Sure, just a little test. You were listening." Aubrey jabs a finger at him, channeling the playfulness he seemed to have in her world. But when he just stares at her quizzically, she lowers her hand. *Keep up appearances, don't get too close to anyone, but try to maintain what's going on in this world.* How is she supposed to do that when she doesn't know what's going on in this world? Or when what's gone on in this world is . . . this?

"I'd have snagged one for you," he says, "but—"

"I was a hot mess."

"I was going to say, 'but I didn't know how you liked it.'"

His leg on hers when she woke this morning, that perfect indent above his hips.

"The tea, I mean," he says, as if he can read her mind.

"Frothy and sweet," she blurts out, which only makes it more awkward.

"Then here." He offers her the sweating cup. "We like it the same way, despite our age difference."

Age. Oh, *oh*, she'd offended him earlier. She hadn't meant to. She accepts the tea.

He remains before her, his tolerance for awkwardness much higher than hers. She swivels her neck, desperate for Mallory and Ilena to save her.

"Okay, then," he says.

He's past her, the whole uncomfortable exchange nearly over when some compulsion makes her say, "Kai?"

He pauses at the entrance to the building and turns to face her.

"I didn't mean it." Her nerves almost get the better of her. "About being young. It's just . . ." *My dead fiancé who's not really dead is only the third person I've ever slept with, and oh yeah, it turns out he's not really dead but Grayson Fields is and I'm more than mildly freaking out and . . .*

Kai's fingers tighten over the folded top of the paper bag, and she feels like a liar because he looks very much like a young twenty-two-year-old (she checked his age in the employee database that morning). And yet, if she's being honest, his demeanor does seem older, more mature than the Kai she met at the outing in her world.

"Thanks for the drink," she says.

Instantly, he grins. "You bet. Best team ever, right?" He says it like it's some private joke she should know.

She holds up the tea in a mock salute as he enters the building and into her head comes "dollar oysters." She and Ethan had been at a bar in the North End when the server finished his rundown of the specials with: "Dollar oysters." The waiter had paused, panic crinkling his forehead as he flipped through his spiral notepad. "I'm so sorry, but I'll have to double-check the price on that."

Ethan's hair had been long in the front then, and it bounced as he burst out laughing. Aubrey tried to cover with a "Probably too rich for our blood," but it only made Ethan laugh harder and the server's forehead crinkle more.

After the server left, she'd said honestly that it wasn't very nice, and Ethan had said, "Babe, dollar oysters. *Dollar* oysters. Check the price. An Aubreyism if I ever heard one."

And he'd given that teasing smile and laughed, and she'd laughed, and "dollar oysters" had become their private joke. Every time someone said something a bit silly or inane, "Dollar oysters," one of them would say. It was their code word if either of them was being held hostage. How they'd work it into conversation, a regular pastime for them after one too many craft beers. Somewhere along the way "Aubreyism" transitioned into a nickname for her, Ethan using it each time she debated a Target pillow or scone from Tatte for too long. He thought it was cute.

She sips the tea, carefully holding the tall cup of brown liquid far from her white coat.

When Ilena and Mallory finally arrive, Mallory sidles up beside Aubrey and says, "Missed you," in a voice soft and oozy like freshly baked cookies.

"I'm not going to like this, am I?" Aubrey says.

Ilena dangles a pair of sneakers. "You're going to need these. And, the answer is no."

Mallory counters with: "Before you say anything, you should know that Ilena thinks she may have trapped Felix with this baby."

Ilena tightens her lips. "And Mallory almost killed Harley."

"Grayson's secretary is a busybody," Mallory says, "which means, we have to move him."

Aubrey's heart clogs her throat. "Well, here's something. Ethan's alive."

Mallory shakes her head. "You win."

Ilena was right. Aubrey doesn't like this. Aubrey hates this. Aubrey couldn't hate this more.

She follows Mallory and Ilena into the service elevator of Grayson's building, a place she never wanted to see again.

"Every time?" Aubrey says. "Every choice? I don't understand."

Mallory leans against the wheelchair she had Noreen borrow from the rehab center on the ground floor of AIM's building with an excuse Aubrey doesn't want to know.

"I don't either, not really," Mallory says, "but a split happens."

"That's not logical," Ilena says, slipping on a pair of blue surgical gloves. "How can a choice create an entire new world?"

Mallory shrugs. "Physics, apparently."

"And that's how we got here?" Aubrey asks. "Physics? Will it get us home?"

Mallory hands Aubrey an identical pair of blue gloves. "Maybe, if we knew enough."

Ilena clucks her tongue. "Great. So one of us gets a PhD in physics, and then we get to go home? Good plan, love it."

Mallory counters with "I didn't say that was my plan."

"You didn't say you had a plan at all."

Mallory taps the wheelchair. "Well, then, what's this?"

Aubrey wriggles her fingers into the gloves, fighting the churning of her stomach. "This isn't going to work," she says softly.

"Maybe not," Mallory says. "But there's no alternative."

But there is. Isn't there always a choice? That's what trips Aubrey up even more than making the wrong choice—the abundance of choices.

Yet if what Mallory said is somehow true, it doesn't really matter what Aubrey chooses. Somewhere, in another place, another Aubrey didn't play Fuck, Marry, Kill at the outing, another Aubrey didn't force herself out of the bathroom stall at the start-up program to eat salad with Ilena and Mallory, another Aubrey didn't text Ethan, and he's still alive.

Like he is here. But with no memory of dollar oysters.

The door dings, opening into an alcove at the back of Grayson's penthouse. Mallory exits first, pushing the wheelchair. Ilena follows, and then Aubrey.

This Aubrey, who maybe didn't forgive Ethan for choosing the arcade for their first date like she did and didn't say yes to a second. Or maybe he never asked.

She moves slowly through Grayson's penthouse, the knowledge of what they're about to do making her skin crawl. Making her think of Ethan, the utter stillness of his body on the hospital bed in the ER.

She aches for him, the him who knew dollar oysters and that she loved peanut butter in smoothies and who'd decide on sushi or pizza for dinner so she wouldn't have to make a pro-con list.

They're not together here. Maybe they weren't supposed to be in her world either. Did she force it? Did she push against the universe and the universe eventually pushed back? Taking away Ethan because Aubrey was too timid to admit that she would have preferred a hip cocktail bar over the arcade? His death a result of a long line of cause and effect, from every choice Aubrey had ever made? Starting with the boy in high school who'd promised her a pool house and a future she was naive enough to believe but that only lasted long enough for her to lose her virginity in his parents' storage shed? Did it even matter that ever since, she's taken her time, doesn't make snap decisions, that she considers and debates and agonizes? She feels like she's drowning, unable to surface long enough to stand.

Hot dog or salad, joining AIM or staying with the start-up that became Tinder, texting Ethan or not texting Ethan. If a version of Aubrey lives every choice taken and not, how will this Aubrey—*how will she?*—ever know what's right?

How will she not make the wrong choice again?

She has to figure out the truth. She has to find out why this Aubrey and Ethan aren't together. If they shouldn't be. If they never should have been. If not being together could have saved her Ethan's life too.

She takes a breath, pushes herself above the surface, and stands beside Mallory as she opens the freezer chest.

14
ILENA

Friday Afternoon
*One Day **After** the Outing*

Ilena refuses to feel guilt. Aubrey saying Ethan was alive ignited deep pangs for not seeking out her husband. Jonah could be someone else's husband. Someone's father, the impossibility in her world not the same here. Or maybe there is no Jonah here. If Ethan is alive here, but not in their world, the opposite could be true of Jonah.

She places her hand on the back of the wheelchair, the bulge of the wedding band from Felix that she couldn't get off judging her from beneath the plastic glove. It doesn't have the right. She's not the one who asked for a divorce.

Aubrey snaps the elastic around her wrist a third time. Ilena bites her tongue. She knows that the last dead body they all saw makes this harder, not easier.

"We shouldn't be doing this," Ilena says as Mallory's and Aubrey's arms lower into the chest, their hands reaching for the edges of the blanket they wrapped Grayson in what already feels like a lifetime ago. "Morally, ethically, legally, it doesn't matter where we are, this is wrong. And it's only going to make things worse because we won't get away with this."

Mallory bends her legs to bear more of Grayson's weight.

Ilena presses, "You can't expect to keep lying without consequences."

"Yes, I can." Mallory grimaces as she heaves Grayson onto the edge of the chest.

Aubrey looks like she's going to be sick, but still she hoists his legs out. She tests letting go, one hand, then the other. The rigidity holds him in place. "I need a minute."

Mallory adjusts her end of Grayson more firmly. "Go."

Aubrey rushes into the powder room in the hall, closing the door behind her.

"She's going to break," Ilena says.

"We'll take care of her," Mallory says. "We always do."

"Do we? Because Ethan—"

"Fucking Ethan. We can't let her get sucked in by him again."

"He's her fiancé," Ilena says. "Who died."

"Unfortunately, not here."

"You didn't just say that."

"We have to protect her," Mallory says, and it's déjà vu.

"And ourselves?" Ilena says. "Yourself? AIM's all-important reputation?"

"Yes. What's wrong with that?"

That Mallory could even ask the question at this very moment, with her hands on a dead Grayson, makes Ilena want to scream. But then Mallory shifts the positions of those hands, revealing how much they're shaking. She bites down hard on her lower lip. It's her tell, the one only Ilena is attuned to. Mallory is scared.

And all the resistance in Ilena dissolves. Despite their differences, this is the same: Ilena would do anything to protect her best friends too.

Mallory leans against the chest and winces. She gestures to her pocket. "Can you . . . ? Texas is a pointy state."

Ilena reluctantly steps into the cold air wafting from the open chest. She slides her hand into Mallory's front pocket and pulls out a key chain. Dangling from it are a dozen charms all in the shape of Texas. One silver with the single word *home* at the bottom, another with the bright blue bonnet state flower, one covered with a fuzzy black-and-white cow print. Their Noreen wasn't the kitschy type. "Did you get anything from Noreen other than her car?"

"You mean, did I ask her if she had 'killing Grayson' as an appointment on my calendar?"

"Okay, yes, that."

"No," Mallory says.

"But there was an outing, at the same place as ours, at least according to the receipt on my desk."

"I know," Mallory says. "It was in my calendar with about a thousand alerts not to forget. Oh, and Noreen asked for the strawberry mule recipe. She wants to make them for us when we go back the night before we go public. For luck."

"That too, then? Same bizarre family tradition?" Ilena drops the keys on the seat of the wheelchair. "That makes Noreen, Ella, the outing, the direct listing, the valuation, all the same." Ilena glances toward the bathroom. "I wonder then if—?"

"It doesn't matter."

"Doesn't it? If the error's here too, we need to know. We have the same obligations. Maybe they were in the middle of dealing with it themselves." And maybe this Mallory's way of dealing with it was to kill Grayson. Maybe that's what her Mallory is afraid to find out.

"Then we let *them* deal with it," Mallory says. "We don't belong here."

But we are here is all Ilena can think. And that comes with certain responsibilities. As she wraps her hands around the arms of the wheelchair they're about to put Grayson in, she stares at the outline of the ring on her finger, grateful she left the emerald one at Felix's. She wouldn't want anything to happen to it. It's how she felt about the opal from Jonah. It had been a family piece. For the first few years of their marriage, the only way she'd wear it was with tape on the back.

She'd meant to take the opal off after they agreed to the divorce, to tuck it away in the box where Jonah kept his cuff links and the old credit cards he was meaning to cut up but never got around to, but she hadn't. It had been on her finger, just like it had been for the past thirteen years, before she woke up here.

From the purse at her feet comes the same sound that woke her that morning. She pulls out her phone. "Felix," she says.

"You have to answer it," Mallory says.

Ilena takes a deep breath and offers a generic "Hello," not knowing if she and Felix share a special greeting like "hey, babe" or "hi, sweetie" or "hello, you." She and Jonah don't. In fact, she can't remember the last time Jonah called instead of texted her.

"How's the singleton doing?" Felix uses the term for a single fetus that must be their nickname for the baby.

"Good."

"Just good?" The excitement in Felix's voice strains her. Jonah had the same, at the start. "Usually you've got some clever euphemism for how he or she's using you as a punching bag."

That this Ilena makes jokes is strange enough, but that she makes jokes about the baby irks her. *Must be nice.*

"Well," Ilena says, "today's been somewhat overshadowed by other things."

"The ultrasound, of course." Felix's tone sobers.

Ultrasound? She'd meant this place, Grayson in a blanket in front of her, Aubrey likely throwing up in the powder room. But ultrasound? For the singleton?

"It'll be fine," Felix says. "Though I'm not supposed to say that. This happens before every appointment, and I understand. You need to feel your feelings, and worry is a perfectly fine feeling. Though how about you let me take that off your shoulders for today? I'll worry for the both of us."

A warmth wraps around her, an unfamiliar feeling as Felix takes on the role she's used to filling. "Okay," she says simply.

"I'll swing by your office in an hour?" Felix says.

Her heart trips. "No, don't. It's just, I'm out lunching with Mallory."

"Ah, of course she'd want to celebrate. Keep her to one old-fashioned, would you? The contract for the appearance requires actual brainpower. I'm leaving it on her desk as we speak."

"Appearance?"

"That's what they call it, apparently."

Ilena goes silent. Being here is like sprinting through a minefield.

"Ilena," Felix says, "I know how scatterbrained Mallory can be, so it's terrifying to have her as the sole AIM founder on national television."

Bombs throughout that entire sentence.

Felix continues, "But let her have *The Shandy Shane Show* herself. You have so much more already."

Ilena narrows her eyes at Mallory. "You're right. Just a momentary lapse. Call it a bit of Mom brain from the singleton."

Felix laughs before describing the lemon-cumin chicken he's making for dinner, and Ilena quickly lowers her phone, checking her calendar to make sure the ob-gyn's name and address is in it. Ilena says "Sounds delicious" and "See you soon" and doesn't wait to see if she and Felix have a special sign-off. She simply hangs up.

Ilena drops the keys onto the seat of the wheelchair. "And

when were you going to tell me you're doing *Shandy Shane* alone?"

Mallory, with a sheepish smile, says, "After it aired?"

A bubble of laughter floats up Ilena's throat. This is what drew her to Mallory—that Mallory was blunt and irreverent and used it to get what she wanted. For a long time, what Ilena wanted too.

"AIM on morning television," Ilena said. "Do you think it's happening at home?"

"And there's the Ilena who doubled our ad revenue twice in the past five years."

She had, she'd made AIM a success as much as Mallory and Aubrey had. Jonah by her side, as invested as she was. Their careers had come first, and by the time Ilena had begun to question if they should, it seemed too late for anything else to find its way into that top position.

"Jonah asked for a divorce," Ilena says suddenly.

"I'm sorry, what? A divorce? I'll kill him."

They both look at Grayson, and terror darkens Mallory's eyes, and Ilena loses her grip on the wheelchair. It rolls, and the keys that were resting on the seat slide off, disappearing beneath the coffee table. Ilena starts to reach for them just as Aubrey exits the bathroom.

"Let me," Aubrey says. "You shouldn't be bending."

Aubrey's eyes are red, her face pale. Being in the presence of a dead body surely makes her think of Ethan. Ilena lost Jonah too, not in the same way of course, but she had. And she hadn't cried once. Ilena begs her heart to beat harder or faster or even explode because she's suddenly afraid it's truly as glacial as her mother's. Is this the kind of mother Ilena will be? One who hides dead bodies?

Aubrey returns to the chest, and Ilena silently rolls the

wheelchair toward it. She holds it steady as Mallory and Aubrey heft Grayson into it, straightens the blanket to cover him, and releases it to Mallory to push to the elevator. There, she waits beside Aubrey as Mallory searches the penthouse for the things a last-minute traveling Grayson would have taken with him: wallet, passport, keys. Ilena wraps her arm around Aubrey's shoulder to try to quell her tremble as Mallory packs an overnight bag. They leave the penthouse with enough evidence of the brunch they were supposed to have had: empty bottle of champagne that Mallory drank a quarter of before pouring down the drain on the counter beside three freshly washed flutes, a fourth juice glass in the dishwasher stacked with the dirty cheese board and set to run, and the floor cleaned of crumbs, dumped in the trash bag they'll dispose of along the way.

In the service elevator, Grayson in the wheelchair between them, Ilena reaches for Mallory's hand. Mallory meets her halfway, anticipating Ilena's need, perhaps having the same need herself.

"We'll have to move quickly," Mallory says, gripping a tote bag of Harley's frozen dog food. "So that means—"

"You take him out the back exit ahead of us," Ilena says, because the honeydew slows her down. And after Ethan, even before Ethan, neither of them would have let Aubrey do it. "Aubrey and I will follow. If anyone's around, I can handle it."

Mallory squeezes Ilena's hand. "Of course you can. The Ilena Cohen I know is capable of anything."

Mallory is the most loyal and fierce friend Ilena has ever had, but she doesn't let her sentimentality show. That she does now, when they are all at their most vulnerable, is as strong a display of friendship as tattooing Ilena's name on her forehead.

Still, for the first time, Ilena wonders where her life would have taken her if she'd never walked into that hardware store in Harvard Square and bought a roll of duct tape.

When the elevator opens, Mallory grips the handles of the wheelchair and elongates her spine, forging ahead, no matter the turmoil—inner or outer. Because Mallory is a walking contradiction with a singular belief that the ends always justify the means.

This is a slippery slope, and Ilena's footing is already off. The lies have to stop. Ilena needs to go have an ultrasound, make sure this honeydew's on track, and then tell Felix the truth.

15
MALLORY

Friday Afternoon
*One Day **After** the Outing*

Mallory releases her grip on the steering wheel. Ilena and Jonah, Jonah and Ilena, they'd never had a cute, combined couple name. They'd started dating before that was even a thing. And even if they hadn't, neither Ilena nor Mallory were prone to making cute couple names.

A divorce, really?

And Ilena waited how long exactly to tell Mallory?

Because they were fighting. About AIM.

Everything comes back to Grayson.

She shifts Noreen's small hatchback into Park in the paved area behind a multifamily home nearly identical to the one Mallory grew up in. "We're here," Mallory says.

In the passenger seat, Aubrey nods, her preferred form of communication since leaving Grayson's building. Mallory looks at the white of Aubrey's coat and shuts her eyes against the memory that's the one thing she wishes this world would erase—the night she told Aubrey she'd found the perfect drink for her wedding reception. The night she betrayed one best friend to save another.

Mallory shakes her head, staying focused on the present. Aubrey here, and Ilena at the hospital. They dropped her off on the way. Incredibly, Ilena is finally having a procedure that isn't about creating a child but caring for one.

Ilena hadn't wanted it, then suddenly wanted it. It wasn't the first difference between them, but Ilena wanting a baby as much as Mallory didn't had been defining them in a way nothing had before. She wished Ilena didn't want it. *What a fucking selfish thought.* But it *has been* her thought. Mallory's mom loved her and supported her in a way Ilena's didn't, yet neither of them had had Norman Rockwell childhoods. Mallory has never felt any urge, no *tick tick tick* inside her; when parents show her pictures of their kids with faces covered in chocolate ice cream, she chokes back bile and offers to buy them napkins.

Still, Mallory had been supporting Ilena in the way she could, sitting by Ilena's side in waiting rooms, reading brochures, listening when Ilena said that Jonah wasn't dealing with it the way she'd hoped. Mallory understood how hard it all was, but honestly, she'd been more focused on how hard it all was on herself.

Was this part of it? Why Ilena wanted to leave AIM? Because it would also let her leave Mallory?

"Good amount of trees," Mallory says, heart racing as she props open the car door. "Nice shielding."

The neighborhood where her mom lives is the same one of Mallory's childhood, though in this world, their particular street is three blocks farther from the Green Line. This Mallory didn't have to fall asleep to the soundtrack of trains screeching against the tracks.

Her mom's contact information listed "Unit 1," meaning the apartment was on the first floor, just like in her world. A quick internet search showed not one but two pandemics in the past fifteen years. Both gave Mallory hope that her mom was still her mom: a low-grade hoarder.

"Bargain shopper," her mom had called it, stocking up on 75 percent–off blenders (even though they already had one they hardly used and two still in boxes) because who knows when you'd get invited to a wedding and need a gift. Shelves overflowed with enough gift wrap to Tyvek a skyscraper because fifty cents a roll is fifty cents a roll even if it was just the two of them and they couldn't really afford a lot of gifts. The $1.99 chicken thighs and two-for-one frozen peas came later, after the first pandemic, the same one this Mallory had lived through.

One text and one white lie later, and they had somewhere to put Grayson until they could figure out something better. Though Mallory suspects she's reaching the end of "they."

Still, Aubrey's here. All five feet four and one hundred and thirty pounds of her—though probably less considering the fit of those pink pants.

Mallory unlocks the back door and enters the kitchen of a railroad apartment just like the one she grew up in. Her mother still loves roosters. Tea towels, a fruit bowl, a sign above the sink, they cock-a-doodle-do at her.

Her mom had assured Mallory that the house was nearly always empty during the day, the owners of the other two units at work or school. Her mom is a physician's assistant here, not a paralegal. But also not a doctor or a lawyer, the same things apparently holding her back from aiming that high in play here too.

Perhaps they needed to be for Mallory to become Mallory in both worlds: ambitious and tenacious enough to found a company worth two point two billion dollars. She can't help but wonder what her younger self would have thought. *Fuck yeah*, or more likely, *Why not three? Four?*

She spies her mother's rooster cookie jar and remembers opening the lid, pulling out two gingersnaps or vanilla wafers or whatever had been on sale that week, and setting them on a carefully torn-in-two paper towel. She'd carry them into the living room where her mom would be laughing at some sitcom as she marked up something from work, getting in overtime, sipping Lipton tea or the occasional "splurge" of cheap prosecco. Mallory's younger self would stare at the silver bangle some boy had given her or her report card filled with As and Bs she only half deserved and wonder why she couldn't be more like her mom—content with what they had, which was more than so many, which was enough. Except that hole in Mallory's chest never closed.

A part of Mallory uncharacteristically wants to pass through the kitchen to the bedroom on the right, the bedroom that would have been hers, but it's nearly eighty degrees, and Grayson's under a blanket in a parked hatchback with the air-conditioning off.

She finds the door to the basement, her mom's private half crudely finished and accessible only through this unit. In the far corner is the white, utilitarian chest freezer. Secured with a padlock. Pandemics bring out the worst in people. She loves that her mom doesn't trust anyone.

Mallory rotates each little dial, lining up the combination, and lifts the lid.

"Goddammit, Mom."

Mallory grabs an empty box from the recycling bin and loads in the equivalent of five chickens, two pigs, and a farm's worth of frozen vegetables. Then, she goes to get Aubrey.

Under the cover of the open hatchback and those leafy trees, they shift the blanket-shrouded Grayson into the wheelchair, trying not to touch his cold skin or imagine the warm fingers that tied those double knots on his expensive loafers, as they half roll, half drag him down the stairs and into the basement.

"It's temporary," Mallory says to Aubrey as they settle Grayson into his second freezer of the day.

Aubrey nods.

Mallory pulls the car keys out of her pocket and hands them to Aubrey. "Listen, grab the overnight bag, will you?"

A nod and perhaps a slight grunt of assent, and Aubrey aims for the stairs. Mallory turns back to the freezer. Her mom thinks it's being stacked with a special mood-enhancing serum that needs to be kept icy cold until AIM begins its giveaway. When Mallory had called, her mom had been thrilled to help. She even said she'd tell her patients all about it, to which Mallory launched into words like "confidentiality agreement" and "first to market" and "competitive advantage" that were enough for her mom to promise to keep it under wraps until she was told otherwise. Mallory's success was the only thing her mom had ever wanted.

And Mallory had given it to her. Despite attention span and focus and all things that would be diagnosed as something warranting help today. Mallory saw her mom's tired eyes and never full enough bank account and used to think life wasn't fair, but then she realized that life doesn't owe you shit. Women like to think that it does, those raised to be "good girls," to be honest and helpful and polite and kind. Deferential, not wanting too much or assuming too much. Do the "right thing." Don't make waves. You'll be rewarded. Good things will come. *Bullshit.* No one grew a company into the billions by making good choices. Good choices left you in overworked, underpaid jobs where brushes of side boob and hands on waists still happened but without the compensation; her mom was proof of that. Her mom did the right thing her entire life and all it got her was a daughter who would do anything to not follow in her footsteps.

So Mallory developed a skill more valuable than anything she'd learn in books: how to read people. She knew the school librarian's self-esteem rose with every analysis Mallory sat wide-eyed through then regurgitated in her book report. She knew the class brainiac would trade math homework for lip-gloss shopping. She knew the boys would let her copy their test answers if she let them drape their meaty arms across her in the halls. All things that never occurred to her weren't okay.

Mallory grabs three racks of ribs to spread over Grayson's legs and accidentally yanks the blanket, which slips to reveal the top of his head, hair like dark porcupine spines. The product he uses must have hardened. *Used.*

A ghastly, violent sob punches through her. Her fingertips instinctually reach out, pressing the pointy tips. There's nothing temporary about this for this Grayson.

What if there's also nothing temporary about this for her? What if this place is all they have?

She pushes back the sleeves of her shirt, tracing the marks on her forearm in the shape of fingers, fingers that must be Grayson's, fingers that reached for her last night with intensity or urgency or anger or fear or all of it combined. She considers extracting his hand, holding his cold, stiff fingers against the lines on her skin to see if they match. Because maybe they don't. Maybe whatever happened last night to cause them wasn't Mallory's fault, maybe someone else was there, maybe she'd tried to stop it. Maybe here, Grayson hasn't manipulated her but someone else. Maybe AIM's valuation is real. And maybe she didn't have a motive to kill him. Maybe, maybe, maybe. Maybe's a good place to be. She leaves Grayson's hand where it is.

As Aubrey returns, Mallory straightens. She trades the overnight bag for the cardboard box full of food that could feed the neighborhood for a week. Aubrey passes Noreen's keys to Mallory, but they're both shaking so much that the charm-filled key chain falls straight into the freezer.

Horror consumes Aubrey's face, and Mallory says, "I've got it."

Aubrey hesitates, shifting the box onto her hip. "I have to ask, do you actually have a plan? Because this . . ." She juts the box at the freezer. "This is starting to feel like scrambling."

Mallory places her hand on Aubrey's arm and chokes back the self-doubt that's nearly strangling her. "I'll figure it out, promise."

Aubrey eyes the frozen cauliflower rice. "Maybe we could start with getting something to eat? This Aubrey's apparently a vegan, and dairy-free cheese is disgusting."

"Understood. I'll meet you at the car. We can see if Gracie's still exists?"

Their favorite sandwich place with the cocktail slushies. She really, really hopes Gracie's exists.

Aubrey's back to nodding, giving a tight head bob before carrying the box of frozen food up the stairs. Mallory stifles a grimace as she slides her hand into the freezer beside Grayson's blanketed torso. She finds the keys, but they resist. She yanks and hears the slight tearing of fabric as the keys snag on the way out. She breathes deeply, shoves the key chain into her pocket, and gently sets the overnight bag at Grayson's feet.

"I'm sorry," she says, realizing she hasn't done that yet. Apologized to Grayson for whatever she might have done.

Her hand lingers on the bag, her fingers grazing his ankle, covered by a sock of purple-and-gold argyle, and this unexpected splash of whimsy suddenly makes Mallory feel weighed down by a knight's armor. She stares at her hand, the pop of blue veins slicing across her skin like a line of mold on some stinky French cheese. Even without her reading glasses on, she's repulsed by it. How could her hands look like this? How could these be her hands? Hands that might have packed her emergency snack bag with the means to kill the man she's not falling in love with because Mallory doesn't fall in anything, let alone love?

The sprout of uncharacteristic tears in her eyes brings back her usual focus. She won't give in to it. She gives a firm shake of her head. She can do this. For all of them.

Her hand disappears into the side of the overnight bag. She slides Grayson's phone into her pocket. She doesn't exactly have a plan, but she has the first piece of it: making Grayson disappear.

She closes the lid to the freezer, plugs a new combination into the padlock, and bounds up the stairs. A Moscow mule, no, a paloma slushie. *Please, Gracie's, please.* But just in case, for Aubrey, she heads for the fridge, hoping for an actual cheese stick to tide them over.

The fridge at home was a matte black, clean and clear, not even a magnet. Here, the white fridge is a jigsaw puzzle of stickies reminding her mom to pick up half-and-half and cat food—*Mom has a cat?*—and of business cards for plumbers and locksmiths and of photographs, lots of photographs. Mallory as a baby eating her own toes, as a toddler dancing with the incoming ocean tide, as an eye-rolling preteen in between her mom and an attractive man holding a World's Best Dad mug.

Mallory stumbles back. That same man beams in half a dozen photographs. A man with the same color hair as Mallory. A man with the same height Mallory has but her mother lacks. A man whose cheek her mother is kissing. A man holding Mallory's hand outside the elementary school.

That very same man in a uniform. Mallory's father is not absent here. And Mallory's not-absent father is a police officer.

They were in shock.

It was shocking.

Death is shocking, but also a part of life, isn't that what they say? But they wouldn't—no one would—if they'd seen it up close. Like we had. We shared something no one else did. We were special.

Bound together, twisted like twine, with a strength that not even the sharpest blade could sever. It is a strange thing to achieve something you didn't even know you were looking for. Yet it creates a hunger. To achieve everything else.

No matter who it hurts.

16
AUBREY

Saturday Morning
*Two Days **After** the Outing*

We're still here.

Aubrey hits Send on the first text she's written in more than a month because this Aubrey didn't have to vow never to text again. The message zooms off to Ilena and Mallory, and Aubrey waits. But no little dots appear, no response comes. What if they're not here? What if it's only Aubrey?

She pushes herself out of the white couch she'd have never bought, because who buys a white couch? She begins folding the throw blanket that she hopes is from Target, because then there's a chance they make it in her world too. A pattern of light green with wispy white fronds, soft cotton on the outside and faux fur underneath, it was like sleeping inside a cotton ball. She couldn't bring herself to sleep in the bed, the sheets smelling of her eucalyptus shampoo but also something heavier, muskier. Kai's deodorant, probably. His baby-smooth cheeks surely don't require aftershave, and oh yeah—sex, smelling like sex.

She found birth control pills in the medicine cabinet last night and took the one marked for that day, and she'll take the one marked for today. If there's another Aubrey in her body at home, she'd like to think that Aubrey's not flaking on taking care of her either.

Though Aubrey did flake, just a little, when she had that hot dog at Gracie's but not Gracie's, the name different but the place still serving the same cocktail slushies, thirty flavors of ice cream, and funky sandwich fillings like mushroom "steak" and pastrami burgers, and yes, hot dogs with buffalo sauce and blue cheese. But the vegan-fed intestinal system she's now stuck with made her pay for it.

So from now on, cashew cheese it is. Aubrey pictures tiny farmers tugging on tiny cashew udders and wonders if Ethan knows how they actually get cheese from nuts, because that's always where her mind goes when she wonders something. And now, once again, she could actually ask him.

She hugs the cloud of a blanket to her chest and drapes it over the back of a low-slung pink chair. A row of perfectly groomed succulents basks on the bump-out of the windowsill, a rolled yoga mat nestles in the corner, a book on birds of the New England coastline sits on a side table, its spine lovingly creased.

It's not that this version of Aubrey has different hobbies, it's that this version of Aubrey has any hobbies at all. The only thing Aubrey has is a pile of rocks, like she's a seven-year-old boy.

She likes succulents, has never tried yoga but always meant to, and birds, well, maybe they're not so bad after all?

She slides open the barn door separating the living room from the bedroom in this cozy apartment in Cambridge that's much smaller than hers. But it's on the top floor, not in the basement, which her real estate agent had kept insisting was the "ground floor." Aubrey forces herself to step into the bedroom and strip the bedsheets, grateful for the washer and dryer in the kitchen, not wanting to do a walk of shame to some communal laundry facility. A phrase she knows she shouldn't be thinking anymore let alone feeling but can't help.

As she shoves the sheets into the washer, something clanks against the inside of the drum. She hesitates, hope battling logic that the painted stone that was in her pocket at the outing somehow got lost in her bed when she fell into it with Kai.

Her collection began after Ethan had pilfered a rock from the dozens perched beneath benches along the river telling passersby to "rest more" and "be proud" and "stand tall." Disingenuous, he'd said of them, the sayings cliché, insisting that words on rocks didn't actually change anything. Except what if what they changed was how a single person felt in that moment? Didn't that make up for the rest?

Cliché or not, the quotes reminded Aubrey of her grandmother, who had passed away not long before. She can still hear her "might's better than fight" and "if tired is a state of mind, tell that to my feet." Without Ethan knowing, Aubrey had returned the one he'd stolen, placing the "miracles happen" rock back amid the rest. A few days later, in a small boutique, she'd bought a round stone with "believe" painted inside a white daisy, feeling like it'd be good karma. It became the first in a collection that grew and her good-luck charm. She'd had it with her at the outing. She untangles the ball of sheets, disappointed at not finding it. Instead, there's a bracelet of tiny wooden beads, a mix of light caramel and dark browns and a smattering of black. Tigereye. Dangling from the clasp is a round silver circle, engraved.

MY KAI,
ALOHA NUI LOA

Aubrey doesn't know exactly what it means, but she knows it makes the bracelet special. Below is:

MAMA

He's probably searching all over for it, scared he lost it, something he brought here from his home in Hawaii. She sighs. She was so looking forward to today being a Saturday, a day she didn't have to see those rather nice dark eyes that would be calming if they hadn't just seen her naked.

She pulls out her phone to search for Kai's number when a text comes in from Mallory.

Are we doing a roll call? Because...

Mallory sends an emoji of a hand raised, and relief at not being alone here helps soothe Aubrey's anxiety over Kai. Ilena's text follows:

Same.

That's it. Like she's saying she also wants to go for avocado toast. Which is good. Ilena's calm mixed with Mallory's determination always guided them best. Aubrey texts: Now what?

Mallory: Calling you both.

A video call appears on Aubrey's screen, and she presses her back against the washing machine.

Mallory's face, then Ilena's.

"Another rule of Alternate World: Put nothing in writing," Mallory says.

"Is that what we're calling it?" Aubrey asks.

Mallory shrugs. "We could vote. AIM 2.0, B-Side, Off-AIM?"

Aubrey offers a smile, a weak one, because this doesn't feel "off" to her. Ethan's alive. She didn't send a text that killed him. This actually feels more right than home.

Ilena cuts in with a matter-of-fact: "Isn't it just our lives now?"

Mallory's eyes harden. "I realize you have a reason to want to be here, Ilena, but I'm not ready to accept this is our fate."

Because then Mallory's fate is prison. Aubrey and Ilena accomplices. Aubrey looks around this apartment she kinda sorta already loves. Do accomplices go to prison too?

"Tell me, then," Ilena says, "if physics and mathematics show that parallel universes or multiverses or many worlds or whatever name someone gives it are possible—"

"Probable," Mallory corrects, her voice higher-pitched than usual.

"Fine. But have you found one piece of evidence to suggest these realities could intersect? That could lead us to how we got here and how we can get home?"

Mallory's entire demeanor fizzles. "I'm still looking."

Aubrey rolls the beads between her fingers. Unsettled is a familiar feeling for Aubrey, and she's accepted it the way some people accept that their skin burns in the sun and don't go to the beach without an umbrella and a gallon of sunscreen. Some things just are. The more you fight them, the more aware you are that you have something to fight, something to lose.

But Mallory? She's never unsure. If she was, she'd surely never let it show.

Aubrey starts slowly, "So what does that mean? We'll simply be these versions of us?" Vegan Aubrey who has one-night stands with her subordinates and does yoga and watches birds and who's apparently "Autumn" to the man she may or may not have been supposed to marry.

"No," Mallory says quickly, her eyes darting like a cornered cat, her fingers digging into her forearm. "We won't. If the worlds intersected once, they'll do it again. We just have to figure out when. And avoid the police . . ." Mallory's voice unexpectedly cracks. "Until we do."

Ilena places a hand on her stomach, silent.

Aubrey's hands shake as she sets Kai's bracelet on the floor beside her. She faces the truth: They don't know anything. Which means Aubrey may have her entire life here or mere hours. She can't wait. She has to figure out if she and Ethan were meant to be together. If her world was right or if this one is.

A flutter of nerves hits like when there's a late bug in an about-to-launch feature. But when that happens, she doesn't let the feelings overwhelm. She doesn't panic. She knows the steps to take to narrow it down, to locate it, to fix it. She has to treat this the same way. A calm, methodical approach. And that starts with a do-over.

Her skin glows orange from the tint of the neon sign screaming Laser Tag. She's outside a brick warehouse that holds all manner of games that let grown men act out their insecurities by shooting at one another.

She chose the arcade perhaps because of the past, because it had been the location of her first date with Ethan. She'd been disappointed then, not because she isn't into games, but because she's always wanted to be more like Mallory, a woman whose profession doesn't define her. As if being into computers means Aubrey isn't into wines that need to breathe and herbs set in place with tweezers. And maybe she isn't, but she could be. Still, she'd liked Ethan, and it wasn't his fault that her white sneakers and zip-up hoodies screamed "tech," prompting him to assume she'd be into the arcade. So on that first date, she'd grabbed an oversize cup of some blue fizzy drink and an enormous tub of kettle corn and played paintball with him even though she doesn't really like anything that involves a weapon. Maybe when this Aubrey went on their first date, she didn't do any of that.

Her phone buzzes.

Kai: Sorry, mud moves faster than the T! Almost there!

Aubrey checks the time. One minute past the hour. Kai's one minute late for meeting her. She's only on time because this Aubrey helped her by labeling all the hangers in the closet according to activity. She tried on the three labeled "date night" before breakfast. And again before lunch. And then an hour before she set the alarm to leave.

Aubrey: You're good.

Kai: Something left to aspire to then.

Aubrey: What?

Kai: Because I aim to be great. In everything.

Heat creeps up Aubrey's neck. Kai's confident in a way that both unnerves and excites her. It makes her wish she could remember their night together, just a little. And even though she can't, here comes a tingling between her legs and a clamminess on her palms. She can't do this. She can't be picturing a naked twenty-two-year-old and especially not a naked twenty-two-year-old who works for her.

She grips her phone and starts to draft a new text when his comes through.

Kai: Let me show you. I'll teach you to surf. They've got a killer sim in this place.

Oh no. No, no, no. What did she say when she asked him to meet her here? She looks back at their text chain. She'd told him she'd found the bracelet and would bring it to the office on Monday, to which he sent about a billion happy emojis before asking if he could swing by and get it tonight. She'd said she wouldn't be home and countered with a We could meet outside the arcade in Southie at 7.

Does that sound like an invitation? For a date?

Her fingers remain paralyzed over the keyboard on her phone. She looks up. *Ethan*. Her actual date. Her breath hitches, the sight of him too much to bear after the image of him still and waxen under the shadow cast by the hospital sheet.

He hasn't noticed her yet. He's pushing back those black-rimmed glasses that make him look both a little nerdy and a whole lot sexy at the same time. And she's kinda glad he didn't get LASIK surgery here. He's fit but not overly so, like someone who goes to the gym out of a love of pasta and ice cream rather than adrenaline and testosterone.

He's early. He'd said "seven fifteen" when she'd gotten up the nerve to search this Aubrey's contacts for his number. He sees her, and she waves, just as Kai rounds the corner, holding a giant pink swirl of cotton candy. Kai reaches her first. He pinches a section of the delicate sugary fluff and presses it above his lips like a moustache. That he twirls.

She bursts out laughing, and when he stands before her, she doesn't react quick enough to dodge his kiss. A kiss she feels in her toes. His hair's loose, free of its bun, and she gets a whiff of her eucalyptus. That he hasn't washed his hair since he did so in her shower sends a strange but pleasant feeling through her.

They part, she steps back, and then her waist is warmed by something. Ethan's somehow at her side and somehow pressing his hand to her lower back. He didn't do that at home. Then again, at home he hadn't seen a strikingly hot guy stick his tongue down her throat.

"Oh, sorry," Aubrey says. "Ethan this is Kai, my, uh . . . he works for me. At AIM."

The heat in her cheeks must be making them ten shades darker than the cotton candy.

Kai's face crumples, but he sticks out his hand to shake Ethan's.

After, Ethan doesn't return his hand to Aubrey's waist, as much as she wants him to.

"AIM'ing high, then?" he says to Kai.

Despite the obviousness of Ethan's joke, Kai smiles politely. "Yes, and I'm learning all sorts of things."

He's disappointed but not embarrassed. The embarrassment is all her, and normally she'd not want to live in this awkwardness for a second longer than she had to, but she resists her urge to mumble a quick goodbye. Instead, she finds herself suggesting Ethan check on the line for tickets while she goes over some "work stuff" with Kai.

Though his forehead crinkles, Ethan leaves Aubrey alone with Kai.

She spins the cotton candy in her hand. "Thanks for this."

"I checked. It's vegan."

Her stomach sinks. "You did?"

He shrugs, and she slides his bracelet off her wrist.

"It's beautiful," she says as it passes from her fingers to his. A jolt she has no way of covering spikes through her, but fortunately he's looking down.

"Appreciate it. Was my grandma's."

"Oh, I'm sorry."

"She's not dead, just stingy. I'd loved it since I was tall enough to sneak it out of her nightstand. Ma added the tag when I left for the mainland."

"A reminder of home," Aubrey says, thinking of the Women Who Code poster.

"And family."

"Family, yes," Aubrey murmurs. Her mom and dad and siblings, all in her home state of Pennsylvania. Are they here? And has she not been back to see them in . . . my god . . . four years? Has it really been four? As long as the years of high school that made her never want to return. "Well, I'm glad it's safe and back where it belongs."

As she says it, she turns to check on Ethan, who's standing at the entrance to the arcade. When he sees her, he smiles, and the guilt and grief that have been keeping her heart pumping get worse not better. She feels that tug down to the place she's been since he died. Her throat's as dry as sandpaper, and she thrusts her tongue against the roof of her mouth, the backs of her teeth, trying to summon saliva that will let her talk, let her try to make it up to Ethan by not letting the same thing happen again here. And the only way to do that is to not pretend. She has to be herself and see if they fit.

She turns to test her voice, to say goodbye to Kai, but he's already gone.

Ethan's the one here, waiting for her by the door, tickets in hand. Inside, he doesn't balk when she says no to playing laser tag. He orders a bright pink drink called a ladybird that smells like coconut and strawberries and is sweeter than the cotton candy. Aubrey chooses a voodoo queen, eyes lighting up at the pretty purple color and the orchid floating on top. The lavender soothes her and the prosecco topper puts a bounce in her step that helps her kick up so much virtual dust as she races her virtual Humvee across the desert in *Storm the Sand* that she easily beats Ethan—or he lets her easily beat him. Though it certainly makes her a bad feminist, she kinda hopes it's that second one.

He's an expert at darts, she's surprisingly good at swinging a golf club, and they're both terrible at shooting hoops. They're so into whacking the mole that they order greasy fries and nachos, hold the cheese, and cancel their reservation at the trendy seafood place around the corner.

Aubrey's drinking some gold concoction that tastes like honey and heaven out of a mug in the shape of a lion's head beside the Skee-Ball when Ethan leans in and says above the pulsing music, "You're so not an Autumn."

His face remains close to hers and she tries to hide the flush she feels coming behind the lion's mane, but he puts his arm on her wrist and draws the drink to the side. Then he kisses her.

The sensation's so familiar and new at the same time that Aubrey doesn't care if it's good or bad (it's not bad), all she cares is that it's happening. Again.

"God, I missed this," she says aloud, and she knows her face is showing her mortification and fear. The old Ethan would have called her confusing comment an "Aubreyism" and laughed and she'd have laughed with him, but this Ethan just looks at her, his lips quirking into a grin.

"Me too. You're right, so right. I never knew how much I could miss something I never even had."

Two columns draw in Aubrey's brain, the start of a pro-con list of continuing down this road with Ethan, knowing what could happen, understanding the risks, unsure of what is in her power to cause or prevent and then his lips press against hers and she erases the list that doesn't matter anyway. Both ways are going to happen, and here, in this world, Aubrey might as well stop living in the past and worrying about the future and just enjoy it.

17
AUBREY

*Six Months **Before** the Outing*

The yellow pad of sticky notes trembled in Aubrey's hand. She'd needed to jot down the potential fix for the load-time lag in the ratings component of "How Wide's My Smile." Of course there was a lag time. The feature wasn't designed for this many subscribers. They'd never expected it to take off like this. More than three and a half million at last count, three and a half million people whose smooth user experience Aubrey was responsible for.

All day in the office, all evening while she waited for Ethan in his apartment, she'd tried to sort out what wasn't working. It hit her right in front of his desk, so she yanked open the top drawer and grabbed the stickies, tore off the top note with scribbles in his handwriting, and wrote down the solution before it flittered from her brain and she was left debating whether it was a back end or database issue even though she'd once been so sure.

She'd placed Ethan's scribbled note back on top and was about to return the pad to the drawer when she realized what it was: a pro-con list. She was rubbing off on him. A smile took over until she read the title: *A lifetime of Aubreyisms.*

Two columns, unlabeled, a line down the middle, and that phrase at the bottom of the second one, circled and underlined. The first column had: *Plays video games* and *Lets me choose dinner ★and★ Netflix* and *Sexy in a geeky way*. The second column had: *Asks so many damn questions about stupid stuff* and *Geeky sometimes annihilates the sexy* and *Codependent AF* and of course that *A lifetime of Aubreyisms*.

The second column outweighed the first. She heard the door to the apartment open, and she quickly shoved the sticky notes back into the drawer.

Three days later, she was drinking a glass of Chardonnay he'd ordered for her even though she never really liked the buttery flavor. She was perched uncomfortably on a cold, metal stool at the bar of a restaurant that was on every Boston "best of" list even though it exclusively served tinned fish that required no cooking, only plating. He was unsuccessfully sawing through the long, skinny razor clam drowning in olive oil that cost more than her last grocery bill when he stopped, set down his knife and fork, and stared at her.

She was sure that she had a smoked mussel dangling from her chin and reached for her napkin. But he'd pressed the burlap cloth, which was really too scratchy for something you used to wipe your lips, back into her lap and said, "This is working, isn't it?"

"Well, not great. Really could use a steak knife."

He grinned one of those grins that didn't come often, the one that puffed his cheeks so much that it brought out those cute lines around his eyes that Aubrey forever longed to see. "Sometimes you're just right."

And she smiled, and when he said they'd been together for

nearly half a year and they might as well keep it going and maybe even make it official, she forgot for a second the list she'd found in his desk drawer.

"Like married?" she said.

"Engaged. Let's get engaged."

And then the list came back. The list that was heavier on the "con" side, and she was overwhelmed with a gripping fear that he'd forgotten, and that if she didn't say yes now, despite the way he asked without actually asking, without a ring, that he'd remember and maybe even add to that second column until it outweighed the first so much that he'd make a different choice. So she made the only choice she could.

She said yes.

18

ILENA

Saturday Morning
*Two Days **After** the Outing*

This is where Ilena's gray lives. The walls of the nursery, which they apparently just finished the build-out and decorating of, are Coventry Gray. She knows it, because she knows every hint of brown, every subtle trace of green, every undertone of blue and black and yellow in every version of gray paint there is. She studied them, tested them on the walls of the living room, dining room, hallway, and mudroom of her and Jonah's house in Newton. This was the perfect one. Pure, no deception. No traitorous eggplant or fraudulent charcoal infiltrating with the second coat.

She presses her feet into the fluffy white area rug that softens the ebony wood. The room is beautiful, everything she could have imagined and things she couldn't have. A gray crib a shade lighter than the walls, cream changing table with black matte pulls, a simple pewter standing lamp above this upholstered chair she's gliding back and forth in. She'd never have chosen the gold sunburst dial mirror or the menagerie of safari animals, proudly stuffed and commanding the bench under the window. The blackout shade she'd wanted in her bedroom hangs above this window, ready to help the singleton sleep by blocking the reflection off the harbor. Her baby will have a waterfront view. What would her mom say to that?

The "her" in "her baby" still gives her a mild case of imposter syndrome, yet she can't deny what she saw at the hospital. A baby, this baby, a "Felix and Ilena" baby curled inside her uterus. She has the picture to prove it.

She rises from the glider and peers over the edge of the crib. Last night, Felix surprised her, first with the meal he cooked of lobster risotto and then by leading her here to see all the gifts from the office baby shower put away and arranged. He'd nestled the photo from the ultrasound inside the crib atop a sheet with little sailboats like polka dots. He'd done all of this while her best friends hid a man's body. Not just any man, a man who had helped AIM to become AIM. A man she considered a friend. One who had been more than a friend to Mallory. Ilena knew, of course she knew. She knew her best friend better than anyone. And as much as Mallory was hiding it, including to herself, she was hurting.

Ilena had cried. And not a little.

She'd cried because of the wood floors she'd have never picked out and the view she never dreamed she'd have and the hydrangeas at home that probably needed watering and the glass-topped dresser in the bedroom she despised and the lingering lemon of the luxurious risotto in her mouth and the house that was hers but not hers and the man that was hers but shouldn't be and the baby that should have been hers and Jonah's.

But it wasn't. It was hers and Felix's. Which is why she couldn't bring herself to search for Jonah's name here. When the technician ran the wand over her skin, Felix had clutched her hand, tears in his eyes even before the ghostlike picture came into focus on the monitor.

"This is everything," he'd said, leaning in to kiss her forehead.

It all disappeared: Mallory and Grayson and the police and

James and the pregnancy stick note and Jonah, everything that had been swirling in Ilena's mind. She was simply present with her baby and the father of her baby. When the technician asked if they'd changed their mind about not knowing the sex, her instinct was to say yes, they had. She had. That's when she knew.

She wasn't going to the police. She wasn't going to tell Felix that she wasn't the Ilena he thought she was, that in her world, he'd married someone else, had a child with someone else. She couldn't risk it, couldn't risk an arrest or jail or an evaluation by social services or a psychiatric ward. Goddammit, Mallory was right.

The lessons Ilena's mother had instilled in her should have made it a harder choice, one she had to think through, struggle with, in order to conquer her dependency on doing the right thing. But nature is stronger than nurture, and she knew instinctually without doubt or hesitation that nothing mattered except this baby. The singleton came first.

Mallory knew it, because Mallory knew Ilena the same way Ilena knew Mallory.

A gentle knock on the nursery door, and there's Felix, holding a box of tissues. "Just in case."

She smiles weakly. "Apparently hormones are a thing."

"Oh? I hadn't noticed." He enters the room wearing an untucked polo and blue-and-white-checkered shorts. "It's clearly my fault though. I wasn't thinking last night. How can one eat lobster risotto without a glass of muscadet? I should have made mac and cheese."

"Please don't. Ever."

"Not even for the singleton?"

She wraps her hands around the top rail of the crib. "Homemade, with Vermont cheddar only, not that imitation crap."

"You got it, Lennie." He winks, and she tries not to startle at the unexpected nickname.

She knows Jonah's mood from the way he slides his phone off the nightstand each morning, can guess what he'll choose off a menu at any restaurant faster than he can, and can time his ejaculation to the second hand of her rose compass clock. After twenty years with Jonah, there's so little that's new or surprising.

As Felix crosses the room, he pauses at the small pegs on the wall beside the door, each home to a little hanger dangling a onesie. Above is a small shelf that she only now realizes holds a framed photograph of her family. Ilena, her sister, and her mom on what appears to be her sister's college graduation day, which threatens more tears. Her sister didn't graduate in her world. She couldn't take the pressure to be the best. There's no sign of her dad, and disappointment fills Ilena to think he was no different here.

At twelve, Ilena had been old enough to understand what it meant that her father was moving in with a woman who wasn't her mom, but too young to realize that the hug Ilena had given him, begging him to stay, was tantamount to her choosing a side and his was the wrong one. The betrayal never left, seeming to linger in her mother's criticism of everything from the way Ilena packed the dishwasher to the shape in which she plucked her eyebrows. Her mother had always been demanding, expecting Ilena and her sister to be perfect daughters, to live up to the reputation of their attorney father and president-of-their-synagogue mother. The picture-perfect family. Her father leaving shattered the image her mother needed, the one that tamped down her insecurities. The one that allowed her to let go of her practical side and be the fourth in their games of Uno or shout out crossword answers as Ilena and her dad bent over the kitchen table on Saturday mornings.

But that mother disappeared just as her father had done. And as much as Ilena knew it was her father's choice to break up their family, she couldn't stop blaming her mother. Sometimes she wished that when her father had left, he'd taken her too.

Yet her father being who he was had set off a chain reaction. If he hadn't left, Ilena wouldn't have begged him to stay, wouldn't have betrayed her mother by choosing him, wouldn't have had to work so hard to be the best at everything. Would she have gotten into Harvard, met Mallory, founded AIM? Her dad's infidelity may be the key to Ilena's success. But it had been the opposite for her sister. When their mother demanded perfection, her younger sister stopped trying because it felt impossible. Yet here, she hadn't. She'd finished college. Ilena couldn't be more proud. Her sister had found a way to succeed in spite of their mother. The same way Ilena had.

"It strikes me that we're overdue. Do you want to invite them?" Felix asks, turning and coming to rest on the opposite side of the crib. "Your mom and sister?"

She nearly laughs out loud. The Cohens operate independently, as Felix's "overdue" and her father's absence from this photo implies is the same here. She's not sure what Felix knows of her family, and now's not the time to find out. She's juggling enough as it is. "Invite for what, exactly?"

"James offered to do a gender-reveal party."

"He did?"

"Well, after I asked him to. But really he owes us for missing the wedding."

"James missed the wedding?"

A fake laugh. "Funny. Sure, sure, we barely noticed bad sushi stopped our best man from attending." He reaches into the crib and lifts the white envelope from the ultrasound technician. "Well, party too tacky?"

She stares at the envelope, then the photograph atop the sailboat sheet. "Definitely, but let's do it anyway. Except, I'll host."

19
ILENA

*Two Years **Before** the Outing*

"We're never hosting again, promise me that," Jonah said as Ilena scrubbed at the chocolate ice cream ground into their hand-knotted cream rug.

"Grab your phone, you can record me." She pressed herself back on her heels. "Never again. They're monsters."

"*Monsters* is too kind. What's worse than monster?"

"Banshees?" Ilena said, dabbing at the rug and only making the stain grow.

"Beast?"

"Chupacabra?"

"Devil children." Jonah plopped down beside her with a spray bottle of rug cleaner. "Even Satan's scared of them. Truly, that's how Bree and Sean got them."

"We visited them in the hospital after she gave birth."

"An elaborate ruse. Trust me."

He ran his hand through his wavy hair. She'd begun to notice more strands of gray interloping among the dark brown. When the first couple appeared, she'd worried he'd go entirely gray overnight and it would age her—make her look older as she stood beside him. But she'd come to appreciate what it meant for their relationship. They'd been with one another long enough to start to go gray together. There was a comfort in that.

She pressed her lips to his cheek before picking up the rug cleaner and reading the back of the bottle. "Crap. I was supposed to spray this and let it sit before even breathing on the stain."

"Well, you've always been a go-getter." Jonah hauled himself to his feet, then pulled up Ilena. "I've been thinking a fern would look great in the living room."

Ilena raised an eyebrow. "Here, right in the middle underneath the coffee table?"

"You never think outside the box, I."

"I? As in 'aye, matey'?"

"As in 'Ilena.'"

"But that doesn't make any sense. That's not how you say my name."

"I'm more of a visual thinker."

"Yeah?"

"Yeah."

Ilena untied the belt of her wrap dress and slipped it over her shoulders so that it spilled onto the floor right on top of the stain. "Then what does this visual make you think?"

Jonah wrapped his arm around the bare skin of her waist above the nude-colored underwear. It didn't match her black bra because they'd been married long enough for that too. "Thank god you're on birth control."

After, they lay in bed sharing the rest of the Bordeaux they hid halfway through the evening. Bree and Sean had abdicated their parental roles the moment they'd walked through the door. Ilena and Jonah had spent the afternoon trying to grill lamb chops and bake dinosaur chicken nuggets while simultaneously stopping a four-year-old from climbing into their kitchen cabinets and a six-year-old from crumbling stolen artisanal cupcake in between the sheets in the guest room. They'd decided Bree and Sean got the Portuguese table wine that Ilena got stuck with during the Yankee swap at AIM's holiday party two years ago.

"Birth control rocks, doesn't it?" Ilena said, rolling the Bordeaux around her tongue.

"Yes, yes, it does." Jonah accepted the glass they were sharing and took a sip. "For now. Though maybe now doesn't have to be so long?"

Ilena sat upright. "What? Did you not see the rug? And I'm pretty sure the little one pooped in the shower and the older one tried to clean it up."

"At least she tried."

"Jonah, what are you saying?"

He sat up beside her and handed her the wine. "We'll be different."

"Obviously. But still, now? AIM's just hitting its stride." If Ilena's focus drifted, Mallory would resent it, resent her. "I'm needed."

"There are two of us."

"So you'll carry it half-time in your uterus?"

"You know I would."

"No, you wouldn't. You step on the scale every single day, freaking out over an extra ounce."

"Noted. So that part's yours. But after. I'm there. We're a team, aren't we?"

Ilena stilled. That was probably what her mom thought once too. She drank the wine, slowly. "We will be, right? If we do this? This is a choice we're making together. We're in. Both of us. All in."

“Speaking of all in . . .” Jonah plucked the glass from her hand and set it on the nightstand.

His hand glided down her torso and wound around to cup her ass and kept traveling farther, and she thought: *This is the man who’s going to take my kids to soccer practice*, before groaning with pleasure.

20
MALLORY

Sunday Afternoon
*Three Days **After** the Outing*

"Dammit," Mallory says as a text comes in from Heidi Hoffman. Her name's all she and Aubrey can see without being able to unlock Grayson's phone. There's a codependency vibe to Heidi Hoffman that makes Mallory sure the woman's not going to wait much longer before doing something. Something that could end with Mallory in handcuffs.

"You really should have asked first," Aubrey says. "I'm a programmer—"

"A genius one."

"Flattery won't help. I studied computer science at Williams College, not on the dark web."

"But isn't there, like—" Mallory flutters her hands "—equipment or something? In the movies they—"

"Do things that are impossible. But, yes, someone could hack his password, someone who has equipment to do so, but that someone isn't me. Besides, even if we could get in, any email or text you send will be encoded with your location, not Barbados or Guam or wherever you're sending him."

"I know that. I am the CEO of a tech company."

"Then why am I here?"

"Because part of my job is to collaborate with experts in their field."

"Thank you."

"You're welcome."

"Still, my field is computer science not organized crime."

Mallory slumps deeper into her sloped dining chair, fiddling with the arm of the ridiculous reading glasses she can't believe she needs. But without them, she nearly cut off her own finger trying to slice an apple. The screen of her own phone flashes with notifications from three different dating apps, and she's gotten two reminders for dates at the end of the week and one to pay last month's mortgage and another to cancel the trial of some streaming channel in all caps, bellowing "FINAL WARNING! DO IT THIS TIME, MAL!"

This Mallory is an embarrassment. The question is which of them is a murderer.

The past purchases on her online grocery orders for the past six months don't show a single box of nut crackers. Either she hasn't bought any or she has and didn't want a paper trail.

Her hand finds the fading marks on her forearm and begins to rub, a compulsive tick she's fully aware of doing and yet unable to stop.

"This isn't like you," Aubrey says, placing her hand on Mallory's forearm. "You understand the consequences of everything. You're a better forecaster than the National Weather Service. So tell me, what are you hoping to achieve? You do know someone other than Grayson's secretary is going to wonder where he is soon."

"Not if she has a reasonable explanation to give them."

"Which would be?"

Mallory hasn't gotten to that yet. First, the phone. She only has one more try before it locks her out permanently.

But Aubrey presses, "Which would last the rest of his life?"

"It doesn't have to last the rest of his life. It just has to last long enough for us to get home."

Mallory feels like she's infested with fleas, her entire body wriggling with every second that passes. She can't stay here in this slouchy chair, staring at that hideous sofa, every night obsessively reading about parallel universes and postmortem signs of anaphylactic shock and how to smuggle hand sanitizer into jail, trying to reconcile the existence of her police officer father, and mourning Grayson. Dammit she can't. This has to stop. All of it. Home, that's all she can focus on. Back to her AIM, to taking it public, to proving that what she's spent half her life on is worthwhile. No matter what Grayson did.

The computer error was like a virus—extremely well hidden and self-perpetuating. Without provocation to investigate, it would have remained hidden—for months, probably longer. And if she hadn't been at the penthouse at the exact right time, she'd have likely never known Grayson was responsible. Those phrases she overheard had cracked her heart as much as they'd inflamed her gut. In shock and knowing he'd only talk his way out of it, Mallory had plastered on a smile and stayed silent that night. She'd spent the next few weeks searching for concrete proof of his involvement. That she hadn't found any didn't mean she was wrong.

Mallory shudders and hugs her arms to her chest. Aubrey gives her a quizzical look, but Mallory can't tell her about Grayson. Telling her means telling her everything, and Mallory can't relive it all again—not the bad and not the bad she'd mistakenly thought was good for nearly a year. So instead, she simply smiles.

Aubrey doesn't smile back, her eyes wander, like she's somewhere else.

"What's with you?" Mallory says.

"Me? I'm trying to help." She grabs Grayson's phone and something sparkles on her wrist.

"A tattoo?" Mallory twists Aubrey's hand to see it better. "You didn't tell us this Aubrey has a tattoo. And a glittery one? Of a lion's head?"

Aubrey yanks her hand back. "It's nothing. It's temporary."

Mallory cocks her head. "Are you mocking me?"

"No, no, it is. A temporary tattoo from the arcade in Southie. It's no big deal."

"Everything in that sentence is a big deal because there's nothing in that sentence that's the Aubrey I know."

"Okay," Aubrey says. "So I went on a date with Ethan."

Mallory's hackles rise, the Pavlovian response to Aubrey's fiancé.

Aubrey strokes the glitter of her tattoo. "It's strange and weird and inappropriate. It is inappropriate, isn't it? Considering everything? But I . . . I had to see him."

And all Mallory can see is the last time they all saw Ethan, the folded-back hospital sheet, the way Ilena squeezed her hand, the stillness of Aubrey, the words Mallory couldn't bring herself to say. "I understand. Did you think I wouldn't?"

"I don't know. I mean, it's not like we all hung out all that much as a group. He's not Jonah or anything."

Mallory's heart sputters. She didn't realize that Aubrey sensed a difference. But of course she did. She's one of the smartest people Mallory knows. Even if Aubrey doesn't see it.

Mallory had never liked Ethan. It was instinctive, from the moment they'd all met at the reception for Grayson's speech. Ethan had that attractive, broody thing that Mallory had no patience for. He'd glommed on to them all night. Mallory had figured he was hitting on her, because Mallory figured everyone was hitting on her (and they usually were). But it was Aubrey who he'd asked out. Aubrey who uncharacteristically overcame her nerves to say yes. And so even though Mallory had a bad taste in the back of her throat like after mis-swallowing a multivitamin, she'd feigned excitement. A second date became a third, and Aubrey was smiling as wide as her grandmother had wanted her to. The chance to speak up was gone.

Still, Mallory would have liked to take Ethan's "Aubrey-isms" and shove them right down his throat. Perhaps Aubrey did wonder about a lot of things like wasn't partly sunny and partly cloudy the same thing. And so what if Aubrey thought it was "curl up in a feeble position" instead of "fetal"? That didn't require five minutes of laughing and Ethan requesting a new partner in charades at Ilena and Jonah's. Jonah had never thrown a punch in his life, but Mallory had watched his hand clench into a fist. But Aubrey had stood and bowed, and they all followed her lead, trying to support her. She didn't make choices easily, and who were they to say this one was wrong?

Though Mallory knew it was. Aubrey was brilliant and deserved someone who treated her that way.

Dying wasn't the ideal way for things to end between them (especially for Ethan), but Aubrey is better off. Mallory has been hanging back, Ilena too, unsure how far they should go to help her see that. Being here complicates it even more. And so Mallory pushes through her guilt and disgust and forces enthusiasm. "And how was it?"

Aubrey's cheeks twinge pink.

"That good?" Mallory raises an eyebrow. "Oh, *that* good, did you—"

"No, no, of course not. It was our first date. Or second, or our hundredth. I don't know, it's confusing."

Mallory stills as she gets a flash from a month ago: the booth in the bar in her world, the woman with the white coat, Ethan running out, dabbing at his shirt, the screaming in the street, the wounded look that came over Aubrey's face and never left . . . until now. "Just . . . we don't know what's going on here so be careful."

Aubrey nods. "I'll say the same to you. Because if all you're looking for is time and don't really care about what the data might show if someone beyond Heidi Hoffman starts looking, well, then, there actually is a relatively easy way of unlocking the phone."

One Mallory isn't sure she can bring herself to do. She closes her eyes. "I know."

"I'll come with you."

Mallory smiles a thanks before reaching into her pocket and pulling out a key chain with a dozen dangling states of Texas. "I've got it. Noreen let me borrow her car all weekend. Besides, I owe you. Because of Ethan and everything."

Aubrey shakes her head. "Don't worry about it. I know you're just looking out for me."

I was, truly, I was.

21 MALLORY

*Four Weeks **Before** the Outing*

Mallory swirled the paper straw through her cocktail, a bright violet thanks to the butterfly pea flower–infused gin. She had no idea what butterfly pea flower was except delicious.

She sipped slowly to keep her head clear. An ambush required focus. Especially one fueled by suspicion and not proof. Fortunately, bluffing was one of her strongest skills. She drew a figure eight with the disintegrating straw and a wad of paper floated to the top of her drink.

Ethan had been a half block ahead of her. She'd seen him exit his building, but she hadn't wanted to do this in the middle of the street. So she followed him to this bar with seductive cocktails and booths with walls that extended nearly to the ceiling. He tucked himself inside one, and she staked out a stool at the bar to fortify herself.

She hadn't been paying close enough attention lately. Grayson and the consistent orgasms had made her not pay close enough attention. Yet if she were being totally honest, she'd admit that it wasn't just him. Mallory was on the verge of becoming a brand independent of AIM. Designers sent her shoes and jumpsuits. She'd been a guest judge on *Top Chef* and *Shark Tank*. All the attention made the little girl inside of her scream "fuck you" at everyone from the teachers who doubted her to her father who left her to that ass in Straus who underestimated her. The constant shower of praise had convinced her that everything coming to AIM had been earned.

Still, hitting two billion should have set off alarms in her head. AIM's stock valuation had been climbing much too fast. If Ella hadn't come to her with those focus group results that seemed off, and if Mallory hadn't decided to lighten the overworked Aubrey's load by using her own strong foundation in coding to investigate, would she have ever realized it? Ever *let* herself realize it? That it perhaps *wasn't* all earned? That she hadn't steered AIM to that sky-high valuation all by herself?

Grayson artificially inflating AIM's stock value was an unnecessary risk. It wasn't exactly the lack of ethics or the abundance of corruption or the threat of actual jail time (well, a little of that last one) that wound Mallory up. It was that he'd overstepped. If anyone were going to toss a grenade into her company, it was going to be her.

She turned and stared at the side of Ethan's sandy-haired head. He wouldn't have been her hundredth choice, let alone first. But the tech giant he worked for also owned the analytics vendor that AIM used. Deep within its data had to be the origin of the glitch. That was how she'd get the evidence she needed to confront Grayson. Her coding skills didn't include hacking. She needed access.

Ilena was insisting on coming clean. They'd lose everything: their reputation, the payday, the big-league press the publicist was on the verge of getting. Everything Mallory had toiled and sweat and strategized and maybe schemed, yes, schemed for. Nearly twenty years of her life wasted. She'd be a forty-year-old woman with sagging breasts forced to buy her clothes off the rack, starting over as some arrogant start-up founder's assistant, if she could even get hired as that.

If the truth came out, AIM would be ruined and Aubrey—Ethan's fiancée—along with it. Professionally, but also personally. Her self-doubt and guilt over missing such an error would cripple her. Mallory hoped it'd be enough to convince Ethan to help. But if it wasn't, she was ready to promise him an absurd amount of shares of AIM to get that proof. Even if that proof would confirm that the last year had been a lie. That Grayson didn't believe in AIM. Didn't believe in Mallory.

Ethan slid to the edge of the booth. Mallory caught a glimpse of that perpetually smug smile that Aubrey just couldn't see. Mallory took a fortifying sip, and when she spun to face him again, he was no longer alone. The corner of a white coat hung down the side of the booth.

Ethan reached across the table and took the person's hand. *The woman's* hand. The woman who was most certainly not Aubrey. Aubrey never wore white because of a fear of spills and her nails were never polished, and she had no engagement ring at all, certainly not a showy one that shined under the glow of the Edison bulb pendant.

Ethan's index finger curled and began stroking the woman's hand. *Bastard.* And in public. *Arrogant bastard.* He dipped his head and his lips brushed her skin.

Shit.

Ethan and Aubrey had been engaged for five months, only now starting to plan the wedding, and this must have been why Ethan had been dragging his feet. This would destroy Aubrey. Without thinking, Mallory extracted her phone from her sailcloth clutch and texted Aubrey:

Drop everything! Found the signature cocktail for the reception. Quick, meet me at...

The point was to get Ethan away from the woman before he cheated on Aubrey. Or cheated on Aubrey again. Mallory looked across the street at a new place she'd never been.

Mallory: Better Bar.

Not best. Way to shoot for mediocrity.

Aubrey: I'm head-down in a potential algorithm issue.

Mallory: It can wait. They say this drink might go off the menu soon. Did I mention it's purple?

Dammit, now she had to find a purple drink at Better Bar across the street.

Three little dots appeared and disappeared.

Aubrey: Okay.

Mallory: Hurry! And invite Ethan. No, insist. Insist that he come. No excuses this time!

Aubrey: I'll try.

Mallory: Tell him I'm buying.

Little weasel was a cheapskate. Hence five months into an engagement with no ring for Aubrey.

Mallory reached inside her clutch, desperate for cash to quickly pay her bill when a booming "Bitch!" silenced everyone in the room.

Ethan launched himself out of the booth, a deep maroon wine stain spreading across the front of his white button-down, a wineglass falling, about to shatter. "You'll regret that," he growled across the booth.

The hand with the large showy ring simply gathered the white coat fully inside the booth.

Mallory ducked her head low as Ethan stormed past, cursing at his phone, which at that very moment must have been buzzing with a text from Aubrey. He jammed his fingers so hard she thought he'd crack the screen.

Whatever Mallory had just witnessed, Aubrey deserved to know. But telling Aubrey about her likely lying, cheating parasite of a fiancé required more support than Mallory could give. She texted Ilena to meet them at Better Bar.

Then it hit her. She needed something from Ethan. And if he *was* cheating, he would need Mallory to stay quiet about this. Her stomach twisted as the thought took root. *Leverage.* Keeping this from Aubrey gave Mallory just that. She could force Ethan to help her find evidence of the inflated numbers, of Grayson's involvement. She could save her company. And all it took was making the choice to betray one of her best friends.

Mallory needed to be sure. She needed proof of what she'd just seen—not from Ethan, from the woman in the booth. Mallory allowed herself time to gather her resolve. Then she took one last sip of the purple drink and laid cash on top of the bar. But by the time she got to the booth, it was empty of everything except the white coat.

22
MALLORY

Sunday Afternoon
*Three Days **After** the Outing*

Mallory leaves Noreen's car running in the driveway. She unlocks the door to her mom's kitchen and files past the photographs on the refrigerator without a single dart of her eye. She's down the basement stairs, in front of the freezer, spinning the padlock and lifting the chest's lid all in a single breath.

On goes the phone, off goes the blanket, and Mallory steadies her quivering hand to level the device between Grayson's face and her own, ignoring the way her heart rams against her rib cage. With the sound of the phone unlocking, the tightrope of tension in her body ebbs. She wrests her eyes from those dark spikes of his hair and replaces the blanket. She keeps one finger on the screen so it doesn't time out as she closes the lid and secures the lock. She's up the stairs and back in the safety of Noreen's car and breathing like she's just finished two marathons when her own phone buzzes and she wants to throttle it along with this universe's Mallory. It's surely a reminder for some absurdity like blindfolded speed dating or instructions on how to unlock her own front door.

But Mallory can't see shit without those stupid reading glasses. She delves into her purse and shoves them on her face. She steadies her breath and opens the settings on Grayson's phone. Her phone buzzes, and Mallory risks a quick glance. On her lock screen are missed texts from Ella and Noreen. This latest buzz is announcing a text from Ilena. Grayson's screen darkens in her hand, and she jams a finger to wake it. She ignores her own texts and finds the setting for facial recognition in Grayson's phone. More incoming messages on her own device: Aubrey, followed by an unknown number.

Ella, Noreen, Ilena, Aubrey, Unknown.

A foreboding grips her chest, but Mallory focuses on the thing that has to take precedence because that thing required the use of a dead body and she's not doing it again. She taps the button for "facial ID" on Grayson's phone.

Enter your passcode.

Well, fuckity, fuck, fuck. If she could do that, she wouldn't need to turn off the goddamn facial ID. Though a scream builds in her throat, she gently cancels and backs all the way out of the settings. She repeats each step. With the same response. Twice.

"Son of a bitch!" She slams the heel of her palm against the wheel. Grayson's phone tumbles from her grip. The screen flashes, but she shoots out her hand and snatches the device before it goes dark.

So she can't shut off the facial ID. So she can't change the passcode. So she'll have to do this here. Find the right wording to shut Heidi Hoffman down, to make Grayson disappear, because the alternative is having to preserve Grayson as a popsicle in her mom's freezer for the rest of her life and of all the things Mallory can live with, that's not one of them.

She scans Grayson's texts: new messages from the names of friends, some of whom she remembers him talking about; a no-show notification for a dinner reservation on Saturday; six "where are you" variations from Heidi Hoffman; and a check-in from his mom. She has no idea if his mom is the type to be worried about him because she didn't even know he had a mom. Well, obviously, of course he would have a mom, technically, but practically? They never talked about their families. AIM and sex and feeling free in a goddamn elevator, that was her relationship with Grayson. It had been enough.

Exiting his texts, she opens his email and addresses a new message to Heidi Hoffman. With the subject line . . .

Family emergency? Heidi Hoffman probably has Grayson's family contacts and their medical histories down to their last bowel movements.

Health issue? Kidney stones or panic attack or nervous breakdown? Heidi Hoffman would scour every hospital and doctor in Boston.

Wellness retreat? But if that yoga and meditation setup in his penthouse was for show, then there will be zero buy-in here too.

Secret fling? Witness protection? Monkhood?

What would Mallory believe? What would be worth missing taking AIM public and an appearance on national television?

Unexpected and urgent business opportunity with tremendous potential. In this, Mallory and Grayson are the same. Nothing would stand in the way of the chance for bigger, greater, more lucrative success.

She reads the email over three times before hitting Send, then creates a generic out-of-office responder for both his email and his texts. The screen dims, signaling a power down that would sever any remaining tie to Grayson.

She could let it go, let it all end, right here and now. She could have no way of knowing the truth: if AIM is a lie here too.

If this universe's Mallory actually did have motive because this Grayson was also inflating the stock price. Ilena wanted to find out. To fix it. Same as in their world. She doesn't understand.

Mallory was a child who wasn't scared of monsters under the bed, who grew into a woman who doesn't shriek at mice. But this? If Grayson was innocent here, if this AIM had reached two billion all on its own, then this Mallory hadn't failed. This version of herself had done what she couldn't.

With the phone dimming, Mallory hurries to open the auto-lock setting before the device goes to sleep. She isn't ready to let go. But she's also not ready to know the truth. So she simply turns off the auto-lock, which she can thankfully do without a passcode. She'll have access to Grayson's phone so long as she never shuts it off. All she has to do is keep it charged. Carefully, she places his phone in the cupholder, wishing she had Bubble Wrap.

She grabs her own phone and reads through her texts:

Ella: We'll have talking points for Shandy Shane this afternoon. How lucky are we?

Noreen: Final paperwork for the listing needs to be signed by y'all ASAP. Or whenever you get a chance because I know the hype has gotten overwhelming and you're underwater but ASAP. I can bring it to you. Just say the where and when!

Ilena: Dinner tonight. A gender-reveal party. Don't ask. Had no choice.

A dinner party? Now? For a baby that isn't actually Ilena's?

Aubrey: Did Ilena text you? Am I supposed to bring a gift? I'd already said yes to drinks tonight with Ethan.

617-555-4090: Mr. Harley's waiting for you at Dog Eat Dog day care! We'll keep snuggling him, but it's an extra $30 per half-hour past pickup!

Aubrey: Can I bring Ethan?

Aubrey: Should I?

Ilena: I'm seating you next to James. See what you can find out.

What are they doing? This isn't real life! We're not just settling in here!

Her hand reaches for the marks on her arm and she kneads so hard that if she had flint in her hand, she'd ignite.

Her phone rings. It's a New York area code. *Shandy Shane.* She has to answer, she wants to answer, but what if they ask about Grayson? Should she act like she knows he's unavailable or pretend she's as shocked as everyone else by his sudden trip? And why does she suddenly sound so very much like Aubrey?

She clutches the phone to her chest. It's going to go to voicemail if she doesn't pick up. She takes off the cat-eyed reading glasses and answers the call. "This is Mallory Latham."

"Ms. Latham, this is Georgina, assistant producer at *The Shandy Shane Show*. We wanted to confirm—"

The wail of sirens eclipses the producer. Mallory presses her finger in her ear.

". . . availability for—"

Flashing red lights ricochet through Noreen's hatchback. A rumble of an engine from behind announces the black-and-white car that boxes her in. A Cambridge police car.

Mallory struggles to summon saliva. "Yes, good, good, all good. I'm sorry, I have to run."

She lowers her phone. Drops it in the cupholder. She's too late. Maybe Grayson's elevator did have a camera or the penthouse had a hidden home security monitor or maybe the goddamn eavesdropping Alexa or Google Home or whatever they have here ratted her out. She's never getting home. She's going to miss everything, in both worlds.

She places her hands on the wheel and waits.

"Step out of the car . . ."

Shit.

"Miss MallieMoo."

Excuse me?

Her rearview mirror frames the driver's-side door as it swings open and a man in a police uniform steps out. He's tall and thick like a linebacker but with the slightest rounded belly and lag in his gait that confirms his playing days are long behind him. Dark gray sunglasses rest beneath a close-cropped haircut that's meant to mask a severely receding hairline. His tight jaw twitches as he approaches. Mallory inhales a breath and opens the car door.

The police officer's arms extend like a T. "There she is. I was starting to think you were a figment of your mom's and my imagination."

Mallory flinches.

"Oh, come on, was it the lights thing?" He lowers his arms. "You used to love it as a kid."

"Kid?"

"I know, I know. Big-time CEO doesn't want to play cops and robbers with her pops anymore."

Pops. He's a "Pops."

"Can I at least get a hug?"

He lumbers toward her, and his arms encircle her stiff torso. Her eyes lower to the gun on his hip and the realization that he's not here to arrest her isn't as relief-inducing as it should be. Because he's not just a "Pops," he's her "Pops."

Inside Noreen's car, a phone begins to ring, playing some

Beatles song she's never heard, which might be because she's not a big Beatles fan or because they have different songs here. Either way, it's not her ringtone. It's Grayson's.

"Let me," the man—her father—says.

Before Mallory's instincts kick in, he's already hunched himself inside the car.

"It's okay, I don't need—"

"Here you go." He plunks it in her hand, and she sees "Heidi Hoffman" on the screen before she hits the decline button and feels her chest and hope deflate as she reluctantly shuts off Grayson's phone.

"Two phones. To think my genes helped create a daughter who's important enough to have two phones. You definitely got that from your mom." He smiles, so wide and genuine and warm, and a thousand thoughts funnel like a tornado in her mind: He's not here to arrest her and he doesn't know about the dead body in the freezer and he seems to love her mom and maybe her. But one single thought eclipses all the rest: *You left me, you left me, you left me, you left—*

"And when did you get a car, MallieMoo?" he says.

23
AUBREY

Sunday Afternoon
*Three Days **After** the Outing*

Aubrey sprinkles blue stars around the base of her wineglass. She plays with them, making a smiley face, drawing a snowman, arranging them in ones and zeros to write code. She sticks her hand in the bag from the party store and grabs a fistful of pink hearts. She mixes the pink confetti into the blue, takes a sip of her rosé, and outlines a crude tulip on the bar top, a single stem like on her "Be you, be true" rock. Is it still on her desk in her world? The same way that glass octopus from Kai is here?

The lion on her wrist continues to glitter, but he's missing an ear. She should probably scrub the rest of the tattoo off, especially before Ilena's dinner party, but she's not ready to let go of last night. If she closes her eyes, she can still feel Ethan's hand on her lower back, his bottom lip tugging on hers, smell his scent that's more clove than it used to be, and she doesn't really even like clove or nutmeg or any of those fall, pumpkin pie spices even though she loves pumpkin—and who decided pumpkin had to be mixed with clove and nutmeg anyway? Everything was the same and everything was different. But still, it was Ethan.

He asked her for drinks. He asked her for a second date. Maybe all this guilt that had been making her lose focus and interest and filling her with so much doubt was misplaced. Maybe this version of Aubrey—maybe every version of Aubrey—is supposed to be with Ethan. Is that why she's here? So the universe can correct itself because of Aubrey's careless mistake? And it brought along her two best friends because even the universe knows Aubrey can't really function alone.

She sends Mallory a message. No gifts? You're sure?

Mallory: I'm sure. And we really need to talk. Where are you?

Aubrey: Meeting Ethan, remember? Best Bar, across the plaza.

Mallory: Best, not Better? At least someone's got full confidence here.

Aubrey: What?

Aubrey: Am I wrong? Is it not Best?

Mallory: Never mind. But get to Ilena's early. OK? I… I just need… just get there.

Aubrey nearly cringes at the desperation of her usually cool-as-a-cucumber friend and sends her an encouraging thumbs-up, except getting to Ilena's early is becoming more difficult with every minute Ethan's late. She flicks a pink heart. Maybe she does have the wrong bar. Maybe she misheard, and Mallory's right that there is a Better Bar and she's sitting here in Best, making him wait.

What if he doesn't? What if he thinks she stood him up?

She seizes her phone, and she sorta hates how quickly she's fallen back into the texting world. She hesitates. She hasn't learned her lesson. What if he's on his way and what if her text stops him? Hurts him. She sets down her phone.

If this is the universe correcting itself, then she shouldn't interfere. Maybe they all just need to stop, give themselves over to the multiverse or many worlds or whatever, and see how things shake out.

The door to the bar opens, and Aubrey straightens her spine, anticipating Ethan. Instead it's a collection of smooth skin and blowout bar hair and trendy rompers and two-day-old scruff. They tumble in, laughing, and heading for a booth across from the bar—AIM employees, including Noreen, Ella, and Kai.

Instinctually, Aubrey waves. Noreen and Ella wave back. Kai pauses, seemingly unsure after last night. Aubrey turns away from them, wishing she'd sat on her hand. She's here waiting for Ethan and she's not supposed to interfere with the universe.

But then again, the universe must be busy. She should meet it halfway, shouldn't she? She has Ethan's full contact information. She could send him an email, less urgent than a text, but maybe if she is at the wrong bar, it'll prompt him to ask where she is. She starts a new message with a casual "Hey," realizes she needs an actual reason to be emailing him, and invites him to the gender-reveal party, after drinks, if he's free.

There. Perfect. Right?

She finishes her drink just as a server sets a second glass of wine in front of her.

"Consider it a thank-you," Kai says, sliding onto the barstool next to her. "For finding this." He wiggles his wrist with the tigereye bracelet, but then his face goes slack. "Maybe that crosses a line? Or is patriarchal? I should have asked. Sorry, yeah, I should totally have asked." He pops off the barstool. His flurry of nerves makes the ones she'd expected to have in his presence again lie dormant.

"It's nice. Thank you." She takes a sip.

"Cool."

"Yeah, cool." She never says "cool." She never feels cool enough to say "cool" for real, or hipster enough to say "cool" ironically, or to even know when to say it which way, or even if hipsters are still a thing. Kai lingers behind the stool, as if it might bite him if he gets too close. "You can sit," she says, the words sliding out before she can stop them.

"That I can. Learned when I was a wee babe."

Her brows scrunch together.

"To sit." He runs his hand through his hair. "This isn't like me. I'm not normally such a cornball. No, sorry, that's a lie. I am. Truly, I'm a cornball. Dad jokes all the way."

"Dad jokes?" she says.

"You've never heard of dad jokes?"

Heat creeps up her neck. Aubreyisms alive and well, Ethan would say if he were here. Then she remembers, Ethan is *supposed* to be here.

Kai grins and dimples indent his cheeks. "They get a bad rap. Highly unwarranted. I challenge you not to laugh."

"I'll warn you, I'm not the hugest laugher."

"You don't laugh?"

"No, I mean, I do, just not like at things other people do."

"Like animals dressed like humans and grandmas tearing down Slip 'N Slides?"

"Do people laugh at those things?"

"Oh, *people* do." Kai's eyes widen in innocence.

She laughs.

"Are you lying to me, Aubrey? Because that sounded like a laugh."

"Just go already."

"Okay." Kai rubs his hands together. "What did the drummer call his two daughters?"

Aubrey stares at him.

He rolls his hand. "It's funnier if you participate."

"Oh, okay, then. What?"

"Anna, one, Anna two." Kai mimes hitting a drum and cymbal. "*Ba dum tsh.*"

Aubrey smiles indulgently.

Kai frowns. "Hardball. I like it. Now, let's see . . . maybe . . . got it. I'm reading this book about antigravity." He rolls his hand again.

"Oh, really? How is it?"

"It's impossible to put down!"

At this, Aubrey laughs, not for the joke but for the way Kai's eyebrows lift in anticipation, the tilt of his body toward her, the energy releasing from him that she can't help but absorb. He smiles easily, as if smiling is easy.

"One more," she says, feeling a lightness she hasn't felt in a long time, even before Ethan's death. She hadn't needed a pro-con list to decide whether she wanted to date Ethan. Just look at him. And look at her. So of course she was always worried about saying something stupid or misunderstanding a joke or *being* the joke without realizing it. There was a weight to living that way. She didn't realize how much until now. She smiles at Kai. "Your absolute best."

Kai nods slowly as if rotating through a database in his mind. "So, yeah," he says like he's in the middle of a casual conversation, "I ordered a chicken and an egg from Amazon." Aubrey's grin comes even before he finishes. He gives a playful shrug. "So, I'll let you know."

The tingling that precedes goose bumps whooshes through her, followed by a ripple in her belly, and her laugh releases from somewhere deep and true. She remembers the feeling she had when she first woke up in this topsy-turvy world two days ago. Not fully asleep, not fully awake, with this warm body beside her and a sense of comfort and contentment that she wanted to burrow into and never let go.

"And there it is," he says. "A laugh. Looks good on you. You can repay me tomorrow by bringing me that succulent you promised. Otherwise, I might have to take back the octopus. We did have a deal." He smiles broadly, and those dimples scoop farther in, and Aubrey resists the urge to trace them with her finger. The bartender approaches, and Kai orders a dark beer. When the bartender asks for his ID, Kai's cheeks flush, and his eyes dart to Aubrey's. To the thirty-two-year-old woman sleeping with a kid. Grad school or not, that's what he is.

Aubrey's phone dings with a new email.

> Hey, Aub, sounds fun, but I'm watching baseball with the guys. Let's make a plan soon? 😉
> —E

"That little shit," Aubrey blurts out, fuming that he didn't even mention the plans they have for this very moment.

Kai's hand drops to the bar, not taking his ID back from the bartender.

"No," Aubrey says. "Not you, sorry, not either of you."

The guys. How many times had Aubrey gone along to watch the Red Sox with Ethan's friends in their frat house of an apartment even though she hates baseball more than she hates cloves?

"Instantaneous" and "Aubrey" do not go together. But still, she turns to Kai. "Do you like baseball?"

"Not especially. But . . . oh, is there a match or something tonight that you want to watch? I'd give it a go."

A baseball "match." A total Aubreyism.

"How about gender-reveal parties?" she asks.

"Cakes that surprisingly burst with blue or pink sponge? Sounds cool. Supercool."

Aubrey smiles. "Cool, for sure. This one's tonight. For Ilena's baby. Want to come with me?"

"Absolutely." His eyes are bright with interest as if everything surrounding Aubrey is something to be explored and he just can't wait. And then, the skin between his brow crinkles. "But I don't have a gift."

24

ILENA

Sunday Evening
*Three Days **After** the Outing*

"Be like you," Ilena half sings, half hums as she perfects the angled pocket of her last napkin and sets it on top of the black dinner plate. She sways as she circles the stainless-steel table, slipping knives, forks, and spoons into the cloth pocket of her napkin folds. It'd look better against a table made of reclaimed wood and plates of white, all things she'd learned by helping her mother, things that ended after her father left.

"Duh, duh, duh, and the man in the moon." Her finger taps her belly to the beat. It's surreal to be in this body, an unmistakable and unceasing reminder that this is a different place, a different life, a different Ilena. When she spins around to get the wineglasses, she sees Felix watching her. "Oh, hey there . . . you." She's really got to search this Ilena's texts and emails for a hint of any pet names.

"What was I thinking, even suggesting James host this? You are in your element."

"So long as no one mushes cupcake under the sheets." She

laughs softly, mindful of causing an involuntary release of her bladder.

Felix cocks his head. "Why would anyone do that?"

A flash of Jonah saying "devil children." "They wouldn't. It's just a figure of speech."

"Is it?"

She tries to brush off the slip by adjusting the hydrangeas delivered with the order of food. Blue, not white. Again, fine if it were a farmhouse table, but it blends too easily with the gray of the stainless. There was a time when she wouldn't have been able to stop herself from channeling her mother and would have marched right back to the grocery store and demanded an exchange. There was a time when Jonah would have done it for her, before she saw the mistake, without ever mentioning that Ilena was still trying to please a woman who could never be pleased. That was a long time ago, before Plum Island. Another life, another world.

A world Mallory insists they get back to. They should, of course they should, except . . . AIM's doing even better here. Ilena checked with marketing, and there haven't been any signs of suspicious focus group results, no strange accounts to suggest the stock value isn't earned. Plus, they're going to be on the goddamn *Shandy Shane Show*, and Ilena doesn't really care if it's only Mallory. Though maybe she should with the unbalanced vibe Mallory's beginning to exude.

Then there's Ethan. Alive. Not that she wants Aubrey to be with him here. But at least, here, the guilt that had become a parasite might finally pass. Everything here is right; everything here is better. Except for James.

And Grayson.

That list doesn't include Jonah. She had to let go. For her, there is no Jonah here. And the one at home might have moved out by now. Maybe back to the city, where he'd been wanting to go. Ilena had kept insisting that you couldn't raise kids in the city. Each time she said that, he simply responded, *Mallory grew up in the city*. A loaded remark inviting her to either speak poorly of her best friend or become a hypocrite.

But it was never about returning to the city. The city was a metaphor for the life they once had, in college, in their twenties and early thirties when they didn't mind smelling their downstairs neighbors' pepperoni pizza through the bathroom radiator or angling the outdoor couch on their narrow porch so they could no longer see the neon G of the Walgreens sign that poked through a gap in the trees. When they were enough for each other.

It was his decision to change that. Something he forgot as conveniently as he forgot that it was their neighbors' use of the common hallway as a time-out space for their shrieking three-year-old that made him want to move to the suburbs. She was the one who'd been unsure initially. The restaurants, the cheese and wine shops, AIM, and most of all, Mallory, all within a short walk, not a drive through traffic that was no longer relegated to rush hour. But eventually she'd come to appreciate their small yard and their own four walls. And yet, she doesn't mind living here, in Felix's apartment. Maybe she'd have been the one to move back to the city after the direct listing, once the divorce was final.

The singleton wallops her, and Ilena swells with renewed purpose. She resumes her table setting and hums, "Hmm, hmm, good time, then, we'll have a good time then."

Footsteps from behind, then Felix asks, "What's that you're singing?"

"'Cats in the Cradle,' you know, silver spoon and all that."

"I don't think so."

"Harry Chapin?"

"That's a new one for me. Is it some kid's lullaby?"

"Not really." Is there no Harry Chapin here or is Felix's

musical taste not stuck in the seventies like Ilena's? "My mom used to play it nonstop. Come to think of it, I remember her singing along to it and realizing it wasn't really all that nice of a song."

"I'm sure it's not what you think. How many lyrics change meaning when you're older?"

"Hmm, yeah, probably."

"What a shame they couldn't come."

"Short notice." That and the fact that Ilena never contacted them. She couldn't bear for her mother to criticize this child inside of her the way she criticized Ilena's role at AIM (why not CEO!), her pixie cut (you're practically bald), and her husband (if only he were a "real" doctor instead of an anesthesiologist). Though Ilena would have liked to see this version of her sister.

"Next time." Felix juts his chin to the set table. "And we've got our extended fam, right here. I'll get on the steak."

Ilena pushes aside the thoughts of her family. "So glad I married a chef disguised as a lawyer. When there's no lobster for the risotto, he pivots just like that." She snaps her fingers before reaching for the wineglasses in the rack above the buffet.

He helps her by sliding the glasses forward, the ones the singleton prevents her from reaching. "I told you it'd all work out. Unorthodox, maybe, but we got this."

"That we do." She smiles broadly. "I'm even thinking an AIM spin-off? Gender-reveal, engagement, retirement, you name it. Parties in an instant?"

"Might as well be your middle name."

She laughs, but Felix doesn't seem to be joking. He returns to the kitchen, and she rubs her stomach. Practical, responsible, that's who Ilena is. And yet she'd once made out with Jonah in the sculptured bronze lap of the *John Harvard* statue—after scouring the yard for campus police, but still, she'd done it.

She'd said yes to the dunk tank at the second AIM outing, and it was legal—Felix—who'd nixed it, which she highly suspected would happen, but no one needed to know that. And she'd handed Mallory that roll of duct tape. But that wasn't because she thought it'd be fun or even for the bigger dorm room, though that was a bonus. It was because even then, Ilena knew how much they each needed the other to become the women they were destined to be. This is who Ilena was destined to become, she's sure of it.

25
ILENA

*Eighteen Months **Before** the Outing*

Ilena stared at the photographs on the wall of the fertility doctor's office. Babies of all sizes and shapes in varying degrees of open-mouthed wailing.

"Are we actually doing this?" Ilena said.

Jonah reached for her hand. "We're exploring our options. Unless you don't want to?"

"Do you not want to?"

"I didn't say that."

"Me neither."

"Okay, then. Options. Exploring. The choice, ultimately, is ours. And remember, we define our choices, not the other way around." Jonah waved the fertility treatment brochure at her. "And hey, good news. We can still have sex during ovarian stimulation. At least until your ovaries expand."

"Expand? They're going to expand? Will I need a bigger belt?"

Jonah pretends to study the brochure intently. "Hmm . . . this suggests you simply walk around naked. Airflow is good."

Ilena tried to smile, to laugh, but she couldn't because she was failing. She let go of Jonah's hand. "This is a lot, and it hasn't even started."

Jonah shifted in the chair to face her. "We're lucky though. To live here, in a state where these treatments are covered by insurance and we couldn't ask for better doctors and hospitals. Your eggs, my sperm, this is top-tier, five-star, champagne and caviar, Four Seasons all the way."

He was trying so hard, and her heart nearly burst with love for him. "I know all that, and I'm grateful for it." Ilena closed her eyes, thinking of all the pregnancy tests she'd taken over the past few months—so sure so many times, and yet all those single lines on the plastic tests added up to nothing. "It's just . . . a part of me is disappointed in myself."

Jonah winced as if he'd been hit by a brick. "We don't even know if something's wrong yet, let alone if it's attributable to one of us."

"I'm sure it's not you."

"And I'm sure it's not you either."

"It's us, then? We aren't meant to be parents?"

Jonah ran his hand through his hair, sending his cowlicks in a thousand different directions. "All I know is *we're* meant to be. That's enough for me."

The door to the office opened, and in came the smiling woman who would help determine their future. As the doctor sat at the desk in front of them, Jonah searched Ilena's eyes, waiting for a response.

"Me too," Ilena said, not realizing how much weight two little words could hold when they became a lie.

26

MALLORY

Sunday Evening
*Three Days **After** the Outing*

From her bedroom closet, Mallory extracts a boxy fuchsia blouse and wide-legged pants, striped in pink and white. "Seriously?" She holds up the offensive pieces. "Is she part clown?"

On the floor by her feet, Harley wags his tail.

"I'll consider that agreement." She riffles through the hangers, past sundresses with fruit on them—*a banana, seriously, Mallory?*—and light-wash jeans and lacy cardigans that skim the floor. There's no consistency here. Soccer mom from 1985, children's librarian, a seventy-five-year-old widow. Her eyes widen. "Think 'I've got nothing to wear' would get me out of this?"

Harley rolls onto his back.

"Yeah, me neither," Mallory mutters.

And her mind returns to her dad. A dad who calls her "Mallie-Moo." A dad who loves her mom. A dad who didn't leave.

A dad who could have her arrested.

Her hand shakes as she scoops up her glass of bourbon, neat. She's trying, without success, to loosen the choke hold on her nerves that came with seeing her police officer father. She'll have to tell Ilena and Aubrey. Except it's not exactly dinner party conversation. Her brain hurts. All she wants to do is have this bourbon, maybe another, and hell, one more, and flump into the couch and eat popcorn and watch *Titanic* to remind herself that things could always be worse—she could have woken up on the *Titanic.*

Ilena's gone full-on Stepford. Among the thousand reasons this dinner party is absurd is that Ilena knows better than to include Mallory. Give her a crowd of a hundred or a sofa with her two best friends, not a table set for six or eight that always winds up with an extra chair jammed around a leg for the solo Mallory. Though at least today Jonah won't be there trying to set her up with some colleague whose descriptions of valve replacements or cartilage scraping would put her to sleep in her lobster bisque—an Ilena specialty.

Has Ilena looked him up? The sinking feeling that she hasn't, that the combination of the unfathomable divorce in their world and equally as incomprehensible Felix and the baby here has caused Ilena's husband of thirteen years to vanish from her thoughts makes Mallory reach for her drink.

She sips her bourbon and fingers the fabric of a maroon sheath dress, the most subdued thing in the closet.

"I'll make it work, I mean, obviously, I will." As she grabs hold of the hanger, her breath catches. Behind the dress is a tan plaid Burberry coat just like the one she and Ilena purchased together. They'd traded it back and forth for years. She's not even sure who has it now. She leans in and sniffs, but there's no hint of perfume from either of them.

She leaves the coat in the closet and carries the dress to the bed. Harley flips himself back over, prancing beside her ankles. She'd texted Ilena back, saying that they didn't have time for this, that they had to concentrate on figuring out next steps. And besides, she couldn't come because of the dog.

Ilena ignored the first part, and for the second, said she would invite Noreen who could watch Harley.

Well-played, Stepford.

Mallory finishes her bourbon and fruitlessly searches the underwear drawer for something other than a bralette, the source of that sag she noticed when she first woke up here. She slips into the dress, which only accentuates the droopiness. She grabs the plaid coat from the closet and sets it on the bed beside her purse.

She then opens her inbox, fighting the urge to touch the marks on her arm. Hope swells at the new email that flies in. It's from the restaurant that catered the AIM outing. She contacted them to request a detailed inventory of every item served. She didn't go through Noreen. The Noreen of here seems more staid than their Noreen, and Mallory wasn't up to conjuring the perfect lie to cover why she was asking, which was to determine if Mallory had means as well as motive.

Like in their world, the food list includes allergen notations for every dish. Crackers of wheat. Crackers of cauliflower. Crackers of spinach. (Spinach?) But none made of nut.

She lets her hand knead her forearm. *Christ, Mallory, what did you do?*

Harley gives his pathetically endearing whine and she grabs his leash just as the intercom buzzes. In her world, someone's always making the rounds for signatures in this neighborhood. Petitions to clean up the river, allow a marijuana festival in the park, save some dilapidated building that George Washington once masturbated inside of; even the stuff Mallory believes in means she loses twenty minutes minimum.

She hooks the leash onto the harness on Harley's back, slides her feet into hideous orange house clogs, and heads down the stairs to the front door. She opens it, rolling her eyes that this time, whatever they want her signature to help them put up or take down or preserve is deemed special enough to bring along a camera crew.

"Not interested." Mallory elbows past a woman in a drapey black tunic and dark-wash jeans.

"I'm sorry," the woman says, a hint of a New York accent assaulting the vowels. "I was looking for Mallory Latham. Maybe I buzzed the wrong unit?"

You did, lives on the tip of Mallory's tongue, but then the dude with a scruffy beard and hair past his ears lowers the camera he's holding. Emblazoned across his T-shirt is the *Shandy Shane* logo.

We wanted to confirm . . . availability for . . .

Shit.

"Georgina?" Mallory asks, grateful for her well-practiced ability to remember names.

"Ms. Latham? Is this a bad time? Earlier, I thought we confirmed—"

"It's fine, completely fine. Remind me, and sorry, it's been a day, this is for . . ."

Georgina shares a loaded look with scruffy bearded dude. "Background, B-roll, walk-and-talk, driving—"

"I don't have a car."

Another look.

"Just an example," Georgina says. "There's lots we can do. If now's still a good time? We're only in from the city for a couple of days. Then we go back to edit, and we'll return with Shandy Shane the morning of the interview at AIM with you and Mr. Fields."

"Yes, spectacular, Mr. Fields, AIM." Mallory's attention shifts to the rumble of a car turning down her block. She gets a glimpse of the black-and-white and the lights on top. Her unfortunate timed run-in with her father must have energized him for some more father-daughter bonding. When the police car approaches with a woman behind the wheel, relief washes over Mallory. (Disappointment too.) "Sure, right. Now is great, this is great."

The police car rolls to a stop right in front of her building.

"Actually." She steadies the tremble threatening her voice. "Why don't you head on up and get settled? Third floor, door's unlocked."

The door to the police car creaks open, and a woman with a swimmer's build and dark hair in a severe bun trains her mirrored-sunglass gaze directly on Mallory.

Shit, shit, shit.

"Really." Mallory steps over the threshold and propels Georgina into the entryway via a forceful prod of her elbow. She lifts Harley's leash, and his head quirks up. She owes the furball for being so damn cute. "He likes his privacy. I'll be up in a jiff."

"Jiff" isn't something she normally says, but it seems to fit this Mallory based on her cheery wardrobe.

From inside the entry, Georgina says, "Uh, sure, Ozzie can get some establishing shots of the condo, if that's okay?"

"Ozzie?"

Scrubby beard sticks out a fist.

Mallory awkwardly meets his cupped hand with her own holding the leash.

The police officer talks into her shoulder as she starts down the front walk.

Right leg bent at an unnatural angle, body still, eyes open, opaque and not moving.

Damn you, Heidi Hoffman.

Mallory yanks the door to the building shut and hurries down the front stairs, Harley tight to her heels. She tries to stave off the police officer, but she's too slow or the officer's too fast and they meet in the middle of the front walk.

"Mallory Latham?" the woman says.

Mallory tries to remember if she left the condo windows open. How good are camera mikes? "Hmm, good day to you."

The police officer cocks her head. "Officer Middlebury. Got a minute?"

"I do, but not sure he does." Mallory lifts Harley's leash, playing into that flighty persona this Mallory apparently has. "I got so wrapped up in the *Real Housewives*, I plum forgot the little nugget!"

Right then, Harley has a bowel movement.

The officer says, "That's settled then, now looks like we got a moment."

Mallory starts to shrug, but then Harley twirls adorably, and he really is doing all he can to earn his keep. "Breed, right? That's what you wanted to know? Everyone does. He gets me stopped more often than a bus on Mass. Ave." She laughs. Officer Middlebury doesn't.

"How long you had him?" The woman pulls down those sunglasses.

"Not long." The dog is her link to Grayson. She has to tread carefully. "Actually, I'm just watching him for a friend." Mallory lowers her voice. "I'm not much of a *d-o-g* person."

"But this friend still asked you to watch him?"

"It was a last-minute thing. Wrong place, wrong time, I guess."

"When was this?"

Officer Middlebury is acting super casual, like they're old friends who just happened to run into each other on their way out of a boozy brunch. But the questions are too pointed, and she knew Mallory's name, and damn you, Heidi Hoffman.

"A couple of days ago." Mallory sneaks a glance up at her condo. "Listen, I'd like to keep this between us, but it was a work thing with too many cocktails, and well, I happened to be there the next morning when my friend had to go out of town unexpectedly. I said I'd watch the dog. Good to try new things, right?"

"Depends on what the new thing is," the officer says. "This friend got a name?"

"Of course."

"And?"

You already know, don't you?

"Grayson Fields, but let's not spread that around. Work colleague, and all." No response, and Mallory clears her throat. "I'm sorry, I'm going on about the dog and my sex life. Did you need something? Is this about the music next door? Let me tell you, at times it's breaking the sound barrier."

Officer Middlebury pushes her sunglasses up on her head in a total power move that makes Mallory's toes curl.

The officer says, "You should file a complaint."

"Oh, I don't like to start things, but if you need another statement, you know where to find me."

"Good to know, because we're just at the beginning stages here."

"How many stages are there to a noise complaint?"

Officer Middlebury's smile drips with condescension. "Perhaps I haven't been clear. The beginning we're at is looking into the disappearance of Grayson Fields."

Nerves make Mallory release a bubble of laughter. "Sounds like a magician show."

The officer doesn't even blink.

"Oh, oh, you're serious?" She draws Harley closer. "But Grayson's just on a trip. Isn't he?"

"You tell me. You seem to know more than anyone. Where was he going?"

"I don't know. He didn't say."

"How long was he going to be gone?"

"A few days," Mallory says noncommittally, then adds, "Grayson's not really the best with details. But maybe you could try his secretary? She's in charge of his schedule."

"But you might have been the last to see him." The officer bends to give Harley a scratch under his chin. "We're still waiting for footage from the building's cameras, but the gentleman with the bad back at the security desk can't remember seeing him leave. We're still trying to nail down a timeline."

Here's her opening. "Well, maybe I can help. We left before he did. I think about . . ." Vague is better, right? "It was after brunch." Mallory scrunches up her cheeks, as if deep in thought. "I'm sorry, we had mimosas, plural, so I'm not exactly sure of the time."

"We, meaning you and Mr. Fields?"

"He had some, yes, and Ilena and Aubrey, my friends and business partners, though Ilena technically only had the juice because she's pregnant."

The officer stands, giving a slight (fake) chuckle. "They stayed over too? You all must be really close."

Mallory refrains from sinking her teeth into her lip, straightens her spine to accentuate the several inches she has over the officer, and lobs that chuckle right back. "They came over in the morning. We were celebrating. Actually, we were celebrating what's happening upstairs. My company—our company—is going to be on *The Shandy Shane Show*. They're doing some B-roll footage today. I really shouldn't keep them waiting. Is there anything else I can do for you, Officer?"

"This interview, is it local?"

"Yes, though I'm not sure if they use an audience. I can ask, if you're interested."

"I only stream. Don't even have cable." The officer hands Mallory a card. "Let me know if you do have to travel for any reason. We might have some more questions."

"Sure thing. I'll also ping him myself. But he'll be back soon. Nothing would stop him from being on TV."

"Really?" Officer Middlebury says with renewed interest.

Mallory wants to kick herself. "You know men with big egos."

"You aren't worried?"

What would someone who has no idea what's happening say?

"I wasn't, but I guess I'm starting to be, a little." She scoops up Harley, the sheath dress doing nothing to hide the fading marks on her forearm. Mallory adjusts the dog to cover. "Is it okay if we check in with you?"

The officer gives nothing away. "Absolutely. Open dialogue."

"Perfect."

"Perfectly perfect."

They stand there, each waiting for the other to blink. Officer Middlebury turns so slowly it's totally another power move—a display the officer doesn't need to make because Mallory's fucked. Because of Heidi Hoffman, because her mom had that damn freezer, because Mallory didn't listen to Ilena and report Grayson's death when she woke up in his penthouse. Christ, why didn't she? Because whatever the truth is, it *would* have been easier to spin it as an accident then.

Mallory watches the officer stroll to her car and is about to turn away herself when the officer pivots, her eyes floating to Mallory's forearm. "You never told me."

Mallory stills. "Told you what?"

"The breed?"

"Cockapoo."

"Cute. Unlike that." The officer gestures to the front walk. "Fifty dollar fine for not curbing your dog."

"I'll be sure to—"

"Just be careful. Wouldn't want to wrinkle that dress."

27

MALLORY

The Day of the Outing

Mallory could barely move among the wrinkle-free, tastefully tattooed bodies flocking to her at the AIM summer outing. She scanned the crowd for Grayson, widening her freshly glossed lips into a welcoming smile to hide the anger and desperation making her heart pound. She hated him. (She did. But also, she didn't.)

"Ooh, are those alpaca?"

"Ms. Latham, can we take a group selfie?"

"With the alpaca?"

Mallory strolled past the life-size tic-tac-toe and led the new interns to the pen of farm animals she already regretted saying yes to. It was the smell. Like being inside a dead whale that gorged itself on Limburger cheese. She angled her head to mask the whisper of a double chin as selfies were snapped before resuming her search for Grayson.

The lawn was full of employees buoyed by the news of AIM's valuation reaching an all-time high: two point two billion. Three months ago, it'd been one point seven. The jump wasn't unprecedented, but it was rare; it marked AIM as a force. It had primed her, Ilena, and Aubrey for the windfall that Mallory had always known was possible. She'd thought it was her doing, her steering of AIM, but it hadn't been her at all.

It had been Grayson, manipulating Mallory for the past year. From that first night after the kickoff party for "How Wide's My Smile," when he'd made her feel like going public was a brilliant idea, second only to falling into his bed. To the night six months later when he'd suggested over French 75s that a direct listing might be more lucrative for them professionally and her spending three nights at the penthouse more rewarding personally. To the stolen moments in AIM's offices, to sneaking around like teenagers, not even letting Ilena and Aubrey know. To late nights that weren't always just about sex, something that had surprised (and terrified) Mallory most of all.

She hadn't fallen for him. (But she had. She completely and totally had.)

Patience, Grayson had that, but also the expertise. He'd choreographed each piece of the puzzle, setting the last one into place by inflating the stock price. He'd ensured the "unprecedented" and "game-changing" increase in users knowing the industry would go wild over it. The kicker was, AIM *had been* booming. AIM had been on track to become what it was now. Grayson and his glitch only accelerated it, Mallory was sure of that. Why hadn't he been? Why hadn't he trusted AIM? Trusted her?

Fucking Grayson—arrogant, egomaniacal Grayson. A simmering in her veins surged as one of AIM's early investors sauntered over, belly testing the limits of his buttoned Tom Ford blazer. Mallory fought her cringe as this man with a ludicrous combover kissed each of her cheeks and placed a hand on her waist.

She backed up. Her heels crunched the shells beneath her feet, and for a second, she pictured it: Grayson's funeral instead of Ethan's. A rush of nausea hit her. Neither of them deserved it, though if one of them did, it was Grayson. If only for Aubrey's sake.

Mallory excused herself with a flash of the smile that had closed more rounds of funding than she could count. The server heading her way was a gift from the universe. Mallory snagged a glass of sparkling wine, catching sight of Aubrey. She came. Good. Because, seriously? Fuck Ethan. And fuck the woman with the white coat that Mallory was sure he'd been cheating on Aubrey with or had been about to cheat on Aubrey with.

Mallory raised her glass and issued a heartfelt smile.

"Why, thank you," Grayson said, startling her.

"That wasn't for you." She meant to say it playfully, but for once, she couldn't pretend.

Grayson had played her so well that if it hadn't happened to Mallory and to AIM, she might have even offered her congratulations.

She steeled herself for the confrontation to come. "I know about the accounts," she said, her breath heavy under her words.

His head tilted, and he started to reach for her, but pulled back at the fury in her eyes. "Whatever this conversation is, let's have it somewhere else."

"As in 'not here'? Does that mean we should leave? Your call, as always." She paraphrased the words she'd overheard in his penthouse weeks ago, the ones that had followed "suspicious accounts," the same day she had discovered the error.

Recognition made his face go slack, and a piece of Mallory fizzled, the whisper of hope that she was wrong. "Right." She would have made AIM a unicorn without him. He stole that chance from her. She could never forgive him. "So this is what we're going to do. You're going to make a surprise announcement that you've become so attached to AIM that you aren't ready to hand it over just yet. You're going to invest so much capital—and I'm talking backing up a Brink's truck—that we can cancel the direct listing without raising suspicion."

His face transformed from that of flirtatious lover to self-preserving shark. "You don't want that. More to the point, I don't want that. So why would I do it?"

Mallory strengthened her resolve. "Because if you don't, I'll leak the error and you as the one who created it for your own financial gain. Understandable that someone of your vintage might be behind on the times, but let's see, Uber, WeWork, ring any bells? High-powered execs forced out for fraud. At least they're not Elizabeth Holmes, trading black turtlenecks for orange jumpsuits. Silicon Valley is not the Wild West anymore, not for something like this, not even for you. You'll be ruined."

"Should I even bother to deny it, or are we past that?"

Mallory hugged her arms to her chest.

"All right," he said, "let's do this, then. I'm not investing any more in AIM. And you aren't leaking anything. In the game of who knows who better, I win." He leaned in, his voice steady as he said, "Aubrey."

Whiplash spun Mallory's head.

"Your CTO," Grayson said. "Apologies, your *tech genius of a CTO*—as you all so often remind everyone—missed such an egregious error?"

The ice running through his veins chilled her to the bone.

"Her stellar reputation would work against her. Not such a leap to believe that Aubrey not discovering the error, not exposing it, and not fixing it, meant she was behind it. Motive, opportunity, and know-how."

Mallory was as repulsed by him as she was in awe. A simple question, a subtle implication by someone of Grayson Fields's stature, would be enough to crucify Aubrey in the press, across the industry, and on Wall Street. Mallory's blackmailing attempt was finished. She had no more cards to play. She faced him, that smug grin and those eyes that she'd once seen herself in. He believed he was smarter than everyone, that he knew best, that he knew all.

He'd better. Because if he didn't, he'd wish he were dead. *Crunch of glass, smell of wine, pooling of blood. Just like Ethan.*

28
AUBREY

Sunday Evening
*Three Days **After** the Outing*

Aubrey studies the row of succulents in her apartment to choose one for Kai. That his collection is octopuses makes her smile in a way she hasn't in a long time. She selects a cabbage-like green plant with pink tips and grabs her keys from the hook by the door. She's meeting Kai at Ilena's. They live on opposite sides of the Seaport, him in South Boston and her in Cambridge, and they each needed to change.

This Aubrey pays more attention to memes, if they have memes in this world. Not a single pair of skinny jeans in the closet. Instead, each hanger holds a complete outfit, labeled with "Work: Mon-Thurs, Summer," or "Work: Fridays, Winter," or "Saturday Casual," or "Dinner Party," and Aubrey is falling just a little bit in love with this world Aubrey. She slips into the "Dinner Party: Summer" full skirt and linen short-sleeved button-down and feels nothing like herself and yet everything like herself.

As she steps into the common hallway, the hair on the back of her neck rises. *Ethan.* Clearly visible through the building's glass front door.

"Aubrey," he says loudly, gesturing to the doorknob.

She doesn't move.

This seems to surprise him, and he raps gently, adding, "Your middle name's Katherine, right?"

"Excuse me?"

He stands her up, refuses to go with her to Ilena's, and now turns up asking about her middle name? He didn't even know her first name a couple of days ago.

He knocks the glass again. "Your middle name is on your website bio. But the other night, I neglected to mention mine."

She hesitantly approaches the door, wondering what she was thinking by telling him where she lived.

"It's Ass," he says. "*I'm* an ass."

"Yes, you are."

"Deserved, hundred percent. You should have called me on it when you emailed. It hit me after I'd already pressed Send. We had plans."

"So that's why you're here? To explain? Or apologize? Because I haven't heard either one yet."

"I'd rather not do it through this thick glass. But I will."

Aubrey stares at him before slowly opening the door. He slips inside and that hint of clove floats toward her.

"The sorry is easy. I'm sorry, Aubrey. There's no world in which I'd ever hurt you."

Aubrey's stomach clenches. She can't say the same.

"The explanation?" he says. "Well, our drinks date wasn't in my calendar, and I'm pathetically dependent on that electronic rectangle to run my life. Make that plural. Rectangles, one for work, one for personal, but I didn't put our date in either one."

"That's not my fault," she says, even though she's spent the past few weeks feeling like everything surrounding Ethan is her fault.

"Actually it is. You were there. Right there, in fact." He leans in. "This close. Remember, you, me, the Skee-Ball . . ."

That was where he'd kissed her, his lips on hers for the first time here but conjuring the thousands of times at home.

"Somehow . . ." His hand settles on her waist. "I was a little too distracted to grab my phone."

Sweat gathers beneath the armpits of her linen shirt, and her body reacts before her mind, pressing against him. He pulls back, and she realizes she's being too forward. He can't understand the intimacy she feels. But then his hand disappears into the canvas messenger bag looped across his chest. When it surfaces, Aubrey's lungs squeeze.

"You are somebody's reason to smile."

Lying flat on his open palm is a rock with a quote painted in yellow. There are no rocks with sayings on them in this Aubrey's apartment, not that Ethan has been in this Aubrey's apartment. She's positive she didn't mention them on their date at the arcade. If he did ever come here, saying she had a collection of painted rocks wouldn't make any sense. And besides, she didn't want him to think she was saccharine or immature.

It's a sign from the universe. This is right. She and Ethan are meant to be.

She leads him into her apartment and to the bed with its freshly washed sheets.

They arrive at Ilena's a half hour late—a betrayal of those perfectly labeled hangers. But worth it. So very worth it.

Aubrey clings to Ethan's hand, her heart still pumping so hard it could keep a team of gymnasts alive. In Ethan's bag is the bottle of cabernet they stopped for on the way even though red gives Aubrey a headache. But Ethan's right that it's more sophisticated for a dinner party.

She texted Kai while Ethan was at the register. She said she was feeling a bit off and might just do a quick drop-in to Ilena's, so he probably shouldn't bother making the trek to join her. He'd responded with a thumbs-up emoji. Kai was sweet and made her laugh, but he was just a one-night stand she didn't remember. Ethan was her past and her present and a future she never got the chance to have. Except maybe now she would.

"Thanks for making me smile," Ethan whispers in the elevator that's nearly the size of her apartment. Felix's condo—Felix and Ilena's condo—is in one of the newly renovated warehouses along the waterfront originally designed for cartons of tea and spices and all manner of imported goods. Maybe she and Ethan could move here, try something new.

The elevator stops on the top floor and the door to the condo opens, revealing breathtaking harbor views through windows that soar from the dark wood floors to the industrial pipes running along the ceiling. Aubrey wonders if she and Ethan moved here if they should get a boat. They could take sailing lessons together. Hobbies bring couples closer, don't they?

Felix excitedly ushers them in. He hugs Aubrey, relieves Ethan of his bag, and Aubrey remembers that this Felix doesn't know who Ethan is. She rushes an introduction, and "thanks for having me" and "congratulations" and "general counsel" and "cloud data storage" and a stream of small-talk pleasantries drift over Aubrey as she enters Ilena's home, trying not to gawk like it's her first time.

Beside a glass bar cart, wearing a plaid coat too heavy for summer, Mallory rocks on her heels, having a conversation with James, though Aubrey can tell she's not paying attention. She hates these things, and presumably this particular thing even more than usual—this admittedly somewhat bizarrely timed celebration of Ilena's baby. Ilena's desire to be a mom triggered something unseemly in Mallory, perhaps simply selfishness, though Aubrey would like to think it runs deeper than that, not that something deeper would make it okay.

Upon hearing Felix's welcome, Mallory turns, her eyes

floating to Ethan, and heat rises in Aubrey's cheeks, even though she's an adult and she's free to have sex with whomever she wants but especially her fiancé. Especially when the sex was so good. Not that it was bad in her world, not always, but there was a degree of awkward, at least for Aubrey. She'd blamed herself, knowing she needed to lighten up, not dwell on past choices of boys and men she wanted who didn't want her, but maybe the only way to do that was to be somewhere without so much history weighing her down.

Mallory continues acting strangely, jutting her chin, pointing with the heel of her strappy sandal and what is she—

"Aubrey, there you are," Ilena says, sparkling water bottle in hand. "Your guest has already arrived. And so very helpful."

"My guest? Helpful? But he's not—"

Kai steps out from behind Ilena carrying a tray of skewers—shrimp, chicken, mozzarella, eggplant, every allergen and dietary restriction accounted for. His slight, unsure smile doesn't give room for those dimples she'd wanted to stick her finger in at the bar. "I was early," he says. "Already here when I got your text, so I figured I'd stick around. Just in case you needed anything."

Her throat's so dry she can't get out a sound.

"Hey now." Ethan plants himself next to her, two lowball glasses already in hand.

Kai tightens his grip on the tray. He doesn't meet Aubrey's eye. He can't see the utter horror that's spreading across her face.

Ethan passes Aubrey a drink before laying an arm around her shoulders. "Genius idea, underlings doubling as servers? Way to be the boss, Aubrey Katherine." He leans over the tray, debating the content of the skewers.

Ilena says, "Oh, he's not—"

"Go for the chicken," Kai says, looking at Aubrey. "It's playful."

In between each bite of chicken is a slice of hard-boiled egg. The sex high Aubrey had been floating on deflates like a popped balloon, and she's overwhelmed with the desire to apologize, to even go back in time, to not open the door and let Ethan in. But that's absurd because Ethan is her fiancé and Kai is an employee whom she barely knows.

Ethan snorts and waves Felix over, pointing at the skewer. "Chicken and the egg. Total dad joke." He gives a little bow to Felix. "Seems you are ready, my friend."

Felix slaps Ethan on the back, and he's the one who "introduces" Ilena and Mallory to Aubrey's dead-but-not-dead fiancé who does a double take at Ilena's stunning blue eyes and Mallory's stilt-like legs. And really, who can blame him? Certainly not Aubrey, who still feels the same awe, all these years later.

Ethan takes his phone out of his pocket and exchanges contact information with Felix, which feels more awkward than Aubrey thinks it should. More small talk ensues, and Kai slips deeper into the living room. Aubrey waits for a pause in the compliments on the harbor view and exposed beams, mumbles something about being hungry, and follows Kai. He's setting the appetizers down on the coffee table when a bundle of apricot fur leaps up.

"Harley!" Aubrey says, to which Noreen suddenly materializes.

"Sorry, y'all, my fault, my fault." Noreen scoops up the dog. "I'm the dog whisperer tonight. Or supposed to be!"

Aubrey smiles apologetically. "Mallory appreciates it. We all do, especially with it being such short notice."

"It's an honor, Ms. Miller, truly. To be included . . . squad goals, right?" She beams and spins to face the windows. "This view, I mean, I've just got to get a closer look." She plucks a chicken skewer, hands a shrimp one to Aubrey with a "Trust me, these are delish," and heads for the balcony.

Aubrey's about to take a bite when Kai says, "That's not vegan. Or is that a lie too?"

Aubrey lowers the skewer. "This . . . it's not what you think."

"Really? You didn't just bring another date to the party you invited me to?"

"Well, I tried to uninvite you."

"That doesn't make it better. Tell me, Aubrey, have you been using me to make that asshat jealous?"

"What? No, I'm not—"

"Because that sucks."

Aubrey rolls the metal stick in her hand, looking past Kai, willing Ilena or Mallory to come help.

"Aubrey?" Kai says.

Ethan's joining Noreen on the balcony, his hand on her waist as he bends his head into Harley's fur. Ethan hates dogs.

"Or perhaps we should stick with Ms. Miller."

She snaps back to Kai. "No, that's not what I want either. At the bar, I was having such a good time." *And pissed at the man I just slept with.* "I had already invited Ethan, and I guess there was miscommunication about him coming. Still, inviting you probably wasn't the smartest move, considering." She keeps fiddling with the skewer and a bit of the coconut it's covered in falls on her shirt. As she wipes it away, she realizes that in her hurry to get dressed, she misbuttoned.

Kai's gaze follows hers, and the reason she was in a hurry must be written all over her face.

"I get it," he says, not with anger or disgust but disappointment. "But I can't stay here. You're not my only boss. Mrs. Singh and Ms. Latham—"

"I'll make it right."

He nods slowly. "Perhaps by seeing if there's an opening in marketing?"

"Oh, that's not . . . you don't have to, or I mean, you shouldn't have to . . . this just happened, I promise. I didn't choose—"

"But you did. Own it, as my grandma says. Fault's in the past, responsibility's in the present."

Aubrey stills, stopping the spinning of the skewer. Kai takes it from her, his hair no longer smelling of her eucalyptus. He places the skewer on a napkin on the table beside a silver gift bag. Aubrey peers inside. There's a small, stuffed octopus with a gift tag that reads, *Warmly, Kai*. She places her hand to her chest, trying to discreetly fix her mismatched buttons but fumbling thanks to the sharp beat of her heart.

Kai tries to slip out unnoticed, but Felix catches him. Aubrey wants to do something or say something, but before she can, Felix is directing them all into the dining room, asking what they'd like to drink with dinner, trying—unsuccessfully—to get Mallory to take off her coat.

Ethan calls to her, "We brought a red. Aubrey?"

"Oh," Aubrey says, a sinking in her gut. "Of course, let me."

Aubrey heads for the hall closet as the dinner guests—which include a couple from the apartment next door that Felix and Ilena are apparently best friends with—compliment Ilena on the table settings.

She finds Ethan's messenger bag hanging on a hook. She has to stand on tiptoes, and as she stretches her hand inside, something clanks. She carefully lifts the bag off the hook and places it on the floor. She removes the bottle, and a phone, half out of its protective leather sleeve, settles at the bottom of the bag. This must be Ethan's personal phone. She goes to slide it fully into its case when a flash of Ethan's face draws her eye. On the lock screen is a close-up photo of him. With his lips pressed against those of another woman.

29
ILENA

Sunday Evening
Three Days ***After*** *the Outing*

Ilena passes the gravy boat to Ethan, who takes it but not the drip plate underneath. As he pours the jus over the rosemary-and-garlic-marinated sirloin, all Ilena sees is red: spreading, pooling, staining everything.

"It's smart, from a business standpoint." Ethan sets the gravy boat down on the cream table runner. "Self-improvement market is set to top fourteen billion in the next three years."

Aubrey's eyes seek Ilena's in apology, but it's Kai, seated across from Ethan, who lifts the gravy boat, dabs at the droplets of red with his napkin, and puts the plate beneath.

Ilena can't wait for the explanation: how Aubrey made them scramble to add extra place settings and folding chairs by bringing both Kai and Ethan to her dinner party. *My God, Ethan.* Who is so very much alive that it makes Ilena's skin crawl.

"Still." Ethan presses those too-hip glasses up the bridge of his nose. "If you're using an app to validate your sense of self, you deserve to be fleeced straight down to your wrinkled ass."

Ilena wills Mallory not to go on the offensive because Aubrey's cheeks are already bright red and she's staring at them with a panicky look in her eyes. And besides, they're only on their second course, and Ilena has timed the white chocolate soufflés down to the millisecond.

"Actually . . ." Mallory spins the stem of her empty wineglass, her tone not aggressive as Ilena feared but strangely defensive. Even when AIM was running on investment fumes and they'd thought a rival app would hit the market before them, Mallory remained unflappable. "Our subscription fee is the lowest of any app in our sector even with the addition of 'How Wide's My Smile.' It was a conscious decision, to thank our users and—"

Ilena interrupts. "More wine? Please, let me live vicariously."

Ethan pours himself more of the red he brought, ignoring Aubrey's half-full glass and Mallory's empty one. His eyes linger on the swell of Mallory's breasts as he says brusquely, "Sure, but going public changes everything."

Ilena hates that she's in agreement. But that's what she's been trying to get Mallory to see. She changes the subject. "We're boring our guests. AIM isn't everything."

"It's not? No one told me!" Noreen says with the enthusiasm Ilena used to feel.

"Me either," says Sun, one half of "Sun and Ava," the couple at the far end of the table that Felix and "fun Ilena" apparently jetted off to Nantucket with over Memorial Day. "We're invested. Or we will be."

Ava crosses her fingers. "Early retirement plan. Not that we've gotten insider information. As much as we and a bottle of mezcal have tried."

Laughter rolls around the table, though neither Ilena nor Mallory can conjure more than a thin smile. The joke hits too close to their other home.

Ilena feels Felix's eyes on her, questioning if she's okay. Jonah would know she wasn't.

"Speaking of," Ethan interrupts. "Is there a friends and family discount? For the stock?"

Aubrey's shoulders creep up. "Ethan, please, we're here for Ilena and Fel—"

"Seriously." He talks over Aubrey, pulling out his phone. "I'll download the app right now, and I'll prove just how wide my smile can be— Oh, wait, Aubrey already knows." Aubrey's cheeks flush an even deeper crimson and her eyes flicker to Kai, who's staring at his plate. This Ethan seems just as terrible as he was in their world, except here, he doesn't cover as well. "Think I can get points for that? But the name, really, 'How Wide's My Smile'? So juvenile."

"No," Aubrey says, softly, then, louder, "don't do that. Don't make fun of it. It was my grandmother's favorite saying."

Her grandmother, whom Aubrey held on the highest of pedestals. Ilena had nearly forgotten. But clearly, Mallory hadn't. Ilena watches as Mallory's eyes find Aubrey's, bonding over losses that can't be said aloud for fear of revealing them as the imposters they are. Ilena blinks, looks away from them and into her kitchen with its marble-topped island and glass-tiled backsplash and industrial pendant lights. Is this Ilena happy with her life? Would Ilena be? Happy without Jonah?

Ilena suddenly feels like she's going to explode. She stands and gestures to the kitchen. "Mallory, would you mind?"

Felix lifts himself halfway, pulling an envelope out from under his placemat. "But I thought we'd—"

"With dessert." Ilena faces the assembled table: Sun and Ava, her supposedly close friends whose names she has to keep reminding herself of; Kai, Aubrey's one-night stand; James, her husband's actual spouse; Noreen, the employee who deserves a raise in both worlds; the reanimated Ethan, still a colossal prick;

and Aubrey and Mallory, her two friends whom she's starting to think she hasn't been all that "best" to lately. "It's a soufflé so . . ."

James rattles his chair back. "Let me."

Before she can form a response, he's already in the kitchen.

"Good man," Ethan says. "Soufflés can go south in an instant. Once they do, well, there's no way back. You can't pluck feathers from a bald chicken."

The words cause Mallory to drop her fork, where it clanks against her plate, drawing all eyes to her. She gives a smile that Ilena knows is forced, though Ilena can't fathom why.

"Okay, then," Ilena says, an unease settling over her. "Probably a better choice, anyway. Not sure Mallory could find the oven with a schematic." Ilena pats her best friend's shoulder, covered in that same Burberry coat they timeshared in their world, as she passes behind her. But then Mallory grabs Ilena's hand. "Love you too, Mal." Ilena chuckles, yet Mallory's grip only tightens.

Ilena bends and whispers, "*Mallory*."

But Mallory squints and keeps running her finger around the emerald of Ilena's engagement ring. Mallory's cheeks pale, making her watermelon blush and bright pink lipstick appear painted on as if by a child fresh from her mother's makeup drawer. When Mallory lets go, her face creases in a way that's hard to discern. Not jealousy or anger or sadness or disappointment . . . fear. It's fear.

They looked afraid. I wanted to tell them it'd be okay. That I'd protect their secrets. That they had nothing to fear from me and certainly nothing from him.

Now that he was dead.

One of them took the other's hand, and I imagined how it must have felt. The warmth of skin against skin, the clasp that erases all space, the bond that transforms separate individuals into one. We all crave it. It is innate. It is how we are meant to live. It is how we thrive. It is how we survive.

It is how they would survive this.

I'd brought them together just when they were about to be split apart.

A twisted repeat of loss—theirs, mine, ours.

The universe might have been willing to let that happen, but I wasn't.

Even though all of us were there, none of us really saw. Because our eyes are the most unreliable of narrators. I should know.

30
ILENA

Sunday Evening
Three Days ***After*** *the Outing*

"This is going to blow up, you do know that?" James says from beside the built-in wine fridge.

Ilena steadies her shaking hands as she checks the egg timer in the shape of an avocado. "Let's hope not. But we are just in time. Two minutes left."

James's freckled cheeks pull as taut as his crossed arms. "Come off it, Ilena. This is insulting, to everyone."

She can't handle this now, not with her heart aching from the sadness on Mallory's and Aubrey's faces that's making her think of Jonah. "I'm sorry, James, I didn't really think you wanted to host this. I figured Felix was forcing you, but if you did, truly, I didn't mean to infringe."

"You are too much. Seriously, Ilena. *Se-ri-ous-ly.*"

"James, I honestly don't know what this is about. But I'd like to. You're Felix's best friend. I want us to be friends." They are already, aren't they? "Stay friends. You know what I mean."

"Oh, this is what we're doing, then? Us, you and me, a couple of Felix groupies who lunch? A scone and a grapefruit mimosa and we'll snuggle your mini me and ignore the fact that you orchestrated this whole thing?"

The avocado cracks open, revealing a pit that begins to bounce, but Ilena doesn't move.

James places his hand on the pit to stop it. "You didn't think I knew? Oh, sweetie, am I the one to tell you? How special."

She forces a swallow. "Tell me what?"

"Hmm, yeah, so, let's just say after a couple of old-fashioneds bestie lips are as loose as, well, you." He scoops up the avocado, sidles next to her, and rests it in her hand. "One night shouldn't change everything. But you let it. You encouraged it. Full throttle, no hesitation. Whatever—whoever—else involved be damned. But for the record, no matter what that hideous thing on your desk says, he wasn't positive. He still isn't."

Ilena's legs go wobbly.

"But he's a better person than either of us because you're here and I'm still sharing a studio with a Berklee student who has a limited conception of hygiene."

The acrid scent of something burning seeps out of the oven.

James strolls past her, and something he said registers. Ilena grabs his arm. "You said 'mini me.'"

He smiles, but in that way of an animated doll about to slash your throat. "It's a girl."

"But Felix said the envelope was sealed."

James winces. "Ooh, yeah, well, Felix lies. Maybe most of all, to himself."

31
MALLORY

Sunday Evening
*Three Days **After** the Outing*

Fuckity fuck fuck.

That night in the bar, the woman Ethan had been about to cheat on Aubrey with . . . Christ. *Ilena.* This can't be happening, but so much is happening that shouldn't be happening.

The Shandy Shane Show filming in her condo.

Officer Middlebury and her menacing sunglasses.

Calendar reminders for "pheromone speed dating."

Grayson's porcupine hair.

Nut crackers, nut crackers, nut crackers!

Her father. Her fucking *father.*

And Ethan. Ethan Sonders, repeating on them like too many jalapeños.

Not to mention that goddamn emerald ring on Ilena's finger.

James retakes his seat just as the smell of smoke wafts over the table. Felix stands.

"No," Mallory says, her gut swirling with panic and fear and disbelief. "This is actually my territory. I'm an expert when things go wrong."

Mallory quickly gets up, feeling the lewd intensity of Ethan's eyes on her, hearing his *You can't pluck feathers from a bald chicken.*

Again, hearing it again.

She slides the kitchen's pocket door closed behind her. "What the hell, Ilena?" Mallory says, keeping her voice low.

Ilena stares at a tray of smoldering ramekins. "These were white chocolate." She floats an oven-mitted hand above the dishes whose tops are as black as asphalt. "Not that you can tell."

"Dessert? We're talking about dessert?"

"What would you like to talk about? Felix was in charge of the steak, and it was perfect. But this?"

"Seriously? You're playing house?" Mallory tosses her hands in the air. "This isn't real, none of this is real life!"

"So you've found the portal?"

"The what?"

"Portal, time machine, wormhole, universe Uber that's going to zoom us back to a world I'm starting to think maybe is the one that's not real."

"Don't you mean the one you wish wasn't real?"

"Do not do this, Mallory."

"What? State the obvious? A squeaky clean AIM, a fawning hubby, and a baby? One that isn't Jonah's, but that doesn't seem to matter to you. So tell me, has it worked? Are you finally happy? Is it everything you hoped it'd be? Even if I go to prison?"

Ilena's jaw clenches. "I thought this was all starting to get to you and I was feeling sorry for you and doubting myself, but, you know what, Mallory, fuck you." Ilena yanks off the oven mitts. She rests her hand with the diamond-encrusted emerald on top.

That ring. Mallory had been so sure that night in the bar: Ethan about to sleep with another woman. But that was only because she'd been looking at it through the lens of Ethan, not the woman. Now her lens shifts to this woman Mallory has known for more than half her life. A woman who has an immutable sense of right and wrong. But she was with Ethan. And never told Mallory.

She seizes Ilena's hand, regretting not bringing her reading glasses. "This doesn't make any sense."

"Mallory, you're hurting me."

Crunch of glass, smell of wine, pooling of blood.

Mallory lets go. "I'm sorry, I didn't mean . . ."

Right leg bent at an unnatural angle, body still, eyes open, opaque and not moving.

Mallory's breaths shorten, and she leans over the marble island, head between her elbows. Ilena met with Ethan. Ethan was at Grayson's penthouse. Is there a connection? Could Ilena be, *shit*, involved? And Mallory thought waking up here was the most lost she could ever feel.

Ilena presses her hand between Mallory's shoulder blades, and the warmth brings Mallory back to the first time she did this, when Mallory was hunched over a grungy dorm toilet. Vodka-sherbet slushies and the special cupcakes Ilena had gotten for her birthday were less colorful on the way out. That was the first time Mallory had met Jonah. Jonah, who has been as much a part of her life as Ilena and Aubrey. She'll lose him too in the divorce.

She misses him. How can Ilena not?

Ilena draws Mallory's long hair back from her face and looks at her with those blue eyes that Mallory still wants to prove herself worthy of, same as when they first met.

"Do you want to tell me what this is about?" Ilena says, sounding very much like a mom.

Mallory squeezes her eyes shut, but all she sees is pieces of herself scattered like a never-finished jigsaw puzzle. She's spent her entire life not being this person. Someone who falls apart.

"Ethan . . . our Ethan . . . I need you to tell me the truth. I know you met with him the night he died."

Shock slackens Ilena's face, and she doesn't deny it. "How do you know?"

"Because I was there. At the bar. I saw you. Or at least, I saw your ring."

"What ring?"

Mallory gently retakes Ilena's hand. "This ring, which I'd never seen you wear before."

"But that's impossible."

"You were there, weren't you? All I could see from my stool was a white coat and a woman's hand, fingernails painted beige, wearing this ring. Just like you are now. But you don't own a white coat."

Ridges form between Ilena's eyebrows. "That can't be."

"It wasn't you?" Mallory says.

A heavy sigh releases. "It was. I'd just gotten the coat, but I left it in the bar and never went back for it. But I wasn't wearing the ring. I didn't own it. It's my engagement ring. From *Felix*."

"What the actual fuck? You're sure?"

"I'm not Queen Elizabeth," Ilena says. "I've got a pretty good sense of what jewels are mine and not."

"Actually, she probably did too."

"Princess Margaret?"

"Better."

"Still . . ." Ilena says.

"What the actual fuck?"

"What the actual fuck."

Mallory saw that ring. She knows she did. What the actual fuck, indeed. She shrugs out of the Burberry coat and reaches for the bottle of bourbon on the tray of after-dinner drinks that will have to serve as dessert, which she honestly prefers. She takes a swig and tips the bottle to Ilena, who considers for half a second before shaking her head.

Ring or no ring, Mallory needs to understand this. "Why were you meeting with him alone?"

Ilena spins the ring around her finger, her face growing more pale with each rotation. "Things weren't great. With Jonah, with AIM, with you and me. Aubrey was sure to find out about the computer error, and well, I needed to know if Ethan loved her, if he truly loved her, if he'd be—"

"There for her? That's why you were in the bar. To talk about Aubrey?"

"Yes, or sort of, but he . . ." Ilena keeps twisting the ring. "This is harder than I thought."

A million ants writhe up Mallory's spine. The woman Ethan had spoken to in the bar with such hatred was Ilena. "Christ, did he hit on you?"

Ilena sets a protective hand on her round belly.

"He did, then. Fucker." Mallory reaches for a glass and pours what feels like a double since these useless eyes of hers won't focus up close. "And we were fighting about going public, so you felt like you couldn't even tell me. My god, Ilena, how did we get here?"

Ilena gives a half shrug, her eyes clouding with guilt.

But Mallory's the one who did this, kept the secret about the night in the bar among so many others she's losing count. She wants, no, she needs to tell Ilena the truth. Starting with the lie that kicked off all the rest. Yet as she confesses to sleeping with Grayson, the look on Ilena's face makes it clear she already knew.

Ilena's eyes are gentle. "I'm sorry, Mal. I should have said it earlier. You cared about him. It's obvious. It's okay to grieve, to truly grieve. Just like Aubrey."

Mallory shakes her head. "Except it's not 'just like Aubrey.'

I'm not accepting responsibility for Grayson's death. Unlike Aubrey, who's clearly been blaming herself for Ethan's. And we've been too distracted to see it."

They live in mutual guilt and silence for a beat before Mallory continues by relaying what she overhead at Grayson's penthouse and the person she's now convinced said it. "Pluck a bald chicken." *Fucking Ethan.*

As she tells Ilena, it all clicks in Mallory's brain. Grayson has—*had?*—an elephant's memory, like Mallory cataloging everything, never knowing when something might prove useful. Like Ethan's position in his tech firm. Grayson surely remembered just as Mallory did and must have enlisted Ethan's help to hide the error in exchange for a job or money or prestige or all of it. Yet Ethan had gotten greedy. That night at the penthouse, he must have been trying to shake Grayson down for more. If that didn't work, Ethan had already secured his backup plan with their best friend.

Ilena nods as they jointly put it together. "If Ethan married Aubrey, he'd have been rich. He'd have insisted on no prenup," Ilena says without a shred of doubt.

"How do we tell her?"

"That her dead fiancé was only with her to steal from her? Maybe we don't." Mallory is surprised at Ilena's uncharacteristic response. Ilena then adds, "At least while we're here. What good would it do?"

"She might hate him. And hate washes away guilt."

"Does it though? It hasn't for you with Grayson." Ilena picks up the coat Mallory had dropped, and Mallory can't help looking at that ring as Ilena continues, "Grayson and the error, it's why you chose him in the game?"

"Plus him threatening Aubrey at the outing. He said if I implicated him in the error, he'd point the finger at her."

"Then he deserved it." Ilena's phone buzzes on the small desk in the corner of the kitchen.

Mallory pours more bourbon.

"Not the actual dying of course," Ilena says flatly, as blunt as ever, and it's more reassuring than anything. "But the choosing." Ilena's phone buzzes again, and this time, she rounds the island to retrieve it.

Mallory sips for courage, not sure if she's fully ready to voice her fears out loud, even to Ilena. "What if it's more than that? What if those crackers we cleaned up in his kitchen were from my emergency snack bag, which shouldn't be possible, but I don't know what other explanation there could be. You know he'd never have had them in his house."

Ilena's hand wraps around her phone. "But it could have still been an accident. Maybe he took them while you were in the bathroom or something."

"Maybe." Mallory sips. "Or maybe I put them out while he was."

"Mallory—"

"I wanted to throttle him. I truly did. Maybe I don't remember because I can't let myself remember because—"

"Mallory."

"Because, I mean, maybe I was actually starting to fall—"

"Mallory!"

"What?"

Ilena holds up her phone just as the pocket door slides open. Aubrey, cheeks sagging and pale, walks toward them, gripping her own phone. With a flash of apricot, Harley scurries in behind her, landing himself beside Mallory's feet and licking her toes.

Ilena and Aubrey share an anxious look, and Mallory's jealous of being out of the loop.

Mallory tilts her head. “What’s going—” But Ilena and Aubrey simply hold up their phones. Mallory squints to see, her eyes shifting from one screen to the other, confirming the same logo for the Cambridge police. Her heart pounds with fear, but she manages to say, “This might be a good time to mention that I met my dad.”

32
MALLORY

A Year ***Before*** *the Outing*

"Is DILF still a thing?" Mallory asked at the DIY craft cocktails pop-up that was exorbitantly expensive despite having no bartenders. You mixed the drinks yourself watching YouTube tutorials. "There's not a single one here."

"Not exactly our demographic," Ilena said.

"Isn't that sexist?"

"Numbers aren't sexist. We're not exactly going after the DILF market with our featuring of celebs like Reese and Shonda."

"But cocktails are universal. Besides, one can still hope." Hope for some no-strings-attached-adequate-don't-spend-the-night sex.

"But I hear Grayson Fields is coming."

"To check on his investment."

"Right, that's why."

Mallory ignored Ilena and watched a young woman wearing a neon pink tee that said "My parents gave me climate change without a gift receipt and now I'm stuck with it" snap a selfie with her rosemary-infused tonic. One of countless attendees shaking organic raw eggs and drinking out of straws made from cactus leaves and touting their love of AIM. A love that led to this, the coveted, see-and-be-seen launch party for "How Wide's My Smile."

It was the challenge that did it: "Seven Days to Your Resting Beach Face!" It had been designed as a one-time thing. Users earned points for self-attesting to the completion of certain behaviors like hitting ten thousand steps or bullet journaling or pleasuring oneself without guilt. Like "Dry January" but with strategically placed ads from their sponsors. Today they celebrated a hundred thousand new subscribers and a new beginning for AIM. The challenge was over, but the points were staying, morphing into their own community-driven channel: "How Wide's My Smile."

All indicators pointed to it eclipsing the rest of AIM's features. That was why Grayson was coming. And why she was having dinner with him after, not that Ilena needed to know that. It was time to explore taking AIM public. Aubrey wasn't the problem—Aubrey was never the problem in that way—but Ilena would take some convincing. Grayson was the start.

"Hey, y'all!" Noreen bounded over and handed them each a highball with perfect layers of blue, green, and orange liquid. "I'm a big DIY-er, so I made you these."

"And you just became my best friend." Mallory took a sip, and her eyes widened at the sweet but savory, citrus-y but herbal concoction. "In fact, you became better than that. I'm in need of a new assistant. Interested?"

Noreen placed a hand to her chest. "Gosh, that's an offer, isn't it? But, Ms. Miller—"

"Aubrey. And she won't mind." Mallory waved her hand. "Twenty percent raise?"

"Well." Noreen's head bobbed. "A girl would be daft to not accept that."

Noreen returned to handing out AIM swag, and Ilena shook

her head. Not a strand of her short cut moved. She was no longer the girl from freshman year with the long, thick hair that Mallory had envied. Her face had grown thinner, with less shine and more lines, yet she was just as gorgeous. More so.

"Shameless, Mal," Ilena said.

"Aubrey won't mind." Mallory took another sip, eyeing Ilena, who hadn't touched hers yet. "Are you . . . ?"

Ilena stuck the straw between her lips.

Mallory nodded. "So that's a no."

"I want to try a different doctor," Ilena said.

"The 'I' implies Jonah doesn't."

"Jonah's . . . tired."

"Maybe a pause would be good? Especially with things ramping up with AIM?" Which would only increase when they went public.

"Don't give me the 'it'll happen when you stop trying to make it happen' speech. Everyone knows someone who magically got pregnant when they stopped trying. But what about all the people who just stopped?"

There was a time when all of this would have been making Ilena do cartwheels, but now all she cared about was what those cartwheels would do to her ovaries.

Look at this, Mallory wanted to scream. Grab Ilena's hands and dance her around this ridiculous pop-up that had a line halfway around the block for entry. They made this, together. What could be better than this? Continuing to do it together, that was what. She loved Aubrey, but Aubrey wasn't in it like they were. Aubrey could never handle the pressure, and as well as Mallory was handling it, going public would take it to another level. She needed Ilena. Ilena was her person.

Mallory changed the subject. "Is Aubrey even coming?"

"Ethan had a thing."

"Sure he did."

"I think she really likes him, Mallory. We're going to have to get used to him."

"He hit on me, did I tell you that?"

Ilena drew back. "And you didn't tell Aubrey?"

"I did. She said me and my long legs always think people are hitting on me."

"She's got a point."

"And you really should try to de-stress. For the baby."

"Touché." Ilena played with her straw. "Do you really think he was?"

"I may be conceited, but it comes from experience. He was hitting on me."

"Then we'll keep an eye on him."

They clinked glasses just as Grayson Fields appeared.

Ilena said, "There's your DILF."

"One, he's not a father, and two, there is no way I'm ever sleeping with our main investor and head of our board. Give me a little credit."

Ilena greeted Grayson, small talk lobbed back and forth, and all the while Mallory did her best not to stare at the tautness of his shirt.

After Ilena excused herself, Grayson lowered his sunglasses. "I'm training for a race. There's a new vegan place in the South End. *Globe* said the meatballs are a surprising aphrodisiac."

Well, shit.

33
AUBREY

Sunday Evening
*Three Days **After** the Outing*

Aubrey wishes she could use the flashlight on her phone. Despite the abrupt end of Ilena and Felix's gender-reveal party (it's a girl!), the sun has already set and the bricks of this sidewalk are really uneven. But if she uses the flashlight, then Ethan will know she's following him.

He turns left toward the Financial District, and Aubrey hesitates. At night, on a Sunday, there won't be much foot traffic in this office-heavy neighborhood, nowhere for her to hide if he makes a mistake in his route and spins around or feels like something's off, the way you just can sometimes. A microsecond flash. Like you've gone somewhere else. Been somewhere else. A prickle up her spine. Could it be this? The intersecting of universes? Maybe that's what déjà vu actually is.

Aubrey turns around, but the only thing she sees is a liquor-infused couple tugging on a closed Starbucks door.

She checks the time on her phone. Past ten, her usual bedtime, and a full hour plus of not responding to a request from a police officer.

Mallory had been shaking, clutching the dog like he was a

stuffed animal. She'd nuzzled his head and said to wait. For both Aubrey and Ilena to not respond to Officer Middlebury asking to speak with them. Mallory's demeanor was enough to convince Aubrey, but still she flexed her power of persuasion, insisting she's going to get them out of it. Her dad—Mallory's dad!—will get them out of it. She figures he's in need of some good karma for hightailing it in her world, and so she'll play the role of daddy's girl, and he'll somehow make this all disappear. Aubrey trusts Mallory, even this increasingly unhinged Mallory, but this . . . the consequences of what happened to Grayson are suddenly real in a way they hadn't been and the only one who doesn't seem to realize that is Mallory.

She acted like it was nothing that her dad was here. Doesn't she have a thousand questions, doesn't she want to know what he's like, doesn't she want to know what she was like with him? Doesn't she need to know if maybe she's the reason he left? And what this Mallory did to make him stay?

Ethan stops. Aubrey stops.

She ducks into the vestibule of a redbrick building. She pokes her head out and watches Ethan enter the only store open, a chain pharmacy. She waits. This is ridiculous. So she asked him to come home with her and he said he had to get up early. So she asked him to share a car home and he said he had to stop at the gym to pick up his sneakers so he could go running in the morning. So she asked him how long he'd been running and he hesitated. It didn't mean anything.

But something tells her that the photo of him kissing another woman, whose face was too obscured to make out, does. So here she is following Ethan. Not trusting him.

The same feeling Kai now has about her. She thinks of him. Sitting through that entire dinner, the gift bag, the pink confetti he threw when she was still too shocked by the message from the police officer to do it herself.

Kai is someone who seems to be nice—genuinely. No drama. No ulterior motives. No posturing. Kai just is who he is. Not to mention he's the first person in a long time to look at her without pity or judgment or the rolling of eyes as she debates Uber or Lyft. And she hurt him. As much as Ethan's behavior at dinner hurt her. No, not hurt, not exactly. Maybe incensed. Whether that's because of a change in this Ethan or a change in her, she doesn't know. Or care. It's simply a piece to factor into this quest of her trying to figure out if they were meant to be together.

Ethan exits the pharmacy with a small succulent in hand. He'd seen them in her apartment and said they were "cute" and she wasn't sure if he truly thought they were or if he thought they were silly, but now, she's so pathetic, following him like some stalker. He's getting her a present on his way to the gym and what was she think—

He stops at one of the new high-rises meant to entice millennials to this residential dearth, with their coworking spaces and in-house dog walkers and casino-grade poker tables. He hits the buzzer on the side of the vestibule and a woman's voice says in a flirtatious tone, "And who might this be?"

He reaches into his messenger bag and pulls out his phone. He holds the screen up to the camera on the intercom, and she laughs, and the door buzzes, and he disappears inside.

Aubrey's heart pounds. Still, the woman behind the voice could be anyone. She could be his mom or his sister—maybe he has one here and she could find out, she needs to find out. Her neck swivels, checking to make sure she's alone. She rushes to the building. Names are written below each buzzer. Ethan had pressed something in the top right.

Eric Rizzoli

Preeti Patel

Lauren Stevens

She pulls out her phone, skips past the male name and searches for "Preeti Patel, Boston." She finds a bio on a local theater site, clicks on the woman's social media links, and sees her on stage dressed as everything from a gumdrop to a queen. She scrolls through photos of her with muffins and lattes at outdoor cafés and picnicking in the Public Garden with friends, but there's no sign of Ethan. Aubrey moves on.

Lauren Stevens seems to have every social media there is—including an AIM account. And there, on the app built from Aubrey's sleepless nights and endless days, is the answer she didn't know she was looking for.

How Wide's My Smile Rating: 10 out of 10
Reason: Engaged!

Aubrey's heart echoes in her ears as she clicks on the linked photo. A tall, pretty woman with dark brown skin thrusts her hand in front of the camera. A sparkling square-cut diamond nearly obscures the man in the background, but he's there, with the smile Aubrey ached for these past weeks.

Oh god, she did this. In this world, she wasn't supposed to be with Ethan. Their date wasn't supposed to lead to another. He was supposed to be with someone else, he *is* with someone else. Aubrey forced it. She made him into a cheater and a liar, she made herself into a cheater and a liar, all because she couldn't live with the guilt of what she'd done. She's been trying to prove that they were supposed to be together in this world in some perverse attempt to prove that they were meant to be in her world. As if "meant to be" made the rest of it okay, made him dying because of her okay.

Aubrey's need to be with Ethan means someone gets hurt. She wanted to know how to not make the wrong choice again. Now she does. Whatever her gut says, do the opposite.

34
AUBREY

*Eleven Months **Before** the Outing*

Her gut told her it was a mistake, but still Aubrey couldn't stop smiling. Behind her two monitors in the communal workspace she shared with her coding team, she squeezed her phone in her hand, then immediately released it, scared she might accidentally delete his text.

Ethan Sonders was asking her out.

Except it couldn't be her, could it? Maybe he had the wrong number? Maybe he meant to text Mallory. Of course he meant to text Mallory. The three of them met Ethan together last week as they mingled at the reception following Grayson's speech at MIT, attended by half of AIM, including Ella and Noreen. Contacts were shared, since they were all in tech. Ethan must have texted Aubrey by mistake.

She closed her eyes, picturing those adorable little lines around his eyes that came out when he laughed in response to her asking his opinion on personal cloud computing. The two of them had been in line for shrimp cocktail. He'd paused, amused at first, thinking she was teasing his profession, slowly gripping the fact that she was not only interested in his work but knowledgeable about it.

"You are unique, aren't you, Aubrey?" he'd said.

"As unique as a website visitor," she'd blurted out, for some reason referencing the metric for counting user visits to a website.

But it had kicked off the longest conversation Aubrey had had with a man who wasn't Jonah or an employee in months. And now he had mistakenly asked her out. This was mortifying. Her cheeks burned as she started typing back, struggling with how to tell him that he'd texted the wrong number. Then she noticed something:

Hey, A, any chance you're free next Friday?

An *A*. Right there between "hey" and "any." *Any* started with an *a*. It was a typo. Wasn't it?

Another message came in:

It's Ethan, BTW. From the Fields's thing? And now I sent a second text, so I'm not a unique visitor. LOL

Unique visitor. Which meant he meant to text her, which meant he meant to ask her out, and oh god, he meant to ask *her* out, and what should she say and where would they go and what would she wear if she went and—

"Aubrey?" Mallory's head quirked to the side as she planted herself in front of Aubrey's desk. "You look both about to toss your cookies and like you've swallowed a rainbow."

"Then I look exactly how I feel."

Mallory gestured to Aubrey's monitors. "How worried should I be?"

"No, it's not the app." Aubrey handed Mallory her phone.

A split second of confusion and then disappointment in Mallory's eyes.

"Oh." Aubrey swallowed. Mallory must have liked Ethan. "I don't have to go, I mean, he's probably not even asking, he's not really asking anything, is he? It's probably a tour of his company. I said I'd be interested. That's what it is, I'm sure of it." She was. That was the only thing that made sense.

She couldn't read people, had never had the skill, she couldn't really even tell what her parents or siblings were thinking, and certainly not boys, guys, men, all versions of the species who would always be defined by the boy in high school who'd promised her a pool house and a future she was naive enough to believe but that only lasted long enough for her to lose her virginity.

It wasn't okay, none of it had been okay, but Miles Perkins hadn't been the only one who'd crossed a line. Aubrey had too. She did something she couldn't take back even though the pool skimmer had been *tap, tap, tapping* against the wall of the shed, the *shed*, not a pool house, not a house, a *shed*. She'd trusted the way he'd made her feel when he trained those blue eyes on hers and asked her out and she'd not trusted the way he'd made her feel when he wouldn't take her hand in the movie theater, when he leaned against the counter as she took a seat at the pizza parlor, when she breathed in chlorine and rested her back on a lounge chair damp from mist. He hadn't even laid down a beach towel.

But he had told everyone. How gullible Aubrey had been. Aubrey lost more than her virginity, more than her reputation, more than the final years of high school. She lost herself, the woman she could have been, to the girl who that day learned that she couldn't trust herself. In the game of nature versus nurture, Aubrey's life was to be shaped entirely by the latter.

Mallory nudged Aubrey with her elbow. "Hey now, have a little faith." She smiled slyly and gave Aubrey back her phone. "See?"

Ethan: Arcade just added paintball. You in?

"Well?" Mallory asked. "Are you going to say yes?"

Aubrey wasn't much into violence, real or imaginary. But this was Ethan Sonders, who smiled like a Greek god and smelled faintly of cloves. The universe gave her but one choice.

"Definitely."

35
ILENA

Sunday Evening
*Three Days **After** the Outing*

Ilena grabs the wet dish towel with her toes. Tiny soap bubbles billow out as she rubs the cloth against the silver rug. At least it's not white. Still, not an ideal choice for a dining room, especially one that'll soon see its share of mushed peas and sweet potatoes.

She draws the end of the towel back. The circle of red remains, bigger if anything, and she wonders if the universe is making some comment on that glass of red wine she tossed at Ethan in the bar in their world—the one Mallory had impossibly seen—because the stain is under his chair. Ilena's not one to ponder signs, to make connections between coincidences, but here comes her husband with a spray bottle of rug cleaner, and she feels a bit dizzy.

"Easy there." Felix rushes forward. "You should have waited for me. Hard for a go-getter, I know."

"Well, you've always been a go-getter."

Ilena's knees buckle.

Felix sets his hand under her elbow and places the rug cleaner on the table. "I think we're supposed to use this first."

"Are we?" Ilena's head swims. "We are, aren't we." She pictures Jonah's wavy hair, those strands of gray peeking out among the dark brown. "I could always cover it with something."

"Like what?"

"A fern?"

Jonah's hair is right in front of her. If she could just reach out, just let her fingers . . . Her hand lifts, and Felix nabs it, encasing it in his as he guides her into the dining chair beside the one Ethan had sat in.

Felix says, "I think maybe tonight was a bit much. You seem a little out of it."

She shakes her head. "A joke. A fern under a chair."

"I've always thought a fern would look great in the living room."

She adds, "Set some new trend."

"You never think outside the box, I."

Ilena's pulse echoes in her temples. She was so sure. For a split second. Jonah, before her, close enough to touch, to hold, to love. She inhales a sharp breath.

"Ilena." Concern strains Felix's voice. The weight of his hands on her shoulders snaps her back.

Is it back? Could it *be* back? Like some reverse déjà vu?

"Ilena," Felix says with a firmness that makes her look up.

"I'm fine." Her whole body trembles, and she gently rests her hand on her belly. "We're fine, but perhaps you were right. Perhaps it was a bit much."

Felix folds his hands around the top of a dining chair. His fingertips press in, hard, before he drags the chair back, twists it to face her, and sits. "What . . ." His voice is low and unsure in a way it never is. "What did he say to you?"

Dark, wavy hair, strands of gray. So close, close enough to touch.

"Nothing," she whispers. "He didn't have a chance."

"He didn't? But you were in the kitchen together, alone, for a while."

Ilena startles. "Oh." *James, he means James.* Here. James, here. She's losing it. She's completely losing it. "We were— Nothing, just chitchat."

"Chitchat doesn't make soufflés burn." Felix's lips tighten. "You don't have to protect him, Ilena. It's my fault."

Felix lies.

"I'm the orchestrator of this."

You orchestrated this whole thing.

"I'm the one who said things I shouldn't have. Things you and I agreed should remain private. I just wasn't sure . . ." He trails off.

He wasn't positive.

"We were figuring it out . . ."

He still isn't.

"But we're here now." The smile Felix offers has so much sadness in it that Ilena audibly gasps. "Another kick?" he says.

Ilena starts to shake her head, but then covers with a "Just one. Gone now."

"She's a soccer player. But maybe I can convince her to switch to tennis."

"She. It really is a girl."

"It is." Felix grins. "I was secretly hoping. Is that okay to say?"

Ilena nods. "I think anything you feel is okay to say." Except she can't take her own advice. What she feels right now more than anything is the loss of Jonah. It's not the same as Aubrey's loss or Mallory's loss, and yet the hole feels gaping, like she's made of nothing but air. She looks at Felix, really looks. He's so very present with her, and yet, there's something, in the wrinkles beyond his eyes, in the overly polite tone and perfect words and this house that is his, that she occupies, but is not hers. And now she's sure it was never supposed to be hers, any of it.

James had said something about bestie lips loosening after a couple of old-fashioneds and she'd assumed he meant Mallory as that's her preferred drink, but maybe it wasn't. Maybe it was Felix saying he'd felt like he had no choice. "Be honest. Did you see your life playing out this way?"

"Ilena, please, just ignore him. James doesn't know everything. He thinks he does, but there's so much here. Happiness is something you can choose, and we did. Celebrate the best. Which is this baby. Which is our friendship."

Friendship. That's what they have. That's who they are. Friends.

"Don't you want more? Don't you want . . ." *That dark wavy hair, those strands of gray. The frustrated lines between his eyes when he'd caught her taking pregnancy test after pregnancy test. The look on his face when he'd asked for the divorce and she'd said yes: pain, but relief.* "Love? Don't you want love?"

Felix blinks, but not fast enough. She sees the tears he forces back as he says, "The more you pursue what you don't have, the more it only reinforces the fact that you lack it in the first place."

Ilena stills. Without intending to, Felix has just summed up the past year and a half of her life.

"You know you can talk to me," Felix says.

He takes her hand in his, rests them both against her stomach, and he's too good, too loyal. And she can't ever forget the moment when she was the opposite.

She calls his name. He turns.

Her phone vibrates, and she reaches for it, letting Felix go.

It's another voicemail from the same Cambridge number. The one belonging to the police officer that's making Ilena's rule-following heart palpitate. Also on her notifications screen is an email from *The Shandy Shane Show*. And a text, from her mom, her mom who demanded perfection and when she got it, demanded more. She can't bring herself to click on any of them.

This baby is a girl, this baby will be a daughter, and Ilena will love her unconditionally, the way her mother couldn't love her. Ilena has always been terrified of impersonating her mother, and maybe this Ilena has been too. Her intentions may have been good, to give her baby the family she'd wished she'd had, but that doesn't make them right.

"What is it?" Felix says. "Is something wrong?"

Can she simply say "Everything"? It's her mom and the dad she shouldn't have loved and Jonah and the life she thought they wanted eclipsing the life they had. And Mallory and Ethan and that night in the bar when they crossed paths but didn't cross paths. And Grayson and the stock price and James despising her and Aubrey's guilt and Ilena's selfishness and Mallory's selfishness and secrets kept and still being kept.

Ilena and Mallory both did things they aren't proud of for reasons they'd justify to the ends of the universe. Only it's turning out that the universe has no end and there's no way to justify anything.

All she knows is that she needs Mallory now more than ever. Because if this baby becomes her baby, she'll need Mallory to ensure she never turns into her mother.

36
ILENA

*Two Months **Before** the Outing*

Ilena made the same promise she always did: She would never turn into her mother. Then, in a well-practiced move, she bunched the fabric of her dress in one hand, held the plastic stick in the other, and squatted over the toilet. She closed her eyes, trying to summon the hope she couldn't let herself feel even though this time was different. This time she was actually late.

Please, just . . . please.

She set a tissue on the sink and the pregnancy stick on top of it. She checked her watch and opened the bottom drawer of the vanity where a dozen more tests waited. She fully believed in science. Flawless manufacturing, not so much. Taking a second test wasn't unreasonable, a third if she noticed a weakness in the packaging or slight discoloration of the plastic.

"Ilena!" Jonah bellowed from somewhere on the first floor.

She pressed her hip into the edge of the vanity.

"Where are your car keys?" Jonah's voice grew louder as footsteps hit the stairs. "Is the wine still in the back or—"

His words became muffled as he reached the top of the staircase and presumably entered their bedroom, where he expected to find her.

She crossed her arms, her index finger tapping her elbows. *Come on, come on.*

Then the door to their guest bathroom burst open.

"Jonah!" Ilena cried. "I'm in here!"

"But why?"

"Oh, I don't know, maybe for a little privacy?"

"Then lock the door."

"Knock."

"You're late," he said.

Her heart lifted that he knew, that he was calculating it too.

"Or we're late, whatever. Of course this whole thing shouldn't sit on your shoulders even though you are the one who offered to host. Everyone's due in five minutes, and the table's not set, and I can't find the wine to decant the red, and—"

"I forgot."

"Forgot what? The wine?"

She hugged her arms tighter, dread building that couldn't be good for the baby, and oh my god, she really thought there was a baby. She swallowed past the lump in her throat. "It's just, AIM was intense today. The valuation is soaring, and I needed to—"

"What? You needed to what?" Jonah pushed himself through the doorway and looked down. "Dammit, Ilena, again?"

"It's not what you think. This time I'm—"

"Having a hunch, feeling nauseous, got a sore right boob, sore left boob, the moon's full, the moon's not full—"

"That's not fair."

"Neither is this."

"Me forgetting a case of wine? If you weren't so precious

about your *Wine Spectator* 'Bottle of the Year' and all the other bottles you're laying down or holding for a special occasion, we wouldn't need me to run out the day of."

"That's not what I meant. I meant *this*." He jutted a finger at the drawer full of pregnancy tests. His eyes briefly squeezed shut, and the tension in his voice ebbed. "We used to love this. We used to love doing this together."

They did, though Ilena always thought she needed Jonah more than the other way around. Jonah reached for everything. Every place and every person was an opportunity. He chatted up strangers like each held the chance to become their new best friend, on planes, in grocery stores, in line for the bathroom during the intermission of *Hamilton*. It almost got them into a couple swap on vacation in Mexico, but it made things memorable. The same way the random things he'd sneak onto her shopping list would make her descend into giggles in the frozen food aisle: "turtle eggs" and "DVD of insect porn" and "bin large enough for a dead body."

"We used to spend hours in cookbooks, coming up with themes," he said. "Remember the bacon? Every course."

Ilena's shoulders relaxed a little. "No one wanted to try the bacon ice cream."

"But they loved it. You knew they would. Doing this used to be fun."

"Fun was a bit easier to come by when I wasn't using my belly as a pincushion."

"And that's my fault?"

"*You* haven't gotten me pregnant. So I shoot up and swallow pills and am ruled by my goddamn calendar app."

"You didn't have to be. We could have done this another way. But you've become so single-minded, there's nothing else."

"Oh, but there is. There's exhaustion. And depression. And

fear and doubt and so many mood swings even I can't keep track. Some days I love you and some days I hate you."

"I know the feeling."

Ilena gritted her teeth. "What more do you want from me?"

"That's the thing, Ilena. All I want *is* you. This. Us. Or the us we used to be." When she didn't respond, his voice hardened. "The dinner you said would be good for us starts in five minutes. We've got no wine to serve, but we do have a hundred useless pregnancy tests."

Jonah had always been a good balance to Ilena's more reserved, practical nature. Yet in this, the first real test of their marriage, she'd come to see his behavior as childish and cavalier. "Nice way to trivialize what's most important to me."

"Since when? I swear to god, Ilena, your need to control everything has no end. This only became important to you when it became something you couldn't do."

"*Me?* Is that what you have to believe out of some neanderthal pride? Is that why you haven't gone back to the fertility clinic for the follow-up? It's been weeks, Jonah, have you even scheduled an appointment?"

"Not since missing the four you scheduled for me."

"I wouldn't have to treat you like a child if you didn't act like one."

The timer on her phone chirped. Jonah looked down, his face revealing nothing, and snatched the stick before she could.

"Give it to me, Jonah."

"Now who's the child? Does someone need to practice sharing?"

"This isn't funny." Ilena's voice cracked.

"No, it's not."

The doorbell rang, the long, protracted sound of Big Ben that reminded them of their honeymoon in London.

Jonah kept the stick out of reach. "Tell me, Ilena, if you're this fixated on a baby that's not even here, what's going to happen when it is? Where will we be?"

"Right here. As parents, just like we've always wanted."

"But we haven't. Shit, I'm to blame for all this. I'm the one who brought it up." He ran his hand through his hair, separating the increasing strands of gray. "Do you ever wonder if maybe this isn't the right choice? If it's all worth it?"

"Are you saying you don't want this anymore?"

Big Ben played again, and Jonah's eyes darted to the open bathroom door. "What would happen if I didn't? Who would you choose?"

Jonah held out his hands, one extended for her to take, the other home to the pregnancy stick.

This wasn't fair, and he knew it. She grabbed the pregnancy stick, and her heart sank.

Jonah was already out the door, lobbing a "You're replacing my 'Bottle of the Year.'"

37
MALLORY

Monday Morning
*Four Days **After** the Outing*

Mallory opens the sliding glass door to her parents' kitchen to find her mother's tongue halfway down the throat of a giant of a man with a paunch straining the front of his police officer's uniform.

"Hey," she says, and they break apart.

Her father stumbles back in surprise, struggling to keep his balance as he falls against the fridge. Mallory stifles a gasp, ripped back to the beach when she was eleven and a figure in the distance lumbered on the hot sand. The figure she had been convinced was her dad. The figure who seems very much like the one before her.

The memory passes like a hot gust of wind, and Mallory manages a "Morning, Mom," but can't follow it with a "Dad," the word too foreign to release.

Her mother eyes her quizzically before turning to her half-packed lunch on the counter. Mallory is too exhausted to pretend to be the happy, perfect daughter. As she waits for the reason she came—to be alone with her father—she opens the door to the pantry, rummaging through every shelf, looking for nut crackers.

"Dinner's in your court tonight," her mother says, straightening the badge on her father's shirt. "Don't forget."

"Never again," he says. "The last time I forgot, you fed me kale salads for a week as punishment. Thankfully MallieMoo taught me how to set reminders on my phone."

She did? I did?

Her mother scoffs. "A double-edged sword. Because that means you also know how to set them on mine. Do you know how embarrassing it was when my phone dinged with a reminder that you loved me every fifteen minutes?"

"Embarrassing, how so?" he says.

"I was in a staff meeting."

"It was sweet."

"And at the same time, creepy," her mom says with a smirk.

Mallory feels like an intruder. This isn't her family. These aren't her parents. This easy, comfortable, loving relationship bordering on soft-core porn isn't something she grew up witnessing. The brightness in this Mallory's life runs much deeper than her wardrobe.

She pulls out her phone and slips on her reading glasses. A dozen tabs lie open in her browser. The articles on the multiverse she'd been trying to read last night scrambled her brain. With the police investigating if Grayson is a "missing person" and requesting an interview with her, Ilena, and Aubrey, she's feeling the scratchiness of an orange jumpsuit against her delicate skin. Is there not a single academic who can tell her in words with less than a dozen syllables how multiverse theory works and how universes can cross—how to force them to cross?

A new email arrives from the morning show, confirming that the team who filmed in Mallory's apartment last night will be at AIM that morning to shoot more B-roll. And there's also a message dictated by Shandy herself regarding the interview the day after AIM goes public:

> Ms. Mallory Latham! My, what a score it is to get you! I aimed high, right? Come wearing the color of money, because you'll be rolling in it!

Added by the assistant:

> Ms. Shane is being literal. She requests you wear green and Mr. Fields wear a matching green tie.

Mr. Fields. No one's told the morning show that Grayson won't be on it.

She starts to forward the email to Noreen for scheduling when her mom sets a hand on her forearm.

"Mallory?" she says. "Walk me to my car?"

"But it's right there." Mallory points to the driveway, anxious to get her father alone. Him being a police officer could have been a hindrance, but considering her mom's saccharine story about the reminders on her phone, she's now sure she can totally use this teddy bear of a man for her own advantage.

"You can carry this." Her mom pushes a tote into Mallory's arms that's as light as a bag of cotton balls. She turns to her husband. "No sausage. Cholesterol, remember?"

The pout Mallory's father issues seems entirely out of place for a man in his sixties and one hundred percent out of character for a man who abandoned his family. He winks at Mallory as she takes off her glasses and follows her mom out the sliding glass door, onto the back porch, and to the small electric car parked behind the house.

"Here you go." Mallory hands off the tote. "Careful, you could strain a fingernail."

"What was that back there?"

"What was what?"

"Come on, Mallory, you're not sixteen, and you're also not being fair."

Should she know what this is about? Other than mom-daughter squabbles that transcend universes?

"He's a grown man," her mom says. "He's in charge of his own choices. You can't blame him for that."

But I can. I really, really can.

"It's me you should be mad at," her mom adds.

"Why would I be mad at you?"

Her mother grits her teeth. "Sarcasm gives you lip wrinkles."

"I'm not being—"

"It was a month. Not even a blip when the span is forty years." She holds up her palm. "I know I hurt him. And you. But don't blame him for taking me back. Blame me for going."

Shock renders Mallory speechless.

"I was curious. I was bored. I was . . . I don't know what I was. Selfish. I was selfish. A woman in her sixties doesn't just up and try out a new life on a whim."

Mallory can't move. She can't even breathe.

Her mother opens the car door and tosses the tote into the passenger seat. She faces Mallory as she slides behind the wheel. "I'll make it up to you both. Just give your dad a break. You know it's not in him to hold on to negativity. So don't try and make him." Her eyes begin to glisten, and she shoves the emotion away. "Come for dinner?"

"I—I can't."

"I know. Busy, busy, busy. My smart girl. Guess I played a role. Serves me right. Reap, sow, and all that. Another time?"

Mallory nods, stepping back as her mother puts the car in Reverse. Her mother tried out another life? What does that even mean? She left her father? The same way he supposedly left in her world? Could there possibly be more to the story Mallory grew up believing?

The car is halfway through a three-point turn when Mallory rushes forward and raps on the driver's-side window. "Was it the first time? The only time? Did you want to before—"

Her mother looks at her blankly, scratches the back of her neck.

"Because he seems invested," Mallory says. "So to leave . . ." A flash of her mom, sipping prosecco, a single bite left of a vanilla wafer, fingers scratching against her skin, the vertigo of déjà vu, and Mallory shakes her head. She's confusing herself. Confusing realities.

"No relationship is perfect, Mallory. We make choices, we make mistakes. Life is simply trying to do the right thing most of the time. And love? Love is being able to forgive when we get it wrong."

Mallory releases her grip on the edge of the window, and her mom drives off. Her mom and her dad, their relationship, one of them always leaving. Coincidence or destiny? Mallory never believed in either.

But what about love? Does she believe in that? She hasn't been able to forgive Grayson. Is that because he doesn't deserve it or because she doesn't actually love him?

And perhaps it's this shared sense of betrayal that gives Mallory the sudden urge to hug her father for the first time in her life. This man she has no memories of but who rents so much space in her head, affecting her in ways she's never let herself truly admit. She rushes to the porch and bursts through the sliding glass door, but her dad isn't in the kitchen. The basement door is open. The light is on. She bounds down the stairs.

Her father stands beside the freezer. The open freezer. With a plastic bag in one hand and a look of anguish on his face. He sees Mallory and holds up the bag. "Sausages. I hit the butcher before your mom woke up. I couldn't put them in the fridge upstairs and let her think I wasn't listening to her. Because I'm listening, I am. I want to make her happy. So I . . ." He looks into the freezer. "I broke the lock, MallieMoo. And I'm sorry, I'm really sorry."

Mallory's legs feel like concrete. "It's . . . I mean, I . . ." She forces herself to lift a foot.

"No!" Her father slams the freezer shut. "Don't come any closer. It's . . . goddamn, Mallory."

Her throat tightens as if a fist were lodged in it. "I don't—"

"At least if someone's got to tell you this, it's me." He balls his hands and takes two giant steps toward her. Before he says anything, he yanks her toward him, and the intensity of the love this man feels for his daughter both breaks and heals her heart.

The badge on his uniform pricks the yarn of Mallory's long-sleeved sweater as he draws back to look into her eyes. "It's Grayson, MallieMoo. He's—"

"Don't say it." She stifles a sob, and somehow, one of the worst parts of all this is knowing she's letting her father down.

"I know, sweetheart, I know." He keeps one hand cupped and runs the palm of his other back and forth over his cropped hair. "No matter how many times I've done this, it doesn't get any easier. We'll get through this. I already called Officer Middlebury. She'll be here any minute."

It's over. Everything's over.

"She has a lead. Something found at Mr. Fields's home. She wasn't sure what it meant, but now . . . I found something similar." Mallory's father opens his closed hand. In it is a silver charm in the shape of Texas with the single word *home*. Just like the one Mallory had seen on Noreen's key chain at Grayson's penthouse. When Mallory retrieved the keys that Aubrey had accidentally dropped into her mom's freezer, they'd snagged on the way out. This must be why.

Ilena and Aubrey. Mallory has to keep them out of this. She can't let them get hurt. No matter what, she has to protect them.

Her father rubs his head. "I don't know how to tell you this, but I'm starting to think this involves one of your employees. Oh, MallieMoo, not just an employee, your assistant—that girl who you really seemed to like, the one who has access to your office, your home, my goodness, your house keys, which means *our* house keys."

What? What, what, what?

"That day, she offered you her car, didn't she?" her father says. "She knew you were coming home with the serum and insisted you use it? It wasn't to be nice. She had an ulterior motive. To cover her tracks in case anyone recognized the car."

"I—I don't understand."

"I don't either. Not fully. Not yet. But this . . ." He holds up his phone. "She was here. Your mom turned off the alerts for our doorbell camera a couple of weeks ago. That beast of a cat the neighbors let hunt the garbage rats kept setting it off. I just went on now and checked the history. The cat's there. But so is a young woman. She was cupping her hands to look through the window on the front door. She had a set of keys in her hand with charms just like these."

A woman? What woman?

Her father is looking straight at her and can't see who she really is.

"The mood-enhancing serum you were storing in here is gone. It's been replaced by something else." His hand clenches into a fist. "She's setting you up. Noreen Parra is framing you for murder. I'd bet anything."

38

MALLORY

Harvard University
Twenty-One Years ***Before*** *the Outing*

Dead presidents weighed down Mallory's pocket. Ones, fives, tens, even a fifty. *Suckers.* Drawn in by Mallory's smokey eyes, round breasts, and knowledge of how to use them. Drawn in by Ilena's everything.

In their new room on the top floor of Straus, Mallory counted their winnings. The story of a boy duct-taped to a wall had spread fast. And opened wallets. More bets had been made—these of the cold, hard, glorious cash variety. The longer the duct tape held and the more freshmen who'd found out, the higher the bets went on if the duct tape would last longer than the pompous kid. He'd made it to dinnertime before he begged to be ripped free.

At his side was the roommate forced to carry their stuff. Even under that tightly drawn hoodie, Mallory could feel his contempt, especially when the resident adviser he'd appealed to agreed to let the results of the bet stand. *Ingenious*, he'd said. *Just what Harvard was looking for.*

Though, honestly, what he'd been looking *at* hadn't hurt.

Christ, Ilena was gorgeous. Lush black hair as thick as wool but smooth as silk, a slender frame curved in exactly the right places, and peacock blue eyes that challenged you, that made you want to prove you were worthy of her looking at you.

Mallory had hated her instantly. Ilena had rolled that stiff new suitcase of hers into their dorm room as if it were a judgment of Mallory's black duffel and cardboard box. She'd smiled deferentially, clutching that anemic white lamp and offering Mallory her choice of bunk as if Mallory arriving first didn't shut that shit down. She was a fucking tourist. Mallory had laughed at them her whole life as they passed through the Yard, rubbing *John Harvard*'s bronze toe for luck, duped that it was some student tradition. Mallory had shoplifted lip gloss and NyQuil from the drugstore across from the circular newsstand. Mallory had reached her first orgasm in the Radcliffe boathouse when she was sixteen. Mallory owned this. Mallory was *owed* this. Eighteen years living with the grind and screech of the Lechmere trolley to living across from Urban Outfitters. She wasn't going to let some chick who lucked out in the DNA department ruin her freshman year.

And then she'd said it. "Did you know Straus was William S. Burroughs's dorm?"

Mallory had stared at her.

"Oh, sorry, William S. Burroughs is a famous writer from the beat generation—"

"I know who Burroughs is." (She didn't.)

"Of course." Ilena gently rested her tony tush on her suitcase. "Supreme Court Justice David Souter too. And Darren Aronofsky, you know that movie, *Requiem for a Dream*?"

"Are you a tour guide?"

"No, I just like to be informed. They all have one thing in common."

"Besides penises."

"Maybe because of their penises." The word didn't quite roll off Ilena's tongue as easily, but that it did at all impressed Mallory. "They each had one of the big rooms on the fourth floor." Ilena surveyed the anchovy tin of a dorm room attached along with three others to an only slightly larger common room. Shared bathrooms at the end of the hall. "A double the size of a quad. With its own bathroom. Two sinks."

"Is that so?" Mallory had said, trying to figure out Ilena's angle. Everyone always had an angle. At least, Mallory did.

"I saw the guys assigned to it."

"And?"

Ilena had lifted herself off her suitcase and unzipped it. "And so I had an idea."

And she'd handed Mallory that roll of duct tape.

39
AUBREY

Monday Morning
*Four Days **After** the Outing*

Aubrey presses the rock from Ethan between her palms. If she had an ounce of the athletic skill of any of her siblings, she'd have tossed it through Ethan's window last night. Except it wasn't his window, it was his fiancée's. And that's the reason why, even if she had any skill, she wouldn't have thrown anything.

"Aubrey?" Mallory's tone is hesitant, unsure, and Aubrey slips the rock into her pocket. "Are we ready? We're ready, right?"

Aubrey can't look at her. They can go over their story a hundred more times and still never be ready to be interrogated by the police. Mallory's father found Grayson. This investigation is no longer that of a missing person.

"Sure, of course," Aubrey says, knowing her face will show the opposite. But Mallory simply nods absentmindedly as she hugs her arms to her chest and lowers herself onto the sofa. Still. Silent.

Beyond the glass door of Mallory's office, AIM buzzes with energy. The typical Monday sluggishness, the trickling in of employees still hungover from weekends at bars or binge-watching or both, has been replaced with an urgency, an air of anticipation and excitement because this is not a typical Monday. It's the Monday before AIM makes history. If its founders don't get arrested first.

"This is happening," Mallory says. "Grayson and—" She hugs her arms tighter, but it can't stop her body from shaking. "We have to deal with this, actually deal with this?"

The tremor in Mallory's voice scares Aubrey. "I'll go find Ilena."

"No." Mallory's head snaps up. "Don't leave."

Aubrey always thought that Mallory could handle anything. But this isn't just anything. This is murder. Of someone she obviously cared about. Aubrey's heartbeat echoes in her ears, and she sends Ilena a quick text. She sits beside Mallory, resting her hand on Mallory's leg, which doesn't seem like Mallory's leg, encased in these pink-and-white-striped pants. Aubrey realizes that she's not the only one who's been wearing someone else's clothes. All three of them have been. But Aubrey's the only one they seem to fit.

"Ethan really hit on you, didn't he?" Aubrey says suddenly. But she knows the answer. She always did, didn't she?

A month after Aubrey and Ethan had started dating, he'd said one of the things he liked most about Aubrey was how easygoing she was, that he didn't have to be a ballet dancer—always on tiptoes—like he'd been with other girls. Girls. Not women, Aubrey just realizes. He'd finish her fries without asking if she were done, saying her bikini would thank him. Then he'd laugh at how witty he was, and she would laugh too because it wasn't untrue. But it was inappropriate. And mean. No, cruel, it was cruel.

Maybe this Aubrey had seen that right away. Maybe that's why one date never became two. With a flush that spreads down her neck, Aubrey tells Mallory about Ethan and Lauren Stevens and the shame of apparently being Ethan's mistress.

"I pushed it," Aubrey says. "I had to know if we were supposed to be together, because if we weren't, then that would mean that I . . ."

"He didn't cheat because of you, and he didn't die because of you." Mallory's words tumble out.

Aubrey studies her perfect cuticles. "I texted him. I'm the reason he wasn't paying attention."

"No, just no. It's not your fault. It's no one's fault. It was an accident. None of us could have prevented it even if we'd . . ." Mallory shakes her head, the stress of today, of all of this, turning her into a version of herself that Aubrey doesn't recognize. "You should never have blamed yourself. But you were, and Ilena and I should have seen it. We failed you, Aubrey, and that's unforgivable."

"It's not, it's okay, really."

"No, it's not!" Mallory is suddenly a fire hose of sweat, and she's chomping on her lower lip like it's a steak. "Wrong, it's all been so wrong and gone so wrong, and we've been wrong. For so long, from the very beginning. I'm not sure I'll ever be able to make it right in any world."

"Mallory, don't—"

"Christ, I don't take ownership of anything. Let me own this."

Aubrey hesitates, her feelings all twisted and tumbled like sheets in a dryer. Mallory's her best friend, Ilena too, and they would never hurt her intentionally. But they never fully accepted Ethan—and, well, yes, that hurt. Maybe they didn't like him, maybe they didn't have reason to mourn him the way she did, maybe they couldn't understand why Aubrey would, because maybe they realized who Ethan was. But they didn't have to mourn Ethan for Ethan. They had to mourn Ethan for her.

Mallory takes Aubrey's hand. "I'm sorry, Aubrey. That's not what best friends do."

Their fingers entwine, and for the first time in all these years of being together, Aubrey truly feels like she belongs. They're close enough friends to fail one another. And be forgiven.

Aubrey squeezes Mallory's hand so tightly, it hurts them both, but neither lets go.

"Fuck Ethan," Mallory says. "You deserve to be loved by someone who forgets to breathe when you walk into a room."

"Yeah, I think, I mean, I do. That's exactly what I deserve."

Through the glass door, AIM stills. Three uniformed police officers stand before Noreen's desk.

Mallory releases Aubrey's hand. "I was sleeping with him. Grayson."

Aubrey nods, not surprised.

"I didn't tell anyone. I thought it would undermine my credibility. And I guess I also thought it was just sex. Spectacular sex, granted, but just sex."

"But?"

"It maybe wasn't just sex."

Aubrey's heart lifts with happiness for Mallory before she realizes that whatever Mallory had, she lost it too.

"I hope I didn't do it on purpose," Mallory whispers.

"Me too," Aubrey says. "But if you did, we'll deal with it together."

As Noreen assists the police officers, Harley scurries to the office door. But then, there's Kai, scooping up the dog and soothing him with long strokes through his soft fur. Aubrey smiles at him. And despite the hot-and-cold game she's been inadvertently playing the past few days, he smiles back. She likes him. Plain and simple. No pro-con list needed. She doesn't have to question it.

What she does have to question is what comes next.

40
ILENA

Monday Morning
*Four Days **After** the Outing*

Ilena straightens the biodegradable carrying tray on the bench beside her. The mingling aromas of strong coffee, Earl Grey, mocha, and peppermint make her slightly nauseous, her superior sense of smell apparently a pregnancy superpower, but she wasn't sure what James liked and she wanted to have options.

Remembering what Felix said about James and punctuality, she arrived early and chose a bench closest to the dock. Across from her is a rainbow of kayaks and paddleboards, stacked one on top of another, looped by a cord and locked, waiting to be rented, their purpose otherwise unfulfilled, in need of someone else to bring them to life. It was the way Ilena had been starting to feel as month after month after month, her body refused to do as she asked.

She couldn't understand why it was just her, why it wasn't the same for Jonah, why he could put it out of his mind the same way he forgot about the time-outs in the hallway that pushed them to buy their house. He forgot this too, the kayaks and paddleboards they'd always talked about renting as they drove past on their way to that exorbitantly priced home with its postage-stamp yard and crumbling detached garage.

He asked for the divorce so easily. He must have been wanting it for a while. And she'd had no idea.

"Mrs. Singh," a singsong voice says.

Ilena puts on a smile. "Thank you for coming, James."

"God, you are glowing, aren't you?" James says with both honesty and derision. "Who thought Ilena Cohen could get more gorgeous? But then again, you're full of surprises."

"Not always good ones, it seems."

"Wait, why are we . . ." James wrinkles his nose, his smattering of freckles dancing. "Is Felix all right? The baby—"

"Fine, we're all fine. Healthy, we're all healthy. Physically, we're all perfectly fine, but mentally, I need you to help with that." She holds up the tray of hot beverages. "Fortification?"

"Do I smell mocha?"

She hands him the mochaccino. Her phone buzzes beneath her thigh, and as she sets the tray back down, she subtly slides her leg aside. It's a text from Aubrey wondering where she is, reminding her, as if she could forget, that the police are coming to AIM.

This is exactly what Mallory feared—that a pregnancy, that a baby, would divide Ilena's time and loyalty. She couldn't argue about the first, but the second, that would only deepen. A baby meant she'd need Mallory even more.

Ilena places her leg back on top of the phone and faces James. "I'd like to ask you some questions, but I don't want you to ask me why I'm asking or say I already know the answer. I just want you to be honest with me. And in turn, I'll be as honest as I can back."

James sips his coffee. "You did hear the qualification in there, right?"

She nods. "I'll do the best I can, that's as much as I can promise."

"On one condition. I get to ask you something that you have to answer with complete honesty."

"All right. That's fair."

He rolls one hand. "Proceed."

Ilena picks up the Earl Grey tea, and her stomach twists. She trades it for the peppermint, her eyes misting as James carefully takes the tray and rests the drinks on the ground, far from her overly sensitive nose. She clears her throat. "How long have you and Felix been friends?"

"You know—"

"James, you agreed."

"Whatever. Six years."

"And you've been close."

"Is that a question?"

"Have you ever been closer than friends?"

"Like do we each have half of a BFF heart necklace?"

"Sure. Or an actual heart? One another's?"

James stills.

Ilena wraps both hands around her tea. "Were you ever romantically involved?"

"Ilena, this—"

"There's a reason, I promise."

One foot begins tapping, gently rocking the bench. "A bit, but we weren't exclusive." His gaze travels to Ilena's pregnant belly. "Obviously."

So it was recent. "Were you in love?"

"'You' in the singular or plural?"

"Whichever. Both."

"Singular, yes. My god, yes. Plural? I can only say I was hoping."

"But I got in the way."

James sighs. "It gives me immense satisfaction to think it was just you, but unless you're some kind of snake charmer for penises, it wasn't just you."

Ilena smiles weakly. "That'd be a résumé builder, wouldn't it?"

"Some doors would burst wide open."

"Touché." Ilena is reminded of how much she'd always liked James. "And yet the door on you two, I closed that." She presses a hand to her stomach. "Me and the singleton."

"Why are you asking, Ilena? What is all this for?"

"Last night you said—"

"A lot of things I shouldn't have. It wasn't the right moment."

"Maybe not, but sometimes we can't always wait for the right moment. We have to make the right moment."

"I appreciate you trying to excuse my behavior, but I was in the wrong. The right moment was months ago. But I was scared. I waited, and, well, I—"

"Ate some bad sushi the day of our wedding."

"Not exactly."

"I figured."

James holds Ilena's gaze. "For the record, Felix wants the baby. He's always wanted to be a dad. I shouldn't have suggested he wasn't sure about that part."

"Then the part he wasn't sure about was me." Ilena's throat goes dry as this world holds up a mirror to the one she left.

Before Jonah had brought up having children, she hadn't really considered it. Being a mom meant risking becoming her mom, creating a family of unceasing disappointment. But Jonah—the Jonah who bought street performers' CDs and made out with her in *John Harvard*'s lap and would have plastered their home with images of cats in glasses and sunsets and rainbows touting "If plan A fails, there are twenty-five more letters"—*that* Jonah would have made sure Ilena was never her mom and would never have reason to be. That's why she'd agreed. She'd wanted to do this with Jonah. She still does. She thought he'd missed all those appointments at the fertility clinic because he wasn't sure he wanted to be a dad anymore. But maybe it's the same, maybe the part he wasn't sure about was her.

An ache comes from deep within her body. "Felix always wanted to be a dad. But he could have been a dad with someone else. Someone he actually loved."

James sets down his coffee. "Is that a question?"

"It's a statement. We're not in love." She tries to absorb the warmth of her tea, but it's already fading. "He's not in love with me any more than I'm in love with him."

"But you knew that going in. What's changed?"

She owes him a truthful answer, so she gives it. "What's changed is wanting it, wanting to be in love. And wanting Felix to have the same."

"So what are you going to do?"

Once again, Jonah is before her, and the warmth the tea denied her comes, flooding her veins, warming her cheeks, swelling her heart. "I have no idea, but I'm working on it."

"Good."

41
MALLORY

Monday Afternoon
Four Days ***After*** *the Outing*

Noreen Parra is framing you for murder.

"Ms. Latham?"

Mallory sits on the couch in her office, trying to act normal despite the policeman across from her (male, late twenties, underwear-model fit), Officer Middlebury to her right, and her father by her desk. On the cushion beside her, Aubrey's index finger digs a trench into her palm. "Yes?" Mallory says.

"I was asking about the timeline?" The policeman flashes a warm hug of a smile. "Starting with the company outing?"

The outing—here. Mallory knows the where and the when. And Ilena had said there were invoices for a raw bar and paddleboard rentals and even dung cleanup. But she doubts that's what Mack Weldon is looking for. The underwear brand was Grayson's favorite, at least in her world.

"Ooh, the outings!" She summons the stupidity she's supposedly known for. "We've held them all over Cambridge and Boston, haven't we, Aubrey? Can't repeat ever. These young people nowadays expect—"

Officer Middlebury leans forward, and the mirrored sunglasses tucked into the collar of her shirt sway. It's like she learned how to be a cop from watching too many B movies.

"I was referring to this most recent outing," Mack Weldon continues in a velvety tone. "What was it?" He starts flipping through a notebook. "Three days ago?"

"Four," Officer Middlebury says, the innocuous word coming out as an accusation.

Make that too many good-cop/bad-cop B movies.

Mallory's father leaves his perch on the edge of the desk and places a hand on Mallory's shoulder. An emotion not in her lexicon makes her lift her own hand and rest it atop his.

"I know you'd prefer bourbon," he says. "Wouldn't we all? But maybe a water, MallieMoo?" He pats her shoulder. "Apologies, Mallory."

"Sure." The use of the nickname in front of the police makes her feel like a child, and he should know better. But then she sees Officer Middlebury's chin tuck, eyes lower to the ground, and she realizes that her father knows exactly what he's doing. It's why he told Mallory to leave their house before the police arrived and to pretend to have no knowledge of what he found in the basement. To be surprised when the police reveal Grayson is dead. To treat this exactly as it had previously been planned: as an informational interview about Grayson's disappearance, scheduled to take place casually, in the office, rather than at the station. He's making it harder for the officers to see her as a suspect.

Even though she is. *She is, she is, she is.*

"Let me." Her father heads for the wet bar, the one place Mallory suddenly realizes she hasn't searched for nut crackers.

She bites her lower lip, her usually rapid-fire brain unable to make any choice. This is how Aubrey must feel all the time. There's an unexpected peace in it, in giving things over to someone else.

Her father opens the refrigerator door. "It's the least I can do. I'm here in such an unofficial capacity that I'm actually in the Dunkin' down the street."

"Dad joke," Aubrey whispers, a soft smile on her face.

Mallory feels like she's just stepped onto a tightrope in a windstorm. She tugs on the sleeve of her blouse. Barely a whisper of an outline remains of the marks on her forearm, yet even when they're gone, she'll still see them.

She accepts the bottle of water from her father, cracks it open, and drinks. (Stalls.)

The sound of tapping draws her attention back to the male officer. He's holding his notebook above his knee. "Sorry, nervous habit." Except he's not actually nervous. Not at all.

He gives one final tap, and from between the pages, a plastic bag slips out. It lands on the floor in front of Mallory. She reaches for it, but Officer Middlebury's quick fingers get there first.

The fuzzy black-and-white cow print. Mallory tries to keep her expression neutral. *The shape of Texas.* She meets the officer's eye. That slip wasn't an accident. This must be the "lead" her father was talking about. A charm found in Grayson's penthouse. Too similar to the one found in her parents' freezer to be a coincidence. Two charms from Noreen's key chain that amounted to one thing.

Noreen Parra is framing you for murder.

Is it possible they all *actually* think that?

Officer Middlebury slides the plastic bag into her shirt pocket, and Mack Weldon nods with feigned gratitude.

"Great." He plants the notebook on his knee. "Where were we?"

"Outing," Officer Middlebury grunts, not as an accusation but as a sentencing.

"Of course. The outing. Exactly what time did you first see Mr. Fields?"

Mallory runs her tongue over her lips. Beside her, Aubrey's about to flay off a layer of skin. And Ilena, where the hell is Ilena? Christ, she's not in labor, is she?

The thought pushes Mallory to step up. If there's even a chance they see her as potentially being framed rather than as a suspect, she's leaning all the way in. "I know that," she pretends to blurt out. "I mean, I know who it belongs to."

Aubrey can't stop her small gasp, which fits in perfectly.

"We have to, Aubrey," Mallory says. "We have to tell them what we know."

Her father hovers near the kitchenette. The officers can't see him nodding encouragingly. He violated investigation protocol by telling her to leave the house after he found the body, the same way he's interfering now. He's trying to help her. Because he must suspect her. He'd be the worst police officer in the world if he didn't. He's protecting her by putting himself at risk.

All she wants is to go home. But the guilt over abandoning this man she barely knows unravels her a bit. She won't let him put himself at risk for nothing. "My assistant, Noreen. That was on her key chain."

"Oh," Officer Middlebury says, her voice rising, "and is there a reason you're so intimately familiar with your assistant's keys?"

"In fact there is. I borrowed her car recently." And now the source of her guilt switches to tossing Noreen under the bus—a figure of speech that conjures Ethan, and Mallory fights to cover her wince. "Accepted her car, more accurately."

Officer Middlebury's eyes flicker to Mack Weldon's. She breaks character for the barest of seconds, but long enough for Mallory to see. Officer Middlebury is surprised.

"I've been a bit sore." Mallory straightens her right leg. "Ooh, yep, still tender. Pickleball's harder than they say." She feels Aubrey's leg begin to shake and places a hand on it. "Anyway, I think Noreen was just being overprotective. Wanting me to drive rather than walk. She even offered me a wheelchair the other day, remember, Aubrey?"

The sound of scratching fills the office as Mack Weldon drops his good cop act and takes notes.

Officer Middlebury sets her sunglasses on the coffee table. She braces her elbows on her thighs and leans in so far that Mallory can smell her perfume. Citrusy, orange, maybe, and the image of Officer Middlebury spritzing the air and darting beneath seems so absurd that Mallory has to bite the inside of her cheek.

"Let's take this further," the male officer says. "Go back to the car. When was—"

A flurry of movement and then a ball of orange fur lands in Mallory's lap.

"Harley!" Noreen cries as she pushes open the office door. "I'm so sorry, y'all! David Copperfield's got nothing on this one."

Mallory laughs politely, Aubrey too, but no one else does—not even her father.

Noreen's gait slows as she approaches the lounge area. She's nervous, without even knowing she has every reason to be, thanks to Mallory's efforts to divert attention from herself.

Mallory has no other choice. She can't go to jail—bring Ilena and Aubrey with her. So she's doing this? Actually doing this to Noreen? *Shit, shit, shit.* She needs to stall for real. To decide if she's actually willing to go this far. Mallory pops up from the sofa, tucking Harley to her chest. "I'll just get him settled."

"Quickly," Officer Middlebury says. "No holding his paw until he falls asleep, Ms. Latham."

"Of course." Mallory's grip on Harley tightens.

With sure-footed steps to mask her inner trembling, Mallory carries Harley out of the office and falls into Noreen's desk chair, black and hard, nothing like the custom-designed coral chairs with the AIM logo in their world.

"The door wasn't fully shut." Noreen closes it behind her now. "I'm so sorry."

Spots gather before Mallory's eyes. Did she hear? *No, no, no, no, no.* Mallory laughs some weird never-before-uttered hyena laugh, and she knows she's losing it. Her sanity along with everything else. "Everyone loves dogs, don't they?"

Noreen crouches as if to attend to the dog, but instead, she looks straight at Mallory, and this is it, this is the end.

"I couldn't hear more than muffled words," Noreen says. "How's it going? Are you okay? If there's anything I can do . . ."

Mallory blinks, trying to focus, looking past Noreen to see the crew from *The Shandy Shane Show* being led by Ella, who keeps tugging at bangs she clearly regrets getting. Ozzie, in the same shirt as the day before, points his long camera lens at the snack bar and rejuvenation rooms, and Mallory trails her fingers through Harley's fur.

"Oh my," Noreen says. "Ms. Latham, I promise I checked y'all's calendar before confirming the, well . . ." She lowers her voice. "The officers."

"No, yes, I'm sure," Mallory mutters, remembering how her mom had distracted her as she'd been forwarding the producer's email to Noreen. Had she never actually hit Send?

Her father pokes his head out of her office. "Breather, I get it. Truly, MallieMoo, it guts me that you have to do this. I'd do it for you in a heartbeat if I could."

She wants to thank him, apologize to him, for not being the daughter he thinks he has, and maybe this too is one of those things that crosses universes—one of them may always be destined to disappoint the other.

"Ms. Latham?" Georgina walks toward Mallory as Ozzie trains his camera on the wall of photographs documenting the history of AIM. Mallory, Ilena, and Aubrey and those micro-green salads at the start-up program, at the endless string of coffee shops around Boston, at the cramped office space barely half a mile from here that smelled like feet and decomposing rats and faintly of yeast from the home brewery below it that Mallory never once missed before now.

Four years. That's how long ago it was. Moving into this space was gradual. They had a quarter of a floor, then half, then the entire thing. And another. The square footage increased along with the number of employees, the original three of them now more than a hundred. They'd have gotten here without Grayson, Mallory doesn't doubt that. But not as quickly. The same goes for this woman in front of her who wants to help, who has no idea that Mallory is in the process of betraying her.

Her father's solemn eyes reach for Mallory's. "The loss of Grayson is devastating, I know."

Georgina stills. "Grayson Fields?"

Mallory has to get out of here. Out of this office, out of this investigation, out of this life.

"The loss of Grayson Fields?" Georgina's in front of Mallory now, with a clear view through the glass office door. "As in missing? As in dead?"

The word draws like a magnet, pulling forward Ozzie and Ella and several of the marketing team Mallory's always threatening to fire and Heidi Hoffman, who doesn't even work here. A camera lens wedges itself between Mallory and her father, capturing Officer Middlebury and Mack Weldon and a terrified Aubrey and a worried Noreen. The camera zooms in, then back out, refocusing squarely on Mallory. Who runs.

42
AUBREY

Monday Afternoon
*Four Days **After** the Outing*

Aubrey's wedge sandals catch in the gaps between the bricks as she spins. The rehab center, the AIM logo, Ethan's building, the deli with the rooibos lattes. The rehab center, the AIM logo, Ethan's building, the deli with the rooibos lattes, again and again, around and around, all blurring into one giant string of malware replicating inside Aubrey until she explodes.

Breathe, breathe, breathe, breathe. She stops spinning, bends at the waist, places her hands on her thighs, her knees, her face that's not even damp with tears. Her heart's pumping too hard just to keep her alive, it has no room for tears. Grayson's dead, and everyone will know it once the footage goes live on *The Shandy Shane Show.*

Mallory, gone, Ilena, gone, she was the only one left when Ella and Kai and Noreen and the rest of AIM all looked to her to explain, to make sense of the police officers and Grayson and what this means for going public, for AIM's future, for their future. A thousand questions to which she had no answer: Mallory's father and the police asking where Mallory was, and why Ilena never came, and why a television crew was filming in the office—filming them—and everything's changed, all of it changed, and Aubrey's jaw locked. Her tongue went limp. Her brain was the only thing going, but not working, swirling, unable to focus, to make a single decision on anything, for any of them.

She'd still be there, hands twisting and eyes wide, if it hadn't been for Felix. He handled everything, or she thinks he did, hopes? She left. Let Noreen carefully guide her to the restroom, her words of reassurance about not giving up hope and how friends stick together and everything will work out okay just white noise. And when Noreen went to check on the dog, Aubrey snuck out. Elevator, lobby, plaza, looking for Mallory or Ilena or the life she had or could have or—

"Aubrey?"

The familiar voice curdles her stomach.

"Aubrey? I thought that was you. I was just about to text you."

Ethan stands before her, his eyes like a snake's behind those black-rimmed glasses. Maybe it's the light. Or maybe it's because Aubrey's no longer in the dark.

"Leave," she mutters under her breath.

"My thoughts exactly. Your place? I've got about—" he holds up his phone "—twenty minutes? Good, right?"

Aubrey fully straightens, a pounding in her temples, a constriction in her throat.

The bed, the curtain, the white sheet. Ethan.

"No," she says.

His eyes flash with annoyance. "My office, then. Shades, ergonomic desk chair, we can make it work. Even got a change of clothes for this exact reason."

Because she's surely not the first woman he's cheated on his fiancée with. She clasps her eyes shut like a child, but she's not a child and she needs to stop acting like one. "I'm so stupid sometimes. Maybe all the time."

"You aren't making any sense." He presses his hand on her lower back. "Babe, last night, your friends, I nailed it. Honestly—"

"Don't! Don't use that word. There's nothing honest about you in any world, is there? I may be naive and needy, yes, sure, I am, but I also trust, and I trusted you, and you used that to get . . . what exactly? What did you want from me? Why me?"

His eyes dart around the plaza. "Let's maybe go somewhere else—"

She wrestles away from him. "To your fiancée's, perhaps?" The word burns like acid.

"My what?" He shakes his head. "Listen, I can explain whatever you think's going on, but not here, let's . . ." He looks past her, a strange expression overtaking his face, before stepping closer, crowding her, and for a moment, she thinks she was wrong. She misinterpreted, and then his hands are on her cheeks, cool against her flush, and the life she had—they had—rushes back and fills her with one desire: to not relive it.

Clove nearly suffocates her, and his lips press against hers. She can't move. He again lands a hand on her lower back, edging down, and she breaks away.

"Last night wasn't enough for you. I get that a lot." He's grinning, strangely, jutting his chin. "Hey, kid."

"It's Kai."

Aubrey turns. It is Kai, holding a leash. Harley bounces upon seeing Aubrey. Kai, pointedly, does not.

"It's not what you think," she says to Kai.

"Oh, but it is," Ethan says with a wink. "Not just once, twice. With a third to come. Pun intended."

Aubrey whirls around to face him. "You don't know me, you never really did know me. But if you did, you'd understand how much it means for me to say 'Fuck you.'"

His lips thin, then he shrugs. "Whatever, crazy bitch."

"Aubrey," Kai says calmly despite the tightness of his jaw. "Do you want to go?"

She nods.

"Do you want me to walk with you?"

She nods again. "If you don't mind."

"No hard feelings, then?" Ethan says, but she keeps her back to him, eyes straight ahead on the logo for AIM beside the front door of the building.

When they reach it, Kai picks up Harley. "Here. Noreen asked me to get him to Mallory before Mr. Fields's secretary took him."

Aubrey accepts the dog despite the scratchiness building in her throat. "I'll get him to her."

Kai places his hands in his front pockets, exhaling, like he'd been punched in the gut. He turns and heads for the entrance.

"Wait!" Aubrey says. "I can explain everything. Well, maybe not everything. There's a lot I don't know how to explain, but most of that isn't important. But what is important, well, I still can't explain that, actually, when it comes down to it. Because how do you explain things you don't know but simply feel? Which is this: I like you."

"I liked you too."

She breathes a sigh of relief. "Great, then great, so—"

"I just don't think I can trust you."

He enters the building, and she can't blame him. She huddles Harley to her chest, the orange fur a surrogate for her grandmother's afghan, and she's back to the day her teenage self curled beneath it, having lost her virginity to a boy she realized too late didn't deserve it or her, knowing she'd never trust herself again. Except, maybe "never" doesn't exist across universes. What she feels right now about Kai, she trusts it implicitly.

43
ILENA

Monday Afternoon
Four Days ***After*** *the Outing*

Three peppermint teas and two scones, apparently that's Ilena's limit. She wraps the third untouched cranberry and orange pastry in a napkin, tips the young girl behind the counter for letting her commandeer the table, and exits into air radiating the perfect amount of summer heat.

She never went to AIM. The police wanted to question her, and she didn't show. Entirely out of character, and yet, Ilena feels fine. Good, even. She wanders down Mass. Ave. toward Boston. There was a time she'd have walked all the way in, to Newbury Street and the Boston Public Garden, even to the Seaport. She wouldn't do it now with her swollen belly and even more swollen ankles. Though part of her feels like she could, like maybe it'd be good for her. She doubts Felix would agree. Would Jonah?

The thought of how Jonah would treat a pregnant Ilena causes her to halt in the middle of the sidewalk. A guy with a backpack the size of a small house knocks into her, sending her off-balance.

"What a loser," a young woman in leggings and a sports bra says. "Are you okay? Come inside, let me get you a water."

Ilena nods, meaning she's fine, but the young woman takes it as agreement to the second part and ushers her inside a warmly lit yoga studio.

"Sit, sit," the young woman says, lowering Ilena into a bean-bag chair she'll never get out of by herself.

"Thank you, but really, this isn't necessary."

The woman brings her a glass tumbler of water that those three teas left no room for.

"Necessary, maybe not. But it makes me happy." She coils her long hair into a messy bun atop her head. "And happiness should be our journey, shouldn't it?" She points to the AIM logo on the window.

"Are you affiliated?" Ilena asks.

"Brand ambassador!" She waves to the check-in counter and the shelves of AIM merchandise beside it. "Certified by Ella—isn't she just the best?"

Ilena nods absently, not really knowing Ella enough to determine that here or at home. She stares at the swag, wondering which of them approved the idea of "brand ambassadors." She wouldn't have. She wouldn't cede that level of control, allowing the AIM brand to be associated with people and places that could behave in ways that would reflect poorly on the company.

Your need to control everything has no end.

She squeezes her eyes shut, but Jonah's indictment remains. She's careful. She's cautious. She does the right thing. Why isn't that okay?

The sliding barn door across from her opens, and heat pours out.

"Excuse me," the young woman says, pushing the water into Ilena's hand.

"But I don't—"

A string of women, mostly young, a few older—well, her age—and a couple of men drenched in sweat stream into the small entryway, slipping their shoes on, chatting about getting drinks or returning to work or recommending their latest binge-watch. A few pull out their phones, and Ilena hears the familiar tone of someone using "How Wide's My Smile."

She presses her feet to the shiny wood floor, trying to haul herself out, but she's stuck. And she's peed herself. Just a little. "Excuse—"

Another ding.

And another.

And three young women move to the stack of hoodies along the wall.

"Fifteen percent off if you buy it here," the woman who helped Ilena says. She turns to give her a wink, and Ilena waves, gesturing for help, but the girl simply waves back.

Perfect. Ilena drinks the water and slumps into the chair for the rest of her life. She checks her phone, expecting a question from Aubrey or a scolding from Mallory, but the only new text is from her mother:

A girl! Your sister and I are so pleased. Felix couldn't wait. Such a catch!

At least her mother likes *one* of her husbands.

Another text comes in, this one a photograph of her mom holding a onesie with a cupcake on it.

Ilena draws in a sharp breath. Does her mother not remember? Did her father not do that here? Bring them special cupcakes for every occasion? Or did he, and her mother's too damn self-absorbed to care?

Her mother couldn't forgive—her father, Ilena, anyone. A wrong had no way to become anything but more wrong in her mother's mind. She relished her anger. She spent so much time being offended by what other people did that she became mean and bitter. Even if her mother had wanted to find love again, who would want to find love with her?

Yet here she is, taking a picture with a onesie. Tall and trim with silver hair and a smile Ilena doesn't recognize. Her mother doesn't smile.

But *this* Ilena's mother does. It's like trying to reconcile something as preposterous as unicorns being real, or having never met Mallory, or Ilena being a mom. She lays one hand atop her belly. If her mother smiles here, what might that mean of her dad?

Ilena opens the browser on her phone and searches for her father's name. It pops up on some social media site she's never heard of, but that she apparently has an account on. The site redirects to an app where she's already logged in, and he's listed as a friend. The last post on his page is from twelve years ago, from before her sister would have graduated from college, from before that photograph of just the three of them in the nursery was taken.

You will be missed.
Too soon.
I can still hear your laugh.

That one was written by her mother.

You would have been the best grandfather.

And this one by her.

All the air leaves her lungs. She hasn't seen her father in person in years, but this, this is . . . this is like nothing she has ever known. A heat builds behind her eyes as she scans the photos on her account. Her family, the four of them, in front of the *John Harvard* statue on what looks to be Ilena's college graduation, her mom and dad wearing "Mr." and "Mrs." tiaras celebrating some milestone anniversary, and Ilena and her sister, hugging in wool hats and ice skates on Frog Pond in Boston Common.

There are also photos of Ilena and Mallory, of Aubrey, of Ilena and Felix, a few interspersed of her and Felix and James. In them, Felix looks exactly the way she feels: in love with someone who isn't their spouse.

An ache deep in her chest makes it hard to breathe. The one person—the only person—she wants to share all of this with won't understand why. She searches his name and finds him in the same place she found him twenty-one years ago: at MIT.

Jonah Gelding, associate professor, physics department.

"Excuse me!" Ilena drops her phone into her purse and waves both hands above her head. "Can someone get me out of this goddamn thing?"

Ilena catches her breath outside the physics building, searching for someone to let her in. She doesn't have a student or faculty ID or an entry card, but she has the next best thing. She taps her stomach and waits. Once inside, thanks to a student more concerned with chivalry than security, she heads for the directory.

Jonah Gelding.

She traces a finger over the letters. A professor. All those nights sitting cross-legged on his bed, quizzing him before the MCATs, vivid in her mind. Maybe he had someone else here, listening to his dissertation.

She wanders down the maze of hallways until she reaches

his office door. Her hand rises to smooth her hair, thinking he hasn't seen her with hair this long in years, which she immediately realizes is silly. She doesn't know if this Jonah has ever seen her. She stretches her neck to get a glimpse of him.

She steadies her breath and knocks.

"Office hours are over. Ergo, I'm still here, so enter." He closes the filing cabinet and faces her. "Oh, sorry. I thought you were a student."

Her heartbeat pounds her temples, and she's swept up by a profound sense of loss. "Not for a long time."

"Wait, don't tell me." He presses a finger to his lips. "Mallory Latham!"

Ilena draws back. "Uh, no, it's—"

"Ilena Cohen. Just having a goof." He grins and that sense of loss ebbs, for just a moment, replaced with longing, desire. "I've been following you. Not literally. Online. Though technically that could still veer into stalker category."

She hovers in the doorway.

"I assure you it doesn't." He rushes to his guest chair to remove stacks of books and papers and a second cardigan, as he's already wearing one, completely the professor cliché. "Please, sit. Your first, right?"

She manages a nod.

"All over the news, you two, and AIM. I like to impress my friends by saying 'I knew them when.' After that first MIT-Harvard mixer, I knew you two would take over the world."

"What happened?" The words tumble out, but what she really wants to ask is if they met here, why aren't they together? Were they ever? And suddenly she fully understands what Aubrey's been going through. The loss, the deep sense of loneliness, the need to know what's right and what's wrong and what role she played in all of it.

"Well," he says, "you two took over the world, that's what."

His eyes meet hers and she can't understand how they can see her now but not have seen everything she's seen, not know everything she knows, the compass rose clock, and Plum Island, and the bottle of the year, and the day he asked her for a divorce and she said yes.

She'd called his bluff. And he'd let her.

The life drains out of her, and she presses her elbows to her thighs, cradling her head in her hands.

"Do you need an ambulance?" She feels him at her side. "Is it the baby? Are you—"

"I'm fine. She's fine."

"You're having a girl? I always wanted a girl."

He never told her that.

Ilena blinks away the moisture in her eyes, embarrassed in a way she hasn't been around Jonah since she was eighteen years old. He smiles warily, nervously running his hand through his hair, still wavy but with less gray. Perhaps because he's a professor and not a doctor. Perhaps because he's not married to her.

He rests against his desk, eyeing Ilena carefully, as if he expects the baby to slide out onto the tile floor.

"You must be wondering why I'm here." Ilena opens the AIM app, employing the ruse she devised on the way. "We—I mean, AIM—we're working on a new challenge."

"So you can become trillionaires?"

"That depends on our focus groups." She smiles to hide the shame that now comes with mention of AIM's valuation. "This challenge is a spin on the *Sliding Doors* concept. Remember that movie?"

He nods. "I'd hoped enrollment in physics would peak after."

"And did it?"

"No, but it's not Gwyneth's fault." He mouths, *It is*, and

Ilena wants to wrap her arms around his cheesy self. "I have full confidence, however, that if AIM even whispers 'parallel universe' our department will be the belle of the ball."

This time she smiles for real.

"So," he says. "It seems you are in need of someone who can speak to what we call the 'many-worlds interpretation' of reality."

"And can you?"

"I can, indeed. Not because I'm a leading expert, but because I have tenure and a thick skin."

"Then it looks like the MIT directory steered me well. I searched the physics department, and there you were."

"This version of me."

Ilena laughs, wondering if she should feel guilty for being attracted to this Jonah.

He pushes himself off the edge of his desk. "What are you looking for, exactly?"

"We're just in the exploratory stage right now," she says, "which is why some grounding in the science will be immensely helpful. The question we're thinking of proposing is this, if there's another version of you living a different life, living out a choice you didn't make, would you want to know? Would it change your life here?"

"A perfect AIM complement," he says. "The intersection of philosophy and science has always fascinated me. We experience time and space as fixed, but mathematically, the world we live in is anything but. Yet the notion of our world not being predictable is philosophically uncomfortable for most."

She leans forward like she would when he'd discuss a complicated spinal tap, seeing that same excitement in his eyes. He circles the desk and settles himself in a wooden chair with arms and spindles and all the hallmarks of this profession he's chosen here. It seems to fit him. Maybe there's something inherent, something that made this Jonah a professor and her Jonah a lover of sci-fi novels.

"For the question you're posing," he says, "we'd look at the theory of multiple realities. In simplest terms, the many-worlds interpretation suggests that every time, say, two things could happen, they both actually do happen. This splits the one reality into two new parallel realities. You, or the you of your conscious self, lives in one branch of what is actually a complex multiverse. The theory goes that there are near infinite versions of you who have made every conceivable choice in your life."

"So I have lived every possible version of my life?"

"Lived and are living. Possibly."

"What about probably?"

"Above my pay grade. Literally. You might need a full professor to answer that. And speaking of, if you're inclined to put in a word . . ."

She laughs, and for a moment, they're back in their original Cambridge apartment after too many glasses of wine, volleying about whose turn it is to take out the trash. But it was never real. He never let her, in the beginning.

She refocuses. "What about this, if we want to ask our users if they'd want to try on this other life, what does the science say? Can they—I don't know the term—choose to move into a different reality? Or at least dip in?"

"Can you cross worlds?" He tents his fingers. "The short answer is no."

Ilena's need to be right begs to protest and offer herself as evidence, but she stays silent.

He fiddles with a button toward the hem of his sweater, barely hanging on by a single thread. "We can think of it like radio frequencies. Even though there are hundreds of different radio stations, you only hear the one that your radio is tuned in to, the one frequency, the station that is what we'd call 'coherent' to your radio. Even though there might be thousands of stations—or alternate realities—you can't interact with them because you don't vibrate coherently with them."

"Never? There's no way to tune in, so to speak?"

"Got me." He places his hand on his chest. "If scientists believed in 'never,' we wouldn't be scientists. Plus, we really do like trying to debunk one another. So is there a theory to support the opposite? Absolutely. And that's 'coherence link,' which in some ways blows apart the reasoning that versions could never maintain consciousness of one another based on things like frequency and wavelength and quantum entanglement . . ." He stops himself. "And you're going to go into labor simply to ease the boredom."

She finds listening to him both fascinating and seductive, but those peppermint teas force her to nod to hurry him along.

He pushes his hair back, accentuating a cowlick and revealing a few strands of gray, which makes Ilena happier than it should. "Theoretically, coherence link would offer a bridge between quantum states."

"A bridge? To travel across? Like a two-way street?"

"Meaning . . ."

"A swap, I guess?"

"A brain swap?"

"Well, it sounds silly when you say it like that."

"It all sounds silly. Ridiculous even. But in this particular case, a swap in the way you are suggesting is highly improbable. More mystical or intentional than the physics allows for. The bridge would simply offer the conditions for one consciousness to access its counterpart in another universe. While the coherence link lasted, consciousnesses could coexist."

"And more silliness, but like two brains are better than one?"

Jonah smiles, and her stomach does a little flip. "While it's conceivable that two sets of memories might exist in the same space, personally, I find the notion of the human mind being able to tolerate such a thing hypothetically challenging."

That must be why she, Mallory, and Aubrey don't remember the lives they had in this world. If only she could tell Jonah she is proof of his conclusion.

Jonah continues, "One set of memories likely suppresses another for a period of time. But it's not a stable state. The more time that passes since the collision, the more the coherence link will fade out, leaving just one consciousness. We have no way of knowing which one."

They could fade. And who knows which versions of themselves would remain.

Jonah seems to note the discomfort on her face. "It's not as out there as it seems. Experiments with collapsing wave function show how a particle that seems to inhabit just one position actually exists in every position simultaneously. We just don't have the means to observe it. With respect to coherence link, for those vibrations to line up, the worlds would have to be very similar in that moment, and the closer they were in all elements, let's say a fortieth birthday party on a beach in Bali—"

"Theoretically speaking or planned?"

"Planned, but only in my mind. So, a party in Bali in both worlds. If most of the same elements were in place, that would substantively increase the odds of the universes bumping."

"As in actually . . ." Ilena brings fist to fist.

"For these purposes, yes. Particles can become entangled, entering a shared quantum state, or, as you say, allow one to 'dip in.' The more alike things are, the more probability of a collision.

It would ignite an active coherence link, and realities would cross. For how long, I can't say."

Puzzle pieces drop into place. The two outings happened on the same day in the same place with most of the same people, even some in practically the same clothes like Mallory and her jumpsuit. They were both held one week before AIM was to go public. And in each one, she, Mallory, and Aubrey agreed to return to the same spot to usher in good luck—in two days' time. Which means . . . maybe . . .

"I should go." She hoists herself up, doing a Kegel to curb the urgency of her bladder.

"Of course." He sounds disappointed. "And it's a wonder he's still single." He gives a self-deprecating laugh.

She smiles politely, though it makes her heart sink a little.

"I hope I answered your question?" he says.

"Yes, you did. You're an excellent professor."

"I was going to be a doctor. But they don't really wear cardigans."

"Which you pull off quite well." Heat rises in her cheeks. "But you would have pulled that off too, being a doctor."

"You think?"

"If only you could see your other-world self."

He smiles and winds around his desk. He holds out a hand to escort her from the office, but part of her doesn't want to leave. "Ilena, can I say something? Aside from it being strange and bizarre and delightful to see you again."

"Same," she says, all that double for her.

"You're asking about choice for AIM, so I have to assume you're looking for an angle related to your app's focus on a fulfilling life."

"And happiness," she says. "The pursuit of it, at least."

"That brings me to my point." He lifts an eyebrow. "Did I

mention my lectures always run long?" She smiles gently, and he continues. "Because happiness is—"

"Don't tell me, a journey."

"Perhaps, for some. But I have to say I'm not that 'woo-woo.' Professional hazard."

"Me neither, despite my profession."

"Then speaking for me and not for the world of physics, I believe happiness stems directly from choice."

Felix had said something similar, about happiness being something you can choose.

"And yet," Jonah continues, "I'm not sure it's about choice the way most people think."

"And what way is that?" Ilena asks.

"That a single choice is the difference between being happy and not. That would mean in one reality you are happy and in the other you aren't. Physics isn't that simple and neither are we."

"Perhaps it'd be better if we were." It was when Ilena's actions strayed from her belief in a right choice and a wrong choice that things began to unravel.

"I'm not convinced. I see it every day in my students who come here hoping the choice of MIT will cause everything else to fall into place. They agonize over internships and job offers and grad schools as if their life literally depends on it. Yet we all do it. We put an extraordinary amount of pressure on our choices. This profession, this apartment, this lover, this Target throw pillow, if we choose the right one, it's all smooth sailing. That's not logical. The lectures you love to give come with the papers you hate to grade. Hypothetically." He smirks. "The apartment with all that light means you pay a small fortune for blackout shades. Again, hypothetically. The partner you go to bed with is the same one who flosses their teeth in front of the open fridge door. Unfortunately, not hypothetically. That relationship didn't last."

Ilena's hit with a little bit of satisfaction. "I'm not sure I'm following."

"Not unusual. Again, just ask my students." He grins, and she didn't realize how much she missed it, the slow parting of his lips, like he's building anticipation for the full reveal.

"Trade-offs, then," she says, "that's what you're saying?"

His finger goes to work on that dangling button. "Sort of. But perhaps being happy is all about choosing—and this is a technical term—the crap you're willing to deal with."

Into her head comes a blur of mice-infested studios, overdrawn bank accounts, investor rejections, the computer glitch, doctors and waiting rooms and shots and fights and . . . She presses her hand to her stomach.

This Ilena and this Felix chose this. They get a baby, a family, a friendship, more than what a lot of people have. But they're giving up something consequential and extraordinary. Though, to be fair, maybe there's something easier about loving someone but not being in love.

She looks at this Jonah with less gray hair in a beige cardigan in a life she can't recognize, in a life she doesn't share. Any hint of desire is gone. She doesn't want *this* Jonah.

She thanks him, puts her number in his phone and his in hers, and says yes to staying in touch. As she leaves, she says, "I hope Bali happens."

He crosses his fingers, and she turns, walks down the hall. Straight into the restroom where she lets in the pain of all she is giving up.

This baby, this baby, this baby, this baby that is not hers, but my god, *is* hers. Could be hers. She falls back against the bathroom stall, squeezing her vaginal muscles, clamping her hands around her balloon of a belly, pressing, pushing, begging, because if Ilena sees her, sees this child, holds this child, it *will* be hers.

But nothing comes.

Ilena strokes her belly. And straightens her spine. Knowing she will never fully forgive herself. But knowing exactly what she has to do. And then she steps out into the MIT quad alone.

44
ILENA

Harvard University
*Twenty-One Years **Before** the Outing*

Ilena stepped into Harvard Yard alone. Her mom had dropped her off at the gate right on Mass. Ave. Her sister hadn't come along for the ride. Lexington was only forty minutes away. It wasn't like she couldn't see them again. Besides, she knew exactly where she needed to go.

She rolled her suitcase into Straus, breathing in the smell of cleaning products and the must and mildew they didn't quite cover. The building was named after the co-owner of Macy's in New York and his wife, both of whom died in the sinking of the *Titanic.* Quite the prophecy that Harvard laid out for the class of incoming freshmen.

Ilena checked her assignment. First floor, roommate, Mallory Latham. Ilena breathed, practiced a "Hey, Mallory" under her breath. The way her hands were shaking came as a surprise. It wasn't like she didn't have friends in high school, but that's what they were. Friends in school, not outside of it. SAT prep, a full slate of AP classes, debate team, and her internship at the top PR firm in Boston didn't leave time for much else. And though

Ilena was never good enough for her mother, her mother also thought that no one was ever good enough for Ilena. Her mother's judgment laced the air in their home, seeped into every throw pillow, lived in the walls like tobacco from a lifetime of chain-smoking.

"*Did you see those tits?*" an excited boy's voice said.

It came from farther down the hall.

"*See it? Felt it. Right here!*" a second male voice shouted before the sound of something large and heavy hitting the floor made Ilena flinch.

She hugged her arm around the white ceramic lamp her mother had allowed her to bring because she *always thought it was a bit too pedestrian anyway* and continued down the hall, arriving at the room that was supposed to be hers. It didn't face the idyllic front of Ivy Yard but instead was on the side that bordered the street. It was louder and less private than Ilena had imagined. And also, full of two boys.

"Uh, you do know that's someone's stuff you just dropped," the first said.

"The faster I drop that someone's stuff the closer I get to *stuffing* that someone—you know, with my dick. Up high! Aw, fuck it, you snooze, you lose, roomie."

A boy in a white T-shirt and baggy shorts raced out of the room, into the hall, flying past Ilena and adding a whiff of sweat and some woody cologne to the already nauseating miasma. A piece of paper, the same size as Ilena's room assignment, fell out of his pocket.

She released her grip on the handle of her suitcase, hating that she wished her mom was here. She pocketed the paper and peered into the dorm room. The remaining boy's back was to her. His hair, a dirty blond, skated down the back of his neck toward the hood of his sweatshirt. He was tall, though Ilena could tell she was still taller, her height the one thing her father gave her that her mother couldn't take away. She was about to clear her throat when she saw him reach into a cardboard box at his feet.

Stealing? He was stealing? She should do something or tell someone, shouldn't she? Or maybe not. Maybe this wasn't her room after all. Maybe there had been some mix-up with the room assignments. She reached into her pocket for the paper the first boy had dropped, when the one inside the dorm room arched his back. Pressed to his face was something lavender. A cloth. No, panties.

He turned. His face was still covered. But his eyes shone with shock and fear. When Ilena remained mute, he began to relax. "You're even hotter than she is." Then he shoved one of his hands down his pants.

Ilena fled. She clutched her pedestrian lamp and grabbed her rolling suitcase and ran down the hall and through the yard and onto the street as if her mother would still be there. This wasn't right. This wasn't supposed to happen. Not here, not at Harvard, the school her mother had made known for the past five years was the only one Ilena could attend to gain her mother's respect—gain, not keep. Hot tears pooled in Ilena's eyes as she gathered both the nerve to report the boy and the words to explain what he did to the roommate she hadn't even met.

Cars honked as an SUV too big for these small, windy Cambridge streets failed at trying to parallel park, and Ilena realized she was standing opposite Straus. She ambled along the wrought-iron fence until she found the window of what she now knew was her first-floor dorm room. The glass was raised, the shade lowered only halfway.

The boy faced her, hoodie drawn low, as he masturbated into that pair of purple underwear. Too arrogant or too oblivious to care that his pumping arm was perfectly visible from the street.

"I'll need those back when you're finished," she heard a distant female voice say.

The boy's arm stopped pumping. His eyes widened, and this time, when he saw Ilena right before he turned around, he didn't smile.

The girl inside Straus, a blur of light brown hair and black shirt, flopped onto the bed with her back to the window. "You can go now," she said, flatly, as if bored.

"I wasn't . . . you can't tell—" the boy stammered.

"You were, and I can anytime it suits me. Oh, and thanks for carrying my stuff from the T station. I just did my nails so . . ."

Ilena hears a zipper and watches as the boy flings the underwear to the ground.

"Crazy bitch," he said.

"Now, now, no snap judgments. You don't know me well enough to ascertain that." She held out her hand to assess her fingernails. "This is going to be a spectacular year. I can just feel it, can't you?"

The boy kept his hoodie low, but his hands tightened into fists. Ilena drew in a sharp breath. *He's going to hit her.*

"Uh, I'd be careful, if I were you," the girl said, jutting her chin toward the doorway where a small group of bodies had clustered.

The boy seemed to take in the gathering crowd before storming out of the room. And then, before this audience of brand-new Harvard freshmen, the girl picked up the underwear with a tissue. "Dammit. My favorite pair. Anyone have quarters for the laundry?"

The titters of nervous laughter couldn't stop Ilena's heart from pounding. This girl—Ilena's new roommate, Mallory—appeared unfazed. Inside, she might have been raging or fighting tears or both, but outside, she was calm.

Admiration twinged with sadness for Mallory wound through

Ilena as she started for the entrance to the building. Then she remembered the boy's room assignment. She dug the piece of paper out of her pocket. Harvard's practice was to list the history of everyone who'd lived in the room before you. As Ilena read the list and compared the location of the room these two boys were assigned to against her own, heat rose in her chest. And then a prank she and her dad had pulled using Ilena's little sister came into her head.

Holding her lamp and the handle of her suitcase, Ilena headed for the hardware store.

45

MALLORY

Tuesday Morning
*Five Days **After** the Outing*

As the first pellets rattle against the bowl bearing his name, Harley scampers toward Mallory, the routine already ingrained. She bought the dry food at the store in Harvard Square. She couldn't stomach the raw chicken nuggets. (Not to mention opening a freezer.) The way Harley rears up on his hind legs in greedy anticipation seems a sure sign that he doesn't miss them.

Not in the way he appears to miss Grayson. The swivel of his head at the jangle of keys, the slight whimper at a deep male voice, the energy that never seems to completely settle down even when she lets him curl up against her, which she's done more and more each night as she wills herself to fall asleep. To shut all of this out.

She ran from the police. And her father made it okay. Well, not okay, but he bought her time. Grief, he'd said, at his slip of Grayson being dead. He used the thing she's feeling, the thing she wouldn't label herself, to reschedule the police interview for Friday, for the day after AIM goes public—a scheduling courtesy often doled out to the wealthy and connected, the latter of which Mallory has thanks to her dad. From what she's seen, he'd do anything for her—even go on the run with her. She's not even sure Ilena would do that.

For now, all she can do is wait. She's living in limbo. She's never lived in limbo, not once in the life she can remember, but she's out of ideas and exhausted.

Mallory ups the volume on the TV as a solemn Shandy Shane in a short-sleeved black sweater and black pants addresses the camera with the gleam of having an exclusive in her eye.

"This morning, I greet you with some grave news." Shandy brings a hand to her throat. She pats, twice, before, slowly, refocusing on the camera. *"Apologies. But it is a shock, still, as I am sure it will be to you at home. Grayson Fields, the devilishly handsome, brilliant entrepreneur with the start-up Midas touch, was to sit here, right beside me—"* she glances to her right, swallowing audibly *"—in a mere two days. After his beloved AIM went public. I am sorry to say we will not get to meet Grayson Fields because Grayson Fields . . . is dead."*

A photograph of Grayson in a black tux. His smile radiates through the screen, and Mallory goes numb.

"You heard that right. But, and this is the kick in your hot pants, folks. We have learned that a police investigation is underway. Lips are tight regarding any foul play or suspects, but we know one place that police are taking aim."

Air quotes. She actually uses air quotes with "aim."

A still of Mallory outside her office yesterday takes over the screen. She looks terrified. She looks guilty.

"Deemed an informational interview, officially, caught on film only by The Shandy Shane Show.*"*

The image widens to include Aubrey and Ella and Noreen with Mallory's dad, Officer Middlebury, and the younger male officer in the background.

"I'm sure we're all wondering how this bombshell will affect the multibillion-dollar valuation of the Wall Street darling AIM. Which

up until now has managed to elude the scandals and greed turning tech into blech."

Another photograph appears. Mallory in that grape jumpsuit, arms around a very alive Grayson. At the bottom of the photo is a tag from a social media influencer. In the background is a path of crushed oyster shells and a giant Jenga. The summer outing, so similar to the one in her world. Except here, the embrace she and Grayson are in appears warm, loving even, with none of the animosity burning in her gut.

"Whatever happens you can be sure that today, at AIM, no one is smiling, wide or otherwise."

Mallory shuts off the TV, leaving the only sound the scraping of Harley's snout against his dish as he searches for crumbs—a sound she no longer minds. She's not going to work today, marking the first day she's not gone into AIM in three years. No vacations, no sick days, no mental health days to frolic in the ocean that's frigid even in August. Her mental health has always been maintained perfectly fine by going to work.

Her phone rings, lighting up with a photograph of her father. She has his chin. If she'd never been brought here, she'd have never known. Maybe he's calling because he saw the news story or maybe he's calling to warn her of an impending arrest. Mallory declines the call.

She falls into the couch, not modern and firm like the one the exorbitant designer she'd hired had picked out, but soft and lumpy and teal and furry like a goddamn Muppet with too many pillows. Mallory can't get comfortable in it. She can't get comfortable here. She has a childhood home not bordering the subway, a papa bear blind to her faults, a company seemingly honestly valued at more than two billion dollars with nary a glitch in sight, a best friend pregnant with the child she's long wanted, another not bereft from her fiancé's death. This Mallory's life is better. (Save for the whole possibly being a murderer thing.)

She doesn't care. She wants *her* life. And not because of the whole possibly being a murderer thing. (Well, perhaps not *only* because of the whole possibly being a murderer thing.)

She wants it because she wouldn't be who she is without it. The good (Ilena, Aubrey, AIM), the bad (lying to Ilena, to Aubrey, to everyone about AIM), and everything in between (swearing off lavender panties and then buying nothing but lavender; building a business on four hours of sleep; suffering through disastrous pitch meeting after disastrous pitch meeting until she could nail them on no sleep; innuendos and wads of cash from investors; breaking the glass ceiling with little regard to where the shards fell because they led to a hundred employees and partnerships with the likes of Reese Witherspoon and Michelle Obama; believing she could be something and becoming that something alongside Ilena and Aubrey).

This Mallory might have done some of that, maybe all of it, but not the way Mallory did for a million reasons and one—one that Mallory could actually try to understand. She grabs her phone and returns the missed call.

"Oh, MallieMoo," her father says, infusing every syllable with worry. "This is all just . . . why is 'pickle sandwich' the only thing I can think of?"

Because you are the human equivalent of Harley.

He exhales a heavy breath. "I'm sorry. How's that? I'm terribly sorry that all this is happening."

"That makes two of us."

"Listen, we'll sort through it, piece by piece, work it out—"

Could he be any more cliché?

This is on her. Did she honestly think he would have some answer to what the universe has done to her? "Right, sure. Sounds—"

His words drown out hers. "—together. Just like we did when we had to retrace our steps to find the stuffed seal you lost in Disney World, and when we realized listening to audiobooks would help with your dyslexia, and when you thought you'd never get into Harvard because you'd assumed you flubbed the essay on what captivates you when you said 'yourself.'"

She can't help but smile at that last one. This Mallory's wardrobe is still bananas, but maybe the two of them have more in common than she thought. "Those aren't exactly at the same level as this."

"They are to me. Because you were hurting, same as you are now. The hardest thing for a father to do is to see his little girl in pain."

Papa. Bear.

And yet, wouldn't her mom in her world say the same?

"Addendum," he says, "see his little girl in pain and not be able to fix it."

A queasiness flips her stomach. *He can't make this all go away.* Part of her believed—*hoped?*—that he could. That he would.

"You can't, then, fix it?" she says, almost in a whisper.

"Not something this big, baby girl."

"But you would, if you could?"

"I'd want to. Course, then I'd have your mom screaming in my ear that even if I could, I shouldn't. Because we raised you right."

Does that imply her mom didn't?

He adds, "We raised you to be able to handle whatever life throws at you."

So that's actually a "no" to going on the run with her.

Mallory blurts out, "Like you did? With Mom?"

"That's private, Mallory, but yes. We all screw up. We all have to make amends. You know I have."

But I don't.

"Listen, MallieMoo, life's complicated. Like this situation you're in. But you know the way out, don't you?"

Not really.

He continues, "It's what your mom did, even if it took her a bit to get there."

She draws in a breath and waits for him to finish.

"Tell the truth."

The bluntness of his words hits like whiplash. Maybe this is his way of hinting that he knows Noreen didn't actually frame anyone. "So spill all?" she says, hunting. "No matter the consequences?"

"As long as you've done all you can to cushion anyone who might get hurt. And you have what you need to deal with those consequences."

"And what's that?"

"Family. Which you have in spades."

A text comes in from Ilena, asking to be let in.

"I do," Mallory says, "we both do."

"Aw, MallieMoo, now you're going to make an old man cry."

She had meant herself and this Mallory. But his interpretation is right too. "Well, just don't go dehydrating yourself because I'm going to need you." She hears him choke back the moisture that must actually be forming, and damned if it doesn't start to incite the same in her. "And . . . Dad? I'm lucky to have you."

She hangs up before he can say anything back. She knows how he feels. But hearing it seems like too much of an invasion of privacy for all of them.

Mallory swallows and heaves herself out of the lumpy couch just as Harley flips his bowl over, scaring himself. She scoops up the trembling dog, opens the door to her condo, and waits just inside as two sets of feet echo up the stairwell. Ilena and her inflated stomach stand in front of a waxen-faced Aubrey.

"We have to go back," Ilena says without any preamble.

Mallory wonders if this is some trick. Ilena wouldn't wear a wire, would she? "So I've been saying."

"So now I'm agreeing."

"Then you've found the portal, time machine, wormhole, universe Uber to take us there?"

"Yes."

Mallory snorts, but Ilena doesn't laugh. "You're serious?" She looks around Ilena to Aubrey. "She's serious?"

"She's Ilena," Aubrey says.

Our Ilena.

Who was going to leave AIM. Without cushioning anyone.

Mallory clutches Harley tighter, her dad's words about consequences echoing in her head. "Everything we left will still be there. All the problems. Everything we did and didn't do . . ." Mallory looks into Ilena's eyes, searching, making sure she truly wants to go back to that world. With Jonah, without this baby, with AIM in peril. If the glitch is exposed, they'll lose everything. *Mallory* will lose everything. She'll lose the self she became because of AIM. The money and the prestige and the designer clothes and the guest spots on *Top Chef* and the money, the money, did she mention the money? She'd be back where she started, in her small bedroom in her mom's apartment, stripped of the armor that made the no father and no partner and no goddamn furball of a dog okay. Even if the glitch never comes out, she still loses because she'll know that in another world, her company hit the same milestones honestly. A lie—that's the world she's returning to. That's the risk she's taking. But Ilena and Aubrey are taking risks too. They're losing too.

Ilena steps into Mallory's condo. "We get a second chance, not at all of it, but maybe enough of it. I'm not turning that down."

Aubrey gives a hesitant nod as she follows Ilena into the living room.

And Mallory lets her fingers massage Harley's stomach, exhaling all that's weighing her down. Who's framing who for murder, Mack Weldon, Officer Middlebury's sunglasses, her parents' sexagenarian foreplay, Grayson. If she gets home, it will all be someone else's problem.

You can't expect to keep lying without consequences.

In Mallory's arms, Harley releases a barely perceptible whine, and unexpected tears spark in her eyes. Ilena's words aren't the same as her father's, but the combination along with this ridiculous stuffie of a dog finally make them ring true.

She tucks her chin to the furry orange head. "I'll fix it," she whispers. "I'll set things right. And I'm sorry." He lets out one more whimper, and her heart breaks just a little. (Actually, a lot.)

46
AUBREY

Wednesday Morning
*Six Days **After** the Outing*

They're going back. Back to a world with no Ethan and with a Kai who doesn't hate her and to an Aubrey who hasn't done all of this—lied and cheated and made a mockery of this other-world Aubrey's life. She needs to let this Aubrey return to her yoga and succulents and the small apartment with the pink chair and the cloud of a blanket and the perfectly organized closet that Aubrey hasn't earned.

Aubrey fluffs the pillows on the bed and scans the apartment to make sure she's leaving it as she found it. With no trace of her left behind, just as Mallory said. Aubrey hopes everything's erased—everything she did, gone from this Aubrey's mind. She wants this Aubrey to be able to live her life without the knowledge of what her genetic match is capable of.

Aubrey pauses in front of the Women Who Code poster. Even if this Aubrey doesn't remember, everyone else here will. There will still be consequences. All Aubrey can do is try to lessen them.

She hurries to the closet and pulls out the outfit she labeled for today. Dark-wash skinny jeans and a coral T-shirt. Yesterday, the day the world found out Grayson was dead, the day the news and social media blew up about what that means for AIM's stock price, the day pundits and critics asked if AIM's bubble had finally burst, relegating it to the rest of the troubled tech world, the day that should have seen her, Mallory, and Ilena not collapsing under the pressure and instead putting out a thousand fires to save the company they built over the past eight years, that day—that day instead saw them shopping.

Aubrey runs her hand along the AIM logo freshly embossed on this brand-new coral shirt. It's not the AIM logo of here. It's the AIM logo of home. Aubrey had nearly forgotten they weren't the same.

She slips her feet into a pair of flip-flops, peels off the price tag, and grabs the tote by the door. It's full of all the ingredients for a strawberry mule, a bottle of sparkling wine, and a facial serum made of lactic acid, which supposedly attracts mosquitos. She slides the rock Ilena painted last night into her pocket. A white daisy with "believe" written across it, a duplicate of the one she had at the outing in their world. It settles beside the glass octopus from Kai. Then she says a silent goodbye to this life she shouldn't feel this sad to leave behind.

Aubrey's finger hovers over the buzzer. Just as she presses the button beside "Lauren Stevens," the woman herself appears on the other side of the glass door. Aubrey knows it's her thanks to her pictures on social media, but also, Ethan's at her side. He freezes when he sees her, his lips thinning, his eyes full of anger. Full of threat.

Drops of sweat prickle the space between Aubrey's breasts, and she's sixteen again listening to the tapping of the pool skimmer against the wall of the shed that wasn't really the pool house the boy said it was, having a first time she would forever regret, twenty-four and hiding in the bathroom stall at the start-up program, thirty-one saying yes to marrying a man who made a list of her flaws before proposing. She doesn't want to be any of those Aubreys.

She straightens her spine and steps back as Lauren Stevens exits the apartment building. "I'm sorry," Aubrey says.

Lauren smiles bemusedly. She's lovely, and Aubrey's going to break her heart.

"We can go around," Ethan says, a hand on Lauren's back, the other balled into a fist at his side.

"I wasn't talking to you, Ethan," Aubrey snaps.

Lauren's face shifts, instantly wary, and again Aubrey wonders about that déjà vu thing. Somewhere, in some reality, does another Lauren Stevens know what's coming?

"I'm sorry I don't recognize you," Lauren says. "Do you live in the building?"

Aubrey shakes her head.

"But you two know each other?" Lauren's voice lifts a pitch. "From work or—"

"Socially," Aubrey says. The way Lauren leans into Ethan, Aubrey almost feels bad. Her words will change Lauren's life. Even though Aubrey thinks she should say them, she won't be here to deal with the consequences. The sense of female loyalty she feels toward Lauren won't make up for that. And maybe this isn't really her choice to make. It's Ethan's. And yet, he's been lying to them both—and maybe they aren't the only ones.

Aubrey pulls the "You are somebody's reason to smile" rock out of her pocket and pushes it into Ethan's hand.

Lauren looks at her with a puzzled expression. "What's that?"

"Just something I needed to return," Aubrey says.

Lauren swivels toward her fiancé. "Return? Ethan?"

"It's nothing," he says, barely covering his growl.

This is as much as Aubrey can do. Once she's gone, the other

Aubrey might not have any memory of all this. How far Lauren pushes Ethan for an answer will be up to her.

Aubrey lets her gaze settle on Ethan, with any luck, for the last time in any reality.

She has one more thing to do. For this Aubrey, yes, but even more, for herself.

She's waiting outside the deli, two iced rooibos lattes dripping condensation onto the bistro table. He pauses when he sees her, lets his hand slip from the door handle. A woman approaches, and he reclaims the handle, opening the door for her, causing his T-shirt to rise, the indentation above his hip to be exposed. Aubrey feels a twinge of desire.

He approaches, and Aubrey holds out one of the drinks. He doesn't take it from her.

"Why am I here?" Kai says. "Can't you fire me at the office?"

"You're not being fired."

"Don't worry, I won't sue you or anything."

Aubrey puts down the tea. "You shouldn't joke about that. It's not funny. It wasn't right, me sleeping with you, and it's not something we should gloss over. We should talk about it."

"It's cool, I told you it's cool. Maybe you think because I'm such a child, you need to keep repeating it for me to get it?"

Disappointment gives way to frustration. "Yeah, so how's that shoulder?"

His brow furrows. "My what? Shoulder, what do you—"

"From the chip. It's heavy, right?"

"That's not fair. You said I was young yourself."

"I did, because I couldn't say what I really wanted to say." Her fingernail finds her thumb and she scratches the phantom mosquito bite. "You weren't Ethan."

"Uh, yeah, I should go." He starts to turn, and Aubrey wraps a hand around his forearm, his muscles taut beneath her palm.

She says softly, "I was glad that you weren't him, but I felt guilty, and I didn't know how to deal with it all."

"Deal with what?"

"This feeling more real than my real life."

"I don't know what that means." He sighs. "I like you, Aubrey. But you're confusing as hell, and I don't think it's just your bullet-train mind. Something's going on with you. And you either trust me enough to tell me or you don't."

Aubrey stares at him blankly, trying to come up with an Aubreyism to explain all this away. He'd never believe the truth. He waits, longer than most would, before resting his hand on top of hers and slipping his arm free.

Her heart deflates. But she can't force him to stay. "At least take the tea."

This time, he accepts it. "I know this is complicated. I'm not naive. But I also know there's something here." He sips the tea, giving her a last chance that she doesn't take.

He's halfway down the block by the time she whispers, "I know it too. That's what scares me."

Aubrey watches him go, her brain launching into overdrive—succulents and her rock collection, Lauren Stevens and Ethan's dirty mug, that pool shed and the start-up program, and the family she doesn't know here and the family waiting at home, and her grandmother's afghan.

She loved running her fingers along the bumps on the blanket, which had perhaps helped her grandmother understand Aubrey's obsession with coding in a way her parents didn't. Coding wasn't all that different from those knits and purls, each strand of yarn important but unable to do much on its own. But together, loop after loop, knot after knot, row after row, the strands formed something new, something complete, something that couldn't be broken.

She sits at the bistro table and pushes her tea to the side. From the tote bag she grabs a pen and the slip of paper with yesterday's shopping list. On the back, she draws a straight line down the middle. She writes "pro" on one side, "con" on the other. And then she makes her list.

Visually, it's clear. On one side of the column, there's a single entry. But it carries a tremendous amount of weight.

She studies it, willing herself not to make the decision her head knows is right despite it tearing off a chunk of her heart. The familiar ache of grief spreads across her chest as she pulls the glass octopus from Kai out of her pocket. She forgot to give it back, not that she wanted to, but she also couldn't leave it in the apartment. She finishes her tea, tucks the octopus back into her jeans pocket, and heads off to meet her two best friends.

47

ILENA

Wednesday Afternoon
Six Days ***After*** *the Outing*

Ilena accepts the handle of the rolling suitcase and sets it beside the teal sofa that Mallory pretends to hate. The dog that falls into that same category edges forward to sniff the wheels.

"This was very sweet," she says.

Felix remains in the doorway. "You at least need a few things if you're going to be staying with Mallory. No offense to the singleton, but you two are no longer the same size."

She smiles and he smiles. There's an awkwardness between them that highlights they aren't a real couple. She doesn't know how she didn't see it before. She gestures for him to sit and offers him something to drink, but he gratefully declines. She doesn't know if his morning beverage is coffee or tea and how he takes it—or if he takes it at all.

He lowers himself into the armchair across from her. "Awful, truly awful. Grayson Fields. How is Mallory? How are you?"

Leaving, we're leaving, I'm leaving. I'm leaving you. I'm leaving this child. I'm so sorry.

She swallows. "In shock, I guess."

"Of course, of course." He shifts uncomfortably. "I appreciate the closeness of your friendship and you staying here to support her. And I want to support you supporting her."

He's out of sorts in a way she's never seen him.

"Felix, if there's something you want to ask, you can. You should."

His head bobs up and down. "It's just . . . is that the only reason you're staying here? I know you were having second thoughts not too long ago, but I thought we worked through it."

Ilena's not sure why this surprises her so much, that perhaps this arrangement wasn't as perfect as she'd thought. "Things aren't the same. Knowing this is a girl has changed me. It's made me want her to have everything."

"She will. Certainly. It's why we exchanged vows. And as we discussed, the condo doesn't have to be forever. When we get to preschool and elementary—"

Ilena holds up her hand. "I'm sure of all of that." She pauses, because if this isn't her child, then this also isn't really her marriage. She treads lightly. "I don't doubt that you will always put her first. But when we decided to do this, we forgot one thing." Or purposely ignored. Or fooled themselves into thinking didn't matter. The wedding photo should have been a sign. The black suit, the traditional gown, like they were trying to prove something to everyone, including themselves. "This baby needs parents who love her and who love each other. But she also needs parents who are *in* love."

His eyes meet hers. No confusion, just agreement, which makes sense as it was him who'd called what they have a friendship.

"We didn't think so," he says. "Not when we decided this."

"We were wrong."

"Were we?"

Ilena places her hand on his. "I think we both know the

answer to that. We do care about each other. And there's an attraction." She gestures to her stomach. "But maybe we aren't a perfect match. It's statistically probable that we are in some reality, but here . . ."

"Something will always be missing." He closes his eyes, briefly, before centering back on Ilena. He's both disappointed and relieved. "We'll never live this down. Your mother being right."

"My mother?"

"She'll be upset, naturally. The baby being a girl will help. Still, she will never let us forget that she thought we weren't focused on what truly mattered in life when we made this decision."

Her mother touting what? Love? Except not *her* mother. This version of her mother, the one who smiles and believes in love and wants to celebrate her granddaughter even though she lost her husband. Maybe it's the way this version of her mother lost him—to a blocked artery or brain aneurysm or whatever it was that took him. Instead of a decision he made to live another life.

The Rebecca Cohen Ilena grew up with did not turtle after her husband left her. Instead, she fanned like a peacock, inviting everyone to look at her, secretly hoping for a sympathetic head tilt or patronizing "How *are* you?" so she could lash out and cut them off at the knees. She was fine. Her family was fine. But she wasn't. They weren't. The love was gone.

Ilena sees her, sighing over the newspaper at breakfast, sitting in the garden, the steam from an untouched mug of tea swirling into nothingness. Were there openings Ilena missed? Could she have tried harder? Was there something she could have done to help her mother appreciate the family she had instead of being pissed off about the one she didn't? Did the Ilena of this world help her mother heal in a way that she never even thought of doing?

The idea steals Ilena's breath. Some things are genetic and some are learned, and the combination makes Ilena question if she missed openings with Jonah too. If she could have prevented him asking her for a divorce. And her saying yes.

Ilena looks at Felix, tucking the life she could have had with him and this child into a corner of her heart. "We're going to co-parent the crap out of this kid."

He laughs. "That we are."

"It's probably best if I do stay here with Mallory for a while as we navigate through this. But I need to ask you a favor."

He nods.

She presses her palms into her thighs. "Help Mallory with this investigation."

His eyes widen. "Is she a suspect? I know the news is insinuating but—"

"Honestly? I don't know. But, and because we're still married I can say this, she should be. Maybe we all should be."

"All . . ." His throat bulges with a swallow. "Whatever you need. And if it's criminal . . . I can find someone."

"Let's hope we don't need to. But I wanted you to be prepared, just in case."

After more talking and tea—Felix likes green best—Ilena closes the door behind him and sits at the dining room table with a pen and paper and Harley at her feet. Once Ilena returns to the reality that is hers, she won't have any control over what this version of herself does. The only thing she can do is describe what it feels like to be loved.

And suggest she look up that boy she once met at the MIT-Harvard mixer: Jonah.

Ilena sets down her pen. She rolls her suitcase into Mallory's guest bedroom, a bright shade of yellow instead of the cream from home. She heaves the suitcase onto the furry pink poof in the corner and opens it to get her toiletries. Freshening up to do anything, including a collision of parallel universes, is something she learned from her mother. Not the worst thing to pass along, really.

Beneath her toiletry bag, Felix has packed the onesie with the cupcake on it. She picks it up and holds it to her chest. She's saying goodbye to so much here, including the mother who bought her baby this, the mother who pressed on after the death of her husband, who seems to be finding joy in life even when it's hard. A lesson Ilena wouldn't mind learning. And then maybe passing along to her own mother.

She reclines on the bed, nestles her head against the bright floral pillowcase, and makes a call.

"How's my baby girl?" her mother says. "Hmm . . . I guess I need to start saying that in the plural."

"Mom," Ilena says, nearly breathless at how her mother sounds the same and different at the same time.

"What is it? Is something wrong? Is the baby—"

"All's good. I really just wanted to check in with you. To see how you were." Something she needs to start doing a lot more of with her mom in her world.

48
MALLORY

Wednesday Evening
*Six Days **After** the Outing*

Mallory tugs a red starfish out of Harley's mouth. What began as her making sure he wouldn't choke on a piece of plastic turned into a game, but only for him.

"Screw it." She releases the starfish, and the gloating Harley escapes into the sandbox she had delivered that morning. The gastropub's here—different name, same kitschy offerings like bacon-wrapped figs and oysters with freeze-dried watermelon. There's also the dock renting paddleboards and kayaks and a lawn full of Adirondacks. A server who earns the "fuck" vote in any game of FMK carried three white chairs to the sandbox thanks to Mallory's smile. (Actually, her breasts.)

She loops Harley's leash around her ankle and lets the deep chair swaddle her as she holds up her phone and reads over her statement to the police. She drafted it here, wearing the cat-eyed reading glasses she's come to despise slightly less, with a view of the river and a glass of sparkling wine—or two.

Details on waking up with no memory of the night of the

outing, insinuating too much to drink followed by panicking—a shock-induced spiral that led to a string of behaviors she can't fully recall let alone explain. She didn't say the truth: that she consciously used her father to subvert the investigation, a part that swells a lump in her throat.

Across the lawn, Aubrey and Ilena arrive together. Like Mallory, they're wearing clothes similar to what they wore to the outing in their world. They settle into the Adirondack chairs, and Harley wheels around in a circle, trying to decide whose toes to lick first. He gives up and chooses his balls.

Mallory rests her reading glasses on the arm of the chair. "I sure hope we're doing this in our world."

"We promised," Ilena says. She's calm, relaxed even. She did her best to dress the same despite her round stomach. Long-sleeved white shirt and a stretchy navy skort. She even trimmed her hair. She looks very much like the Ilena of home. "We promised Aubrey we'd gather for luck the night before AIM goes public. So, yes, we're there."

Because Mallory and Ilena owe Aubrey. They will forever owe Aubrey.

Aubrey opens the tote bag and pours two glasses of pink liquid from an insulated water bottle. "No doubt about it."

"That's definitive," Ilena says.

"I'm trying it out," Aubrey says. "Plus, I'm still waving that dead fiancé card at home. No one says no to that."

Ilena looks at her. "And you're not here?"

Aubrey shakes her head.

"Seems I have some catching up to do," Ilena says.

Aubrey smiles slightly as she hands Mallory a bottle of sparkling wine.

Ilena lifts her glass, and Aubrey's arm darts out. "It's not a virgin. I'm sorry, I didn't think—"

"It's fine. The doctor even said so. Just a little. Special occasion and all."

"Let's hope so," Mallory says, trailing a finger along the seam of the cheap grape jumpsuit she hopes to never see again. "Special enough that all this disappears." As she says it, Ilena touches her stomach, and Mallory wishes she could take it back. "Oh, Ilena, I'm sorry."

"It's fine." Ilena blinks back tears, and Mallory's heart sinks. "I mean, it's not fine. Of course it's not for a thousand reasons I know and ones that I can't yet fathom." Ilena presses her ballet flats into the grass. "But this baby isn't mine. She belongs to this Ilena and this Felix. It's not my place to stay here."

Aubrey bends to pet Harley. "What makes you so sure?"

"Because I have my own place."

Mallory knows that Ilena can say this with such confidence because her place has been with Jonah since the day they met.

Mallory never thought she needed what Ilena and Jonah had. She had Ilena, and then, Aubrey. More was a distraction. Grayson proves it.

He hurt her, the her who was letting herself feel something for him, something she hadn't let herself feel for anyone. She's not sure if that makes it more or less likely that she could have killed him. But she's choosing to believe the crackers were an accident. And so she's not confessing to murder, but she is taking control, feeling more like herself, and giving this Mallory the best shot she can. She put the top criminal lawyer in the city on retainer that afternoon.

"When were we supposed to get here?" Mallory asks.

Aubrey checks the time. "In about ten minutes."

"Perfect." Mallory holds up her phone. "So there's this. I drafted a statement for the police, telling them everything except I left you two out of it." She's cushioning anyone who might get hurt, for the first time in her life following advice from her dad. "Let that register just in case the versions of you who are left behind retain any memory of all this."

"But, Mallory . . ." Ilena's face pales. "You could go to jail if—"

"If I actually did it? Maybe. And believe me, that's not high on my bucket list. But what you said about lying without consequences—" Harley pops up from the ground and launches himself into her lap. The furball understands English, fluently. "Honestly, it's mostly bullshit. I'm a really good liar. But just in case, the only consequences I actually care about are the ones that hurt the people I love."

Which includes the father she will never get to know here.

"That has never been in doubt," Ilena says.

Aubrey's eyes begin to well.

"None of that." Mallory swats the air in front of Aubrey. "I hired this Mallory a lawyer so expensive I'm positive she can bribe her way to an acquittal."

At that, Aubrey takes a long swig of her drink.

"I'm kidding, of course," Mallory says, hoping she isn't, wondering if she could have paid extra for that. She looks past her friends and out on their uninterrupted view of the river. The path that runs alongside is transitioning from moms and the occasional dad behind a stroller to that irritating class of exercise fanatic who runs back and forth to the office. A dog on a leash barks, and Harley rams his foot into Mallory's crotch. "Oh shit. The dog."

"Noreen." Ilena unlocks her phone. "I'll text her to come just in case. Tie the dog to the chair."

"No," Aubrey says, quietly. "I'll take care of him. Because I think, because I might . . ." She inhales, inflating her chest, stretching her neck, growing taller. "I'll take care of Harley because I'm staying."

Lightning snaps through Mallory's body.

"Staying?" Ilena's brow crinkles. "What does that even mean? You won't return with us?"

Tears overflow Aubrey's eyes, and she wipes at them with the back of her hand. "That burns." She blinks. "The lactic acid."

Immediately, Mallory and Ilena reach for their purses.

"I have a tissue," Mallory says.

"Water bottle, I'm sure I have one," Ilena says. "Just blot some liquid on the tissue and—"

"You two . . ." Aubrey smiles. "At least we really are making this as close to our world as we can." She rubs her palms together in her lap before clutching them between her thighs. "But that's the problem. Our world doesn't feel like mine anymore."

"And this does?" Mallory says curtly. "Have you truly thought this through?"

Aubrey doesn't respond. Conflict has never been in her nature. Mallory needs to appeal to Aubrey without anger or accusation. Aubrey is a coder with an understanding of math and logic. Reason is the way to convince her to come back with them.

Mallory forces an outer calm. "Remember what Ilena said? You might be here with no memory of where you came from. Or perhaps with every memory. I'm not sure what's worse." Mallory pauses to let that sink in. "But let's say you can do this. Let's say you can just decide to stay. And you do. Let's even say your consciousness remains. So what then, you've simply replaced the version of you who was here? How is that okay?"

Ilena leans forward. "Maybe the universe has been showing us that we shouldn't be the ones judging what's okay and not okay."

Twenty-one years of loyalty, huh, Ilena?

"Oh," Mallory says, "is that whose side you're on? The universe's?"

"No, Mallory," Ilena says, "there are no sides, not anymore."

Yes, there is, there's mine.

Which by extension is theirs. Mallory knows what's best for all of them.

Aubrey rubs the back of her hand, then stops. "It's just that *replaced* isn't the right word, at least not in the way you're suggesting. That's too narrow a view of what we now know is possible. See, I've been thinking . . . maybe there are slips all the time—like I had this déjà vu the other day and thought—"

Mallory gives a dismissive wave. "Come on, Aubrey, that's not relevant."

Aubrey's cheeks flush the way they do when she makes an "Aubreyism."

"And that's not fair," she says, not with embarrassment. With hurt. And a little anger. "All I was trying to say is that it's highly improbable that this is the first collision ever and might not even be the first for the three of us. Any one of us could have been in another universe before and not even know it. For a second or for a lifetime. Intentionally and unintentionally. Maybe we slide all the time but can only see how the world we happen to be in at the time is playing out."

"Schrödinger's cat," Mallory says, remembering the research she did. (Reluctantly.) "The role of observation in determining the state."

Ilena nods. "Jonah said something similar about the frequency we're tuned to. And it doesn't contradict what Aubrey's suggesting, that a brief cross could be like déjà vu."

Mallory gets the feeling that Ilena has more experience with this than she's letting on. "Regardless, a brief cross is not what we have. We have time to think things through, to make decisions."

"That according to the multiverse theory causes more splits," Ilena says.

"Which really messes with your head, right?" Aubrey says.

And when did this turn into a Philosophy 101 debate?

"But also," Aubrey continues, "like, I mean, it reinforces that anything's possible, doesn't it? That consciousnesses might not be fixed, even. In this universe, maybe I decide to stay, but in another, I decide to go. And in another it's possible we all stay or maybe you do, Mallory, or Ilena does and one consciousness remains or the other one does or even they merge, and on and on. We have to accept that it's not as simple as one version or the other. This isn't binary. It's not two worlds. It's likely millions or even billions . . . every variation of this plays out, and every version of us lives every possible outcome. There's no 'replacing' because everything happens. We all exist somewhere."

Mallory's head is spinning. Everything Aubrey is saying feels one hundred percent right and wrong at the same time. She manages, "It's still a big risk, Aubrey."

"It is." Aubrey hesitates. "And I never take risks. You always have, Mallory. Maybe it's time for me to know what that's like."

No, no, it's not, Mallory wants to scream. Because Jonah also said that to increase the probability of universes crossing and a coherence link engaging, the circumstances needed to be nearly identical. That means all three of them. Aubrey staying here risks *all of them staying here*. Jail and no Jonah and a dead Grayson and all because of what? Aubrey being too timid to pursue sex with Kai in their world? So selfish, so incredibly, terribly, unceasingly selfish.

Mallory hunches over Harley, the betrayal burning like acid in her throat. Harley wriggles in her lap. She works her fingers into his belly. Aubrey wants to stay. No matter what it means for Mallory. And the pain and fear contained within her every cell her entire life breaks free.

"You're running away," Mallory blurts out. "Whatever multiverse jargon you want to use to justify it, the bottom line is that instead of coming home to your life with your problems, you're staying here where it's easier."

It's so still, you can almost hear the grains of sand in the sandbox shifting.

Finally, Aubrey says, "Easier?" in a tone so wounded that Harley gives a whimper, and Mallory almost wishes Aubrey had shouted instead. "Easier, maybe, if I have none of my own memories, yet that assumes this life is perfect, and I think we all know that no one's life is perfect. But if it works the way I feel in my gut and I'm still me, tell me, what about living in an entirely new world *alone* is easier? Because it's terrifying. Or how about this? What's easy about staying in a world where my flea of a fiancé is alive? The one who conned me into sleeping with him when he's engaged to someone else?"

She grows more animated. "Not only will I have to risk living in the same city and seeing his stupid smug face, but seeing his stupid smug face that hovered above me as I had the best sex of my life? Seeing that face that *is* stupid and smug but that will always remind me of the role I played in his death in our world? Add in seeing his fiancée, who may even come to me with questions I'll have to answer in a way that changes her life? And then there's this: Facing the employee I slept with, who I'm pretty sure hates me but who I'm also pretty sure I'm falling in love with? Which means confronting the notion of an actual relationship, which is nauseating and scary and something I'd actually love to run away from? Let's see, what else? Oh, being a possible accomplice to murder and if not murder at the very least a cover-up and let's not forget lying to the police? I think that's all the opposite of easier?"

Mallory trails her shell-shocked eyes to Ilena, who says, "Aubrey, let's take a breath and—"

"I'm not done," Aubrey says, sitting up straighter. "I haven't gotten to the biggest one. Or ones. The two of you. Because leaving you feels impossible. There is nothing easy about the idea of not being with you—the you I know and love. But it's because I know and love you that I'm worried about these other versions of you. We screwed things up here. No matter how we each want to try to justify it, we've changed their lives—and the lives of Felix and James and Mallory's dad and probably everyone at our company. What if these versions of you don't remember what's happened? What becomes of them without someone to explain it all?"

Ilena places her hands on her belly. "I hadn't thought of it that way."

Wait, what? Is this Ilena giving in? Without even talking to Mallory in private?

Aubrey extends her hands toward the two of them, but her arms aren't long enough to reach. "We play the odds this way. We give all of us the best chance."

Unintentional as it likely is, Mallory feels judged, like hiring a lawyer was the thing that was selfish.

Aubrey draws her shoulder blades together. "No matter what happens, I'm ready to stop looking behind me, at every mistake and every failure, and start looking forward. Making no decision at all is worse than sometimes being wrong. I'm hoping you two can help the me at home learn the same."

Mallory looks at Aubrey, her protégé, her partner, her friend. She looks at the healthy color in her cheeks, the straightness of her back, the unbitten cuticles, the ease with which she's come to carry herself here.

What's wrong with me?

Mallory's selfishness is failing her best friend here, the same way it failed her at home. That night in the bar, she thought Ethan was cheating on Aubrey. And she wasn't going to tell her. She can pretend all she wants that she hadn't made the decision and that his death meant she never had to make the decision. But there was no decision to make. She was going to use the woman in the white coat as leverage over Ethan. No matter the consequences.

Crunch of glass, smell of wine, pooling of blood.

And some secrets aren't just too terrible to tell, they're too terrible to know.

"I'm going to miss you," Mallory simply says.

Aubrey launches herself out of the Adirondack, tears sliding down her cheeks. She circles Mallory's chair and wraps her arms around her neck from behind. She kisses Mallory's cheek and whispers, "I owe you everything, Mallory. I'll make you proud, I promise."

"Aubrey, you already do. You always have." If only the opposite could be true.

The screeching of tires, the shattering of glass, the pounding of her heart, the reaching for Ilena's hand.

Mallory watches as Aubrey kneels in front of Ilena, rubbing her belly, clasping her hand, touching the ends of her shorter hair. Aubrey lifts herself to peck Ilena's cheek, and Mallory lowers her eyes, struggling to hold in the sob building from the depths of a soul she wasn't sure she had. When she looks up, Aubrey's holding some sort of glass figurine in one hand and setting the rock with "believe" written across it on her chair with the other.

"I'll get to take care of you the same way you took care of me," Aubrey says. "And finish what we started by taking AIM public amid a murder investigation. Thanks for that, by the way."

She smiles with such confidence that Mallory almost wants to stay to see the woman she'll become here. Mallory always thought Ilena was her person. And she is, but so is Aubrey.

But then Aubrey's smile fades and hints of her old self slink in. "I do want this, but we are AIM, always. If you truly think this won't work if I'm not sitting beside you, I choose you. Us."

Mallory fights the seizing in her chest. This is the thread she can grab ahold of, the way to force Aubrey to come back. And in some universe, that's exactly what Mallory does. But not in this one.

Here, in this universe, Mallory gives her choice to Aubrey. She puts on her widest smile and makes a decision that goes against her every instinct. "*Nearly* identical. That's what Jonah said. Two-thirds feels 'nearly' to me. Go home, Aubrey. We'll see you in ours."

Against every instinct but one: to stand by her best friend.

Aubrey grabs each of their hands and squeezes one final time. She then scoops up Harley. With a final nod of goodbye, Aubrey chooses her life and walks away.

Mallory reaches for Ilena's hand at the same time as Ilena reaches for Mallory's. They're both shaking and their eyes meet. The impossibility of this working at all collides with the impossibility of this working without Aubrey. What if it doesn't, and this is all they have? Mallory sees everything in an instant: chocolate ice cream all over the face of Ilena's baby girl; an engagement ring gleaming on Aubrey's finger as her hand entwines with Kai's; AIM breaking every Wall Street record; Mallory visiting Grayson's grave. The multiverse theory means they get to live every life, for better or worse. They get to do everything. Here, at least whatever they do, she's certain they'll do it together.

Ilena says, "That was very brave. I'm proud of you. Truly, you really are an exceptional liar."

"Shut up." One hand still holding Ilena's, she looks out at the river and all those people running, ponytails of brown and black and blond and red swaying, backpacks filled with work clothes weighing them down, all aiming for home. Mallory picks up her phone and hits Send on her statement to Officer Middlebury.

"She's going to be okay," Ilena says with the confidence Mallory has known for more than half their lives. "And so will we."

Your neighborhood book club chooses *Anna Karenina* and you profess to love it. Your girlfriends from college call all male authors misogynistic and you agree. The women at your ladies' night out insist tequila doesn't give hangovers and you toss back your third shot and say you read it's because of the low sugar content. Your yoga friends extend Dry January through April and you stock your fridge with drinks made of hemp and adaptogens. Your work friends blame their chronic carpal tunnel on bosses who feign Excel ignorance and colleagues who can't unpack the dishwasher and you pull on your wrist brace and say you'll absolutely refuse to plan the next holiday party. Your mom frowns during your third rescheduled coffee date as you clutch your latte, create a spreadsheet of coworker allergens, and insist you don't mind that it's not in your job description, the company has been good to you. Because you believe that it has. In that moment, at that time, you are sure.

Not because you are a liar, but because you are a chameleon. You slip in and out of versions of yourself, consciously and subconsciously fitting in with friends old and new, colleagues and bosses, partners and siblings. As many versions of yourself as there are seasons of housewives who claim to be real. Though some say there are only three: the one you see yourself as, the one others see you as, and the one you truly are. Maybe it's that last one that all the others are trying to find.

And maybe, finally, I have.

49
AUBREY

Thursday Morning
*Seven Days **After** the Outing*

The Day AIM Should Go Public

Aubrey knows exactly what to do, but she keeps messing up. She keeps scratching at the back of her hand and now she's drawn blood and she doesn't have a Band-Aid and she's wearing this outfit labeled "Special Occasion, Summer" and she doesn't want to get blood on the white-flowered skirt.

She blots the blood with the side of Harley's leash and whispers an apology and a promise to buy him a new one. He lies at her feet in agreement, and she doesn't hesitate, she knocks twice and fast like the beating of her heart.

Dark hair rumpled, bare chest creased from bedsheets, eyes still crusted with sleep, Kai furrows his brow in confusion. He's not the reason she stayed, but she hopes he'll become one of the reasons she's glad she did.

"Aubrey, what time—"

She hands him the succulent with the pink tips. "It's 6:23 a.m. I've always liked numbers. They're concrete. They just make sense to me. There's no need for a pro-con list, no weighing of options. There's a right, and there's a wrong. But deciding which flavor of yogurt to have for breakfast? I give up and make do with the dregs of the latest vendor-sent bribe of a gift basket at work. Jerky, by the way, it's always the jerky."

"Aubrey, I—"

"Life isn't like coding, it's not an algorithm, and I've never known how to deal with that."

His hand rises to smooth his messy hair, and his grandmother's bracelet glides down his arm. "We all make mistakes. And I told you, I'm cool. This wasn't a mistake for me. I understand if it was for you, but—"

"That's the thing. It wasn't. But it also—" She was going to say it wasn't her choice, but that's not really true. Mallory may have made the rules and Aubrey may have followed them, but the choice, the choice of Kai in the game, that was all hers. And it led her here. To this place she decided to stay in, not knowing what would happen. But she's herself, with all her memories of the world she came from, with all the memories of the past week of being here. Nothing before it. It's scary. It's also okay. Especially since, deep down, somehow she is sure that in some other world, the Aubrey of here lives a different path, another version of this life they all share. "I wasn't sure it was something I could trust."

"And, what, you're sure now?"

"It's not that simple." She takes her time. And that's okay. In this place, with Kai, she trusts the way she feels and the way he makes her feel. Like she isn't playing a supporting role in her own life. "I spent my life waiting for everyone else to take the lead. But now here, with this . . . I like you. I'd like to see if there's something here."

At that, Harley pops up and circles three times before settling himself on Kai's foot.

Kai's head tilts down. "Totally cheating. You do realize that?"

"I'm playing the odds."

"Yeah, well, you warned me you were good with numbers."

Kai begins to tug her into his apartment, where she really, really wants to go. She places her palm on his bare chest and nothing has felt so right since the day she forced herself out of that bathroom stall at the start-up program to have lunch with Mallory and Ilena. Which is why she taps his chest and then presses the leash into his hand.

"Let's see how you do with numbers," Aubrey says. "Walk him at nine, noon, and three. Feed him at four. Walk at five."

"But I thought . . ." His brow furrows before he nods in understanding. "The direct listing. You must have a thousand things to do. Let me know if there's anything I can help with."

Ethan never said anything like that. And if he had, it'd have been with the assumption that she needed help, more a statement about what she lacked rather than what he wanted to give.

"Today's going to require some David Copperfield–level magic to make everything happen, but after . . . dinner. Takeout. I don't know what time but—"

"I'll be here."

"Me too." She's so glad she is.

"But, Aubrey, who's David Copperfield?"

Young, so very young, but it'll be fun to teach him things.

Once she's back on the street, she calls Noreen, who answers instantly. "Big day!"

"Very. Because we made a decision." Aubrey's never used the royal "we" before. As she walks to the subway, she explains what she needs Noreen to do.

"I'll see to it faster than small-town gossip," Noreen says.

Aubrey pauses before hanging up. She knows how it feels to be an outsider. "Lunch soon? All of us?"

"Oh, that's . . . nice, just real nice. Thank you, Ms. Miller."

"Aubrey. It's Aubrey, and I'm sorry not to ask sooner. We've been a bit too self-absorbed lately."

"Aren't we all?"

Aubrey lets herself into the condo, holding her breath. Mallory's lying on the sofa. When Aubrey shuts the door, Mallory's eyes flutter open.

"I'm still drunk." She groans. "Am I still drunk?" She sits up, clutches her head, looks down at her jumpsuit. "Oh shit."

Aubrey's chest seizes. It didn't work. This is still her Mallory, her Mallory who hates the color of—

"What is this?" Mallory licks her index finger and rubs the fabric. "Hot sauce? Did we even eat anything last night? Dammit, my favorite jumpsuit too."

Mallory lifts her head, meets Aubrey's eye. "Are you . . . Did you stay here last night?"

"No, I didn't. But Ilena—"

"Here." Ilena pads out of the bedroom in a white faux fur robe that doesn't quite close thanks to her round stomach. "Did my no-booze willpower break? I feel like I did when I shattered my record for most Jell-O shots in one night."

"New Year's Eve, 2005. Epic before epic was a thing." Mallory presses a hand to her temple. "But when did we get home? I don't remember getting home."

Aubrey sits in the armchair across from her. "What do you remember?"

"The last thing?" Mallory contemplates. "A lot's jumbled, but I'm clear on the outing that we just had—"

"A week ago." Aubrey places her phone on the coffee table so she can show them the date.

Mallory's brow furrows as she looks to Ilena, who excitedly totters forward and sinks into the couch beside Mallory. She points to the date on the phone. "Ooh, is this a prank? Did Felix set this up? Like some kind of babymoon bachelorette party."

"Splendid opportunity to message that stripper I accidentally swiped right on," Mallory says.

"Accidentally, my hemorrhoidal ass," Ilena cries. "Bring it, Aubrey!"

Jonah's theory of coherence link gave a hypothetical reason for how the transfer between universes could happen. But he didn't know what it might mean for their consciousnesses, for who would know what, who might remember what. He did say one set of memories might supplant another. That's what it seems has happened, leaving nothing but a blank in this Ilena's and this Mallory's memories. Jonah also seems to be spot-on about the improbability of a "swap." These women didn't "go" into Aubrey's original world—or if Jonah is wrong and they did, they have no memory of it. For them, it's as if the past week didn't exist. Aubrey was right that they'd need her.

She's going to have to tell them everything. "Um, it's none of those things. The outing really was last week."

"Christ cakes, what was in those drinks?" Mallory says. "I haven't been this fuzzy since homecoming freshman year. Weed gummies and blackberry schnapps. Don't, take it from me, and just, don't." She nuzzles Ilena's stomach. "Did you hear that, Singleton? I got your back, kiddo."

Aubrey tries to cover her surprise at Mallory's enthusiasm. Ilena, though, taps her belly and says, "Listen to your aunt. Well, not on everything, but this, yes, listen." She then shoves Mallory off. "Aubrey's just doing a test run for the listing. If I promise not to let Mallory drink so much the night before that, can we skip this?" Ilena reaches for the TV remote. "The humidity, is it going to be like this all day?"

"Ilena, wait—" Aubrey says, but on the screen is Shandy

Shane, the AIM logo hovering next to her head with an *X* through it.

"What the hell?" Mallory says. "Turn it up."

Eyebrows pinched, Shandy Shane begins, *"Frowns all around this morning as the news comes in that Wall Street darling AIM has gotten cold feet. In a move that industry experts call 'unprecedented' and 'alarming,' AIM has canceled its direct listing mere hours before it was to begin. While no official statement has been made by AIM or its founders, it's hard to imagine this last-minute decision and the shocking news of the death of one of the company's largest investors are unrelated. For more on—"*

"Investor? Who?" Mallory leaps off the sofa, jarring Ilena. "My phone, where's my phone? I'm always losing that damn thing. This has to be a mistake, all of it. Or a PR stunt? Ooh, that company we hired must be building buzz. Especially because today isn't the day of the listing, it's only . . ." Her eyes fall on the date on the television screen. "That's not . . . Aubrey, you aren't doing a test run?"

Ilena's glowing cheeks dull. "I should call Felix. He must be able to explain . . . Is that my suitcase?" As she turns, her hand reflexively goes to push hair off her shoulder but meets only with air. "Did someone cut my hair?"

"We're all looking for answers," Shandy Shane continues as a photograph of Mallory and Grayson appears on the screen. *"But they won't come from CEO Mallory Latham. The live interview with Ms. Latham and Mr. Fields that was to air tomorrow has been canceled."* Shandy's face turns grim. She presses a finger to her earpiece. *"But what's this?"* She pauses, listening, or pretending to listen. What she's about to say reached the morning show before the program began. Noreen assured Aubrey it would. *"In an unexpected turn, the behind-the-scenes cofounder we see so little of, Aubrey Miller, will be joining us next week. So the plot thickens,*

AIMers, and you can be sure of one thing. You'll see it unravel here first. In other news—"

Aubrey shuts off the television.

"Aubrey, *The Shandy Shane Show*?" Mallory circles the coffee table. "You're going to be on it? *I* was supposed to be on it? With Grayson? I'd need an outfit. Did I have an outfit? Hot damn, the PR team nailed it! Ella was right to have us hire them. But they canceled? I don't understand. Ilena?"

Her palm bounces against the short ends of her hair. "I'm . . . confused."

Aubrey lifts herself out of the armchair to stand beside Mallory. "This isn't the way I wanted you to find out, but it might actually make this easier." She looks at Mallory and then Ilena. "Let me just confirm, the last thing you both clearly remember is the outing?"

Mallory nods, as does Ilena, who says, "Aubrey, what does that have to do with all this?"

"Everything." A ding comes from Aubrey's phone. A text from Ethan.

Mallory slips on her reading glasses and reaches for the phone. "Ethan Sonders?"

Aubrey's cheeks grow hot. "It's nothing. It has nothing to do with this. Let's just focus on—"

Mallory bites her bottom lip. "Ethan Sonders. Why does that name sound familiar?"

Aubrey tries to reclaim her phone. "We went on a date, a few months ago."

"The tech guy?" Ilena struggles to push herself out of the soft couch. "The one you met when you bumped into him outside our office? Wait, are you dating again?" As Aubrey's hand wraps around the phone, Ilena grabs her wrist. "Aubrey! Is this a tattoo? Why didn't we all go? Get matching ones?"

Aubrey's phone dings with another text. This one from Noreen. She quickly swipes.

> **Noreen:** The police called me in for questioning. I'm worried I may need a lawyer. Mallory's going to need one too. And still all I can think is poor Grayson. Oh, and y'all need anything? I've got my mom's muesli muffin recipe memorized!

"Aubrey . . ." Mallory says slowly, apparently having read over Aubrey's shoulder.

"It's going to be all right," Aubrey says. One hand takes Mallory's, and the other intertwines with Ilena's as she leads them back to the couch. "I think you should both sit down."

And—as if Aubrey being in charge isn't unusual—they do.

50

ILENA

Thursday Morning
Seven Days ***After*** *the Outing*

The Day AIM Actually Goes Public

Ilena wakes to total darkness. She fumbles to free herself from the silk eye mask, but it's still too dim to make out anything but the barest of outlines. A frame on the opposite wall hanging above something long and squat . . . a driftwood chest. *Her driftwood chest.* She casts off the duvet and rushes to the window, yanking the cord on the blackout shade so hard it snaps.

White flowers burst forth amid lush green leaves on the ring of hydrangeas encircling the manicured lawn of the small backyard she never quite used enough. She presses a palm to the glass, her opal ring tapping against it, and breathes.

She leans against the window, her body taking longer than she expects to meet the sill. This body—her body—is as foreign as it is familiar. She wraps her arms around her midsection, telling herself that you can't lose something you never actually had. Unlike Mallory, she's never been a very good liar.

She stays there, accepting the sorrow she knew would come. As the pink of the sky gives way to blue, she turns to check the time on the compass rose clock. Not even 6 a.m., but Jonah's side of the bed remains smooth, not a corner of the white bamboo sheet out of place. She clicks on the lamp. It's the only object on a nightstand usually crowded with medical journals and chargers and his stack of sci-fi TBRs. She nears the driftwood chest and opens it. His sweaters remain, but his running clothes and polo shirts are gone. He's not just on call for the night. He's living somewhere else.

For how long? Since when? She has no memory of what's transpired in the time she's been gone. Maybe she and Jonah discussed his moving out at length. Maybe they didn't discuss it at all. Or maybe he just told her and she just said "fine" like with the divorce. As she circles the bed, she passes the clothes she wore to the outing here. She must have worn them last night, just as they'd planned. Unless the outing *was* last night.

She lunges for her phone, housed in its usual crisp, clear case. The same amount of time has passed. Part of her was wishing it hadn't, as if that would confirm it all having been a dream and not something she can never really explain. She starts a text to Mallory, debating what to say. Something that won't make her seem unhinged if this was all a delusion, something that'll tell her if she's the only one who remembers the other reality or the only one who made it back.

Ilena: I'm not pregnant.

Three little dots appear.

Mallory: Thank god.

Mallory: But I'm sorry. It looked good on you.

Ilena: So that happened then.

Mallory: Christ, this is wild. How are you?

Ilena's eyes sweep over the linen-tufted headboard and the blue porcelain lamps that she and Jonah picked out after having lunch on Newbury Street. The bottle of wine they split meant they spent more on the lamps than they would have otherwise. More than they should have. But they've never regretted it. It was the first thing they bought for the house.

Ilena: It's difficult. But—

She was going to say *right*. But she's not sure if it is. A feeling she's going to have to learn to live with.

Ilena: At least we're here together.

Mallory sends an uncharacteristic string of hearts that Ilena is sure is a direct result of Harley's influence.

Ilena: I'll check on Aubrey.

She sends the same text to Aubrey, whose response brings both relief and sadness.

Aubrey: Oh, oh, I didn't know you thought you were! To find out the same day as we go public and with Jonah moving out. I'm so sorry, Ilena. If you need to skip the bell ringing at the office, M and I will cover. Xoxo

So that's it: This Aubrey won't share the same memories of the past week. She won't have slept with Kai or learned that Ethan was an ass. She won't understand the loss Ilena's feeling and the relief that Mallory is. But she knows about Jonah and the apparent separation. Though she has no memory of doing it, Ilena is glad that sometime in the past week, she must have told her friends. And Aubrey remembering means she was here—somehow she was here. They all must have been. It strikes her that they could write a damn good academic paper on the many-worlds theory.

Ilena assures Aubrey that she'll be at AIM and returns to her text chain with Mallory, filling her in on Aubrey's memories as well as the celebration at nine thirty, when trading begins on Wall Street. When AIM goes public.

Public, AIM's going public. Problems and all. And not insubstantial ones. But for the first time in a long time, Ilena's excited to fix them—provided the same thing hasn't happened here. That thing being Grayson. He may be an arrogant manipulator, but that doesn't mean he should die by nut cracker.

Ilena: Grayson. Do you know if he's…

Mallory: Slithering around like the snake he is? Yes, and apparently I've taken a passive-aggressive approach. Since the outing, it appears we've been communicating solely through Noreen and Patrick.

Ilena: I'll take passive-aggressive. Better than the alternative.

Mallory gives a thumbs-up. Followed with a Do you think she's okay?

Ilena: Aubrey?

Mallory: Our Aubrey—both of our Aubreys. And us.

Ilena: Absolutely. No doubt whatsoever.

Mallory: You're a good liar too. See you at AIM. One tiny benefit of not being pregnant... 🍾🍊

Into Ilena's head comes the mimosas they faked at Grayson's apartment. They have ruined the drink for her for a lifetime.

Mallory: On second thought, NO.

She sends a peach and a bell, and Ilena understands. Peach Bellini. That's what it means to know someone for twenty-one years. The same amount of time she's known Jonah. She turns off the lamp and grabs her purse. Then she trails a finger along the Coventry Gray wall that's as perfect as she remembered.

She picks up cupcakes on the way, from the same bakery her father would frequent, the bakery whose box she was carrying the day Jonah held the subway for her. Still in business after all these years. Proof that good things can last.

A note in her phone lets her know that Jonah had checked in to the B&B four blocks from the apartment in Cambridge where they lived for most of their married life. They had snuck in once on their way home from work, back when they used to time their schedules to come home together. Through the B&B window, they saw the flickering flames in the fireplace, the table of charcuterie, the bottles of wine, and the cans of local beer. Jonah had grabbed her arm and whisked her inside before she knew what was happening. He'd started talking loudly about being famished from following the Free Trail all day. The clerk behind the desk with long, dark hair and a streak of white like a skunk's running down one side politely corrected him with "Freedom Trail" and suggested he relax in front of the fire and enjoy the guests-only happy hour.

That Jonah is staying here fills her with hope. He's not here for the B&B. Jonah is viscerally repelled by grandmotherly vibes of frill and flowers. Which means he's here because it reminds him of that night. Of who they used to be.

"May I help you?" a voice says.

Ilena turns to see the same clerk from all those years ago, her hair no longer streaked but fully white. If Ilena believed in signs, this would be one. And why shouldn't she believe in signs after what she's just experienced?

Ilena greets the clerk and explains she's looking for a guest, her husband, and the woman cocks her head.

"That's it!" the clerk says. "That's why he looked so familiar. He was with you, and you—I hope it's not inappropriate to say—cannot be forgotten."

Ilena smiles politely as the clerk points to a bulletin board behind her. Thumbtacked to it are photographs beneath a handwritten note that says, "Crashers."

Ilena grips the cupcake box as a baby-faced version of herself and Jonah stare back at her. "That's been hanging here all this time?"

"You two gave us the idea," the woman says.

"I'm sorry. We were young, and, well, we did know better." She sets the box on the counter and reaches for her purse. "Let me make it right. We had two glasses each and—"

"A loaf of bread and a pound of that cheddar."

A voice she would recognize in any universe.

"Gouda, I think," Ilena says over the frenetic beating of her heart.

The clerk nods. "Women always remember better. It was definitely Gouda. Back then I took home the leftovers, and I hate cheddar. No more leftovers now. Lactose intolerant."

Ilena again forces a smile before she returns to rummaging in her purse for her wallet.

Jonah steps toward her. "I've got this. It was my idea." He faces the clerk. "Are we adjusting for inflation? Interest added?"

The clerk's cheeks flush as Jonah smiles at her. Ilena knows the feeling.

The clerk gestures to the cupcakes. "How about you leave those, and we'll call it even?"

"Hard bargain. Counteroffer: I keep the chocolate–peanut butter, and you've got a deal."

The clerk lifts her chin. "And how do you know there's a chocolate–peanut butter?"

"Because I know my wife as well as she knows me." From a shopping bag in his hand, he pulls out a smaller pink box. "We both hate sleeping alone."

Ilena's heart tumbles over itself.

He opens his cupcake box. "Congratulations on the listing, and I'm an asshat."

The ache in her chest morphs into laughter. Across each of the six chocolate–peanut butter cupcakes is written one letter, the sum total equaling "asshat."

"You're not an asshat," she says.

"Jerk?"

"Pea brain?"

"Clod?"

The clerk interjects, "Partial to 'chowderhead,' myself. Keep it local."

Ilena leaves her box with the clerk and takes Jonah's, carrying it into the small sitting room where they ate all that Gouda. Jonah follows, a hand pushing back the abundance of gray hairs absent from their photograph on the bulletin board. She places the cupcakes on the coffee table and sits on the settee that is even harder than its stark frame makes it look. He takes the chair across from it.

"It feels so long ago," she says.

"And not."

"And not," she says. "Would you do it again?"

"Considering what they charge for a single night, we should have crashed happy hour every week."

"That's not what I meant."

"I know." His smile is sad and pained, which is both so much worse and so much better than the expression he's worn around her lately. That expression has just been blank. Feeling something means they each still care. "I'd do it again. With better choices, though, so we never end up here."

Ilena shakes her head. She believed that was possible once. Not anymore. "But you couldn't know. Hindsight is the only way a choice becomes right or wrong. All we can do is recognize it and adjust. I'm starting to think life is one big pivot."

He grins, at her, and it feels glorious. "Since when do you speak like a desk calendar?"

"Since I realized what life would be like without you."

"And how is life without me?"

"No one steals the covers."

"I don't—"

"And no one complains that they don't steal the covers. But also, there's no one to share the covers with."

"You could find someone else. Someone who wouldn't mind that you accuse them of stealing the covers."

"I could, but then that someone would probably floss in front of an open fridge door."

"Revolting."

"Right?" This is how it felt on the subway when she was eighteen. "And besides, I don't want someone, I want you."

His breath is heavy, laden with all they've been through and all they'll have to go through. "I want you too. It's why I was bringing these cupcakes to celebrate with you at AIM. But our problems, they don't magically go away."

Ilena never thought problems would magically disappear. But the woman she was before all of this would have insisted that if she only tried harder, did everything perfectly, she had the power to eliminate them. Happiness might not be the journey, but it's also not something static, that once achieved means everything falls into place.

"No, they don't," Ilena says. "But these are the problems I'm choosing to work on. Because the trade-off is so very worth it."

The lines around his eyes crinkle. He looks at her as if seeing her for the first time but also seeing every version of who she has been and will ever be. The heat of embarrassment sneaks into her cheeks in a way it hasn't since before they were married.

"Let's go to Plum Island," he says.

"It's horsefly season."

"Then let's embrace those little demons and let's talk. I want to talk."

"Me too." She picks up the box of cupcakes. "But first . . . how late is checkout?"

As she follows him up the creaky staircase with the butterfly wallpaper, she pulls her phone from her purse. She can't miss the opening bell at AIM. Just enough time. She lets her phone fall back into her bag, where it clanks against something hard. She pauses, puts her hand inside, and feels around. *Impossible.* There's no part of coherence link that explains this. This is . . . something else. Still, she knows it, somewhere deep inside, before she sees it. The diamond-encrusted emerald ring that Ilena wore in another reality, that Mallory swears she saw Ilena wearing here, the night they watched Ethan die.

51
MALLORY

Thursday Morning
Seven Days ***After*** *the Outing*

The Day AIM Actually Goes Public

Grayson steps into Mallory's office, and reflexively her arms entwine around him. Her chest aches with guilt and her head with relief and other parts with desire.

"A week of silent treatment and now this?" Grayson pulls back from her to close the door. "I realize we have much to discuss, but first things first. These glass walls of your office have blinds, correct?"

The life in his limbs, the animation in his eyes, the puckering of his lips are all in such contrast to the Grayson she left behind that when he touches her again, she recoils.

"All right, then," he says with a resigned sigh. "No sex in the office rule stands."

Her head's thumping and she curses the fact that hangovers can apparently cross universes.

"Mallory?" Grayson says with concern, with none of the arrogance or harshness of his words on the day of the outing. He shakes his head. "Still? Not ready to have a mature conversation about this?"

Right leg bent at an unnatural angle, body still, eyes open, opaque and not moving.

"Mallory?" he says.

Crunch of glass, smell of wine, pooling of blood.

Her heart thrums as she tries to reconcile the images of the only two dead bodies she's ever seen. They're connected across universes. Because of her. She has to do what she can to make things right.

She slowly circles to the chair behind her desk, taking comfort in the familiar view of the river outside her window. "We need to talk about Ethan."

Grayson remains standing. "Patrick sent a sympathy gift—premade dinners, I believe. He says there's always too many floral arrangements."

He's uncertain, evaluating, the way he would when she'd bring him the financial statements and an unorthodox idea he always said yes to. She'd forgotten that. He never said no. Until the day of the outing. Maybe that's why it infuriated her so much. Hurt her so much.

She knits her fingers together in her lap. "Do you really need me to say it?"

"I'll say it." Grayson carefully removes his suit jacket and folds it in two. "He really was a prick, wasn't he?" Grayson lifts his palm, his muscles bulging beneath his button-down. "Not supposed to speak ill of the dead, I know, but the lying bastard led us here."

"Don't you mean the two of you lying bastards?"

"I mistook you for more evolved than a woman scorned, Mallory." He takes a seat in front of her, spreading to fill every inch of the chair. "Is every woman simply Taylor Swift at heart?"

"Enough." Anger jabs like a bee sting. "You're resigning. I'd like to say 'today,' but I'm not a masochist. Not even to get back at you. Give it a month. Then you're out of AIM."

Her tone causes the flirtatious glint in his eye to fizzle out. "Or?"

"Or I tell the truth. You used Ethan Sonders to create and perpetrate a fraud on all of our investors, employees, and the public for your own financial gain. It'll tar my reputation, Ilena's, Aubrey's, maybe even end AIM. But I now know there are worse things."

"You don't believe that. You're bluffing."

"I was the first time at the outing. But now . . ." She shrugs. "We'll see."

"Believe what you want, Mallory, but I had nothing to do with it, not until after it was done. Our valuation was going up and up, and you and I were riding high in more ways than one. The duplicate accounts were a brilliant idea, which is how you know I'd take ownership if it was actually mine. Little prick had the nerve to call me and solicit a thank-you. He followed it with a demand for a payoff, laughing like we were in some boys' club."

"But I was there," Mallory says. "I heard you both."

"What you heard was me staving off a blackmail attempt, which apparently then became an unfortunate pattern. It's astounding, truly, that Mr. Sonders actually thought he could gain the upper hand. But no one fucks with me or this company. I haven't believed in a business more since my first—"

"That's bullshit. Don't rewrite history, Grayson. You never believed in AIM. You never even used it."

"I don't have to use diapers or chemotherapy to believe in them." He seems so genuine, like when they'd mapped out the plan for going public. They were on his couch, the catered meal from the oyster bar around the corner untouched, including the two bottles of wine. They'd gotten so immersed in what AIM could become. His shoulders hunch, nearly imperceptibly. "Be logical, Mallory. Let's say I'd done what you were trying to force me to do at the outing, suddenly invested a substantial amount of money in AIM so you could use that as your reason for canceling the direct listing. What then? The media wouldn't have stopped digging until it found our every skeleton. I had to preserve AIM, even if it made you hate me. You would have done the same thing."

Her head swims, and all she can think is he's right. That's partly how he had been able to thaw the heart she'd spent a lifetime hardening. He accepts her for who she is.

Her mother had said that love was being able to forgive when we get it wrong, and Mallory might have done just that. She'd been falling in love with him, and maybe that would have meant she would have forgiven him for undermining her. For being that selfish. She'd been that selfish with Ilena and Aubrey. He's right that a version of her might have done the same thing. But she wouldn't. Not anymore.

"I probably would have," Mallory admits. "Once. And that's something I have to live with. But what I don't have to live with is you." Mallory brushes past him and opens the door to her office. "Goodbye, Grayson."

"You'll miss me more than you realize."

"Maybe. But it's better not to have someone than to have a shitty version of them."

She is a strong, independent woman who will squeal at mice because they're terrifying and will ask for help changing a tire because she pays a fortune for manicures, and she never needed a romantic relationship before and she doesn't need one now. But wanting is an entirely different thing. She wants love. Grayson has shown her that. He's also shown her that she doesn't want it with him.

She stares into those eyes she still sees herself in, knowing she'll work to change that. "And one last piece of advice. Carry a damn EpiPen."

She doesn't watch him go. She moves to her window and stands in the reflection of the sun off the glass, hoping for a brief flash of déjà vu, so she can know if her alternate self is okay—and thank her. Harley too.

Footsteps softened by the expensive carpet resound, and her throat swells. She turns. Sees Ilena. And Aubrey. Mallory wants to grab her and hug her and say she's sorry, so very sorry.

"Mallory," Ilena says pointedly, as if she knows Mallory is about to break. "It certainly is an emotional morning for all of us." She gestures to the clock on the wall. "The opening bell, it's almost time. After everything, it's almost time."

Mallory and Ilena hold each other's gaze as if they were holding hands.

"No!" Aubrey cries. "Not today."

Mallory scans Ilena's face, but the creases on her forehead make it clear that she's not following either.

"This." Aubrey jabs a finger at each of them. "You have entire conversations in a single look, and I get it, I know you've been friends for a really long time, but you invited me to that table, and I sat there, shaking and doubting myself every second I was with the two of you then and every second since, and Mallory fighting with Grayson and Jonah moving out and my nerves over all of it may have sent us into our own worlds for the past week, but we're not doing this today, on the day AIM goes public, because this is ours. All of ours. And I want in. All the way."

Ilena's face crumples. "Oh, Aubrey, did we do that, did we make you feel that way?"

"No," Aubrey says, "and yes. And ever since Ethan, things have been, well, we've all been distant? Strained? I can't do it anymore." Her lower lip trembles as she faces Mallory. "I know you never liked him."

"Well, I—"

"And maybe you had a reason. Maybe I had a reason. I didn't always like him either. But I did love him. I still do."

Ilena places an arm around Aubrey's shoulder. "And you should. You're also right. We haven't been there for you, not the way you deserved. That ends now."

Even though it was Mallory's idea not to, in this moment, she wants to tell Aubrey everything. About AIM's "error" and the alternate reality and, especially, their role in Ethan's death. Doing so feels both right and wrong. Sorting that out means looking into the eyes of the woman who has been her barometer for more than half her life. But Ilena's expression lives firmly in the in-between. And so Mallory does the one thing she knows without question is right.

She takes Aubrey's hand. "Ethan's death is not your fault. If you've ever trusted me on anything, trust me on that."

There's so much more to say, so many secrets still tying them together and pulling them apart, but as the clock hits nine thirty and cheers echo throughout AIM, they stand, ready to face everything together. Because secrets can destroy friendships. Especially when they're told.

52
ILENA

Four Weeks ***Before*** *the Outing*

This would destroy their friendship. If Mallory knew where Ilena was and what she was about to do, the past twenty-one years wouldn't matter.

Ilena stared at the "If at first you don't succeed, don't try skydiving" graffiti on the wall of the ladies' restroom and sipped her Scotch. Neat. The Scotch and the graffiti. It was one of those bars that left Sharpies on the shelf above the feeding trough sink beside free tampons and temporary tattoos and butterscotch-flavored condoms.

She hadn't been to a place like this in years. That she was here now was entirely Mallory's fault. When Mallory had come to her a few days ago with the discovery of the computer error, Ilena had thought they'd see the same solution—the only solution. But Mallory's refusal to even consider postponing the direct listing was reckless. What right did Mallory have to be the final say on their company?

Ilena felt like she'd swallowed a book of matches, each one lighting and burning a hole in her gut. Did she share the blame? Because of what she'd let Mallory get away with in the past?

Ilena might not have always liked Mallory's methods, but she couldn't deny the enjoyment that came with reaping the benefits. But this surpassed anything Mallory had done so far, even forcing Ilena to attend the "dinner party" in that San Francisco mansion, knowing full well that it was actually a weekend-long "cuddle puddle," with all the caviar and MDMA you could want. But there were investors. The tech elite. And that was all that had mattered.

Ilena was done. If Mallory wouldn't listen to reason, she wouldn't have a company anymore. Ilena finished her Scotch and set the empty glass beside a plastic model of a boob that purported to show women how to do a breast self-exam. She reapplied her lipstick and set out to meet Ethan.

Ethan's hand flattened against the table. "The satisfaction in seeing the glamazon Ilena beg is more than I could have imagined. Give me your hand, I'll show you."

Bile billowed, and acid from the Scotch seared her throat. "That wasn't begging," she said, keeping her tone even.

"Something to look forward to, then." He lifted a finger, cocking it like a fake gun that he aimed at the bartender. "Drink? Let me guess, pinot grigio?" He slapped the table. "Fuck that, you're a sweet Riesling girl."

She swallowed her revulsion. "Are you buying?"

"Sure, my hard-on and I owe you."

Without a beat: "Pinot noir from the reserve list."

"Got it." When a server came to their table, he said, "House red, merlot if you've got it, two of them."

"Dick," Ilena muttered.

"Careful there, babe. Your negotiation skills are starting to show why Mallory's in charge."

"Don't babe—"

His lips lifted into a smirk. He was goading her. "Though is she, really? What with Grayson Fields behind her. Or is it on top? Underneath?"

Her disgust at this man-child who was the type to leave the seat up on an airplane mixed with her desire to defend and protect Mallory, which was the exact opposite of the reason she was here. She'd been doing it for so long, it was ingrained.

"I'm wasting your time." Ilena started to exit the booth. "I should go."

Ethan's arm crept out, and he laid his index finger against the back of her hand. "Not yet. You can't just ask me to manipulate my girlfriend and—"

"Fiancée, and not manipulate."

"That depends on your perspective."

"For which?"

"Both?" He stroked her skin, and that bile flooded her veins. "Let's see . . . for what you're asking, I would accept stock options. Unless you have something else to offer?" He tucked his chin, leaned over the table, and pressed his lips—and his tongue—against her skin.

She jerked her hand back. "You're disgusting."

"And you're a liar. You don't want Aubrey to help you postpone the direct listing because the financials aren't in order."

The revulsion of his tongue on her skin met with sickening fear. "What other reason would I have?"

"That's exactly what I'm waiting for you to tell me."

She was holding all the cards, and somehow he had the upper hand. She was out of her league. She wasn't Mallory. She had no idea how to do this. She felt dirty. All Ilena wanted to do was go home and cleanse herself in the glass-tiled shower that she thought would make her house and life as perfect as it seemed on the pages of the *Boston Home* magazine.

A sudden flash of bumping her belly—*her pregnant belly*—

against a marble-topped island beneath a set of industrial pendant lights that matched nothing in her kitchen and Ilena couldn't breathe. Like some form of déjà vu.

She shook it away and gathered her resolve. She was going to have to tell Ethan the truth. She needed Aubrey on her side. They had to be a united front if they were going to stop Mallory from proceeding with the direct listing. Because if reasoning didn't work, their combined votes could force Mallory out of AIM.

"AIM has a problem with its user base," Ilena said, swallowing past the lump in her throat.

The server dropped off their wine, and Ethan pulled his phone beneath the table to make room. "Go on," he said when the server left.

"We can't go public. And I need Aubrey's help to ensure Mallory understands that."

Neither of them touched their wine as Ilena gave a high-level overview of the situation and how vital it was for the direct listing to be postponed—no matter what it took, including pushing Mallory out. She hadn't planned to say the words, but they spilled out before she could stop them. And yet, somehow, it felt okay, even right, because the more Ethan knew, the better prepared he would be to support Aubrey when she found out about the computer error. The news would devastate her.

Ethan lifted his glass and took a long sip. "Let me see if I have this right. AIM's newest and flashiest feature, the one that everyone says is thrusting the valuation into the stratosphere isn't. What's causing AIM to break records is, what, a software malfunction? One the company's cofounders are actively hiding from the public? Is that about right, cofounder Ilena Cohen?"

Ilena shook her head. "Forget it, this was a bad idea. I'm leaving."

"Are you sure about that? Are you actively refusing to explain AIM's position on this to the public? Let it be known that Ms. Cohen had her chance to comment."

"My . . . what?" Something wasn't right.

Ethan lifted his phone. The counter on a recording app ticked up.

"You son of a bitch—"

He'd hit the red button to stop recording before she'd gotten the first word out.

"Delete it," Ilena said, her heart racing at the idea of what she said coming out—what she said about Mallory. "Now. I came to you to ask a favor as a friend, one I shouldn't have, I realize that now, but it was to protect AIM, to protect Aubrey, the woman you love."

"*Love*'s a strong word, though, isn't it? It doesn't convey the reality of enduring all the mediocre meals she cooks and the even more pedestrian intercourse that can't in good conscience be called 'fucking.'"

Ilena's heart sank. Mallory had never liked Ethan. Ilena hadn't either, not really, but she'd tried to, for Aubrey. She thought she was doing the right thing. She wasn't.

Ethan continued, "But love can make someone ignore sound advice like having a prenup. Even someone whose company is about to make their new husband a fortune."

Ilena blanched. "You're using her. All this time? For money?"

"You truly are the brains of the trio."

"So it's all an act? Your whole relationship?"

"It's not entirely without pleasure, I'm not that much of a martyr. I dove in with Aubrey just to see where things might take me. What opportunities might arise. I had no idea it would lead to more money than you all deserve. True, it'll take marriage, then eventually divorce. But we can save her from it—you and I. I'll delete the recording if you sign half your shares of AIM over to me right now."

The rest of those matches in Ilena's stomach flamed into an inferno. "This is unethical—" He laughed at her—hard and full and with so much derision it made Ilena embarrassed, doubting herself. She forced herself to speak slowly, softly, even though it made her throw up in her mouth. "If you make that recording public it will destroy Aubrey. But it will also ruin AIM, which matters to so many people and—"

"All righty, then maybe you aren't the brains of the trio."

"You're out to destroy AIM?"

"What's the phrase? Payback's a bitch?"

Ilena shook her head. "I don't understand."

"Of course you don't. You're Ilena and Mallory and nothing can touch you. You fuck with everyone, thinking you won't ever get fucked back. Your actions have consequences, Ilena." He rammed the back of his head against the booth and spit out, "They duct-taped everything. My door, my backpack, my head to the fucking pillow. Asshole told everyone it was my fault. But he's the one who made the bet, and he's the one who lost it. Fuck. They called me Barney Jizz for weeks. No one wants to hang with Barney Jizz."

Ilena went numb. She couldn't process his words.

"I dropped out. My parents nearly divorced. Wouldn't pay a cent. I went from Harvard to community college and worked my ass off, and it didn't matter. I never thought I'd get this chance. And then . . ." He gave a perverse grin. "'Nice to meet you,' that's what you two self-centered bitches said at Grayson's speech. Like I'd never existed. Then Aubrey said the same with a look on her face like she was orgasming right there. The universe owed me, and it finally paid up." He leaned across the table. "Oh, and tell Mallory I've still got the panties. Picked 'em right out of the trash. Gave them to Aubrey for our one-month anniversary. Course, they didn't fit. Her ass is just too fucking big."

Instinctually, Ilena's arm darted out and red liquid spread like a bloodstain across his white shirt. Ilena set her empty wineglass back on the table.

"Bitch!" He propelled himself out of the booth, slapping at his chest before flinging his hand at the glass, which fell but didn't shatter. "You'll regret that." He spun around, grabbing his buzzing phone from his pocket. He mumbled something Ilena couldn't quite make out. His fingers tapped, and he said clearly, "Office, clean shirt, then I burst this motherfucking AIM bubble. Ingenious this, you crazy bitch."

A drop of red wine rolled onto the web between Ilena's thumb and index finger, and she dried it with a cocktail napkin despite the trembling in her hand. A text came through from Aubrey. They were all meeting at some place just down the street, Better Bar. She breathed in methodically as she gathered her white coat.

Ethan, goddamn Ethan.

How could she have come to this pissant excuse for a man? One who couldn't get past being a boy.

She slid to the edge of the bench seat, far enough to look at the floor-to-ceiling windows at the front of the bar. There he was, outside, leaning against the window, his hand clutching his phone. Then, he pushed himself off the window, on the move.

Panic unfurled inside her, and she rushed out to the street, the chill in the air prickling goose bumps as she left her coat in the bar. Her heart pounded her chest and dark spots crowded her vision as she whirled around to find him. She caught a glimpse, his arched back, his forceful stride, jaywalking across the street toward the plaza with AIM on one side and his office on the other. She couldn't let him reach either.

She shouted to him, calling his name, one she never actually knew in college; she'd have never recognized him, her only interaction was with him in that low-drawn hoodie. Ethan didn't hear her, or he heard her and didn't care.

She started to run. Her heart nearly burst when she caught a glimpse of the long, bronzed hair she recognized as well as her own. Mallory was on the opposite side of the street, heading away, in the direction of the bar in the text. But Ilena needed her, needed her help to fix this. She missed her best friend and she missed her husband and missed the woman she'd been when she met them both.

"Mallory," she cried. She pointed to Ethan, her fingers shaking, her throat dry, her words hoarse and desperate. "Stop him, we have to stop—"

Whatever Mallory understood in that moment didn't matter. Ilena had asked for help and Mallory gave it. Mallory cupped her hands around her mouth and screamed, "Ethan!" His stride slowed, but he didn't stop or look their way. Ilena opened her mouth, and the next "Ethan!" resounded in unison, their combined power strong enough to make him freeze.

He turned away from the oncoming traffic and toward them.

It all came at once. Screech, honk, sparks, the shattering of glass, the pooling of blood.

Ilena felt as though she'd been lifted out of her body, seeing it all from another time, another place. A place where she could agree to words she would have never imagined.

When Mallory said, "Aubrey can never know," Ilena hesitated

for a microsecond before she nodded and reached for Mallory's hand, letting her lead them to meet Aubrey at Better Bar, making a promise to herself that Mallory would never know the full truth either. She'd never tell her that she had met with Ethan in order to betray her best friend.

53
ETHAN

Harvard University
Twenty-One Years ***Before*** *the Outing*

He drew the strings tight, and the fabric molded to his head. The hem of the hood rested heavy against his forehead.

"Ingenious," the resident adviser said, rubbing his beard. Several strands of duct tape remained affixed to the wall. The RA assessed the adhesion visually, then with a slight tug of his calloused index finger and thumb. "Truly remarkable. This is just the kind of innovation and tactical thinking Harvard is looking for." He faced the girl with hair the color of a dead crab and tits big enough to nurse a cow who'd tricked them into carrying her fucking low-rent box from the subway stop. He wasn't a fucking valet. Or a moron. The moron was his jackass of a roommate who'd actually put their fucking killer dorm room on the line.

It was the other chick's idea. The stuck-up one with eyes of ice, and he hates himself that he'd do anything to fuck her. Still. She'd made him do it. Staring at him from the doorway with gleaming hair and fluttering lashes, teasing him, testing him. His dick throbbed, about to burst.

Now he'd lost his goddamn Hugh Hefner dorm room to the cunt.

The RA walked the pair, who must have gotten in off of blow jobs not SAT scores, down the hall. The crowd who'd gathered to hear the ruling dispersed.

"Come on." His fuckwad of a roommate picked at the hair on his arms. "I'm sticky as shit."

"Fuck all, if I care." He kicked at the strands of duct tape coiled like a molted snakeskin.

The roommate stilled, rolled bits of adhesive between his fingers. "Your fault, dude."

"You made the bet."

"Never woulda been offered the bet if you hadn't jizzed in her roommate's underwear. Chicks stick together, dumbass." This made a couple of dudes turn back to listen, and the fuckwad added, "So it is actually your fault, Jizzum."

"Name's Ethan, you dipshit."

"Not anymore, Barney Jizz." The roommate called to the guys up ahead. "Yo, wait up, burgers at Mr. Bartley's on me."

Ethan yanked on the string of his hoodie so hard, it broke. He didn't know how and he didn't know when, but when the chance came, he'd take the bitches down.

I always believed in fate. I just didn't know what mine was until that text message arrived. Ilena admitting to a cover-up. The release of that video would ruin everything.

That was never the plan.

That was never *my* plan.

Little did I know he had a plan of his own. Ethan's plan could not be allowed to succeed. Not when it was at odds with all I had done. All I had risked. And endured: humoring him, pretending he was the one in charge even though I was the one who'd done it all to raise our company to the level it deserved.

They deserved.

They would see, they would know, they would thank me.

That night, a month before the outing, they took each other's hand and walked away as one. United by a secret they could never tell. *I* did that. I saved them from losing each other. I was supposed to save us all.

The reveal of the computer glitch was supposed to have come from me—a feat to be perceived as astonishing yet simple in practice as I'd created it. I'd only used Ethan and his position within his company to mask the error's existence until I said otherwise. The valuation, the attention, the success. *Me, me, me.* I'd intended to explain it all. And they would understand that I was the one who had manufactured the error and taken us to the brink of greatness, the wealth of users, the wealth those users would shower upon us, and they would embrace me as they did you.

That was the plan. To play out on my timeline. Not his. Ethan got greedy. He sought to blackmail his way to a windfall.

First Grayson, then, when that failed, Ilena. The text message Ethan sent me from the bar with the incriminating recording of Ilena could not come to light. It was quicksand. I was drowning. Y'all were drowning. He had to be stopped. And quickly. What none of us knew was that fate had already stepped in to help.

Fate made the printer jam on the document that had to be signed in the morning. Fate made me stay at AIM until it was too dark to comfortably cycle home. Fate made me walk past the stop just as the bus arrived. Fate made me choose to stand in front rather than sit in back. Fate made me see it all coming. Clearly. In an instant. The way out.

They were on opposite sides of the street.

Ethan was in the middle.

My hand found the bus's emergency stop.

My voice cried, distracting the driver.

The shrieking brakes, the wrenching halt, the thundering shouts, the heaving pain, so much in the moment, so much to come. But they had taught me: one a means to an end; the other right and wrong. This was right. This was the only way it should end. In Ethan's death.

After we went public, they would see. They would know. They would thank me. They would love me. That was my plan.

That the game annihilated.

One second I was crossing the lawn of the gastropub in my white linen dress to round y'all up, and the next I was lying in white linen pants in a lumpy futon in the living room of the studio I apparently shared with a Tufts grad student. Except I lived alone.

The smell of meat smoking on an open fire from the barbecue restaurant down the street wafted through the open windows, a constant I've come to find comforting, but that first day, I ran to the bathroom, gagging. That was when I saw my hair. Red. I never wanted to be anything but the blonde I was.

Time travel was my first guess, yet aside from the hair and toned calves, which I would come to discover are the result of an apparent affinity for heels, I looked the same age. As did all of you.

Panic is not something I do. Methodical, that's in my DNA. That first morning, my phone had sounded with a reminder to set up the AIM conference room for a meeting with Grayson Fields. No such meeting had been scheduled in what I would come to realize was our universe. I knew little of what was happening then. My mind remained on what I knew of our world and what I had to protect: all of you.

Y'all were easy to find. This phone tracks all things Mallory: her laptop, her phone, herself. She must have trackers on all the things she might lose. I didn't even change, just hurried to Grayson's penthouse, and there you all were at the door with that dog that's so cute it demands to be kidnapped. Then I heard: *"Watching the dog while Mr. Fields goes on an unexpected trip."* A lie from Mallory's lips. At odds with the meeting surely in everyone's calendar. Y'all were heading to AIM, but I didn't know if y'all *were* y'all. I stayed out of sight and hurried to AIM to find out.

I was dumping that bougie tea in sachets when you ran past. I waved, but you continued on as if you didn't even know me. I was alone here the same way I had been in our universe. It wasn't fair. It wasn't right.

That was when I knew why I was here. To right all the wrongs. The wrongs y'all have done to me.

When I tracked down Ethan, I suggested a painted rock might be just the trick to connect with you, the success of which he relayed to me on the balcony at Ilena's dinner party. When I learned Kai had a crush, I reminded him that you don't drink caffeine and told him to buy you another rosé at the bar, because who doesn't love a love triangle? Poor jilted James, that's who. The fury in his eyes when he took my musings over those old-fashioneds Mallory loves to mean his dear Felix had been trapped? My, oh, my.

Not that everything went to plan. When I realized at least one of those hideous state charms on my key chain was missing, I searched everywhere before trying the Latham home. The doorbell camera I learned about later was unfortunate. Still, I was intent on creating chaos. And I did. Scheduling the *Shandy Shane* visit for the same time as the police interview and making sure Heidi Hoffman was there played out even more brilliantly than I'd imagined. Ironically, that was where it all fell apart.

I was the one who nudged the door open and encouraged Harley to interrupt. Seeing how frightened y'all were crushed me worse than a stampede of wild horses. I had to do something to help fix what I'd done.

This wasn't me. It wasn't who I wanted *us* to be. Why I had done all I had in our universe. Y'all were *here*. And so was I. This was our chance to come together. I knew exactly where to start. The river. The event I suggested you re-create in our universe.

That day, none of you came to work. I took a chance, and there you were, huddled around that sandbox. I had no idea what you'd intended. I just knew I needed to be there too. To come clean. To have us come together, finally, as one. Fast as small-town gossip, I ran alongside the river, weaving through all those people running home from work, my ponytail bouncing like I was on a trampoline. But then you walked away.

And now they are gone.

But we, we, are here. And we will be the best of friends.

Two hands encase Aubrey's, the warmth at odds with the piercing cold sparking gooseflesh along her skin. She looks to the table in front of them. She's reassured by the knot of jet-black hair and the person to which it's attached.

Aubrey extracts her hand, sliding it past the half-finished old-fashioned across the table and the untouched one in front of herself. She manages a half smile despite the nausea blooming in her stomach at what she'd just heard. Ethan, her Ethan, *had* been killed—just not by Aubrey. "The plan, your plan, did it extend beyond, to anything else? Anyone else?"

"Mr. Fields?"

She smiles so genuinely with such affection that Aubrey almost feels sorry for her. For how lonely she must have been. Aubrey thinks of the night of the outing in the world that had once been theirs, the night she came to them with drinks and a desire to please, the night Aubrey had invited her to stay. She hadn't. Yet she must not have strayed far. She must have been spatially close enough to move between worlds when they bumped. But not quite close enough to return when Mallory and Ilena did.

It was the David Copperfield that sparked Aubrey's suspicion. When Aubrey had tried to explain the reference to Kai, she discovered that the man doesn't exist here—at least not as a magician that everyone knows. But this woman was here. And she knew David Copperfield too. She'd said it when Harley interrupted the police interview.

"Y'all know that Mallory sometimes asks me to restock her emergency snack bag," she says, having slipped back into using their first names. "I like to surprise her. Change it up."

This Mallory has no memory of anything after the outing. She admits an attraction to Grayson but swears they never slept together. If she went home with him after the party, that was the first time. She had no reason to keep her emergency snack bag free of nut crackers. An accident, that's what her lawyer is insisting.

Could this help? If Mallory didn't pack her own snack bag, she could be cleared entirely, not even that involuntary manslaughter they're floating would have a chance. Mallory would no longer have to worry about being in jail when the newly separated Ilena gives birth to her daughter. Mallory could accept an invitation to *The Shandy Shane Show* for something other than as part of a scandal. She did go on, they all did, to explain the postponement of the direct listing as a result of the tragic loss of Grayson Fields.

Aubrey gently tugs Harley closer. "Grayson, then. The crackers being made of nut . . ."

"An unfortunate twist of fate."

Relief bubbles up inside Aubrey's chest before her mind takes it one step further. Because this woman admitted that she woke up here, same as them, with no idea that she was in a different universe. With a different Grayson. A Grayson who didn't actually know the secret that she had already killed to keep. Was she leaving anything out?

"Not planned?" Aubrey says carefully.

"Not by this version of me," she says. "Perhaps the other Noreen . . . well, I guess we may never know."

ACKNOWLEDGMENTS

Writing a novel is all about choice. You make choices constantly, endlessly, obsessively. You start with nothing but a blinking cursor and rising panic and then decide *everything*: the premise, the characters, who falls in love, who falls on their face, who sets up the twist, who survives the twist, and how to do it all without anyone seeing it coming. You also, of course, have to choose each and every word, which forms each and every sentence, which forms each and every paragraph and chapter and on and on. By the end of a writing day, I have decision fatigue, where the question of sparkling or still water can spiral into a five-minute existential crisis.

But choices aren't just a writer problem. They're a human problem. What to major in. Which job to take. Which city to live in. Whether you should have bought that sparkly throw pillow at Target because it *definitely* matched the rug better. We treat choices like they're Jenga blocks, where one wrong move will collapse the whole tower. Honestly, it's amazing we ever choose anything at all.

This novel started with its high-concept hook: a twist on a familiar conversational game. But it turned into something deeper. I was writing this novel during a period of my life when it seemed every choice I made was the "wrong" one. The decisions and the consequences incited a paralysis for making any choice at all. That was when I realized how much pressure we all put on ourselves, as if a single decision has the power to change everything—for better or worse. The characters in this novel wrestle with this question of "what-ifs," if the grass is truly greener, and how to live your best life because of and in spite of those decisions.

One of the best decisions I made during the formation of this book was to share it with some good friends and early readers. A huge heartfelt thanks to Charlotte Huang, Natalie Mae, Chelsea Bobulski, and Jen Malone for their savvy insights and unceasing encouragement. A special thanks to Lee Kelly, my "parallel universe" consultant (still unclear if this is an official job title, but if not, it should be). Every writer needs these types of friends and readers willing to go the distance with you. With this book, my good friend Chandler Baker offered invaluable advice, not just on the manuscript, but on thinking strategically about both professional and personal choices. This book would not have been published without her unceasing support and friendship.

I'm grateful to my agent, Jill Marr, and the brilliant team at the Sandra Dijkstra Literary Agency for bringing me and this novel to my editor, Meredith Clark, at Park Row. Meredith supported me at every stage of telling this story—even when we went back and forth over a not-so-tiny plot point before she (generously and bravely) left the decision up to me. (No, I won't tell you which one.) Meredith, thank you for believing in both me and this story.

I also want to thank my film agent, Mirabel Michelson at UTA, for her tremendous enthusiasm for translating this story into a visual form (stay tuned!). My gratitude also goes to Francesca Melis, whose cover design may or may not be my favorite of all my books (okay, it is, but don't tell the others—they're very sensitive). I am grateful to the marketing and publicity teams at HarperCollins, as well as Emily Miles Terry, a good friend and the best book champion a writer can have.

A special nod to each and every one of my students over the past ten years, especially my accountability cohorts and the Woods Hole crew, who give me more inspiration and professional and personal fulfillment than they know. It's an honor to share this creative road with you.

Some people I didn't exactly choose—at least not originally. My family. Thank you for reminding me that even if I wrote a list of my favorite Taylor Swift lyrics and called it a novel, you'd still read it, probably with pride, possibly with notes.

Readers, this is the part where I get sincere (brace yourselves). Every time you pick up one of my books, you've made a choice to spend *your* limited, precious time in *my* head. You could be scrolling TikTok or reorganizing your spice rack by color, but you chose *this*. Thank you for your reviews, your DMs, and your continued support. It means everything.

And finally, Marc—my husband, my sounding board, my "are-you-sure-that-works?" guy. Seven published books in, I'm surely repeating myself, but that's because it's still true: none of this happens without you. This book especially was a high-risk, "what-am-I-doing?" gamble. In another life, with one different decision, it might not exist at all. But here we are. He supported me in trusting my instincts when all signs were pushing me not to. Ultimately, the choice to take the risk was mine. The reward? It's in your hands.

READING GROUP GUIDE

Please Note: In order to provide reading groups with the most thought-provoking questions possible, it is necessary to reveal important aspects of the plot of the novel, including the ending. If you have not finished reading *Kiss, Marry, Kill*, we respectfully suggest you may want to do so before reviewing this guide.

1. As we meet Aubrey for the first time, we discover that Mallory and Ilena are her best friends. However, Aubrey is the newest member of the friendship trio. In Aubrey's mind, Mallory and Ilena have "silent conversations that always remind Aubrey how much longer the two have known each other." Can friendships in odd numbers ever truly feel equal? Do you have personal experience with being a friend in a trio?

2. Choice is the overarching theme of the novel, including the weight we all put on our choices, often believing a

single decision has the power to determine the course of our lives. How does the problem each character is grappling with in the alternate universe play into their approach to choice and consequences? Who changes the most? The least?

3. The novel takes place mostly in the alternate universe. It uses flashbacks to allow the reader to see elements of the story from the "real world," which influence our understanding of both the characters and the lives they are trying to return to. Was this a successful device? Why do you think the author chose to show the flashbacks that she did?

4. At the end of the novel, Mallory, Ilena, and Aubrey believe they know how to return to "their" world. As they are preparing to leave the alternate universe, several choices are made. Ilena decides to have a conversation with Felix about their marriage, ending in the realization that they are not in love but want to be—with other people. She leaves a letter to the Ilena who will "return" to this life, describing what it feels like to be loved, to encourage her to follow her heart. Do you believe Ilena had the right to do these things? Should she have left this world without addressing what she came to believe was a mistake—one the other Ilena and Felix were too afraid to admit?

5. Mallory decides to send a statement to the police. She doesn't admit guilt, as she truly doesn't know who—if anyone—was behind Grayson's death. She aims to clear her father, Ilena, and Aubrey of any wrongdoing and take any blame to come herself. However, that self will be the "other Mallory." It's quite possible that the "other

Mallory" *did* have a hand in Grayson's death. She has no way of knowing. So she leaves it to the police to decide, putting a high-profile lawyer on retainer. Do you think Mallory did the right thing? What other options does she have?

6. Aubrey makes the decision to stay in the alternate universe. She knows the risks, but she says "making no decision at all is worse than sometimes being wrong." Aubrey's decision has consequences. It makes it theoretically more challenging that Ilena and Mallory's "return" will succeed. It also has unclear ramifications for the "other Aubrey." The evidence, such as it is, suggests that this isn't a "Freaky Friday" switch, and the "other Aubrey" is not in their "real world." But Mallory poses the question to Aubrey of what will become of this "other" version of Aubrey. Were you surprised by Aubrey's decision? How do you feel about her making this choice for herself? How did Mallory's and Ilena's reactions resonate? How do you think the story would have changed if Aubrey didn't stay? Why do you think the author had Aubrey make this choice?

7. The novel ends by revealing two additional twists: that Ethan had been at Harvard with Mallory and Ilena and was involved in the "duct tape" incident. When Ethan reconnected with the two women, his long-held grudge pushed him to try to hurt them, and he used Aubrey to do it. Were you surprised by this twist? Do you think Ethan "got what he deserved"?

8. In addition, it turns out that Noreen from the "real world" was also transported to the alternate universe, and unlike Aubrey, who makes the choice to stay, Noreen gets stuck.

It is Noreen who has been the narrator of the "I" interstitials in the novel. This was a red herring. Did you have a guess as to who was narrating these sections?

9. In Noreen's confession to Aubrey at the end of the novel, Noreen explains how she was the one behind the computer glitch, something done to position her as a "hero" who saves the company and is then accepted into the friendship she desperately wants to be a part of. What do you think of Noreen's reasoning? Noreen goes even further, admitting that she was the one who pulled the emergency brake on the bus that ended in Ethan's death, something Aubrey has blamed herself for. Noreen believes she made the right decision—the decision that protects the women she cares about, which is not dissimilar to justifications both Aubrey and Mallory use in their climactic decisions. How do you feel about the lengths Noreen was willing to go? What does this say about her as a person? Do you believe the friends had any role in the extremes Noreen went to?

10. The novel is fiction, but principles mentioned, such as the many-worlds interpretation, were part of the author's research, and some believe the notion of the universe splitting with each decision is possible. What do you believe? Do you think there are alternate or parallel universes? Do you think there are other versions of you? Would you want to meet your "other self/selves"?

Q & A WITH LORI

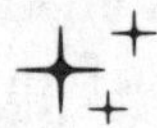

Where did the idea for *Kiss, Marry, Kill* come from?

This novel came to me in nearly an instant. Some story ideas hit you that fast. I was watching a television show where the characters were playing a game of Kiss, Marry, Kill the usual way. My brain immediately seized on the game being a great catalyst for a novel, but there had to be a twist. Today, most novels being published are what we call "high concept," meaning they can be explained easily but have an unexpected element that elevates the story. When I come up with any potential premise for a story, I'm always thinking about how I can make it more high concept. Enter the parallel universe. I'm a big fan of alternate universes, time loops, and time travel stories, so this speculative bent was one I felt entirely comfortable pursuing.

The novel has a strong theme of choice. Did this come from somewhere personal?

In most of the novels I've written, it takes me a little time to settle on the theme or what the story is *really* about. *Kiss, Marry,*

Kill is the exception. After the spark hit me, the next thing I did was think about the theme. Inherently, of course, choice plays a role. But why it became the central theme is directly related to where I was in my own life.

I was in a period where it seemed every choice I made was the wrong one, and for a time, it made me like Aubrey, simply unable to make any decision for fear of making the wrong one. But that got me thinking more grandly. I realized I wanted to explore something I think we all feel: that a single choice can truly determine the course of our lives. We put so much pressure on ourselves to be making the "right" choice in everything from the jobs we hold to the partners we choose to the cars we drive to if our blueberries should be organic or not. I wanted to examine what happens when you think the grass is greener—that the other choice would have made you happier—and you realize that's not true. Your life is still full of problems, just different ones. As alternate-universe Jonah says, choice is actually about "choosing the crap you're willing to deal with."

The novel is written in three points of view and multiple timelines. Why did you choose to structure the story this way?

Because I'm a glutton for punishment! I've actually written in multiple POVs previously, and I find it an extremely enjoyable and efficient way to tell a story. It's a great fit for my strengths, which center on voice and fast plotting. I was less worried about that aspect than I was about executing the timelines. But I knew that this book's hook was the characters entering the alternate universe.

The trouble with this is that the reader doesn't get to spend much time with the characters *before* the flip. The flip is obviously an enormous stressor on the women and will dictate their behavior in the alternate universe. But how do we know who they were before? The solution came in the form of flashbacks. I could show some of the key elements of the story before the flip to the alternate universe. An understanding of the relationships we don't get to see, like how Ilena and Mallory met, how Ethan entered Aubrey's life, how Grayson and Mallory interacted, as well as how Ilena and Jonah's marriage deteriorated, became the essential moments to tell. These are actually some of my favorite passages in the book.

While the novel reads much like a contemporary novel, to explore this "what if" question, it adds a speculative element. How did you go about integrating this into the story?

I really enjoy these types of stories where a character gets a glimpse into another version of themselves. Whether it's a parallel universe or a time loop or time travel, I think when the stakes are so high and the character is thrown so far out of their comfort zone, there's tremendous opportunity for that character to have to learn to adapt and adapt quickly. It also allows for a faster-paced style of storytelling, which is what I gravitate toward. I love telling stories that happen over a few days' time.

One challenge I had in creating this story was to figure out how to bring the alternate universe to life in a way that is both accessible and grounded in scientific theory—theory that is extremely complex. I'm not a physicist, but I did have a little bit of knowledge of this particular space simply because it's an area that interests me. But I definitely had a lot of homework to do in order to understand the theories out there regarding the multiverse, many-worlds interpretation, coherence link, and more so I could craft a story that, while fictional, is remotely possible. I wanted the novel to touch on the theories but not overwhelm the reader, and I wanted to leave the door open to perhaps a more mystical explanation too, which I do with a couple of unexplained pieces of the story, including a mysterious ring. I want readers to form their own opinions and spark their own discussions with their friends, families, and book clubs.

Read an excerpt from Lori Gold's
Romantic Friction,
available now!

ABOUT THE AUTHOR

It's a commonly held belief that in order to be a good author you have to be drunk or tortured. To be a great author? Both. I am a great author. I am occasionally drunk (though not at present). But I am not prone to sprawled-on-the-bathroom-floor bawling. I have not, nor will I ever, utter the phrase: "Please don't make me adult today." And I am not the least bit disturbed by crawling into a king-size bed alone.

All that's to say, I am not, nor have I ever been, tortured.

But there truly is a first time for everything.

The bookstore buzzes like an active hive. Beyond these rolling partitions masquerading as shelves, cushioned folding chairs cradle bums of all shapes and sizes and stages of cellulite. They are here for me. As I am here for them. This is my hometown. And this is the bookstore in my hometown that Jocelyn and Torrence and Callum and little Vance built, word by word, page by page, chapter by chapter, book by book. That I share with no one.

I am not a charity.

My coattails are not for riding.

Tell that to Lacey, my publicist for the last ten years. I already did. Multiple times and with only one expletive. (Which honestly is the definition of *restraint*.) And yet, I am here. Because

Blaire, my agent with a heart mushier than a ripe peach, intervened on Lacey's behalf and asked me to be.

Listen, that this industry is harder to navigate than Gen Z slang is not lost on me. I'm not completely averse to the idea of paying it forward, even though when I was starting out no one gave me so much as a linty nickel. But you can be damn sure that if a bestselling author who helped to define my genre had invited me (via said publicist) to a bookstore celebration of their blockbuster series, I'd have been on time.

Not late. By twenty minutes—and counting.

I reach for the partition cordoning off this back room, my rose gold bangles clattering as I wiggle free a chapter book—a tale about monsters hiding in school cubbies that must be the bane of every kindergarten teacher's existence. A ghost of a smile plays on my lips, affection for my kindred spirit of an author who came up with this. I set the book aside and peek through the slim gap.

Heart-shaped helium balloons kiss the ceiling, "library" candles that smell of old books and lavender flicker on the windowsills, and my favorite cushioned armchair beckons from behind my usual signing table, an old desk with legs fashioned out of stacked books. Hanging above the register is a poster of the first nine titles in this series I nearly gave a kidney to make happen (don't ask).

The dozens who have traveled from as close as Boston and as far as Iowa wait with more patience than me alongside half the residents of this small seaside town.

With so many bodies, the room temperature rises. The air turns electric. And I come alive. I wriggle my head out of my introverted shell and gorge myself on the energy of the crowd. I'm no longer a little girl with debilitating stage fright, convincing my teachers I'd been bitten by a squirrel or had a seven-foot-long tapeworm in my belly to get out of an oral report. Turns out I've always been good at lying.

Lies, fibs, fabrications, tall tales. That's all writing is, really, being good at making things up, convincing others that a little boy with freckled cheeks and a mop of carrot-colored hair can bend universes in one breath and giggle at fart jokes in the next. Ah, little Vance—everyone's favorite character. Which is why he had to die. My socials will be flooded with heartbreak emoji and death threats when fans get their hands on this last book.

My god, do I love my job.

"Sofie, our little Sofie."

I would take these words as a slight, given my five-foot stature, if they weren't coming from a woman slipping behind the partition with arms outstretched, a half dozen tiny pencils poking out of her salt-and-pepper bun, and a "Roxanne (as in *Bel Canto*!)" name tag on her ample left breast (the right is ample too, but there's just the one name tag).

"Sofie Wilde, the hero of the harbor." Roxanne repeats the same refrain each time I enter this store, be it through the back for an event like today or the spontaneous (read: always-staged) drop-ins through the front to "casually" browse and be photographed with some new release Roxanne's exuberance and penchant for underdogs caused her to overbuy. She posts them on the store's Instagram. Knowing this, some of the younger authors, freed from the decorum handcuffs of my generation, have been bold enough to send extra copies of their books to the store. The feed for Harbor Books is the only place you'll see me posing with a novel that isn't mine. It's my rule. Roxanne, somehow, over all these years, remains the exception.

"Tell me," Roxanne says, wiggling her phone and pressing the side button to shut it down. "And not even Instagram will hear. Will Vance be able to restore the cosmic balance in time for Jocelyn to choose Torrence? Because she will, naturally. It must be Torrence."

My face remains hard as steel.

"Sofie," Roxanne coaxes. "It's me. We did this together. We built this store as a team. This is ours."

Roxanne also has a penchant for hyperbole.

Still, these days, my fantasy romance series—what this Gen Z, grammaphobic world now calls "romantasy"—is a *New York Times* bestseller, and I have more than half a million followers on social media. But fifteen years ago, I was a thirty-five-year-old woman with mousy brown hair, clear plastic-framed eyeglasses, and self-made bookmarks rolled off my laser printer in need of a yellow cartridge. A self-published author without the financial means to promote myself. That's when I met Roxanne.

When I walked through the door of Harbor Books with my sack of sad-looking bookmarks and shoddily glued-together manuscripts, Roxanne didn't even wait for me to finish my plea to support a local author. She was already slapping price stickers on the back and arranging them in a three-foot-tall window display. Hers was the first store to stock my books. She was the first bookstore owner to host an event with me. In return, I've held every launch party here, and Harbor Books is the only store where readers can preorder signed copies with one-of-a-kind swag. Whenever I have my last launch (a very, very, very long time from now), it'll be here.

Roxanne bats her eyelashes. "I can better serve you and the book if I know how to respond to customer inquiries." She gives me that syrupy smile we both know is exaggerated. "Truly, there were no advance reader copies printed? Not even for Jenna? Reese?"

"Not a one," I say, firmly, though of course there were. Stripped of the cover with *confidential* and *sharing prohibited upon penalty of death* written across the front (though, as I think about it, no one ever confirmed the use of that perfectly reasonable suggestion).

A small number of advance reader copies are always necessary in this industry that relies on prepublication buzz to anoint its best-sellers, and my publisher plays the game well, distributing copies to high-profile outlets for review. I could have secured one for Roxanne, but Vance's death is *the* surprise of the series and she's terrible at keeping secrets. A photo of her still hangs on the wall of shame at the single-screen movie theater across the street for telling everyone that Bruce Willis's character in *The Sixth Sense* is actually dead. (Ooh, did I just pull a Roxanne? Whoops.)

A ding announces the opening of the front door. Roxanne peers around the partition to confirm it's her.

"Break a spine!" Roxanne says, whooshing out.

Instead of following, I pause to peer through that tiny gap on the bookshelf.

My "invited" guest, the author who will ask me a few questions and then moderate ones from the crowd, hovers at the front of the store, seemingly unsure, eyes scanning the room. Silver hair past her shoulders, flowy cotton skirt, well-worn canvas tote bulging with what can only be useless buttons and cheap pens and glitter tattoos she paid for herself. She has no marketing budget for swag or anything else. She's only here because of me.

No one had heard of Hartley West until a month ago. As happens (usually thanks to a hefty Venmo transfer), an influencer "discovered" Hartley's self-published debut, *Love and Lawlessness*. That influencer gushed about it and set off a trend among her fellow movers and shakers—leaders of the "next wave" of how books are found, even branded as such by an article in the *New York Times*. Like a snowball, more and more readers "found" and recommended Hartley's book. Said it reminded them of me.

The next Sofie Wilde. That's what they're calling her. Over my dead body.

"Ms. Wilde?"

I turn.

"Are we missing anything?"

The bookstore employee—Amy (as in *Little Women*!) according to her name tag—lifts a large wooden tray as if making an offering to the gods. On it are three black Sharpies with an ultra-fine tip, a pad of sticky notes (blue), six peppermint-flavored lozenges, two glasses of water, no ice, and a bottle of hand sanitizer disguised as hand lotion.

I'm not a diva. (Despite how it sounds.) I've simply paid my dues. I've earned the right to be here, to be doing this, and I intend to do it well.

"It's perfect, Amy," I say just as on the other side of this partition, chair legs scratch against the floor.

I return to my peekaboo window. Hartley West has circled the table. She drops her bag on the seat of the armchair. The single armchair. The chair that is mine. She puts her back to the room. Her eyes are closed. Her hand presses against her breastbone, and I wonder if this is her very first event. I'm positive it's her very first event like this. I remember the feeling. And by feeling I mean fear. Maybe that's why she was late. I feel a momentary surge of empathy toward her, understanding what it was like to be just starting out, to be hoping and praying to all the gods and no particular god (to cover all the bases) for the doors of publishing to open even the tiniest crack.

I watch Hartley's chest inflate and deflate, and suddenly I feel like I'm intruding. I lower my gaze, but I can still hear her on the other side, the faint mumbling as she repeats her pitch one final time. Rehearsing the quippy soundbite that we authors spend more time writing than the actual book. We are actors without training. Performers without a safety net. We are thrust into the spotlight despite our desire to avoid it being what led most of our introverted selves to become writers in the first place. When we stand before a crowd, be it one or one thousand, we must be witty and wise.

I am.

Is "the next Sofie Wilde"?

Honestly, what *is* that? Is it supposed to be a compliment? Me being replaced? Isn't that called a coup?

Flump.

Flump, flump, flump, flump.

I resume my spying. Hartley West is plopping stacks of bookmarks on the table beside a two-foot-tall tower of books that she must have pulled from her Mary Poppins tote.

She then reaches into that bag and draws out a single sheet of paper. I watch as she carefully folds it in two. Printed on the front, in big blocky aquamarine letters, is her name and underneath: CO-PANELIST.

I text Lacey: Hartley West, what did you say to her?

Lacey: She's late, I know. Roxanne's been hounding me.

Me: She's here. With a "co-panelist" name card.

Lacey: WTF?

Me: My thoughts exactly.

Lacey: Looping in Blaire.

But Blaire wouldn't overstep. She may have a heart that bleeds so much she needs daily transfusions, but she defers to Lacey on all things publicity related. Lacey started as my in-house publicist, working for a publisher where she had more authors to handle than romance authors have euphemisms for *penis*. Lacey hung out her own shingle after helping me hit the *New York Times* bestseller list with book four, and I became her first client.

Blaire: It must be a misunderstanding.

Lacey: Damn straight, because if you look up the definition of limelight, you will see Sofie right here and now. Not Sofie and Hartley West. She came out of nowhere at the pinnacle of Sofie's career. Sofie cannot validate this flash in the pan at her own event.

Sofie: Isn't that what I said to you? Right before you hit "click" on the posts promoting this entirely predictable debacle?

Lacey: I'll fix it.

Lacey could talk a lobster into a pot of water—then get it to use its own claw to turn up the heat.

And yet . . . in exchange for a blurb, I once offered to donate a kidney to a bestselling author on dialysis (I said not to ask). I had to fight for every reader at the start.

Just like "the next Sofie Wilde."

And if karma exists, I need it on my side. Today marks the beginning of the end for Jocelyn and Torrence and Callum and little Vance. I mourn them. A part of me always will. They've rented space in my head for more than ten years. I know what they eat for breakfast and what they'd wear to a funeral and the fears that paralyze them. Things I barely know about myself. But it's time to let them go, and along with them, shifting universes and alternate dimensions and three-headed beasts. At least for a little while. I'm not leaving romance behind—I may have my flaws, but self-sabotage is not one of them. But the idea of penning a meet-cute that doesn't involve fantastical elements like a talking dolphin or a sidekick with yellow feathers makes me all warm and fuzzy (though honestly, that could also be the hot flashes).

Hartley West places her name card in front of her, testing its ability to stand on its own. I see Roxanne with her phone to her ear, Lacey surely on the other end. Roxanne's lips thin, and she marches forward, a tiny pencil falling to the floor behind her.

I calmly roll the partition aside. I step forward, cutting off Roxanne, secure enough in my books and my fans and the legacy I've built to, just for tonight, share this table in this bookstore in my hometown. I face the crowd here to celebrate with me. And stand behind the table next to Hartley West. Solidarity, women supporting women, one of us rises, all of us rise—yes, yes, yes—all things touted by filtered faces and artsy quotes on Instagram.

Yet if it turns out that this woman *is* trying to make a name for herself by mooching off mine, I'll consider it a declaration of war. And Hartley West won't write so much as a grocery list.

Hartley presses her forearms hard against the table. Wishing she could push through and disappear into a portal that leads to another realm. Or maybe that's just me. Because this is more awkward than I anticipated.

Grooves darkened with time and dust line the top of the wooden table. Amy hurriedly brought in an extra chair, but it's one of the folding ones and the height is a mismatch for the table. I need to scoot to the edge just to land my feet on the ground. I can't see readers beyond the first row, which means they can't see me. But they can see her.

Hartley towers above me, even though we're both seated. She has yet to look at me. Not a word of gratitude. No visible appreciation for how rare this is. No acknowledgment of the shift from announcer to co-panelist. (Though "co" is generous any way you slice it.)

Hartley chews on her bottom lip, unaware that the hem of her blue-flowered skirt is caught beneath the leg of her chair, tugging the waistband down. The top of her underwear is showing. (Red, for the record.) Her brown crocheted cardigan hangs half off one shoulder, the fuzzy pom-poms at the hem dangling like rabbit tails. She's hippie meets prairie with a dash of disheveled that many authors exaggerate to seem more relatable.

I don't think she's exaggerating.

My go-to event outfit is black pants with a hint of sheen and a crisp white blouse. Varied only by a scarf that matches the color of my latest cover. Today it's aquamarine. In honor of the tenth and final book in my series, which officially releases next week.

On the table, a single wireless microphone lies between us. I don't need it. Early on, I was plopped onto hard-core sci-fi and fantasy panels stocked with men and their bassoon voices. A bloodbath for the meek. It was survival of the loudest, so I hired a voice coach. Now, my voice can project to those seated in the cheap seats of auditoriums and ballrooms. It most certainly reaches all who await in this crowd that stretches to the back of the store and halfway down the stairs to the bargain basement where unsold books live out their final days.

I signal to Roxanne with a tilt of my head that I'm ready. She stations Amy at the register and weaves her way through the crowd. A hush swathes the room. Her arms cradle a book-shaped rectangle wrapped in aquamarine paper. It is the magnet that drew everyone here. (And the words you're searching for, Hartley, are *thank* and *you*.)

"Welcome to Harbor Books," Roxanne gushes. "Weeks away from St. Paddy's Day, but the luck of the Irish who founded this town is with us." Roxanne raises the gift-wrapped book, and clapping strikes like thunder. A hoot or two (okay, three) echoes off the shelves.

I can feel the table shift as Hartley drives her forearms into the top. I don't swivel my neck. I don't let my eye slide even a millimeter in her direction. I don't allow the humble half smile

I've perfected to slip into resting bitch face. The internet slays you for that.

Roxanne raises her hand to settle the crowd. "Now, she needs no introduction, but—"

I clear my throat, and Roxanne pauses. She forgot Hartley, and let's just put "forgot" in quotes. Roxanne isn't one to eschew potential book sales, but Hartley bringing her own books without discussing the terms first means Roxanne might not get the cut she rightly deserves for providing this customer base (though technically, I'm providing it).

Roxanne nods to Hartley. "But first, a Harbor Books welcome to Hartley West, another local author our great state has birthed!" Roxanne faces me. "And a fan of the woman we are here to celebrate. Now, *she* needs no introduction, but I'm giving her one anyway because she deserves it. She also hates when I make a fuss."

I don't.

"Our very own Sofie Wilde has graciously agreed to let our little store make history. And to let you all be a part of it."

This is my cue, not planned by Roxanne but internalized by me. "To be fair," I begin, and I swear there's an awed gasp from the self-help corner. My adrenaline surges. This feeling, addictive and inimitable, is why I do this. There is no point without it. "Casinos are bigger than this town. And it's February. Tonight, our local events calendar consists of this or an iPad class at the senior center."

Laughter rattles the windows framing the carnival cutout in the shape of a lobster across the street. My fans make much use of it, filling their social media feeds after every event with faces flanked by red claws and topped with pointy antennae. That fish market owes me kickbacks.

Roxanne gives the spiel she has memorized, light on the

years spent with dirt under my fingernails clawing my way up the ranks, heavy on the weeks atop list after list.

Hartley listens, a somewhat glazed look on her face as if Roxanne is describing what a landline is to a seven-year-old. But Hartley must be about my age, meaning she's also newly obsessed with the weather and with identifying birds (is that a black-capped chickadee?). She's old enough to understand the difference between how it was and how it is—and that means she should be kissing the ring my finger would be wearing if it weren't for this goiter-like arthritic bump at my knuckle.

I sat in fungus-scented elementary school gyms with a table of my books beside women selling homemade penguin-shaped candles and men hawking neon cephalopod fishing lures. My first series was about a scorpion-loving peasant growing an army of the venomous arachnids to seize the dying realm from an even more poisonous queen. It did not garner me an agent nor a traditional publishing deal.

I self-published in the days when it meant running off copies in Staples. Before it saw the first wave of authors who earned themselves a solid payday and a foothold in the industry. I watched as self-publishing gained a get-rich-quick-on-grammatically-mangled-drivel reputation, experienced the rise of e-books, muddled through the inevitable oversaturation and the back-and-forth of it being "the" place to be or the death of publishing, praised and maligned in equal measure for years. The controversy has largely gone the way of video stores and dial-up internet. Self-publishing is now acceptable for authors big and small. A new breed of hybrid authors extols the virtues of releasing books on their own as well as through traditional publishers.

I am part of that species, thanks to my fans. My scorpion-loving peasant has had a resurgence despite the oft-cringeworthy dialogue and derivative world building. Along with my two standalones and one mediocre series that attempted to invent a brand of superheroes born of constellations.

Roxanne smiles warmly. "Sofie Wilde put our little town on the map."

Well, me and the four miles of unspoiled coastline.

"She built this bookstore."

Not literally. Not with brick or drywall or even the numbers in my bank account.

"She treats us like family."

I'm not even sure I treat my family like family. I just don't understand the word *all* without *in* trailing it. Deadlines and touring rule my life. I wouldn't have it any other way.

Roxanne comes to the end of her introduction and taps the gift-wrapped book she's still holding. "Now, as you already know, these treasures are under lock and key in our storeroom until next week—"

A bit of grumbling and a "we won't tell" come from the crowd.

Roxanne talks over them. "Even so, Sofie has planned something special as a thank you for being here tonight."

And by that she means Lacey planned it.

Roxanne continues, "Anyone who preorders the final book will receive a one-of-a-kind bookplate designed by the cover illustrator, which Sofie will sign and personalize to you tonight! These won't be available anywhere else and will be included in addition to our exclusive Harbor Books swag." A roar of applause. "And as always, Sofie is happy to sign any of her other books, which are also available for purchase."

Roxanne has a bookshelf dedicated to my past titles that she's planning to roll out right before I begin signing. How convenient.

Because like some decree chiseled in stone and adhered to

with more fervor than any religion, publishers only release books on Tuesdays. But this Tuesday, for the first time, I won't be in my hometown.

This year on release day, I'll be in Chicago hanging with the Obamas and hunting down the Bear (the cutie who looks like a young Gene Wilder, not the footballers or the actual carnivores who we've apparently trained to eat from trash cans).

My loyalty to Roxanne, her launch sales, and her Instagram feed is why we're here tonight for what we're calling (or rather what Lacey is calling) a "Celebration of Sofie Wilde."

And, apparently, Hartley West.

Roxanne spreads her arms and gestures to the room. "We here at Harbor Books are honored to welcome Sofie back, in celebration of *Light As*, the final book in her *Weight of Feathers and Stone* series. Tonight, our every question will finally be answered—unless it spoils the book, of course," she adds, winking. She directs that saccharine smile at the prize nuzzled by her bosom. "My heart has never beat faster. Inside are the words that will either set it soaring or shatter it to pieces. But I, like all of you, will love it and her either way. She's the reason we are here."

Roxanne turns toward me, this a planned cue, but just as I begin to rise to my feet, a soft bubble of words releases from the chapped lips of the woman beside me.

"Quite literally," Hartley West says. "She saved me. Sofie Wilde saved my life."